Leaving 'Berengaria'

Hammerton Press,
31 Piercy End,
Kirkbymoorside,
York YO62 6DQ

ISBN: 978-0-9540960-1-4

British Library Cataloguing in Publication Data
A catalogue record of this book is available from the British Library

Printed in Great Britain by Print2Demand,
Westoning, Bedfordshire MK45 5LD

Front and back cover images reproduced by kind permission of Cunard from
original Cunard brochure illustrations by A.K. Macdonald.

'Leaving *Berengaria*' is a work of fiction. Apart from Danny, who is very loosely based on my dad, a Liverpool seaman who was a waiter on RMS *Berengaria* in the 1920s (he was 47 when I was born in 1943), all shipboard characters are fictitious and bear no resemblance to any person, living or dead.

Acknowledgements

Grateful thanks to Jim Pewtress for unstinting help whenever the computer wouldn't behave, and to Jimmy Pewtress for more unstinting help with the cover layout.

Thanks also to my cousin Hugh Gribbin for authentic shipboard information from his years at sea, and to both Adrienne Silcock and Federica Leonardis for valuable editorial comments on an earlier draft.

Research material:

'The Liners of Liverpool' by Derek M. Whale
'Ocean Liners: The Golden Years' by Rupert Prior
'The Romance of a Modern Liner' by Captain E.G. Diggle RD RNR

For the three nicest men I've ever met:
my dad, my husband, and my son.

PROLOGUE

The train journey from Southampton dragged on, and Danny was tired, cold, hungry, and bored. He picked up a discarded newspaper left open at the sports section and idly skimmed through the football results before turning, yawning, to the front page.

He stared at the headline, suddenly alert. And then, rubbing his chin thoughtfully, he read the report...

THE MANCHESTER GUARDIAN, 24th September 1925:

BOMB HOAX ON THE LINER 'BERENGARIA'.

"Official explanation was obtained yesterday of a remarkable occurrence on board the great Cunarder 'Berengaria' when she was 1,200 miles out on the voyage from New York to Southampton. The captain received a wireless message from the company's New York office; a bomb had been placed aboard, timed to explode at five o'clock on Friday afternoon last. An unsigned letter was received at the Cunard offices in New York giving information of the plot to blow up the vessel, which was taking some 1,600 people, including crew, across the ocean.

The captain took immediate steps to have the ship searched. All luggage was inspected and every corner looked into, but in a 52,000 ton liner there are many places where an object of this nature could be stored and escape attention.

The precaution was taken of getting passengers to a place where in the event of trouble they would mostly be within reach of life-saving apparatus. Preparations to meet the terrible possibility were completed, although only one or two men knew of the possible danger. A fire drill was called twenty minutes before the bomb was due to explode. But nothing happened.

Officials in New York are uncertain whether the letter-writer was purely mischievous or a plot had miscarried. It was officially stated that no notice would be taken of the hoax, in order to prevent recurrences."

He lowered the paper. Hoax letter, eh?

Well, maybe it was best left at that, because Danny was in no position to reveal how close the *Berengaria* had come to joining the most famous liner of all time on the ocean bed.

He stood as the train swayed and juddered its approach to Lime Street Station, lifted his bag from the overhead luggage rack, tossed the newspaper onto his seat, then as an afterthought - why not keep this bizarre memento of everything that had happened on his last ever trip on the *Berry*? - pocketed it before heading along the platform and out into Liverpool's noisy, smoky, welcoming familiarity.

PART ONE: FIRST NIGHT AT SEA

1

"A Berengaria *sailing is tempestuous, with the exploding of flashlights, the pursuit of reporters - everything about the* 'Berengaria' *is on the grand, opulent scale. She is sensational; sensational people board her."*

So ran Cunard's publicity blurb.

But although highly effective (who wanted to board a ship with anyone less sensational than oneself?) in ensuring only the elite - the seriously rich among the merely rich, the aristocracy, the movie stars and assorted celebrities - graced the First Class saloons of RMS *Berengaria*, when safely out of earshot the crew at their beck and call frequently used more colourful and less flattering descriptions.

And so, while for First Class passengers the Sailing Night Dinner was a see-and-be-seen occasion to greet old friends and sift new faces into the relevant categories of self-promotion, potential romantic interest, business contact, future name-dropping opportunity, or boring nonentity to be avoided at all costs, for the dining saloon waiters it was just the start of another three thousand mile voyage: six days of long hours and unremitting hard work.

But as each trip had its own unique blend of personalities and agendas, either an uneventful crossing lay ahead, or the Last Night at Sea Dinner and Farewell Party couldn't come soon enough, and Danny could tell straight away which this one would be. This one had Trouble written all over it. And he'd put money on the man he was about to serve being involved.

'Smoked sturgeon, sir...'

The man gave a dismissive grunt.

He was aware of two debutantes sitting opposite eyeing the flashily dressed spiv with interest as they toyed with their *Grapefruits au maraschino,* and hoped their finishing school had taught them that sharks weren't only to be found in water.

The fourth occupant of the table, dressed in the sort of dark suit and dog-collar worn by the clergy, was also sneaking a speculative glance from behind a large black prayer book. Danny, recognising him from previous trips, smiled faintly; it was the victims who'd need prayers when this vicar revealed his real profession, because he was a highly skilled card sharp.

'Oysters on half shell, sir...'

The clergyman thanked him and closed his prayer book, and Here-Comes-Trouble summoned him back with a click of the fingers and a loud sniff.

'Yes sir?'

A podgy finger pointed at the untouched dish. 'Tell the chef Mister Stonefeather doesn't expect to have to add his own lemon juice. Can't smell any in this.'

'Of course, sir,' Danny nodded respectfully. As long as you don't mind some blood mixed in it when Alec Baxter hears about it, he added under his breath.

However, judging from the profanities echoing around the kitchens (situated well out of sight, sound, and smelling range of first class diners, naturally), Alec's pan-hurling rage was already in full flow. And the victim was Joey Smith, who looked near to collapse from worry and exhaustion - and had prepared this particular dish. Danny listened as jeers at Joey's uselessness, not just in the kitchen but in all areas of life, progressed to total control over his future: 'The slightest fault with *anything* you produce - and believe me, I mean the least, minutest detail - there'll be a D/R in your Book!'

It was the threat they all lived in fear of. Anyone with a D/R (Decline to Report) stamped in their Seaman's Discharge Book would never be signed on this, or any other, ship again. And jobs were scarce. Nudge-wink Prohibition dodging and flappers dancing the Charleston on taxi bonnets didn't have the same ring if you were at the bottom of the heap and desperate for work of any kind, no matter how brutal the conditions. And Joey was desperate. He'd recently got engaged. Danny knew how much this job meant to him.

He stepped aside as another waiter, arms laden to the elbows with bowls of *Consommé Aurore* and *Potage Solferino,* bustled to the 'Out' swing door, and looked at the smoked sturgeon nestling on its bed of perfectly chopped shallots, beets, red onions, chives, and dessert apples, topped with quail's egg and caviar, all arranged with meticulous care. Complaints from first class diners were rare - everyone made sure there was nothing to complain about - but if ever there *was* the slightest dissatisfaction he knew perfectly well it must be reported, despite triggering more vilification for Joey. A waiter taking matters into his own hands was unheard of; the possibility of it happening would occur neither to the Head Waiter nor kitchen hierarchy. It certainly wouldn't occur to the passenger.

And it wouldn't occur to the waiter either if he had any sense, thought Danny as he slipped through the 'Out' swing door, trekked back to the dining saloon, and courteously placed in front of Mister Stonefeather (now upgraded from mere involvement in mischief to odds-on favourite to singlehandedly leaving a trail of mayhem from here to New York) the dish he'd just sent back.

'Mister Smith has the honour of creating this for you, sir.' The tone was quiet and friendly, and lowered confidentially to add, 'That's who Prince Nicolai Romanoff always insists prepares his smoked sturgeon personally.'

Lexie Stonefeather looked at the dish, then up at Danny.

'He won't have it done by anyone else.' Danny bent slightly towards Mister Stonefeather's oil-slick black hair, well aware he was digging himself into a deeper hole with every word he spoke, and that instead of just one seafarer with a D/R in his Discharge Book there'd now probably be two. He hadn't a clue whether there was a Prince Nicolai Romanoff or not; he just had to hope Mister Stonefeather (and the vicar, now listening with interest to this far-fetched bilge) didn't either, and said a silent prayer that the man scrutinising his 'replacement' *hors d'oeuvres* didn't turn out to be some sort of expert on Russian aristocracy, with intimate knowledge of the entire Romanoff dynasty.

He began to sweat. He was committed now. There was no way out of this but to keep going.

'Mister Smith was trained at the Waldorf-Astoria Hotel, sir. His speciality dish, smoked sturgeon, comes with his precise dash of lemon already added. But of course, if you'd prefer the more obvious drizzle over the top...?'

Mister Stonefeather inspected the dish in silence, and the silence was ominous.

Nobody quite knew how he'd made his money. There were whispered rumours, of course - and vague rumours suited him just fine, because all anyone needed to know was that the man who could pull a fast one on Lexie Stonefeather had yet to be born. And if he had been, he'd wish he hadn't when Lexie'd finished with him.

He continued to frown at the unparalleled creation produced by the maestro of smoked sturgeon - which looked exactly the same as the one he'd just sent back - and gave another doubtful sniff.

Danny desperately ratcheted up the flattery: 'Mister Smith delights in preparing his most exquisite creations for true connoisseurs, sir.'

There was a glint of amusement in the eye of the vicar.

'My dear departed Aunt Matilda once met a Romanoff,' he announced, blinking earnestly at Mister Stonefeather. 'Although I gather he was a connoisseur of Russian triptychs. Or... now let me think... was it Easter eggs?'

Mister Stonefeather looked at him with open contempt and decided, rather than returning the dish a second time, to get a move on before this idiot parson whipped out his prayer book again and start praying over him (everyone knew vicars lulled you into a false sense of security with tales of batty aunts before going in for the kill with Repent, The End is Nigh. Or the church roof/organ/bells fund appeal. Or both). And tomorrow night, he'd make sure he found a table with more congenial company than the dead losses on this one; gormless debs, not even attractive, and an inane vicar. He nodded briefly at Danny, selected from the array of solid silver cutlery at either side of the dish the correct knife and fork, and set to work.

And Danny, heart pounding, took the girls' orders for the next course and set off back to the kitchens. Short term success could mean long term disaster for both himself and Joey, who'd never been anywhere near the Waldorf-Astoria Hotel; all it needed was Mister Stonefeather boasting about preferential treatment when everyday excellence was good enough for common-or-garden Royalty and other first class passengers - and the irony was, it'd be only a matter of time before whatever was going on between Alec and Joey came to a head anyway. They had the whole of the Atlantic to cross yet.

He knew intuitively that he hadn't heard the last of this. But Joey was an old mate, and if you couldn't do a favour for a mate, well, you weren't up to much.

As for the 'vicar', he'd obviously used the occasion to slip into his adopted role for this trip. Not that Danny disapproved. He'd try it himself if he thought he'd get away with it. Who'd be a waiter, if the odd touch of skulduggery here and there meant someone else carting plates around while you selected whatever you desired from a menu to tempt the palates of kings and emperors?

Alec's attention was taken up with some drama at the double ovens, and Danny took advantage of a short wait for the girls' *Noisettes d'Agneau Maltese* and *Ris de Veau Osielle* to motion Joey across.

'What was all that about?'
'All what about?'

Oh. He was in one of those moods, was he. Here they were with thirty seconds if they were lucky, and Joey had to waste it with What-are-you-talking-about, everything's-fine rubbish.

'Alec Baxter.' Danny could be abrupt, too. He'd just put his own job on the line.

'Nothing.'

'Yeah. Looked like it.'

Joey gave an exasperated sigh. 'All right, since you won't drop it. He's going to make sure I'm unemployed by the end of this trip. Happy now?'

'But why? Why would -'

'Leave it, Danny. I mean it.'

Danny had no option. His order arrived, and Joey deliberately turned away and went back to his station.

There was a lot more to this than met the eye, and whatever it was, it was serious. Usually they chatted and joked together as they came on board in Southampton, but on this occasion Joey had left it until the last possible minute, and arrived looking drained and haggard. In fact, the only time Danny had seen him look so utterly wretched was at the end of the first voyage they'd done together, when they'd both sworn never again to endure such misery.

He was thoughtful as he returned to the dining saloon with the girls' orders, because the exhaustion and despair on Joey's face brought it all back; his own face had frequently worn the same expression during that trip, when a wink of support from Joey had saved him from collapse more than once...

It was 1919, they'd both found themselves marooned in Canada for different reasons, and they both needed to get back to Europe. In Danny's case it was because everyone who'd served in the Canadian Expeditionary Force had to return to Canada from Europe to be discharged, despite the fact that he was English and his unit was in France at the end of the war. But he had to make his own way to a British port, and the only way he could do it was to work his passage. And as he'd had

13

word that his mother was seriously ill with Spanish flu, he needed to take whatever job he could get, on the first home-bound ship he could find. The only vessel signing on crew in Saint John, New Brunswick, bound for Liverpool, required stokehold firemen - a job Danny wouldn't have touched if he hadn't been desperate.

Joey also needed to get back to England, but for different reasons. The ship he'd arrived on had sailed without him when he'd got too drunk to report back before she left port. He was in trouble, he was penniless, and he was stuck in Canada with no identification papers of any sort and no belongings other than the clothes he stood up in. Joey was desperate, too.

They'd both signed on as firemen.

Four hours at a time, working two shifts in every twenty four hours, day and night, it was long recognised as the toughest job in the world. In sweltering heat, each man, stripped to the waist and with a piece of wet cloth around his neck, blinded by coal dust, unable to breathe in the choking fumes, and trying to stay upright as the deck plating rose and fell with the movement of the ship even in calm conditions, had to shovel two and a half tons of coal into a white hot furnace during each shift. Seven minutes at a time was the maximum possible for any man to do, with a gong struck, prize fighter style, to allow a brief break for breath before clanging again for another seven minutes of furiously shovelling coal into the insatiable mouths of the furnaces. Nostrils, mouth, eyes, and lungs clogged with coal dust, the back-breaking shovelling went on for four endless hours at a time, alternating with the equally brutal but necessary job of clearing the furnaces of clinker with long-handled slicers, again in seven minute bouts signalled by the gong.

The firemen they worked with were broad and muscular, with a fearsome reputation. Joey, also broad and muscular, managed to adapt, but Danny's slight build marked him out for derision as a puny weakling, which was why Joey's support had meant so much. He could have managed it for a week in order to reach home quickly, but the ship was given orders to change destination and proceed to Australia instead, which meant a voyage starting in February eventually ended in August, with Danny close to physical and mental breakdown.

And when he did eventually arrive home, it was to find he was too late. His mother had died.

But while the horrific voyage had affected the health of both of them to differing degrees, it created a bond that would last a lifetime. And whatever happened on this voyage - and Danny knew that if Joey was pushed too far, something *would* happen, and it could end in serious trouble - he'd be embroiled in it.

Just because Joey looked near to collapse from worry and exhaustion didn't mean he'd meekly accept being tormented for the rest of the trip, if deliberately pushed to breaking point. Joey was a rough, tough Scouser who'd take anyone on (Danny had seen him in action), and no matter how badly he wanted this job, it would probably be only a matter of time before he used his fists on Alec Baxter. As Alec, of course, knew only too well.

All crew members were aware that any such outburst would, for the short-lived satisfaction of seeing blood pour from a bully's mouth, result in spending the rest of the voyage chained up in the ship's hold before serving the long and savage prison sentence that would follow, and ending up unemployable with a prison record at the end of it.

So whatever was behind all this - and he'd find out more later, when they finished their shifts - if that was what Alec Baxter had in mind, there was every chance he'd achieve it.

And no amount of bamboozling Mister Stonefeather with flattery that he was among the elite few to be favoured with Mister Smith's extra-special masterpieces was going to stop it.

Many of the diners had already left, and Danny was clearing the table when the Head Waiter swept regally across with an elderly couple and deposited them at the adjoining two-seater, and he guessed they'd deliberately postponed eating until the saloon was relatively quiet. They were ill-at-ease; the woman's

15

body language was timid, the man's verging on truculence to overcompensate for feelings of inadequacy, and both seemed over-awed by the size and splendour of the room, which ran the full breadth of the ship and was nearly three decks high. They gaped at the domed ceiling with its leaded glass windows, the marble columns, the opulent mahogany and walnut fittings, the orchestra playing some unfamiliar classical piece; took in the sophisticated women in the most expensive of gowns, the men, utterly self-assured, accustomed to wealth, power, and influence.

He held the chair for the woman as she sat. She was wearing a plain grey dress, with a sash of lighter grey tied around the hips, and a stole of the same material. Danny, although no expert on women's clothing, guessed the outfit was home-made.

'Thanks, son.'

'It's a pleasure, madam,' smiled Danny, nodding at her husband, who nodded awkwardly back.

'Oh, my name's Mary.' She indicated her husband. 'This is Sam… Oor son's paid for a' this,' she went on, hiding large workworn hands under the table and obviously feeling the need to justify the presence of riff-raff in such illustrious surroundings. 'For oor Fiftieth Wedding Anniversary.'

'Well, that's terrific,' replied Danny, 'He'll be wanting us all to look after you, and give you the very best of attention. And that's just what we're going to do, so you just sit back and enjoy it.'

He warmed to the couple. He'd love to do the same thing for his own dad, who in his youth had crossed the Atlantic in very different conditions; on sailing ships bound for San Francisco via the storms of Cape Horn (and still known locally as Frisco after a fellow lifeboat crewman coined the nickname) as well as Canada and Australia.

He saw the woman's eyes drawn to the bewildering array of cutlery at her place setting, behind which were two wine glasses, a water goblet, a champagne flute, and a sherry glass, and heard the intake of breath as she instinctively raised a hand

16

to her mouth, then lowered it hastily under the table again to hide an unsightly bandage on her left thumb.

The man was staring in horror at the *Carte du Jour* Dinner choices. Danny saw the large hands, used to a lifetime of manual work, shake slightly, and guessed the problem. Five courses, all in French... and the Head Waiter, instead of leaving them to quietly find a table where they'd be discreetly hidden from view, had escorted them to one of the most prominent in the room. The man's panic-stricken thoughts were as clear as if he'd spoken them aloud: I don't understand any of this! How do I order? What am I going to end up with?

Well, Danny mightn't be able to treat his dad to a trip on the *Berengaria*, but he could ensure this couple's voyage wasn't spoilt by unfamiliarity with a French *Carte du Jour* and a glut of unnecessary knives and forks. And although it wasn't within a waiter's remit to make suggestions, he knew instinctively they'd find it even more mortifying if the Head Waiter swept across to rescue the situation.

'Could I recommend something for you, sir? Tell me, what's your favourite food?'

Favourite food? The man stared at him, his mind a blank. Bad enough making a holy show of themselves by arriving late, without having to cope with all this as well. Anyway, he didn't have a favourite food, he just ate whatever Mary put on the table. He thought for a moment. The fish suppers she brought home from time to time from her job at the fish and chip shop were all right, he supposed.

'Fish... have you got any fish?'

'Good choice sir.' Danny pointed to the *Sole Frite avec Vinaigrette a la Lime.* 'How does Fried Sole sound?'

'Aye, that'll do. I don't want any of this... this First Course stuff.'

'I'll have the same. Thanks, son,' the woman nodded.

'And how about...' Danny pointed to the *Boeuf Roti avec garniture au Sauce Raifort* and *Pommes Nouvelles*. 'Roast beef with horseradish sauce and new potatoes to follow?'

'To follow? Ye mean, as well as the fish?'

'Yes. And then there's dessert. Anything you want, anything at all, you only have to ask, and I'll make sure you get it. Like I said, sir,' smiled Danny, quietly removing the oyster forks and fruit spoons from the place settings. 'You just sit back, enjoy your son's Golden Wedding treat as he'd want you to, and don't worry about anything at all.' Or anybody, he added silently as a couple of elegant dowagers glanced with barely-concealed disdain at Mary's dress on their way out.

He swiftly moved position, blocking her view before she became aware of it and was wounded.

Whatever else might happen on this voyage - and although it might seem like a melodramatic cliché to compare his intuitive unease to an awareness of pressure building inside a volcano before the eruption, that was the phase that came to Danny's mind - Mary and Sam's trip of a lifetime would not be spoiled by anxiety about correct table etiquette, incomprehensible menus, or being regarded as gauche outsiders by a couple of haughty prima donnas, if he had anything to do with it.

2

The vicar sat puffing at his pipe in the first class Smoking Room, which was a replica of an old English inn, complete with half-timbered walls and ceiling, oak carved pillars, and stag horns over a large open fireplace.

After a discreet but expert assessment of his fellow smokers, his attention focused on Mister Stonefeather, who was now deep in conversion with (as he discovered thanks to a chair conveniently placed for eavesdropping) a New York industrialist by the name of Lemuel Hoffmann.

One of the junior pursers entered, and looked around the room.

'Good evening, gentlemen. Just an informal warning... we understand there may be card sharps aboard on this trip.' His eye alighted briefly on the clergyman. 'It's our duty to ensure you are alert to the possibility of falling prey to these people, so do please be on your guard if you choose to play with strangers. That's all, gentlemen. Thank you.'

There was silence as he went out.

'Card sharps? What did he mean? I don't think I've heard the expression.' The clergyman looked around the room. 'Would any of you gentlemen be kind enough to explain?'

Mister Stonefeather glanced at his companion, and winked.

'I don't think you need to worry about cards sharps, Reverend. I don't suppose you play much poker, do you?'

'No,' agreed the dog-collared cleric, shaking his head. 'Why? Is it a complicated game?'

'Well, there's a bit more to it than Snap!, if you've ever played that?'

'Oh yes, I've played Snap!, and I must admit I do enjoy a game of Patience sometimes. And of course Whist with the Elderberry Club.'

The man winked at his companion again and strolled over to the table, on which lay a deck of cards. He shuffled them with competent but unexceptional ability. 'Lexie Stonefeather at your service, Reverend. I'd be happy to explain the intricacies of poker to you. How about a little game right now?'

The invitation was accepted with diffident courtesy, and Lexie laughed to himself. A vicar, of all things, who from the look of him had probably given hundreds of sermons on the evils of gambling, asking about card sharps and poker! He was going to have some fun on this trip. Blameless innocent boarding the ship in Southampton, degenerate gambler disembarking in New York...

Come to think of it, what was a clergyman doing travelling first class, anyway? Didn't they have to take a vow of poverty? Or was that nuns? Well, if ministers were supposed to live austere, puritanical lives, Lexie'd be doing him a good turn, wouldn't he, if he helped bring him in line with that aspect of his faith by the time he reached the other side of the Atlantic? He vaguely remembered some convoluted explanation to the debutantes over dinner about a religious convention in New York - he'd gone glazed-eyed and stopped listening half way through - and the man was presumably sufficiently high up in the organisation to warrant a first class passage, which meant he must have been provided with enough money to make it worth Lexie's while to re-route it into his own pocket with the lure of cash for fancy new pews, or a super-duper organ, or whatever ecclesiastical furniture vicars lusted after.

He'd have to tread a bit warily with Lemuel, who obviously hadn't yet worked out what was going on under Lexie's surface friendliness, because Lemuel could prove an equally useful cash cow of a different variety; lucrative contracts when they reached New York, where it was important that he was seen as a serious businessman, not some huckster playing poker with nincompoops for amusement. But that still left the prospect of some very rewarding sessions with the vicar on the way.

And just think of the mileage in amusing anecdotes for the Golf Club!

Jack Dalton had more important things to think about than storing up amusing anecdotes to impress golf club members. Funds were running low. On his last trip he'd only made enough, after the cost of his ticket and expenses, to purchase the Rolls Royce New Phantom he'd earmarked as a replacement for the Silver Ghost, and now he needed to bring the kitty back to a more healthy level.

The demonstration/instruction poker game was a convenient way of assessing the level of expertise to expect. No big stakes of course, just 'a bit of innocent fun.' When it was his turn to win it was laughed off as beginner's luck; when he allowed them to win they couldn't resist showing off by explaining the various points of the game while he listened attentively, murmuring, 'Well! What a fascinating game!' and shaking his head in wonder.

It would be on the last night of the voyage, in the privacy of one of the suites or staterooms when he played for serious money, that Lexie Stonefeather - who was obviously only too ready to fleece a dim-witted vicar - would find out just what a card sharp who meant business could do.

'*Now* what are ye doing?'

'Just giving the place a wee tidy.'

'*A wee tidy?* What for? The stewardess will do that!'

'We can't let the stewardess see it like this, Sam!'

Sam shook his head, bemused. 'But it's her job!'

'Och wheest! It'll only take a minute.'

He huffed in exasperation. He'd already side-stepped his way through the minefield of what Mary would wear for tonight's Ball, now he had to wait while she cleaned the bathroom as well. No wonder they called ships 'she'. No matter how you tried to steer them to where you wanted to go, they had the same contrary determination to head off in some other direction.

The dress, for example. For the life of him, he couldn't see why she was moaning that she had nothing to wear. Of course she had things to wear. What about the dress she'd bought on the market? Or the ones she'd run up herself on a friend's sewing machine? The grey one she'd worn for dinner looked all right to him. Why couldn't she wear that?

Mary stopped wiping the washbasin, and looked at her face in the mirror above. Old, lined, tired... She looked down at her hands. Large, wrinkled, workworn, a grubby bandage on her left thumb... She thought about the dainty white hands she'd noticed on other women, hands that had never toiled in a cold damp factory, gutted a fish, or scrubbed a floor, and were pampered night after night with the best quality creams money could buy.

And she thought about the grey dress, so obviously home-made; the cheap material, the pathetic lack of adornment and accessories. Everyone at the fish and chip shop had admired it, but here, as she compared it to the other gowns and evening dresses on display, she saw it for what it was, and was mortified. She thought of the contrast between it and the fabulous *haute couture* gowns bought in the fashion houses of Paris as other women, beautiful, stylish, and supremely confident of their allure, made effortless conversation while she sat mute and ashamed.

She gave the washbasin another automatic wipe. Well, she had two choices. Either they lurked out of sight in here like hermits for the entire trip - which would hurt and disappoint Michael, who'd paid for it (and wouldn't do much for marital harmony), or...

She bit her lip. If she delayed much longer the Ball would be over anyway, and that would settle the issue. And she did so much want to see one of the fabulous *Berengaria* Balls she'd heard so much about...

Daphne absently fingered her Sailing Day Present diamond brooch, and scoured the First Class Passenger List which was placed in every suite and stateroom, together with the Dining Reservation Card, greetings telegrams, various invitations, flower arrangements, crystal decanter of sherry, selection of chocolates, and bowls of choicest fruit.

One needed to know who else of note was on board. An unacknowledged but tangible social pecking order marked out each voyage, and it helped to ascertain at the start to which clique it was in one's best interests to belong. And as dinner hadn't exactly produced an overflowing harvest of opportunities - they'd been paired with an overweight American widow and a retired professor who was stone deaf - they'd better get down to some serious perusing if they wanted to salvage the rest of the evening, if not the entire trip.

'Darling, it's an absolute *disaster*! We don't know a *soul*!'

Theodore gave a noncommittal grunt as he took off his full-dress coat and dropped it on the bed for the steward to brush down and hang up.

'I mean, it's bound to be rather an anti-climax after last time,' conceded Daphne. 'One quite appreciates that. After all, the Prince of Wales can't be aboard on *every* trip.'

'And even if he was,' Theodore raised a sardonic eyebrow, 'He'd be permanently obscured from view by the usual coterie of brash American floosies.'

Daphne said nothing, and returned to carefully scouring the Passenger List. Good heavens, this was catastrophic! There must be *somebody*...

Of course, the aged widow and deaf professor - together with that boorish spiv, vicar, and insipid girls on the neighbouring table - quite obviously presented no threat to this trip's main aim: an invitation to dine at the captain's table. Theodore's elder brother had recently dined for the third time with the captain on the *Aquitania,* and it rankled that Theodore had never been invited to do likewise, despite making numerous transatlantic trips on Cunard liners over the years. It rankled even more with Daphne, who had to keep up the pretence of indifference at the irksome fact that they were the only ones at dinner parties unable to toss in a throwaway line introducing some riveting anecdote: 'When we dined at the captain's table on the *Berengaria*...'

But secret glee at the lack of competition was one thing. Spending the entire voyage surrounded by a collection of nonentities and social inferiors was quite another.

She finally came across a familiar name.

'Oh. The Countess of Knotworth.' She sniffed, unimpressed. 'And Miss Caroline McLean. That'll be the ghastly American sister Penelope told me about. Apparently she absolutely *ruined* her last dinner party!'

Again Theodore grunted, adjusting his cuffs. Daphne took the hint and stood up. Time to head to the Sailing Night Ball.

'Oh well,' she sighed, 'Needs must, I suppose. If there's nobody else, we'll just have to make do with them.'

Theodore looked across. 'Aubrey not with them?'

'No...' The word was loaded with innuendo.

They glanced at each other. Well quite honestly, who could blame him? Poor, poor Aubrey, saddled with that dreary, half-alive, *ungrateful* creature. A most unsatisfactory state of affairs altogether. It really was too, *too* bad.

'Wasn't he the dreamiest creature you've ever seen?' sighed Caroline as she expertly re-applied lipstick, blotted her lips, and reached for her gold compact.

The Countess of Knotworth had to agree about that. He certainly was. She'd privately thought much the same thing herself when the ship's officer in question hurried past as they watched the military band playing on the quayside, the crowds waving to friends and relatives aboard the ship, the winches embarking the last of the heavy baggage, the shore gangs waiting to cast off the mooring ropes, the tugs making ready to take up the strain of the hawsers, and the steward beating a gong and shouting 'All visitors ashore!' But seven years of carefully saying only what was expected of her meant the habit was now too deeply ingrained to drool over the physical attractions of a man, however delectable.

'Just as well I'm chaperoning you on this trip,' she murmured instead, in a tone of vague reproof befitting an older married sibling assuming responsibility for a giddy young thing on the *Berengaria,* a liner famous (or, to those sections of society who placed a high value on decorum, notorious) for amorous shipboard adventures. 'Heaven knows what debauchery you'd get up to by the time we reach New York if you were travelling alone. You're just a natural born flirt!'

She knew she'd been wasting her breath, so the response wasn't altogether unexpected. It was the contempt in Caroline's Long Island drawl that made her flinch.

'You betcha sweet life I'll get up to debauchery! I'd consider it a complete waste of time if I didn't. I'm gonna flirt with every hunk in sight!' She finished powdering her nose, snapped the compact shut, and began applying kohl all around her eyes, smudging it outwards. 'You ain't chaperoning some goody-two-shoes convent novice here, Reverend Sister Sophie. So just remember that at tonight's Ball!'

'Caroline, I'm not trying to stop you having fun, I just -'

'Good. Because I plan on having lots of fun on this trip.' Caroline turned to face her sister. 'Like you used to, before that cold fish you married sapped all the *joie de vivre* out of you!'

Sophie cast about for a response to laugh off the jibe without revealing the deeply painful nerve it touched, but none sprang to mind. Not that it would have made any difference if it had; Caroline fully intended having the sort of talk she knew Sophie would avoid at all costs during this voyage, and she had no intention of being sidestepped by lectures on avoiding the temptations of the flesh.

And as the topic had, coincidentally, veered towards flirtation and debauchery, then right now seemed as good a time as any for it to continue veering towards a topic she knew would be even more unpalatable; the state of Sophie's marriage.

'You used to be such good company when you were young,' Caroline reminded her sister. 'Now look at you - twenty seven, going on seventy two. He's buried you alive, Sophie!'

'Look. I don't want to talk about Aubrey.'

'I know you don't. But we're going to, because until you hear it said aloud you'll keep on denying that marrying that creep was the biggest mistake of your life...'

She broke off. The stress and strain on her sister's face was so pronounced that continuing with this would just result in floods of tears, and achieve nothing. Okay. It could wait.

And anyway - she glanced at her Cartier watch - the evening's festivities were about to begin. Who wanted to dig into marital disasters when there were dances to enjoy, men to flirt with, and a host of male hearts to captivate at *Berengaria's* legendary Sailing Night Ball? And if Sophie was too prim to take full advantage of these delights (purely to dissipate nervous tension of course), Caroline would willingly make up for both of them.

Time enough to hold the matrimonial inquest in the morning.

Caroline allowed herself to be escorted back to her place by her latest waltz partner, a young ship's officer who introduced himself as Tom Burnett.

She had, of course, spent much longer than Sophie in choosing tonight's evening dress, finally settling on a flamboyant red number which flattered her dark hair and showed off her trim figure (if you've got it, flaunt it - who wanted to merge into the background like some reticent Victorian wallflower?). Sophie, who planned to sit out most dances, settled for a more demure dark green dress which nevertheless suited her tawny hair and slight frame.

Tom held the chair for her as she sat, enquired if she'd like a drink, thanked her again for the pleasure of her company, requested another dance later, and backed respectfully away.

'Yeah, not a bad dancer,' she agreed in response to the friendly compliment from the elderly couple at the adjoining table, who had introduced themselves as Mary and Sam. 'Couldn't hold a candle to the Prince of Wales, of course.' She fluttered her eyelashes at a German princeling with whom she'd danced earlier, and then fluttered them even more at a very fetching Polish count with whom she'd also danced.

'The Prince of Wales?' gasped Mary, trying to hide behind the table in a homely grey dress and self-consciously keeping her hands out of view.

Even her husband took notice. 'You danced wi' the Prince of Wales?'

'Sure did. In this very ballroom. Last year. And believe me, he really is the best I've ever danced with.'

Another gasp.

'Only problem is, he's set the benchmark too high for all the rest.' Caroline broke off as her sister was escorted back by her dance partner - coincidentally the dark-haired ship's officer they'd earlier nicknamed the Promenade Deck Hunk - who thanked her for the dance and then (to Caroline's indignation) asked the taller of two giggling flappers at a neighbouring table for the next waltz.

'Sophie, meet Mary and Sam... My sister, Sophie.'

Mary and Sam, after introductions, explained that he was a retired shipyard worker, she a factory hand. They'd both put in extra hours, he at the yard, Mary as a cleaner and in a fish and chip shop, so their son could attend college. Michael had emigrated to New York, prospered, and was now treating them to a holiday in the United States for their Fiftieth Wedding Anniversary, travelling first class on the *Berengaria*.

Sophie nodded, interested. Despite her ambition to marry into English aristocracy, she was no snob. Both she and Caroline had a healthy American respect for anyone who accumulated wealth through their own efforts; Pop's grandparents had been penniless immigrants when they'd first arrived in America.

'Your sister was just telling us she's danced with the Prince of Wales,' prompted Mary, who'd rather hear about Caroline's exotic dance partner than discuss fish and chip shops and office-cleaning.

'Yeah. I was on the way back to the States with Pop. The Prince travelled under the title of Duke of Renfrew, but you can bet your bottom dollar it wasn't long before everyone knew!'

'What was he like?' asked Sam, sipping his whisky.

'Sociable. Debonair. Handsome...'

'I think Pop hoped there might be a romance,' smiled Sophie.

'Him and me both. I certainly wouldn't have said no,' sighed Caroline wistfully, and they all laughed.

Mary was obviously eager to hear more.

'On Sports Day,' Caroline told her, 'He took part in the tug of war. And he went to the Carnival Dinner and Fancy Dress Ball that night.'

'What did he go as?' interrogated Mary, eager for every detail to relate to the chippie regulars when she got home.

'An Apache.'

'What did you go as?'

'An Arabian Princess. Should have gone as an Apache squaw, shouldn't I?'

Mary clucked sympathetically.

'And he played a ukulele with his coat of arms engraved on at the Ship's Concert.'

'Pity I wasnae aboard,' grinned Sam. 'I could have played the Jew's harp along wi' him!'

Mary gave him a sharp nudge. Sam was obviously under orders to be on his best behaviour, curb his thick Glaswegian accent, and speak only when necessary. He was doing his best to be obedient, but his accent was becoming more pronounced as the evening wore on and his alcohol intake increased.

'And -' Caroline broke off as a buxom woman in a blue crepe-de-chine evening gown, accompanied by a portly man with a florid face and thinning hair, bore down on them.

'Sophie darling! *There* you are! We saw your name on the Passenger List, and thought how utterly divine to meet up again!'

Caroline was the only one to notice her sister's face fall momentarily before automatically assuming the professional Countess of Knotworth smile that didn't quite reach her eyes.

'What a lovely surprise!' Sophie exclaimed politely. 'How nice.' There was a slight pause. 'Now this is unforgiveable of me, I know. Do be kind and remind me... Where...?'

The woman chuckled conspiratorially. 'Oh, I do *quite* understand! Dilly's parties do have that effect on one, don't they? We always escape as soon as we can!'

Sophie remembered now. Daphne and Theodore. One of Dilly's dinner parties. But far from agreeing with the derision Daphne offered as a common bond, Sophie was unimpressed by 'friends' who accepted hospitality and then belittled the hostess later. And she was fond of Dilly, who was warm-hearted and

30

kind, and one of the few people who'd made her feel truly welcome rather than grudgingly tolerated. Daphne and Theodore were wrong. It wasn't Dilly's party, but they themselves she had no particular wish to remember.

'Oh... yes. Yes! Of course. How nice to see you again.'

'How's Aubrey?' enquired Theodore, fixing her with what Pop would have described as a very old-fashioned look.

'Very well, thank you.'

The woman lowered her voice discreetly. 'Is he not travelling with you?'

'No. Not on this occasion.'

'Ah...' A knowing look passed between them, and Sophie could almost hear them add, 'Not on any other occasion either, if he can help it.' There was a slightly awkward silence.

'I don't think you've met my sister?' she continued, to fill it. 'Caroline, do meet Daphne and Theodore.'

Caroline in turn nodded and smiled, but was far from happy at the way things were developing. No wonder Sophie's face had fallen with the arrival of this gruesome twosome; the cloistered world of the English aristocracy had now infiltrated the anonymity and distance provided by the ship, and they looked likely to attach themselves like limpets and act as unofficial secret agents, spying on Sophie's every move and reporting back, if not directly to Aubrey, to mutual friends who would ensure any gossip safely reached his ears.

Well, they might dictate the terms at home, but they'd strayed onto her territory now, and *she'd* call the shots on this one. Sophie may not be in a position to discourage them, but Caroline, the American sister who doubtless mixed with heaven only knew what disreputable dregs of humanity back home (no accounting for taste when it came to Americans) knew exactly what would ensure they didn't hang around too long.

'Why, howdy doody, folks!' The volume increased, the American accent was exaggerated to the point of burlesque, and Caroline gave a lascivious wink. 'Say, you just gotta meet our

31

new friends, Mary and Sam, as well! Let's make it one big son-of-a-gun party!'

Sam immediately staggered to his feet, almost knocking the chair over, and held out a huge workman's paw. 'Pleased tae meet ye! Put it there, if it weighs a ton!'

Daphne froze, mute.

'Of course, maybe you folks already know each other from back home?' enquired Caroline innocently.

Mary smiled goodnaturedly, indicating the empty chair beside her. 'Sit yersel' doon here, hen. Plenty room for a wee'un, eh?'

Daphne blinked at Sophie, horrified. What on earth were these ghastly people doing here? Had they wandered up from second class by mistake? But there was strict segregation - why hadn't they been ejected?

Theodore was having similar thoughts. Obviously the most tactful way of dealing with this was to summon one of the waiters, who would attend to the problem.

He snapped his fingers. 'Waiter!'

Then, in deference to Aubrey, who would be mortified to discover his wife hadn't had sufficient presence of mind to deal with the situation herself, he provided the face-saving excuse for calling the waiter. 'Can I get you a refill, Sophie?'

'Thank you. Another Americano.'

'Caroline?'

'The same.'

'Darling?'

'Brandy cocktail I think please, darling.'

There was a pause as Theodore looked at the waiter, who happened to be Danny, then pointedly directed his eyes at Sam and Mary in an unspoken instruction for their removal to be effected quickly, quietly, and with the minimum of fuss.

'Aye, thanks. Hauf an' a hauf. Laphroiag.' Sam held out his empty whisky glass to Danny, drained his pint glass, and held that out too. 'Thanks, son.'

'I'd be quite happy with a nice cup o' tea, masel',' nodded Mary, smiling at Danny.

Theodore gaped at her, dumbstruck. Riff-raff from the slums of Glasgow, calmly ordering cups of tea and whisky - Laphroaig of all things, if you please! - in the first class ballroom of the *Berengaria*!

And the waiter, instead of indignantly hustling them out, was taking the order, the implication being that they had every right to be here!

Which meant he was now committed to joining not only Sophie and Caroline but this uncouth navvy and his wife with her cheap clothes and scarecrow-like hair, because he had no choice but to take Mary's adjoining chair as Danny pulled back another chair for Daphne. Even worse, he had an uncomfortable suspicion that under the impeccable courteous deference, the waiter found the situation amusing in some way.

Well, the only possible course was to ignore the interlopers altogether.

'I say, Caroline,' he remarked jovially, 'Jolly good show, that Charleston earlier, what!'

'Ra-*ther!*' Daphne had adopted the habit, fashionable with Bright Young Things, of placing emphasis on the second syllable of the word. '*I* certainly couldn't attempt an energetic dance like that after tonight's meal!'

'Well, speaking of meals,' replied Caroline. 'Mary works in a fish and chip shop.' She turned to Mary. 'What's your professional opinion of *Berengaria's* fish course, Mary?'

Daphne's eyes travelled down to the home-made grey dress, which was presumably what one wore to work in fish and chip shops, and Danny quietly placed a tray containing teapot, milk jug, sugar basin, and cup and saucer in front of Mary as a second waiter replenished the cocktails and Sam's half tumbler of whisky and half of bitter.

One had to make allowances for Caroline (no accounting for taste when it came to Americans), but Sophie... well, really. American she may be, but the Countess of Knotworth should surely have more respect for her own title and position. Courteous small talk with social inferiors as and when appropriate, yes of course - but that certainly didn't apply to the first class ballroom on the *Berengaria*.

'Och, I don't cook the fish masel'! Naw, I jist gut them.' Mary held up the thumb of her left hand, encased in its huge bandage. 'Daft clot that I am, I nearly sliced off my thumb, ha ha! So easy wi' a fish-gutting knife, isn't it?'

Daphne looked helplessly at Theodore.

'Yes, I suppose it must be,' he agreed vaguely.

'Have the ship's doctor keep an eye on it, Mary,' advised Sophie, as Danny and his fellow waiter moved away. 'It looks nasty. You don't want to spoil your stay in New York.'

Mary craned round Theodore to smile at Daphne, and include her in the conversation. 'Aye, this is us going on oor holidays! To New York!'

'Really.' Daphne nodded politely. Where did the idiotic woman think everyone else was going?

'Aye. Oor son's taking us tae see a Broadway show, *'No, No, Nanette'*.'

'How exciting.' Daphne's tone was cool, indicating that the level of small talk she was prepared to tolerate had now been reached, and it was time for this ghastly pair to take themselves off.

'Ye'll have heard of it, aye?' enquired Sam, nodding encouragingly at Theodore.

Theodore shook his head. 'I'm afraid not.'

Mary was incredulous. 'Och, ye must have done!'

Daphne sipped her cocktail, staring at a point above Mary's head. Were they incapable of taking a hint?

'Well, don't worry, ye'll hear the orchestra play something from the show soon,' Sam leaned across Theodore and patted Daphne's knee reassuringly.

Daphne hastily moved her chair further out of range and, as if on cue, the orchestra finished *'Yes Sir, That's My Baby'*.

The conductor turned, and smiled directly at them. 'Ladies and gentlemen, something from the new Broadway show, *'No, No, Nanette'* for Mary and Sam who celebrate their Fiftieth

34

Wedding Anniversary when we reach New York. So let's hear it for - *'Tea For Two'*!'

Amid enthusiastic applause, and to Mary's undisguised delight, the conductor smiled again and bowed to her before the orchestra swung jauntily into *'Tea for Two'*.

'Good for a singalong, eh?' Sam took another swig of whisky and began to hum an out of tune accompaniment. 'Ye'll have heard of this one, surely?'

'Tea for Two,' explained Mary helpfully, in case they hadn't heard the conductor.

'No, I'm afraid I haven't. But then I don't suppose you've heard of *'le roi David'* either, have you?' Theodore's tone was icily polite.

'Eh... is that a Broadway musical as well, aye?'

'It's an oratorio, Mary. A bit like an opera,' explained Sophie quietly.

Sam, still shaking his head in wonderment that neither Theodore nor Daphne had heard of *'No, No, Nanette'*, accent growing more pronounced as the whisky had an increasing effect on his tongue, fought a losing battle with the sequence of no's, knows, and No's, which finally ran away with him altogether.

'Ye no' know *'No...?'* Ye no' know, know, *'No...?'* Ye no' know *'No, No, Nanette'?'*

Caroline giggled, and turned to Theodore. 'I just *knew* you'd love meeting Mary and Sam!'

'Tch!' Theodore had had enough of this nonsense. He and Daphne had done their bit by coming across to offer companionship to the Countess of Knotworth, but if she and her brash American sister chose to repay their kindness by continuing to hobnob with a drunken oaf of low intelligence bleating non-stop about some vulgar show, instead of gratefully engaging in stimulating conversation with himself and Daphne, well...

As everybody had said all along, American heiresses might have oodles of money... but...

Sympathy anew for Aubrey flooded him. Poor chap, saddled with this wash-out wife, this dreary creature who failed so utterly to cut the mustard as Lady Knotworth, because of his obligation to preserve Weedmoor Hall. What a self-sacrificing example of *noblesse oblige*! No wonder he endeavoured to spend as little time as possible with her, and escape to London whenever he could. Who could blame him?

Daphne's thoughts ran along similar lines (even if her ulterior motive was to ferret out as much as possible about the state of affairs between Sophie and Aubrey). What a tragedy this marriage had been. Poor, poor Aubrey.

Well, decided Theodore, obligatory courtesy now observed, they could avoid Sophie and the dire American sister for the rest of the voyage. Even better - and a blessed excuse to escape - he'd just spotted two familiar faces making their way past the potted palms towards a table next to the pillar in the seating area.

'Darling! I've just spotted Julian and Arabella! You must have missed them on the Passenger List!'

'Really? Where? How super! Oh, we *must* go and say hello!' Daphne rose from her chair with obvious relief.

'Do excuse us, won't you, Sophie.' Theodore hauled himself out of his own chair. 'It's been marvellous seeing you again. Do enjoy the rest of your evening!'

'Oh, I will,' Sophie promised, with a wide and genuine smile.

'Caroline. Lovely to meet you. Look forward to chatting again soon.' He gave her a courteous nod before turning away.

'Me too,' lied Caroline.

Daphne aimed a kiss at Sophie's cheek. 'Simply divine to see you again...' She turned to Caroline. 'And I'll look forward to another spirited performance of the Charleston, Caroline, with your ever-growing band of admirers!'

'Yeah, you and me both.'

Sam raised his whisky glass in a toast and grinned, although he hadn't actually been included in Theodore's farewells.

'Cheerio noo,' smiled Mary.

Neither Sophie nor Caroline could prevent the fit of giggles that overtook them as Daphne and Theodore made their way across the aisle to the other side of the seating area. Caroline gave Mary a hug. 'Mary, you and Sam have just done us the biggest favour imaginable!'

Mary and Sam looked at each other blankly. Favour? Of course they'd do anyone a favour if asked. But as far as they were aware nobody had requested any favours... Had they missed something here?

'You must come and visit us at Long Island while you're in New York,' continued Caroline.

'And bring your son,' added Sophie. 'He sounds like the sort of young man Pop could do business with.'

Again Mary and Sam again looked at each other, mystified.

American heiresses who burst out laughing for no reason, thanking them for non-existent favours and inviting them to Long Island (which could mean Michael making another influential business contact - he'd be pleased about that); English toffs who'd never heard of '*No, No, Nanette*' and didn't want to join in a singalong...

Och well. Live and let live. They'd been told they'd meet all sorts on the *Berengaria*.

They shrugged and joined contentedly in the chorus again, forefingers moving from side to side like piano metronomes:

'*Tea for two, And two for tea, Me for you, And you for me...*'

7

'Rather hot in here, don't you find?' Clive Willis winced inwardly as he spoke; it sounded corny even to him.

It was a line he'd used to good effect many times in the past, but on this occasion he had no devious ulterior motive. He was speaking the truth. It *was* hot in here - probably because the last dance had been a particularly energetic polka.

He'd danced during the evening with partners ranging from a coy debutante to the wife of an ambassador with no apparent preference for any of them, but partnered the tawny-haired lady in a dark green dress for the polka, his favourite dance, and it ended with them both bursting out laughing from sheer exhilaration.

But there was another reason it wasn't a line. There was absolutely no likelihood of a shipboard romance with this particular woman even if he *had* been interested - which he wasn't - because during the lull when the orchestra had a break he'd heard from Tom Burnett, who obviously fancied his chances with her companion, that they were sisters. And apparently she was a countess.

A countess, begorrah. That was upping the stakes, even for him.

Of course, the reassuring thing about shipboard dalliances was that everyone knew the score; fleeting episodes of frothy, light-hearted fun, amusing and uncomplicated, ending with a maudlin hug and a collection of autographed menu cards when the ship docked - and never, ever, intended to be taken seriously. But although Clive laughed along with the rest in the purser's office at the usual banter about potential female candidates for this trip's amorous interests, they all knew that while women were there to flirt with on a superficial level, his career came first every time. Never would he jeopardise that for any woman, on this trip or any other.

He had the makings of a very successful purser. He was suave and amenable with a ready smile and an easy manner, able to converse knowledgably on economics with high-ranking financiers, discuss politics with more astuteness than the politicians with whom he discussed them, indulge in salacious gossip about the aristocracy with whichever members of it happened to be currently on board, and flatter vacuous film stars with chatty inside information about the film industry. All of which was important, because part of his job involved keeping up with news about those sections of society likely to travel on the *Berengaria,* to avoid embarrassing scenes with ex-lovers, feuding rivals and so on.

He was also extremely attractive to women. It was all there: the tanned features, the dark flashing eyes, the muscular build, the panther-like grace, the affable naval-officer confidence - the archetypal women's journal heart-throb. Complete with uniform.

And in his capacity as Senior Assistant Purser he was expected to be at the First Night at Sea Ball. And although this countess was very different from the ones he usually met (buxom dowagers with shrill voices, for whom part of his job was to turn on the gently flirtatious charm) she was strictly a no-go area for any ship's officer intent on furthering his career. So it was a perfectly proper invitation after an exhausting dance to suggest to his glowing partner with a smile, 'Would you like to go out on deck for a breath of fresh air?'

Sophie was feeling more relaxed than she had for... well, for years.

They admired the flower arrangements supplied by the ship's gardener, commented on the twinkling fairy lights casting multi-coloured reflections on the water, and leaned over the rails in companionable silence.

It had been a therapeutic evening. Giggling with Caroline about Theodore and Daphne had released a healthy dollop of the tension that had followed her onto the ship, chatting with Sam and Mary had drained away still more, and the exuberance of that last wild polka with the Promenade Deck Hunk (as she'd begun to think of him, although he'd introduced himself as Clive) had made further inroads; just standing quietly, looking at the vast expanse of ocean illuminated by gentle ripples of silvery moonlight, its movement mesmerising and calming, brought its own stillness and peace.

And because of that very stillness and peace, she gradually became aware of an almost subconscious knowledge: this trip wasn't just a physical crossing from one continent to another. Her own life was simultaneously moving from one phase to the next.

She shook her head slightly. Where on earth had that come from? Too much wine at dinner? Even more incomprehensible, a sense that there was something... she searched for the right word... familiar, somehow, about the man standing next to her, which *must* be the wine, because he was a complete stranger.

To dispel such absurd flights of fancy she broke the silence to ask about the possibility of seeing any whales or dolphins during the voyage.

'Some dolphins were spotted near the ship earlier,' he replied, and smiled. 'I'll let you know of any future sightings.'

'Trust me to miss what might be the only occasion they're seen,' she sighed, peering hopefully over the rails.

And as Clive explained that this was their rest time, their 'logging' period when they swam slowly and quietly near the surface to allow each half of their brains to rest in turn, the thought unexpectedly occurred to him that she seemed... familiar, as though he'd met her before somewhere - which was very strange because he knew for a fact that he hadn't. He gave himself a brisk mental shake to dispel such out-of-character notions, and wondered where her husband was. Not that it was any of his business.

He glanced at his watch; he had a full day tomorrow, and after a busy Sailing Day was ready to hit the hay.

He stood upright to indicate it was time to escort her back inside.

Caroline, whirling around the superbly sprung dance floor in the arms of Tom Burnett, listened to his enticing murmurings.

Rather hot in here, didn't she find? Would she like to go out on deck for a breath of fresh air? It should be rather pleasant on deck this evening, a relatively calm night with an almost full moon.

It had better be, thought Caroline. Who wanted to be blown to smithereens in a howling gale, with one's carefully set hairstyle completely ruined, clutching at one's evening dress and shivering?

She fluttered her eyelashes as Tom gazed admiringly back, awaiting her answer.

She *would* like to? Was she sure? Oh, how super. Because actually, he'd rather relish some fresh air too...

But of course when one was held in the arms of a deliciously attractive ship's officer on a moonlit night on the promenade deck of the *Berengaria,* surrounded by garlands of flowers and romantic fairy lights, fresh air was the last thing on one's mind - as was Sophie, Mary and Sam, and the myriad other revellers dotted here and there along the spacious deck (five laps around the ship equalled one mile).

As for whales, porpoises, and dolphins, if a hundred of them somersaulted in a spectacular synchronised leap over the ship from one side to the other, performing triple pirouettes on the way, neither Caroline nor Tom Burnett - so nobly and willingly sacrificing his off-duty hours in the interests of *Berengaria's* passenger satisfaction - would even have noticed.

8

The contrast between the opulence of the first class area and the quarters for the lower rank catering crew couldn't be more marked. With each level of the ship, the luxury of the decor lessened, the level of comfort lessened, and the structure of the ship became increasingly evident. No effort had been made to disguise the rivets, joists, and sweating bulkheads down next to the engine room, where huge pistons thumped ceaselessly and massive shafts revolved non-stop to control the speed and direction of the mighty turbine-driven propellers. Why should they? No fare-paying passengers ever visited this part of the ship.

Danny clattered down a succession of steel companion-ways towards G Deck and the warren of 'glory holes' which were home to the bellboys, waiters, junior chefs, and kitchen porters. He was the last down. The rest appeared to be already asleep. But no matter how tired, no matter how his feet throbbed, no matter how the ship rolled, no matter whether a freezing gale, driving rain, or falling snow waited outside, Danny always filled his lungs with fresh air before going down to the crew's accommodation.

But tonight, he'd had a narrow escape.

The designated outdoor deck relaxation area for all crew was the aft mooring deck. All other areas, and in particular the first class promenade deck, were strictly forbidden. But it took time to reach the aft deck...

He'd stepped out onto the promenade deck, distancing himself physically and mentally from the ceaseless activity on board. From the captain to the ship's cat, from Royalty to the Huddled Masses in steerage, to whom the Statue of Liberty extended her famous welcome as long as they were kept safely out of sight and sniffing distance of the rich and famous who were given a much louder and far more exuberant welcome, there was, in any period of twenty four hours, somebody, somewhere, doing something.

There had to be. The ship was virtually a self-contained floating city, and like any other city operated on a twenty four hour time scale. Officers on the bridge navigated her. A doctor was on duty lest anyone took ill. Night stewards were on call. Wireless operators received weather reports and information about other ships, plus news from land which was passed in turn to the printers, who were now getting ready next morning's edition of the ship's newspaper. Engineers serviced the miles of pipes and wiring needed for lights, heating, hot water, refrigerated storage areas for fresh food - everything from the massive engines powering the ship to the bells in staterooms for summoning a steward.

Somebody, somewhere, doing something.

Except, for these precious few minutes of freedom, Danny.

As he'd hoped, it was deserted except for an A.B. (able-bodied seaman) further along the deck, securing a loose mooring rope on a lifeboat; the sounds of the orchestra in the ballroom and occasional burst of laughter were far enough away not to intrude. He leaned on the rail, relishing the solitude after the noise and heat of the kitchens and to-ing and fro-ing from the dining saloon. But there was another reason he wanted to be alone: to think about his future. Because some weeks ago he'd met and fallen deeply in love with the woman he knew he was going to marry...

There was a slight sound. Someone was approaching. He froze; he was trapped. Worst case scenario, ship's officer. Slightly less catastrophic, but still potentially disastrous, passengers.

To try and escape would only make matters worse. He prepared to launch into the first excuse that came to mind: 'I thought I heard someone being seasick, so came to see if I could help...'

43

''Ello.'

It was a woman's voice, deep, hoarse, and unattractively guttural. Danny couldn't pretend he was unaware of her; she was illuminated in a square of light thrown by the glass panel in the door. Tall, gaunt, and pale, she was shrouded in an old fashioned black floor-length coat, with a folk-art headscarf providing an incongruous splash of colour.

'Good evening, madam.'

Bony fingers groped towards him. 'American? English?

From the overpowering reek of alcohol on her breath she was stockpiling enough in her liver to outwit Stateside Prohibition for the next few months.

'English, madam. Can I help you?'

'I like English men…'

'Are you in need of assistance, madam?'

The fingers tightened their grip on his arm. 'I am Russian...' She pronounced it Rarshan.

Well wasn't this just dandy. Not just a passenger, she had to be Russian as well. All he needed now was Mister Stonefeather turning up too and asking if she knew Prince Nicolai Romanoff, so she could inform him that no such person existed.

'My husband is Russian,' croaked the voice.

Danny nodded, gently easing his arm from her grasp.

'Russian men...' She made a gesture of contempt. Danny thought she was going to spit at him, and shuffled awkwardly sideways. 'Russian men no good! Always drunk...' The fingers edged after his arm. 'My husband, he is in bed, drunk...'

Danny clucked sympathetically, keeping his arm well out of reach.

'*Ty mne mravisha*... (I like you…) '

Uh-oh. Time to leg it. Bad enough being found in a place he had no right to be, without getting caught up in wherever this conversation was going. Self-preservation took precedence over courtesy, every time. He heard a muffled snigger and looked at the A.B., who'd stopped work on the lifeboat and was leaning on the rail, grinning at the cabaret.

Danny turned politely back to the woman. 'I'm sorry madam, I must go. Perhaps that gentleman over there could help you?'

Your turn for the starring role in this comedy, mate, he added under his breath as he quietly escaped.

All was (relatively) quiet in the sleeping quarters. The usual snoring, the odd cough or snort in someone's sleep, but nothing to compete with the ever-present thunderous vibrations from the propeller. He looked at Joey, asleep like the twenty others in this section - or pretending to be, which amounted to the same thing. Joey's two precious sets of kitchen whites hung at the end of his bunk, together with the only suit he owned. He, like the rest of them, had obviously done his best to clean his uniform with a damp cloth, leaving it to dry overnight because all laundry had to be paid for and uniform wasn't provided.

There was a slight movement… Danny said nothing as he headed towards the washing area, but was aware of Joey noiselessly climbing from his bunk and following. He wasn't asleep after all.

'Well?' Danny prepared to clean his teeth.

Joey poured water into an enamel mug, and took a long swig. 'Well what?'

'Same as I asked earlier when I got my head bitten off. What's going on with Alec Baxter?'

'I've already told you. He's going to make sure I'm unemployed by the end of this trip.' Joey took another swig. 'Either by making out I'm useless at my job, or provoking me into laying into him in front of a kitchen full of witnesses. One way or another, that's his plan. So there you are. Now you know.'

Danny stopped cleaning his teeth and looked at him. 'Now I know? I know less than I did before!'

'Well, you know as much as you need to. Or to put it another way, as much as I'm going to tell you.'

'But why?' Danny wasn't going to be brushed off so easily. 'He's a nasty piece of work, we all know that, but why would he target you specifically?'

45

Joey sighed. 'Let's just say because it suits him. Don't worry, I'm not going to let him. I'm going to be a good boy, behave myself. No complaints in the kitchen. No violent outbursts.'

'Yeah. We all know what a paragon of restraint you are.' There was no need to tell Joey about the smoked sturgeon episode. But violent outbursts… that was something else.

Joey ignored it. 'He was just throwing his weight around as usual, and making sure I knew where my place is; bottom of the heap. That's all.'

It quite clearly wasn't all, but Danny knew when to stop probing. Joey obviously didn't want to go into further detail about Alec's sudden determination to make his life a misery, and you didn't need to know all someone's business to be a good mate. If Joey, who wasn't prone to wild imaginings, said Alec was out to get him, then that was good enough for Danny. The reason would no doubt become clear in time; for now it was enough to be aware of the two potential areas of danger, and to help if and when he could.

He changed to a safer topic. 'How's Clara, anyway?'

'Pregnant.'

'Oh! Well… congratulations!'

'It's not mine.'

Danny stared at him. It wasn't Joey's? Well then… who…?

'So you'd have to ask her how she is. If she's got time to answer you, what with the wedding coming up and all.'

'Wedding?'

'Yes. She's getting married. But not to me.'

Danny's hand slowly dropped from his mouth. Alec being determined to hound Joey, for whatever reason, was a grim enough prospect, but - although challenging to say the least - one that was at least *possible* to avert. But this! This bombshell left him thunderstruck. Joey and Clara hadn't been all that long engaged! The obvious question hung in the air, unspoken. How did you say to an old mate, 'So, er, who's your fiancée marrying, then?'

46

'And before you ask - to the father, obviously.' Joey emptied what was left of the water and replaced the mug. 'And I've only told you this because I know it won't go any further.' His voice held an unmistakeable note of warning as he turned away. 'But as far as Alec Baxter's concerned, in case you're tempted to say anything when you see him having a go, Danny, leave it. I'm serious. I'll sort this out my own way.'

Danny nodded slowly as Joey made his way back to the glory hole, climbed into his bunk, and turned deliberately towards the bulkhead.

9

Talk was cheap. Everyone knew it, including Joey, just as he knew perfectly well that the line he'd spun to Danny about being a good boy, behaving, and not letting himself to be goaded into any violent outbursts, was a load of baloney. He'd known before he set foot on the ship what he'd be in for on this voyage.

But there hadn't been any other option to reporting for duty. For one thing, he'd already signed on for this trip at the end of the last one, which meant he didn't have his Discharge Book so couldn't try for another ship. For another, there was nowhere to go ashore. On a purely practical level, he had no choice.

But there was a deeper level, more difficult to define. Was it a sort of perverse defiance, an unspoken, 'I ain't running away mate. I can take everything you throw at me, so go ahead and do your worst!'? A weird urge to test his own self-control? Or just a subconscious desire to wait until they reached New York and then sort out Alec Baxter for good down some deserted alley, ensuring that when the bloodied victim was found there'd be no trail leading back to him? Because his hatred for Alec Baxter ran deep after what he'd learned in Southampton.

And Joey was a fighter, through and through.

His dad had been a bare-knuckle fighter - or at least, he took a beating, with never a hope of winning, time after time for the half a crown (twelve pence) offered by the professional fighters to anyone in the watching crowd who'd get in the ring for the entertainment of the rest of the audience. He'd done it to supplement the meagre wages he earned at the barrel works; he was willing to be thumped black and blue every week to make sure there was enough food on the table for his wife and child. Half a crown was half a crown, and if it meant they didn't go short of food and there were a few extra bags of coal for the winter, shoes for Joey and enough clothes for him to attend school without having to wear, like some of the other children, an elder sister's cast-offs and be either barefoot or in ill-fitting holey socks, and a few small treats for Christmas (Joey had never forgotten the year his dad bought him a pair of football boots, the only pair he'd ever had. Second hand and ill-fitting they may have been, but they were precious beyond words to the ten year old child, who wore them until he could no longer get them on his feet) then Joe Senior was prepared to suffer a few - if he was honest, a lot, and they hurt - cuts and bruises.

And young Joey had watched, learned, and picked up enough from his dad's coaching, and the professionals who sparred playfully with the young boy desperate to protect his dad in the ring, to use his own fists at an early age. Years of experience had honed those skills; they'd served him well in many a Liverpool dockside pub and similar dives in other ports worldwide, and his hands had been itching to use them tonight. But what would it achieve to end up chained next to Alec's corpse in the hold?

Nothing. It would have to be Plan B: how much self-control could he muster?

The problem was that despite his assurances to Danny, he already knew the answer. It was highly unlikely he'd make it to New York without pulverising his boss in full view of the entire kitchen.

10

Danny finished in the washing area.

He quietly followed Joey back to his bunk, sat down on one of the forms at either side of the old wooden table in the middle of the sleeping area that separated the two lines of triple-tier steel bunks, eased off his shoes, automatically massaged his feet, and then sat motionless at the table.

'...Either by making out I'm useless at my job or provoking me into laying into him in front of a kitchen full of witnesses...'

Alec Baxter would go for the second option.

Well, as he had no choice but to respect Joey's wishes and stay out of it, he might as well keep to his habitual routine. He padded to the small metal locker provided for each man to store personal possessions (just as well he didn't have many; you couldn't fit a lot into eighteen inches square), got his writing pad and pencil to write to his Love - he'd thought of her as that within days of meeting her, and knew he always would - then had second thoughts and put them back again. Somehow, after what he'd just heard, he wasn't in the mood for writing the sort of trivial shipboard gossip he usually included in his letters.

He got into his bunk, pulling the threadbare blanket up over his ears in a futile attempt to cut down the noise from the propeller and snores from neighbouring bunks. Within the space of half an hour he'd encountered two deeply unhappy people; Joey, with a fiancée who'd betrayed him and a boss who was out for his blood, and Mother Russia, rich enough to travel first class on the *Berengaria* yet lonely and wretched enough to prowl around the promenade deck propositioning total strangers. It made you wonder how many others had secret woes and worries that had followed them on board on the ship, despite (if travelling first class) being surrounded by opulence, popping champagne corks, and merry laughter. If you had money, you could at least be miserable in comfort. But if you weren't travelling first class... if you were an emigrant, for example, like middle-aged man he'd seen boarding the ship earlier... Danny, seeing the bleak despair in his eyes, had slowly raised his hand in a gesture of hope, but the man turned away and continued plodding grimly up the gangway.

Danny understood. He knew all about emigrating in steerage. He had first-hand experience of being cooped up with emigrants beset with fear of the unknown. His parents had moved the family to Canada in 1911 when his dad left the sea, and following a childhood of poverty in a small cottage on the Wirral side of the Mersey shore it seemed at first like an adventure leading to all sorts of opportunities, and wealth galore, for fifteen-year-old Danny.

The voyage soon put paid to that.

They had more luggage than most. Some they'd travelled with had a box or bundle or two, others nothing but the clothes they stood up in. He remembered the men chatting uneasily as they wandered around the confined space during the interminable voyage to Canada, and the women nursing seasick babies and children. He could still hear the sound of one particular child crying, and a woman's voice crooning a comforting lullaby before breaking into sobs herself...

The family arrived in thick fog in Newfoundland, and settled in Ontario. But the War put an end to many people's dreams and hopes, theirs among them; they returned to England, reluctantly leaving the two eldest sons, Tommy and Danny, who were now of an age, and only too eager, to enlist in the Canadian Expeditionary Force.

Danny knew he was edging on to dangerous territory with this train of thought, but his mind was now too active to sleep. The propeller's incessant thump-thump-thump took him back to tramping along endless French roads, in endless rain, in an endless column of men carrying sixty pound packs, under endlessly dripping sodden capes. He thought about the day - a

51

day of tedium, overlaid with a heavy sense of impending doom - when the arrival of a huge consignment of apples sent by one of the boys' families in the Bay of Fundy had lifted everyone's spirits and brought laughter, banter, and youthful high spirits to the camp. A Canadian apple for each man! He'd never forgotten that day in late June, a few days before the Battle of the Somme began on the First of July...

He gave himself a strict order: finish right there, before the nightmares started again.

He focused his mind on the entrancing sight he'd seen earlier in the day when he'd escaped to the aft deck during a meal break before the Sailing Night Dinner preparations started in earnest: a school of dolphins, swimming away from the ship.

During Atlantic trips no one was allowed on the foredeck, which meant nobody would have actually seen them at close quarters on this occasion. But things were more lax on the winter Caribbean Cruises, and he'd often been on the foredeck then, watching them play in the bow wave for hours. It was a sight he never tired of. Not only was it a true privilege to watch those graceful silvery bodies flying out of the water and diving back in for the sheer enjoyment of it, it was healing for mind, body, and spirit.

And it helped Danny to finally relax, and drift off to sleep.

TWO: THE FLOATING PALACE

1

There were genteel chuckles behind hands in some of London society's well-appointed drawing rooms when, at the launch of the *Imperator* in a Hamburg shipyard in 1912, a steel hawser snapped and apparently narrowly missed the Kaiser.

He in turn got much amusement from publicity posters depicting a German captain on the bridge of the *Imperator* flicking ash from his cigar onto the deck of a smaller, far less impressive British liner chugging along at her side, trying in vain to keep up. The *Imperator,* at 900 feet in length, had been specifically designed to be the largest, fastest, most luxurious ship to cross the Atlantic.

So when Cunard announced that the length of the new *Aquitania,* to be launched in 1913 at John Brown's shipyard at Clydebank, would be 901 feet, there was predictable outrage in Germany and a huge bronze eagle figurehead was immediately attached to the *Imperator*'s bow to add another seventeen feet. (Unfortunately, the wings were torn off during an Atlantic storm in 1914.) And for an additional show of playground one-upmanship, a buoy weighing 20 tons, with a circumference of 75 feet, was specially made to moor her; the largest buoy in the world for the Kaiser's favourite toy.

But despite her superior length and her eagle and her buoy and her two Imperial Suites, furnished to the most luxurious standards to be found anywhere afloat and intended for use by himself and the Kaiserin, the *Imperator* spent the war moored up in Hamburg. Then, under the terms of the Treaty of Versailles in 1919, Germany was obliged to forfeit her. Although never stated, it was tacitly accepted that this was in reparation for the sinking of the *Lusitania* in 1915. What was also never actually put into words, but equally understood by all, was that this was calculated to inflict the biggest humiliation, the most mortifying loss of face possible, on the defeated Kaiser.

As a further insult, following her sale by the Shipping Controller to Cunard and her name being changed to *Berengaria* (for the queen of Richard the Lionheart), the Kaiser's pride and joy was put into service on the Atlantic run, operating from Southampton to New York as one of the most prestigious British liners afloat. So prestigious in fact that British Royalty travelled across the Atlantic in the Imperial Suites intended for the Kaiser's exclusive use. And of course, if Royalty crossed the Atlantic on the *Berengaria,* the rich and famous also had to be seen crossing the Atlantic on her.

But neither Royalty, nor the famous, nor the wealthy, had any authority over the Atlantic wind which, during the night, had increased from Force Two, a gentle breeze, to Force Six. Cunard, aware of her tendency to list and roll, had tried to correct the problem by replacing the original marble baths in first class suites and staterooms with metal ones, pouring extra ballast of pig iron into her hold, and chopping nine feet off each of the three funnels which made her top-heavy.

But for all the difference it made they may as well have not bothered. She still listed and rolled, and Danny, shifting weight from one foot to the other as he dried his face in front of the small plain mirror (he was the first to admit he hadn't been blessed with film star looks; dark eyes, dark wavy hair, laughter lines, and that was about it), gave a wry grin as someone reminded them about the charge for any broken crockery being deducted from their wages. Then, watching Joey head morosely up the companionway, he silently assessed the odds on his friend getting through the day without incurring a charge of GBH against Alec Baxter.

They weren't high.

In the first class dining saloon, the *Carte du Jour* listed a Breakfast choice to indulge the most discerning of palates.

And in the kitchens, each corresponding section was busily preparing for the orders that would soon start flooding in.

The Breakfast menu started with Fruits: Grapefruit, Oranges, Compote of Fruit, Baked Apples with Cream, and Figs in Syrup. Juice was now being extracted from oranges and lemons, and cores removed from grapefruit and apples.

This was followed by Cereals, which had become popular in recent years, as well as the perennial favourite, Porridge, a huge pan of which was left overnight to simmer in the traditional manner. Everything was being made ready for the waiters to deliver quickly and easily.

Next, Fish: Boneless Codfish with Cream Sauce, Fried Lemon Sole, and Kippered Herring, all being prepared under the direction of the *poissonnier* (fish chef) in readiness for orders to be produced speedily and with the minimum of fuss.

Eggs and Omelettes followed, with sauce cooks readying the hundreds of eggs needed for the omelette mix, assembling a vast variety of fillings, and preparing both the bain-marie for the poached and scrambled eggs and the automatic egg-boiler which could be set for three, five, or seven minutes, as required.

Entrees came next: Calf's Liver, Chicken Hash, and Smoked Beef in Cream; the preparation of these was being supervised by the *entremetier,* or entree preparer.

For the Grill: Wiltshire Smoked Bacon, Mutton Chops, Cambridge Sausage, Devilled Beef Bones, and Cumberland Ham; the *grillardin* (grill chef) was ensuring his section had everything ready for all possible orders.

And then Potatoes: Mashed, French Fried, or Jacket. Potatoes were already boiling in huge steam saucepans, while others were being chopped into delicate potato chips.

Then came the Selection of Cold Meats, now being carved in readiness by the *garde manger* (pantry chef), together with Accompaniments: Spring Onions, Tomatoes, Cucumber, and Radish, all of which had to be ornately sculpted and arranged by the *legumier* (veg chef) and his assistants.

For the Various Breads listed next, the huge arms of the dough machine were kneading sacks of flour at seven minute intervals to produce batches of rolls, while in the ovens were every kind of bread a passenger could possibly ask for: Swedish, Vienna, Corn, and Hovis bread, Cottage Loaves, Muffins, French toast, Soda Scones, Sally Lunns, Scotch Oat Cakes, Croissants, and thousands of waffles and griddle cakes.

And the urns were boiling for the gallons of tea that would be called for; Ceylon, China, Blended, every possible choice as well as Coffee, Cocoa, Horlicks Malted Milk, and Buttermilk. All would be ready when the waiters brought in the first orders.

And no matter how extensive the choices on the *Carte du Jour*, there was always something someone would ask for that wasn't listed; an unexpected request that must be respectfully and speedily provided, no matter how extraordinary, outlandish, or awkward to produce.

And no matter how high the Atlantic waves as the ship pitched and tossed onward, the work of producing whatever first class passengers may desire stopped for nothing. Certainly not for Joey Smith who, trying to cheer up a fourteen year old homesick kitchen boy overcome with fatigue, poured a bowl of milk for the ship's cat, only to be startled by Alec Baxter's coarse voice: 'Here! Never mind feeding the bloody cat! Get cracking! And bear in mind what I said, because that cat's just lent you its last life!'

2

The most opulent suite on the *Berengaria* or the cheapest dockside pub in any seaport in the world, it made no difference; vomit, urine, and stale wine, beer, and spirits smelled exactly the same wherever you were.

Billy Saunders gagged as he opened the door. He'd looked forward to being promoted to first class bedroom steward on this trip, thinking it would mean not only bigger tips, but looking after the famous, the fascinating, and the fabulous.

Not so. Certainly not in this case, anyway.

He looked at the man lying in bed, who was neither famous, nor fascinating, nor fabulous, and had vomited the previous night's intake over every item of bedlinen in range. Blankets, sheets, fitted eiderdown, silk counterpane; all were soiled, and the overflow formed yet more vile mess on the carpet.

'What you staring at?' snapped the bloated, unshaven face on the silk pillow.

Billy put the Early Morning Tea tray on the dressing table. 'Are you ill, sir? Do you need the doctor? He can give you something if you're seasick -'

The man actually laughed. 'Lexie Stonefeather's never been seasick in his life, boy.'

Billy gaped at him. 'Oh. I, er… Obviously you couldn't make it to the bathroom, so I just assumed -'

'Oh, a clever-clogs, eh? Well, stewards aren't paid to *assume* things. Just stick to skivvying, boy.' Lexie nodded at the tray. 'Before you start cleaning up - milk, two sugars.'

The ship rolled and pitched.

Balancing himself against the dressing table, Billy silently poured the tea and, carefully avoiding the mess on the carpet, made his way to the bed.

'And run my bath,' went on Lexie Stonefeather, taking the cup. 'With my clothes laid out ready. The brown suit... You listening, boy?'

Billy noticed a wet patch half way down the counterpane. The man had actually urinated in the bed, as well as fouling it with what he'd spewed up.

He tried not to retch. 'Yes, sir.'

'Then I'll have breakfast. I don't feel like going to the Dining Saloon this morning. Bring it here instead. Porridge. Then bacon and eggs.'

'Yes, sir.'

Strictly speaking the steward's job was to bring early morning tea, not provide a full breakfast service. But what first class passengers wanted, first class passengers got.

'No. On second thoughts I'll have orange juice.'

'Yes, sir.'

'No... No, I'll stick with porridge. Have it here ready as I get out of the bath. You can bring the bacon and eggs while I'm having my porridge.'

The ship gave a particularly violent roll, and Billy instinctively stepped forward to steady himself. His right foot ended up in the mess of vomit; he lost his footing, slipped, and landed on his side in the slimy filth.

Lexie Stonefeather watched him struggle to his feet. 'Now you know why *I* had no intention of risking life and limb getting to the bathroom, boy!'

Billy steadied himself on the dressing table, trying to avoid smearing it with the vomit on his hands, jacket, and trousers, then lurched towards the bathroom to carry out a temporary fumigating operation with one of the towels. The urge to rip off his soiled clothing and get into the bath he began to run for Lexie was overpowering, but washing his uniform - and underwear, also contaminated as moisture soaked through the top layer - had to wait. First he had to strip the bed when Lexie vacated it, and clean up the revolting sight on the floor. There was no one to complain to, and no point in moaning about it; as

59

far as Cunard were concerned, that's what they paid stewards and laundry crews for, as well as the laundries ashore. (The ship was equipped with its own laundry, but the daily volume so great that by the time they reached New York or Southampton over one hundred thousand items of table linen, towels, sheets, pillowcases, blankets, counterpanes, and dry-cleaning items like eiderdowns and pillows, were delivered to the laundries that catered for transatlantic liners on the completion of each voyage.) And although each item was recorded, if the odd piece of bedlinen ended up beyond salvation its loss was a drop in the Atlantic to Cunard, compared to the overall profit of the trip. Fare-paying passengers, especially first class ones, were a lot more valuable than stewards, who were ten a penny.

If Billy didn't like his job there were plenty more waiting to take it, as the Chief Steward regularly pointed out. The dole queues were full of men who'd be grateful for a steward's job; he could swap with them any time he liked.

3

Lexie left the dirty water in the bath and was strolling from the bathroom in his bathrobe as Billy, now in clean mess jacket, trousers, and underpants, knocked and entered with his porridge.

Lexie stared at him. 'What's this?'

'Porridge, sir.'

'I didn't ask for effing porridge, I asked for orange juice!'

'Yes sir... but then you changed it back to porridge.'

'Don't you tell me what I did and didn't ask for!'

Billy looked at the floor.

'If I ask for orange juice, then orange juice is what I expect to get, not what you decide to bring! Take it back. Tell them you got it wrong, it should be orange juice!'

'Yes sir.' Billy turned to go.

'Oi! *Oi!* Don't you *ever* turn your back on me while I'm speaking!'

Before Billy realised what was happening, Lexie whirled across, bathrobe flying open, and knocked the bowl through his unresisting hands. Porridge cascaded down his clean mess jacket, dribbled down his trousers, and splashed onto his shoes and the carpet.

'*Nobody* walks out on Lexie Stonefeather when he's speaking, boy!'

'But you just told me -'

'Don't argue with me!'

For less than a second they stared at each other. Words were unnecessary. Communication took place in the eyes of both of them. Billy's clearly expressed contempt and deep dislike, and Lexie's blazed with fury; *no* underling ever regarded him with anything less than cowed deference.

It was an unequal confrontation, and there could be only one winner. Lexie nodded slowly at the carpet, and spoke with insulting clarity: 'Clean it up.'

He watched as Billy knelt to wipe the carpet with the linen napkin that accompanied the porridge. 'And then see if you can get the order right this time. Orange juice. *Orange juice.* And bacon and eggs, sunny side up.' He turned to the mirror, slicking his hair. 'Just in case you're unclear which role is yours and which is mine, let me remind you. I've paid for first class service. You're here to provide it. And so far I'm not impressed, either by your ability or your attitude. ' He glanced round. 'Have you got that?'

Billy nodded silently.

'I said, have you got that?'

'Yes sir.'

'I'm not sure I like the look in your eye, boy. I hope you *have* got it, or I'll be adding insolence to effing useless when I complain to the Chief Steward. Go on, get out!'

4

Elsie Parkinson needed both hands to carry a tray bearing a teapot, milk jug, sugar bowl, dish of sliced lemon, two cups and saucers, a side plate of biscuits, and a beautifully wrapped bouquet of long-stemmed red roses provided by the ship's gardener together with their accompanying note, which meant she was unable to keep to the age-old rule: one hand for the ship and one for yourself. Instead, she leaned against the bulkhead (she must remember to use the ship's terminology for walls) to steady herself as she staggered from one side of the corridor to the other each time the ship rolled.

She lifted a knee to balance the tray as she knocked on the door and opened it with one hand, feeling nervous and queasy; the Chief Stewardess's sarcasm if the new girl, who obviously hadn't made much of an impression so far, was seasick on her first Early Morning Tea run of the trip didn't bear thinking about.

Elsie hadn't expected to be a first class stewardess after just one voyage, but she certainly wasn't going to complain. Her first trip had been spent in the Nursery, looking after thirty three children varying in ages from six months to nine years old, and it had been exhausting. And for the most part, boring. The only thing she'd enjoyed was organising the birthday party for the nine-year-old, to which all the other children were invited. The kitchens had provided the usual sandwiches, fancy pastries, jellies, orange juice, and birthday cake, and she'd organised games for them, and amused them by drawing simple pictures for them to colour in; cats, dogs, horses, beautiful ladies in their elegant dresses, the ship... she'd discovered a natural flair through art materials provided for the children, and had been complimented on her handling of the event - and then wished she hadn't, dreading being stuck in the Nursery for ever as a result, looking after children for a straight twelve hour shift every day.

But even that was better than being unemployed ashore, as she had been before she got the job - and that was only because her uncle was a steward who'd died of a stroke in his fifties. His widow was offered work as was the custom when a breadwinner died, but hadn't wanted it because of looking after an aged mother, so put in a request for twenty year old Elsie to have it instead.

So far, she much preferred first class. She loved the fashionable clothes the ladies brought with them. She'd never seen anything like the beauty and elegance of the gowns, the grace and style of the designs, the gorgeous shades ranging from the most delicate pastel to deep rich tones of the same colour, the skill of French *haute couture* seamstresses' to adorn a dress with just the right finishing touch or decorative embellishment, the exquisite silks and satins that shimmered in the light. And the sheer amount; an outfit for every occasion, from practical linen frocks for deck games to the most sophisticated evening gowns and cocktail dresses. What a contrast to her uniforms, which she'd made herself because they weren't provided and she couldn't afford to buy them: two morning sets of blue and white striped dresses with white cuffs and a celluloid collar, and two afternoon navy blue dresses, also worn with celluloid collar and cuffs, and a high-necked apron.

On a practical note however, she was even more relieved to be in first class this morning, high up and near the centre of the ship where the motion was least. She tried to ignore the queasiness as she closed the door with her foot and made her way through the salon, with its writing desk and chaise longue, to the bedroom, where her passengers lay propped up on silk pillows in magnificent oxydised silver beds.

'Good morning, Miss Parkinson... oh, what beautiful roses!' smiled Sophie.

'Good morning, madam.' Elsie carefully put down the tray on the satinwood table, wedging it against the side 'fiddle' so it wouldn't slide off as the ship rolled.

Caroline yawned. 'Morning, Miss P.' She nodded at the roses. 'They for me?'

Elsie laid the bouquet, with its accompanying card, on Caroline's silk counterpane. 'Yes, madam.'

Caroline wagged her finger in mock-stern reproof. 'Well I sure am glad to see you're not putting them in the closet!'

Elsie blushed, and said nothing. When they'd arrived on board, Caroline had told her to put her shoes 'in the closet' as she unpacked the trunks, and she hadn't realised the word meant cupboard; she'd only ever heard 'closet' used when referring to a W.C.

'You're gonna have to learn some American English before you get to New York!' teased Caroline, idly examining the bouquet.

Elsie fumbled with pouring the tea, making it obvious that she wasn't being impolite by not answering, but was too busy ensuring it didn't slop over into the saucers. She wasn't sure how to respond. Her role as stewardess meant that anything other than respectful courtesy to passengers was stepping on to very thin ice covering a very deep, dangerous lake; you didn't risk it if you had any sense of self-preservation. They could joke with easy familiarity to you, but you never knew the moment you'd overstepped the mark if you answered in the same vein. Older stewardesses, who had a lot more sea miles under their belts, had cautioned keeping within strictly drawn demarcation lines, and it was advice she intended to take.

'Milk and one sugar for me, please,' Sophie instructed Elsie.

'Yes, madam.'

Caroline dropped the bouquet to concentrate on what her admirer had written on the accompanying card. 'Disgusting habit, putting milk in tea. Lemon for me.'

'Yes, madam.'

'Aren't they lovely. Who are they from?' asked Sophie, indicating the roses.

'Oh...' Caroline dropped Tom's note. 'Tom. You know, the ship's officer from last night. He's busy working today. Wants to meet me at Sports Day, tomorrow afternoon.'

Sophie smiled. 'That's nice.'

'Well, he'll do to start with. But I've absolutely *nothing* to wear...'

Elsie gasped. Between them, they'd brought ninety trunks. She'd drooled as she'd helped with the unpacking, lost in wonder as she hung garment after garment in the huge mahogany wardrobe while they decided what would stay with them for the trip and what could be sent down to the main trunk room in the ship's hold.

Sophie, aware of the astounded gasp, reverted to Countess of Knotworth mode and brought the conversion back to a more fitting level. 'Would you be terribly kind, Miss Parkinson, and run my bath? Thank you.'

'And then let's have something to eat,' suggested Caroline, turning back to Elsie as Sophie nodded. 'We'd like to have it up here instead of going to the Dining Saloon, Miss P., if you wouldn't mind. Heaven forbid I'm seen in public before going to the hairdressers! Fresh orange juice, waffles, and coffee, please.'

She patted her hair, all interest lost in the roses lying abandoned by her feet. The rest of the trip was still ahead, and the collection of captivated male suitors had yet to start in earnest.

And she'd expect all future bouquets to far outclass Tom's offering (which had cost him a week's salary) in ostentation, abundance, and sheer extravagance.

5

Elsie entered the kitchens, shy in the presence of so many men.

They all seemed so totally at home, and she had such a lot to learn about the job, the ship, the way things were done. Also, a few of them used terms which were vulgar. She didn't necessarily know what they meant, but knew intuitively they were in poor taste, like the occasion on her last voyage when one of them asked for 'double shit on a raft,' (two Cambridge Sausages on toast) which had made her squirm with embarrassment. Most of them, though, modified their language and were kind to her.

She recognised the steward she'd seen coming out of the opposite suite earlier, standing further along the counter and frowning at the floor. She smiled hesitantly as he, sensing someone watching him, instinctively looked up. She didn't get an answering smile. In fact he looked as if he was ready to commit murder.

The waiter she knew as Danny came in through the 'In' swing door, saw her standing in the melee of scurrying waiters, and made a space for her.

'Here y'are love, get in here.'

He let her give her order safely before giving his own, then spoke to the steward she recognised.

'Aye aye, Billy. All right?'

'No.'

'Oh aye? Like that, is it? What's happened?'

Billy jerked his head at the door. 'Some pain-in-the-ar -' He glanced the young stewardess standing awkwardly nearby. 'Er, neck, by the name of Lexie Stonefeather, too lazy to go to the bathroom to throw up. Puked over everything in sight.'

Lexie Stonefeather? Any slight feelings of guilt Danny felt about the smoked sturgeon chicanery evaporated, but although his sympathy for Billy was genuine - he'd worked as a steward and done his share of mopping up other people's vomit; he knew how that felt - it was wise to keep that bit of business to himself. Even one other person knowing was one too many.

'Oh, no!'

'Oh yes. Of course, I had to slip over in it. And the bas -' Billy again glanced at Elsie. 'He'd peed in the bed as well.'

'Ugh!' Elsie shook her head in disbelief and forgot her shyness in her desire to commiserate with him. 'How awful for you, having to face that! And to fall over in someone's vomit.'

'Oh, that was just the warm-up act. We had the breakfast performance next. He ordered porridge, and then swore he'd ordered orange juice. So I got porridge knocked all over me as well. Two uniforms down.' There was no self-pity in the tone, just a very noticeable lack of Christian readiness to turn the other cheek and a very noticeable un-Christian eagerness to repay the treatment, with interest, if he ever got the chance.

Elsie, horrified by what she was hearing, nevertheless found herself noticing Billy's attractive brown eyes.

'Well,' Billy looked at the bacon and eggs as his order arrived. 'Let's hope this doesn't go the same way as the porridge. I've borrowed Phil's mess jacket until I can wash mine. He won't be too happy if there's orange juice and egg yolk thrown all over it.'

'I know I shouldn't say this,' said Elsie, but said it all the same. 'But I hope it chokes him!'

'So do I,' said Billy quietly. 'Before either he makes sure I never work again, or I make sure he never eats again.'

He was gone.

She and Danny looked at each other. Elsie saw wisdom and experience as well as kindness in his eyes, and guessed that he'd probably seen some of the best, and worst, examples of human behaviour in his time, even though he only looked about thirty. He was obviously old enough to have been in the war, and everyone knew how that had affected those who'd been involved, quite apart from the widows, orphans, and all the other broken lives left in its wake.

He sensed her anxiety, and took time to reassure her. 'Don't worry. Most passengers aren't like that.'

She nodded, more interested in finding more out about Billy.

Of course, she knew that the whole point of discipline on the ship, with strict segregation between male and female crew, and fraternisation forbidden, was to avoid on-board romances, although she'd picked up from other stewardesses that most of them considered themselves above stewards and waiters anyway.

From Cunard's viewpoint who was above whom was irrelevant. They had enough problems with passengers' matrimonial affairs without more from the crew; the story of a celebrity couple on another ship who'd met on one voyage, got married on the second, and separated after a monumental row on the third was legendary. That was probably why the steward she'd been allocated to work with on the section was old Reg, everyone's favourite grandad.

But Billy...

She wondered what he looked like when he smiled. She wondered if he had a sweetheart at home. She wondered if he had any idea the effect his brown eyes -

She became aware of Danny nudging her, and came back to the kitchen. Her order was waiting on the counter, and the chef was staring at her.

'Better get going,' said Danny, 'Before he comes back and says Prince Charming decided he didn't order Orange Juice and Bacon and Eggs, it was Figs in Syrup and Devilled Beef Bones.'

And he mightn't be so careful about his language next time, he added under his breath.

6

'There's all sorts of things going on,' announced Mary as she and Sam strolled arm in arm towards the shops in the long gallery after breakfast. The original candy and cigarette kiosks had evolved into slightly larger premises and been joined by several other shops during a recent re-fit. 'There's a new kinda thing called Yogo, or some name like that. They're all lying on the floor in the gymnasium with their arms stretched oot and their legs kinda...' She gestured helplessly.

'Are you going to have a go?'

'Me? You're joking! If I got doon on the floor like that, I'd never get up again!'

They stopped to look in the window of the first shop, which sold fancy goods.

'Michty me!' Mary was almost (but not quite) speechless. 'Have you seen what they want for a handbag?'

Sam had. He shook his head in wonder.

'Who do they think is going to pay five pounds - *five pounds!* - for a couple o' bits o' leather sewn together?' gasped Mary. 'Ye can pick one up in the market for a shilling!'

'Well somebody must do, or they wouldnae sell them,' shrugged Sam.

They moved on to the next window - a display of top quality French perfumes, created with the most expensive ingredients available by the most distinguished perfumiers; *'Shalimar'* by Guerlain, Patou's *'Joy'*, and the latest collection by Lionceau: *'Nuit D'Egypt'*, made from the oils of rare Egyptian flowers, *'Parfums Pour Blondes'* in jade green bottles, *'Parfums Pour Brunes'* in coral red ones, and *'Le Fleur Bleu'* in unmistakeable black ones. There were scents to suit every taste: sophisticated New York career girls, mature matriarchs, fashionable flappers, sporty athletes, glamorous stars of stage and screen, gold-digging adventuresses...

'Hmmph!' grunted Sam. 'Look at the price o' a' that rubbish, and all they need's a good wash with a bar of carbolic soap!'

Also on display were beautiful Houbigant compacts, face powder, talcum powder, and various brands of cosmetics and make-up. Sam blinked at the pictures of Clara Bow, the 'It Girl', and cast an anxious glance at his wife. He loved her dearly, but cupid's bow lips were never intended for the mouths of women who had done a lot of laughing, crying, talking, and kissing in the course of nearly seventy years of life. To his relief she said nothing about purchasing make-up and lipstick to supplement her daily beauty routine of a dollop of cold cream night and morning, but he had a strong suspicion that may well change before the voyage ended... heaven help us.

Next was a tobacconist. Sam slowed down and looked cautiously in the window, which was full of Meerschaum pipes, pipe racks, cheroots, cheroot holders, cigars, and cigar cutters.

'I've run oot o' fags,' he said. 'I wonder how much they rush you for a packet? Three times as much as at home, probably.'

'Aye well, I doubt it looks the kinda place where they'd sell one or two ciggies on their own,' agreed Mary.

Sam decided to risk it. 'Probably more than I earn in a week!'

'Get me a bar of chocolate while ye're in.' The tobacconist stocked a selection of chocolate bars, and the candy shop was still some way off.

'I see ye're no' giving me a bar of gold to pay for it,' grumbled Sam.

Mary ignored him, and strolled to the jewellery shop next door to gaze in awed fascination at exquisite rings, bracelets, brooches, men's and women's watches, and solid gold necklaces inset with the most precious stones to be found anywhere on earth. But the most prominent display, in the centre of the window, was a tray of engagement rings; the enterprising shopkeeper, well aware of the demand created by shipboard romances, catered for every choice from the

71

discreetly elegant to the brashly ostentatious. And judging from the easy accessibility of the tray, conveniently placed to be whisked from the window before either party could have second thoughts, this particular line was highly profitable.

Mary sighed. She'd never had an engagement ring; every penny had to go on rent and food. But she'd never quite given up hope, even after fifty years of marriage.

Sam, emerging from the tobacconist with cigarettes and chocolate, saw her scrutinizing the merchandise in the jeweller's window and apprehensively followed her line of vision.

Engagement rings. Surprise, surprise.

Well, she deserved one, he admitted to himself. He'd willingly propose - with a ring - if he had his time over again. He'd always meant to buy one for her when the time was right and he had enough money... but somehow, the time never *was* right and he never *did* have enough money.

He scanned the window for the cheapest one. Twenty guineas. Well, that was the end of that. May as well be twenty thousand guineas. He blinked, turned away, and moved on to the next shop; Ladies Fashions. Hi ho, feet - get ready for a long wait here. We won't be going anywhere in a hurry once she claps her eyes on this.

He was right. Mary, in common with the rest of womankind, found it biologically impossible to walk past a shop window displaying ladies' fashions - even though this one could only, because of its size, stock a small sample of off-the-peg frocks as a taster of what could be bought at the parent establishment in Bond Street, London, or the New York branch. Merchandise for sale consisted mostly of bathing costumes, underwear, stockings, scarves, and gloves.

Sam passed her the chocolate bar, which she took without moving her gaze from an afternoon tea gown, a coffee coloured georgette slip with wide ribbon shoulder straps and side drapes, covered by a cream lace overdress with long sleeves, and decorated with white lace flouncing all down the centre, so that

72

the total effect was a delightful blend of coffee, cream, and white froth.

'Seven guineas!' gasped Sam. Her eyes were riveted on the garment; his were riveted on the price tag.

Mary made no comment. She unwrapped the chocolate, broke off a piece, and passed it to him, her eyes never leaving the tea gown.

'I can't see any difference between that yin and the dress ye got on the market for three shillings. Looks just as nice tae me, anyway.'

Stony silence. If he'd hoped to convince her, he'd failed. Time for a conciliatory gesture.

'Well, if you want to treat yersel', we could afford a pair of gloves.'

Mary looked down at her hands, red, wrinkled, work-worn, chapped, left thumb still encased in its bandage.

'I wouldn't even dare go in!'

He grinned. 'You could ask if they take Provident Clothing Coupons!'

(Provident Clothing Coupons were a way of saving a small amount each week, which could then be used to buy a new item of clothing at certain stores.) She gave him a mock clip over the ear and they moved on, he hastily, she with a backward lingering glance at the coffee and cream creation which, a printed note advised, could be purchased in all sizes at the New York branch...

The final shop was a gentlemen's outfitters. Now it was Mary who became disinterested and Sam who stopped to look in the window.

'A week's wages for a pair o' socks,' he marvelled.

'Aye. Your turn to ask if they take Provident Clothing Coupons.'

They surveyed the price tags adorning shirts, ties, pullovers and jumpers, pyjamas, gloves, and underwear in bemusement. Sam had his eye on a well-cut white shirt. He'd always worn blue heavy-duty ones for the shipyard. Strange to think he'd never ever owned a white shirt in his life.

'Imagine anyone being daft enough to pay that price for pyjamas,' scoffed Mary, eyeing a pair propped up on a stand. 'Who's going to see them, in bed?'

There was movement behind the semi-opaque glass separating the window from the main shop area. Two figures could be seen. Mary looked more closely, and recognised Theodore's portly silhouette.

'Here, isn't that whatsisname, you know, yon chap we spoke to last night?'

'Oh aye,' nodded Sam. 'So it is. I wonder what he's buying?'

They cupped their hands around the sides of their eyes to cut out the reflective light and peered through the glass.

Daphne, who happened to glance up at that moment, glared indignantly at the two faces squinting in between displays of men's apparel in the window. Those awful people from last night's Ball! How *dared* they gawp in at her and Theodore like that! What *impudence!* She turned pointedly away to shame them into moving on before the transaction was completed; the senior salesman was now wrapping the purchases in tissue paper, and placing them carefully in a bag.

She needn't have bothered. As the junior salesman opened the door and they emerged, the first thing Theodore saw was Sam's grizzled head.

He groaned. Oh please, not *this* pair again.

'Hello there,' Mary smiled and nodded in friendly curiosity. 'Have ye been shopping?'

'Ah. Good morning,' said Theodore distantly, and made to move off, his wife close behind.

Sam nudged him, grinning. 'I'd buy some gloves and socks, but they cost an arm and a leg!'

Theodore glanced at Daphne. Neither, it seemed, shared Sam's sense of humour. They made to move off again.

'Well, lovely to see you, but we must -'

74

Again they were too late. Sam was already peering into the outfitter's bag. Striped pyjamas, identical to those Mary had commented on, were clearly visible through the tissue paper. 'Oh... ye've treated yersel' to some new pyjamas, aye?'

Theodore stared at him in disbelief, and transferred the bag to his other hand.

'Sam never wears any,' Mary informed them chattily.

'Really. How unfortunate... or perhaps fortunate... for the Gent's Outfitter,' murmured Daphne.

'Well, nice to see you again,' said Theodore again, a little more testily. 'And now we -'

'Have ye seen the prices in yon jewellery shop?' continued Mary, as it was obvious that Theodore had no wish to prolong the conversation about pyjamas. She belatedly noticed the bag Daphne was carrying, bearing the name of the jeweller's shop. 'Oh aye, I see ye have!'

And it wouldn't be some cheap twenty guinea ring either, thought Sam, wisely refraining from contributing to this particular topic.

'Have you bought something sparkly?' went on Mary, nodding encouragingly. How nice to pal up with new friends, share news of what they'd all bought at the shops, discuss prices. She missed the wee blethers with the customers at the fish and chip shop.

'Yes,' said Theodore shortly. 'And now we really -'

Mary picked up on the lack of enthusiasm to discuss purchases. Well, that was fair enough. And it wasn't as though she and Sam could contribute much anyway; Sam buying cigarettes and chocolate wasn't quite in the same league as a wee trinket from the jeweller, and pyjamas that cost almost ten pounds. Time for a change of subject.

'Lots of activities going on, eh? Golf, tennis, shuffleboard... And I see there's a even a fencing display later! Spoilt for choice, aren't we?'

'Yes,' replied Theodore again, his voice rising slightly. 'Do enjoy yourselves. Now, please excuse -'

'And that's just on deck! As well as a gymnasium and a swimming pool,' marvelled Sam. 'What a place that is, eh? Have ye seen it?'

'Yes. On numerous occasions,' murmured Daphne.

'I havenae got a bathing costume masel',' confided Mary. 'But it's nice to see the young ones enjoying themselves, eh?'

'Yes,' said Theodore. 'Now please excuse -'

'Oh aye, I won't hold you up if you're in a hurry. But before ye go... talking of young ones, I see there's a college band travelling second class and they're giving a concert on the promenade deck this afternoon. Are you going?'

'Erm...' Daphne glanced at Theodore. That could well depend on whether Sam and Mary were likely to be there. 'We've no definite plans yet for today.'

'Well, we're going,' nodded Sam. 'Will we save a couple of seats for youse, aye?'

'No,' said Daphne hastily. 'Really. It's too, too kind of you, but... don't do that.'

'Och, it's nae bother!'

'But you see, we may decide to... erm... do something else!'

'Aye well,' said Mary. Strange folk, these English toffs. In a blinding hurry to get somewhere, but didn't seem to know where they were going or what they were going to do when they got there. 'What aboot Sports Day tomorrow? Ye must be going to that, surely? We heard everyone goes to Sports Day!'

'Probably,' snapped Theodore in the tone of voice he used to bring business meetings to an abrupt end. *Everyone* got the point when they heard that tone. Even these dimwits couldn't fail to get the underlying message. And Sports Day was safe enough. Sam was right about that; everyone would indeed be there, so it would be easy enough to avoid them. 'And on that note, we really must -'

'I hope you and me are on the same team in the tug'o'war,' grinned Sam.

I most fervently hope we're not, thought Theodore, momentarily floored. He'd never actually met anyone who didn't immediately grasp and obey the unequivocal command in the tone of voice he'd just used.

Mary was stepping up her efforts to be friendly with Daphne. The poor lady obviously suffered with her nerves; perhaps she'd benefit from being taken under a motherly wing. 'Aye. You and me could enter the Egg and Spoon race together, couldn't we, Daphne?'

Heaven forbid, thought Daphne, making a mental note to keep as far away from the Egg and Spoon Race as possible. Were they destined to be pursued by these ghastly people wherever they went on the ship? It was too, *too* tiresome, it really was. How on earth could anybody miss Theodore's unmistakeable cue to part company?

'Terribly exciting, isn't it. But we mustn't be selfish and expect you to spend all your time with *us* -'

'Oh, don't say that,' Mary protested, shocked. 'I'd be only too happy to have a pal to enter with! Mind, there'll be some things I'll no' be able to go in for. My legs are no' what they used tae be.' She appraised Daphne's stout legs with interest, searching out varicose veins in the couple of inches visible above her ankles. 'None of us are getting any younger, eh?'

Daphne closed her eyes.

Theodore decided this had gone on long enough. 'Come along, darling. We really mustn't hold up these good people any longer.'

'Och, ye're not holding us up at all,' Mary assured them kindly. 'So that's settled then. We'll all sit together tomorrow afternoon for Sports Day, and decide what we want to go in for, aye?'

'*What* a kind offer. Too, *too* thoughtful. But I'm quite sure you'd rather be entering races and... and... meeting new people,' said Daphne desperately.

'Och, away wi' ye!' Sam reassured them. 'We'd be only too happy to look out for ye!' He patted Daphne's hand. 'Don't worry, hen, we'll make sure and stay wi' ye all afternoon, so ye won't be lonely!'

77

Daphne's mouth went dry. 'Darling, we really *must*...'

'Indeed so,' agreed Theodore emphatically.

'*So* nice to see you again,' said Daphne, edging purposefully away. 'Do excuse us, we -'

'What time will we all meet up? Two o'clock, I think it starts,' suggested Mary.

Theodore scowled at her. If this stupid woman couldn't take a polite hint - and heaven knew he and Daphne had moved heaven and earth to be unfailingly courteous - he'd just have to make the meaning so clear even *she* would finally get the message, and if she was hurt or offended, too bad.

'We wouldn't dream of monopolising you, this afternoon, tomorrow, or any other day. There must be lots of other people on the ship who'll enjoy your company. Do enjoy the occasion, won't you. Now, good day to you.' He gave a curt nod, clearly indicating that the conversation was at an end, held out his arm to Daphne, and turned away.

Undaunted, Mary took Daphne's other arm. 'Oh, that's nice, we're all going the same way. We can all walk alang together, the four of us, can't we!'

Daphne and Theodore finally managed to shake off those dreadful, *dreadful* nuisances with a web of elaborate excuses, the most effective being that they simply must visit the ship's bank. Such a bind - tiresome chore and all that, but they were sure Sam and Mary would appreciate that sometimes it was necessary to attend to these matters.

In private.

Sam and Mary bid them an affectionate farewell after reassuring them they'd be sure to look out for them at Sports Day, and drifted off, he to lean on the rail and stare at the ocean, she to the Ladies Writing Room. And Theodore and Daphne heaved a joint sigh of relief, promised themselves they'd keep well out of sight at the Sports Day festivities, and settled down once more to enjoy the morning.

Shopping in the long gallery was so much more relaxing than Bond Street, where you had to watch out for traffic all the time. Here it was pleasantly warm, and there was a thick carpet instead of a tarmac road and dirty pavement, with tables and chairs and comfortable settees all along one side, ideally placed to sit and admire the merchandise in the shop windows, relax after each purchase, and - equally important - consider what to buy next.

But all this activity did rather take it out of one after a while. Daphne sank into one of the superbly upholstered sofas

'Darling,' she suggested, 'I think a cup of tea might be welcome. Shall we ring for a steward and have it here, or trot along and mingle in the Winter Gardens?'

'I think the Winter Gardens,' decided Theodore. 'I have an overwhelming desire to re-connect with intelligent forms of life. Thank *heavens* for Julian and Arabella!'

7

Caroline opened the discussion on her sister's marriage by asking bluntly what, exactly, Sophie proposed to do about it.

Sophie sighed. There was no point in holding this conversation, but equally no point in saying so to Caroline.

Instead she answered, 'What *can* I do? I've made my bed, as the saying goes - now I've got to lie in it.'

'That's just rubbish!' snorted Caroline. 'Listen, honeybunch, the only people who deserve to lie in a badly-made bed are the ones who are too lazy to get up and re-make it!'

'Easy for you to say. What about Pop's money?' countered Sophie.

'I know exactly what he'd say about the money. Let it go, learn from it, and never throw good money after bad.'

Sophie stared at the rattan table in the small enclosed veranda, where Elsie had brought their mid-morning coffee. Last night the Ball had rescued her from this confrontation, but there was half an hour to kill before this morning's hairdressing appointment, which Caroline had obviously earmarked for this purpose.

'Come on, you don't have to keep up the Lady Knotworth act with me,' she went on quietly. 'You need to confide in someone you can trust, Sophie. Let it out.'

Sophie shook her head. She'd spent years successfully suppressing tears behind a dam of sheer determination and she wasn't about to allow it to be breached now. However, it was obvious Caroline wasn't going to let this drop, so - well, maybe one or two trickles through a safety valve would silence her, while ensuring the dam itself remained secure.

But somehow, once she started, the dam ruptured and the trickle became an unstoppable flow. Everything poured out; the hurt, the slights, the humiliations, the utter disillusionment...

Caroline listened in silence.

Although she'd die rather than admit it to anyone but close family, Sophie had made the trip from the United States seven years before as an heiress hoping to emulate her heroine Jenny Jerome, who'd cemented her position in high society by marrying Lord Randolph Churchill. If Jenny Jerome could do it, why not Sophie McLean? Everyone said she was far more beautiful, and Pop made sure she was dressed in the most sumptuous Paris gowns and fashionable jewellery money could buy to enhance that beauty.

Pop had hoped she'd marry a Scottish clan leader, but Sophie had no intention of being stuck in some draughty castle surrounded by mountains and peat-digging yokels, or, even worse, some gloomy rain-soaked island eternally battered by Atlantic gales. No, she was a city girl. She liked the good things of life. Clubs, parties, fun. And shopping. So when she first arrived as a lively twenty year old, armed with a launch-pad of the sort of invitations needed to generate a lot more, she prudently kept the field clear of undesirables in order to concentrate on the main goal - the English aristocracy.

She'd been successful. The courtship with the Earl of Knotworth, who'd succeeded the title in his early thirties following his father's sudden death, took place in a variety of exotic locations, the society wedding was of course financed wholly by Pop, and Sophie was so engrossed in basking in the glory of being Lady Knotworth that as the requests gradually increased for Pop to stump up more - and more, and more - money for ongoing repairs to the handsome but crumbling house that was now home, she happily concurred. Pop, proud of his daughter's success, hadn't minded. Not at first, anyway.

Just as she, at first, hadn't minded her husband's diary abounding with social occasions which appeared to exclude her in favour of the clique of young men who always seemed to surround him. At first she found his popularity among his male friends endearing, and his shyness with her enchanting. At first the fact that the marriage was never actually consummated, although disappointing and surprising, didn't unduly worry her. At first she put the half-hearted attempts on her husband's part which ended in disaster down to the fact that he still hadn't quite outgrown his public school way of life; everyone knew English public schools were obsessed with cold baths and rugby to the exclusion of everything else. At first she was confident that her allure, her beauty, her own sensual nature would be sufficient to overcome these initial problems, and banish the uncomfortable suspicion that people seemed to think it must in some way be *her* fault that an heir had not yet put in an appearance.

And at first it didn't matter that she never quite managed to grasp the nuances of speech that could mysteriously change the entire meaning of a sentence for those in the know; never quite managed to overcome the sense of being either deliberately or unconsciously left out when people everyone else knew, but she didn't, were discussed at dinner parties.

It was a strange form of education. Nobody told you anything, you picked things up as you went along. Snippets of information delivered with an arched eyebrow when the ladies withdrew after dinner; what was acceptable as long as it was kept discreet, what was not...

As to the physical side of her marriage, when the truth finally dawned it left her feeling idiotically naive and utterly humiliated. How could she possibly have failed to see what was so obvious to everyone else? She'd gone hot with shame at the thought of the hilarity it must have caused in so many drawing rooms. Not to mention the servants, who always seemed to know more about one's business than one did oneself.

That was when she saw clearly that the romantic courtship, the proposal on the stone terrace overlooking the lake, the position in society, the invitations piled up on the desk in her husband's study, all the advantages in fact of the title that was now hers, were merely the exchange rate of a Faustian agreement she'd been too much in love - as she thought at the time - to take at anything other than face value. The whole thing had, on Aubrey's part, been nothing but a business arrangement. He needed money; she (or rather, Pop) had it in abundance. It was as simple as that.

If he'd been honest about his preference for men at the start they could at least have formed a meaningful friendship, rather than the distant formality that had developed between them. But she'd had to face reality and make her choice; either she accepted the situation gracefully and made a life for herself independently of his, apart from those occasions where a joint appearance was necessary, or she went through the trauma and disgrace of divorce. And then what? An ignominious return to New York, after all the fuss and newspaper publicity covering her romantic English Society Wedding? What did she tell her father?

And that was another thing. Pop had poured thousands of dollars into Weedmoor Hall. Why should Aubrey have the freedom divorce would bring to pursue a life of hedonistic pleasure, his home conveniently rescued from dilapidation, renovated throughout, and decorated with those elegant finishing touches only the best (Pop's) money could buy?

No. There was too much invested, on every level, to walk away. She was committed to the arrangement for life. And she was better off than some. It was whispered that one high-born lady in a neighbouring county had actually been beaten by her husband; the worst Aubrey could be accused of was indifference. She had the position she'd coveted. What she didn't have, and never would have, was love. Aubrey hadn't even come to Southampton to see them off. He was too busy attending a 'meeting' in London...

Caroline had remained silent throughout.

Still saying nothing, she went into the bathroom and ran a flannel under the Cold Fresh Water tap. She'd already guessed what would come tumbling out. It was Sophie who needed to hear it spoken aloud.

'Even if you weren't coming home to visit Pop, I'd have gotten you away from that set-up somehow. What you need,' she diagnosed as she gently bathed her sister's puffy, bloodshot eyes, 'Is to escape from slobbery, snobbery Aubrey and his entourage - preferably permanently, but I guess temporarily is better than nothing.' The mischievous smile returned. 'And if that Promenade Deck Hunk you danced with last night is a sample of what the *Berengaria* can offer on the way - hey, tell His Lordship to go pee up a wall, sling your chastity belt over the side, and throw the key after it!'

Sophie couldn't help it. A smile, faint, tremulous, but genuine, broke through the tears.

She had no intention of embarking on some meaningless shipboard romance - and even less a meaningful one - but who could stay miserable for long in the face of Caroline's totally ridiculous rehabilitation strategies?

She'd been right to confide in Caroline. It had been cathartic.

Once she'd admitted to making a complete mess of her life instead of trying to be someone she wasn't, and put into words her overwhelming sense of failure and deep unhappiness over the state of her marriage - everything, in fact, she'd determinedly smothered for so long - it had lessened the power of its hold over her. Now that she'd distanced herself from the situation, she could see how damaging it had been physically, as well as mentally, to take on a role to which she was temperamentally wholly unsuited.

And, having cleared the air, it was time to enjoy what the ship had to offer. A spot of pampering at the manicurist had followed the obligatory trip to the hairdressers.

And then Caroline, who decided to pop along to Ladies Fashions for (another) headscarf in case they went up on deck to play quoits and shuffleboard later, ended up buying the prettiest bathing costume she'd ever seen. It sat in the window, in front of the coffee-and-cream dress, an irresistible temptation simply *begging* to be bought; a beguiling shade of apple green with darker green frills around the modesty skirt covering the tops of the legs, and just the flirtiest glimpse of flesh where the straps went over the shoulders, the whole effect finished to perfection by the most elegant little white belt around the waist, drawing it in with flattering emphasis on Caroline's slender figure. And it had the dearest little matching bathing cap to protect one's hair - although naturally one would just go straight back to the hairdressers again after a swim - while guaranteeing the desired effect.

Well, one had to look one's best for these things.

In any case, it was always possible she might decide to swim more than once in *Berengaria's* Pompeian pool, so of course she'd need far more than the dozen she'd brought with her, because obviously one couldn't be seen in the same costume twice. And for those stress-inducing last minute bouts of indecision about which one to wear, which was the most flattering...

Oh, why not.

Sophie, waiting for her sister to come out of the shop, was shaken out of a relaxed reverie by an attractive male voice: 'Hello there!'

She looked up to find the man she'd danced with last night smiling at her. Clive, the PDH.

'Can't stop,' he explained, 'I'm in a tearing hurry. How's things? Are you enjoying the trip?'

'Oh yes, thank you.' (Who wouldn't?)

'Jolly good. No sign of any more dolphins or whales I'm afraid, but I'll definitely let you know of any sightings. Must rush, I'm afraid. Might see you again, hopefully - perhaps at Sports Day tomorrow? I'm co-organising it.' He rolled his eyes in mock dread.

'Yes. That would be nice. We'll probably enter for one or two things,' replied Sophie, and smiled as he hoped she'd enjoy it and bade her good day.

She watched as he strode off and was lost in the crowds, and wondered why, once again, he seemed so... *familiar.* It wasn't as though they'd spent much time together last night, and there was nothing remarkable about it when they did; a couple of dances and a brief chat on deck about dolphins.

She frowned slightly. For once, she was glad Caroline took longer than anyone else on earth to buy a headscarf. If her sister had witnessed this perfectly innocent conversation, she'd put two and two together and come up with ninety-nine.

Suddenly restless, she stood up and sauntered into the shop, just as Caroline was about to leave. Lying on the counter, where the senior saleslady had obviously got out the entire selection from the mahogany drawers at the back for her sister's perusal, was a most unusual shimmering golden brown bathing costume. She stared at it.

She didn't need a new one any more than Caroline, as she was the first to admit. But almost without a conscious decision to buy it, she found herself paying for it, and had the strangest sense that far from being some frivolous impulse buy, it was an object which, in some way as yet unknown, held great significance for her future.

She watched as the senior saleslady carefully wrapped her purchase, and shook her head slightly. What a ridiculous, fanciful notion - where on earth did that come from? It was just a perfectly ordinary bathing costume, although an extremely attractive one. Nothing more.

8

'Having lunch with the countess then?'

Clive looked up from detailing particulars of each crew member as required by the U.S immigration authorities; rating, place and date of birth, description, length of sea service, last ship in Cunard and discharge book number, all of which must be accurate on arrival in New York.

'Don't be so silly.'

'Oh. Touchy this morning, aren't we?' Tom Burnett grinned as he checked the time. Another five minutes to lunch break.

'Why on earth,' Clive turned back to the crew lists. 'Would I want to meet up with some boring old countess?'

'She didn't seem boring last night,' Tom pointed out, and sighed. 'Wish I was having lunch with her sister!'

'You'd *be* lunch. She'd eat you alive,' said Clive, remembering Caroline's coquettish eye-play when he'd asked her sister to dance. 'Don't tell me you've fallen for her?'

'Ra-*ther*!' admitted Tom. 'I've got a date with her on Sports Day. Should have a couple of hours off then.'

'More fool you for wasting them. Why be the consolation prize for the latest American heiress on her way back home after failing to bag an English lord?'

Tom tutted in disgust. 'You grow more cynical by the day, don't you, Clive.'

'Well that's what most of them make the journey for, with their equally ambitious mamas, isn't it?'

'Not in this case. I gather Caroline's been put off by her sister's experience.'

Clive looked up again. 'Oh?'

'Yes. She's been visiting her in England. It seems the marriage is in trouble.'

'Oh. No dastardly ulterior motive for Sports Day then; merely giving Miss Yankee Doodle Dandy the benefit of your vast marriage guidance experience to help things along for her sister, eh? How noble of you!'

Tom tutted again. '*You* might think it's clever to be flippant about someone's marital problems, but it's no joke for her!'

Clive shrugged, hesitated, then decided not to mention the fact that, coincidentally, he'd bumped into Sophie earlier and, in the course of polite but meaningless small-talk as he hoped she was enjoying the trip and so on, he'd said - more out of courtesy than as a statement of truth - he hoped that their paths might cross again, perhaps at Sports Day or some other occasion. Wasn't as if it was significant, or important.

And he certainly wasn't going to mention the curious sense he'd had at the time of some sort of sub-text taking place beneath the normal everyday civility of greeting a passenger with whom he'd danced the night before. The notion sounded crazy even to him. What could 'Are you enjoying the trip?' possibly be a coded message for? It was hardly a conversation loaded with meaning and innuendo. In fact it couldn't have been more inconsequential. He shook himself slightly.

'Obviously a classic case of Be Careful What You Wish For,' he said, after a slight pause. 'In case you end up getting it.'

'You really *are* a cynic, aren't you!'

'Yes.' Clive turned back to his lists. 'Good job I'm not wishing to fall in love with anyone, isn't it?'

9

'Something light for luncheon, I think.' Sophie perused the *Carte du Jour*, and looked up at Danny. 'Quail consomme to start, please.'

'Tomato juice for me,' decided Caroline.

A surprised voice broke in. 'Say Caroline! I didn't know you were on board!'

Caroline recognised the voice at once.

'Cyril! *I* didn't know *you* were on board!' She turned to Sophie as Danny headed to the kitchens. 'Sophie, you remember Cyril, don't you?'

'Vaguely,' smiled Sophie as Cyril took her hand and kissed it with flamboyant gallantry. It gradually came back to her; the son of a steel magnate, a neighbour in Long Island. Years ago she'd met him at the parties of mutual friends. He was three or four years younger than she was - more of an age with Caroline, and a sort of on-off member of the set to which Caroline belonged. Sophie had left all that behind with her marriage. Even Caroline, it seemed, hadn't seen him for some time.

He was, he informed them, returning from a visit to friends at a French chateau.

'Great to see you again!' he grinned, holding Caroline's gaze for a few seconds longer than was necessary for an affectionate greeting between old friends. 'Got a lot of catching up to do, *n'est-ce pas?*'

Sophie saw the look in Caroline's eye as she took in Cyril's perfectly tailored slacks and hand-knitted Fair Isle pullover. He'd indulged his sense of sartorial elegance and style even in his teenage years. Things hadn't changed, obviously.

Oh dear. Poor Tom.

Last night's contender had obviously been flushed completely from mind by this latest suitor who was more handsome, more sophisticated, and infinitely more wealthy.

Tomorrow morning's bouquet would far eclipse Tom's, because any flowers sent by an American playboy with a limitless budget who was intent on impressing a lady would naturally be unequalled in extravagant ostentation.

There wouldn't be any point in the gesture otherwise.

10

The Pompeian pool was advertised, with some justification, by Cunard as being the biggest swimming pool next to the Atlantic itself.

Three decks high, it was overlooked by a balcony, encircled by eighteen pillars, and lit underwater by sunken cluster lights. The sea water in the pool was kept constantly fresh through a decorative fountain cascade, the marble benches at the sides were continually warmed by inner copper steam piping, and the adjoining marble and bronze dressing rooms were fitted with well-upholstered sofas and led on to the Turkish steam baths, saunas, and massage rooms.

It was the perfect place to show off one's new bathing costume. Which meant, of course, one's figure. So Caroline was glad it was too windy to play deck games. She and Sophie arranged to meet up with Cyril later that afternoon at the pool instead.

However, the idea of lowering oneself into a tank of cold water (it was heated, but that was beside the point) held limited appeal. While admittedly useful for displaying one's charms to the admiring glances of those to whom one wished to display them, it didn't necessarily mean one wanted to be immersed in it for any length of time. A brief dip was quite enough. One didn't want to end up catching pneumonia.

So Caroline climbed up the steps by the cascade fountain, and perched seductively on one of the heated marble benches in the new costume...

Only to find that Cyril, who was a strong swimmer, spent the first fifteen minutes ploughing up and down the pool without paying her a single compliment, and with hardly a glance in her direction.

She glared petulantly at him. Of all the cheek! Too busy showing off his own powerful crawl stroke to the other occupants of the pool, including a couple of giggling female admirers on the balcony, to pay the adoring homage she expected as she sat fiddling with a beguiling tendril of hair she'd allowed to peep from under her cap... and adjusting the shoulder straps... and re-arranging the modesty skirt at the tops of her legs...

Before giving up altogether.

Well, one had absolutely no intention of sitting here indefinitely, waiting for that braggart to take notice. It was he who'd said they had a lot of catching up to do. About time he got on with it then, instead of showing off to all and sundry.

She decided to take a shower, get dressed, and flop onto one of the richly brocaded settees in the balcony above the pool to watch the swimmers. Which meant, swimmers other than Cyril. Because he wasn't the *only* Adonis in the pool with an attractive male physique; she'd spotted a rather delicious dark haired Rudolph Valentino look-alike executing a perfect dive just along from where she was sitting...

Though not as strong a swimmer as Cyril, Sophie found just being in water deeply relaxing, and swam slowly and sensuously, completing length after length. She'd decided against wearing the new gold-brown costume. The dark red would do.

And as she swam, for the second time that day she had the mystifying and unsettling sense that this pool would, in some unexpected way, be instrumental in her future.

Most odd. Why would she imagine that?

She gave herself another mental shake, turned onto her back, waved up at Caroline who had now appeared on the balcony, and made a conscious decision to focus on unremarkable everyday things like having coffee and visiting the hairdressers again, to banish these ridiculous, and most unwelcome, fanciful notions.

11

'I wonder where Daphne and Theodore are?' Mary scanned the deck impatiently.

Sam, tapping his feet as the band belted out *'If You Knew Susie'*, shrugged. 'Och, stop worrying about them. They'd be here if they wanted to be here.'

'But I've kept seats for them so they don't miss the concert -'

'Never mind *them* missing the concert, *I'm* missing half of it wi' you wittering on! Sshh!' He tapped his feet again as the band swung into *'Yes sir! That's My Baby!'*

Silence.

Then: 'Maybe they're -'

'Aye. And maybe they're busy admiring Theodore's new pyjamas,' said Sam, and immediately regretted it as she shot back the predictable answer:

'Aye. Or Daphne's wee present from the jeweller's!'

Sam shuffled uncomfortably. He'd walked right into that one.

Well, now he was finding his feet a bit on the ship, maybe it was worth turning his mind to whatever opportunities there may be for a spot of gambling. Nothing major - no poker schools, he had more sense than that - but wherever there were men, be it a shipyard or first class on a transatlantic liner, there was sure to be some form of gambling. Maybe he could make a bit of money there. He'd heard about the ship's pool, for instance. He'd try and find out a bit more about that...

The Smoking Room was a popular retreat. Quite apart from bonhomie and business opportunities, it provided the means of a discreet after-lunch snooze without the indignity of retiring to one's stateroom like a geriatric old buffer. Or, if one didn't wish to huddle in a blanket on deck staring at the grey Atlantic in a

Force Six gale, or listen to a gang of high-spirited students giving a band concert, one could escape to the gentlemen-only Smoking Room under the pretext (so much more dignified and weighty) of engaging in the sort of serious business talk that was too complicated for pretty little female heads to concern themselves with, and spend a few hours either contentedly dozing in a corner, or whiling away the time in congenial male company as one's contemporaries indulged in masculine banter, loud guffaws, and bawdy jokes around the ornate fireplace.

Sam observed the companionable clique that was beginning to form, at the centre of which was Lexie Stonefeather and Lemuel Hoffmann. He had no particular desire to be a part of it (not that he was likely to be invited), so made no attempt to join in the conversation.

And he also observed the clergyman on the periphery, never intruding or drawing attention to himself in any way, but well within earshot, quietly reading the ship's newspaper.

Sam smiled at him, picked up a magazine, and sat down nearby. You could learn a lot by just sitting and listening...

12

'Well, that's two more meals got through without you ending up in the hold for mincing up Alec Baxter in the meat shredder,' commented Danny wryly. 'Three down. Only another twenty or so to go…'

'I told you I was going to be a good boy. No complaints, no outbursts,' answered Joey.

They'd escaped to the aft mooring deck (there was no staff room or communal recreation area) for a break before preparations began for Afternoon Tea, and then Dinner.

'I'm surprised you've lasted this long,' admitted Danny. 'I thought you'd have decked him that first night.'

'I did, in my mind's eye.' Joey finished his cigarette, and threw the butt over the side. 'Think I'll go down for a kip. I didn't sleep much last night.'

Danny nodded. He also felt in need of a period of quiet and solitude. He sat down against the rail and got out his paper and pencil to write to his Love.

But as he started, Billy appeared, carrying a bucket containing the uniforms he'd earlier left soaking in the glory hole.

'Aye aye,' greeted Danny.

'I've washed this lot five times!' answered Billy. 'They're permanently contaminated. I've rinsed and swilled til my hands are nearly washed away and still can't get rid of the stench!'

Danny shook his head in sympathy. There was no difficulty in getting washing dry; hot air was always circulating below. The real problem for Billy was trying to persuade his nostrils that the smell of Lexie Stonefeather had finally left his clothes, because that would take a lot more than a few buckets of water.

'I wish I could just sling the lot overboard.' Billy began spreading it all on the deck, weighing down each item so the wind could purify it without blowing it all the way back to England.

'Well, here's something that'll take your mind off it.' Danny knew what would cheer him up. 'That lass this morning -'

Billy cut him off.

'Yeah, I know, I know. I'd no right to take it out on her. Save it, Danny, I'm not in the mood for a lecture.'

He'd already had this conversation with himself; he didn't need Danny beating him up over it. He'd been a bit short with her, which was unfair because it wasn't her fault Lexie's performance had not only caused the entire morning's work schedule to be delayed, but left him with two sets of uniform to be scrubbed. She was an attractive little thing, apart from an ever-present anxious frown which was probably due to being new on the section and under particular scrutiny from the Chief Stewardess. Either that or seasickness. Not that there was much to choose between the two.

'I was only going to tell you -'

'Well don't bother.' Billy moved away as he continued spreading items of clothing out on the deck.

Danny shrugged. If the daft bat stopped wallowing in all the bad things that happened to him on this trip, he might see something good right under his nose - like that young lass who clearly thought he was the dishiest thing on two legs. Well, Danny's time off was just as precious as Billy's, and he wasn't going to waste it in trying to get the numbskull to hear what he was too blind to see. He had his own concerns to mull over, the main one being whether he, a bottom-of-the-heap waiter with little prospect of ever being anything else, could summon up enough nerve to propose marriage to someone so far above his league...

She was the second eldest of seven children and her father, Pat Higgins, was a self-made bookmaker, an ambitious Liverpool Irishman who'd started out with nothing but confidence, bluff, and a sound knowledge of horses, walked

96

from Liverpool to Aintree Racecourse carrying a large bag apparently full of coins and, once there, set himself up to take as many bets as he could, jangling his bag to attract prospective punters.

Or rather, to take as many bets as he could get away with. Because the bag wasn't full of cash, but nails, covered by a top layer of coins to present with loud, crowd-drawing congratulations, to the winners. It was the most dangerous gamble of his life; if there weren't sufficient losers to provide him with enough money to pay out when his float had gone, he'd be lynched by a furious crowd.

He survived the day, which meant he could return the following day with more confidence. And fewer nails.

He brought home increasing amounts from each Race Meeting, and became established as a professional bookie, gradually travelling further and further afield; first Chester, Haydock Park, and Manchester, then Doncaster, Nottingham, Beverley, Redcar... All transactions were meticulously recorded in a ledger book; amount for each horse in each race, outgoings - tic-tac, clerk, tax, digs, fares, meals etc - and overall result.

The years also produced yield of another kind; a growing family. And there was great excitement among the children when they moved from Liverpool to a newly built house less than five minutes away from the sandy Mersey shore in New Brighton, which in Edwardian days bore no resemblance to the urban sprawl it was to become over the next hundred years. Still a child's paradise of clean golden sand when the tide was out, there were small sandstone cliffs and sandhills leading onto heathland to explore in the direction of the estuary, and upriver, the site of the former Magazines, where all ships entering the river had to deposit any gunpowder while in port. And Mother Redcap's tavern with its smugglers' tunnels and hidden doors and secret passages and rumours of buried treasure, and history of violent confrontations with excise men and press gangs, and tales of dark deeds in the days of wreckers who inhabited the coastline in the previous century.

So in fact Pat Higgins' children had grown up by the sea, just as Danny and his own brothers and sisters had done before they emigrated to Canada.

But now they were adults. And Pat Higgins, having prospered considerably over the years, would be none too keen on one of his daughters associating with a waiter, no matter how honourable Danny's intentions. In fact the more honourable his intentions, the more likely it was that he'd be told to clear off and look elsewhere.

Danny, however, had no intention of being frightened off by an irascible tongue and an overbearing 'I'm-head-of-the-household-and-what-I-say-goes' frame of mind now that he'd fallen deeply, and irrevocably, in love.

He'd been captivated by her unusual slate grey eyes, her brown hair fixed in a bun at the nape of her neck, and her air of thoughtfulness, which spoke of innate kindness and generosity of spirit; there was a quietness about her, a gentleness, coupled with a good sense of humour which he found irresistible. And her name was as unusual as her looks - Honorah, after an Irish ancestress in wild Connemara, shortened for everyday usage to Norah.

And Danny wanted to marry her, if she'd accept his proposal.

As for Pat Higgins, he had his own way of disarming him. Danny was blessed with a personality that overflowed with genuine warmth, cheerfulness, and willingness to help; he was likeable, excellent company, and a natural raconteur with a ready fund of entertaining stories about life at sea, particularly on board a transatlantic liner packed on every voyage with the sort of passengers most people saw only in films, or read about in newspapers.

And he had another invaluable asset: a positive, optimistic outlook on life.

Which was just as well, because he'd need all the help he could get when he formally proposed to her. And that, he resolved, would be in the very near future. He'd deliberately held back until now in order to give her both time and opportunity to meet someone else with more prospects, more status, and more money.

Which wouldn't be difficult.

True, on occasions a steward or waiter could bring his basic wage up to a decent level with tips on a really productive trip. On occasions. But on the whole, even with tips, you were hardly the catch of the century. He imagined the conversation between some of her brothers and sisters: Who's that fellow Norah's knocking around with? Oh him. He's a waiter or steward or something. Seagoing. Let's hope it runs its course and fizzles out before she does something stupid like marrying him, because she could do better than him!

And the worst of it was, Danny knew they were absolutely right. She could do much, much better than him.

He stared quietly at the sea, an endless expanse of dark grey-green waves under a gunmetal Atlantic sky, and made a decision.

It was impossible to get up to Liverpool and back during turnaround time in Southampton. So, although he had a steady job here and as yet none up there, this would be his last Western Ocean run on the *Berengaria.* When they arrived back in Southampton he'd collect his Discharge Book, head up to Liverpool, and propose.

He'd left it long enough for her to meet a host of more eminent suitors, all of whom he knew would far surpass him in looks, career prospects, and all the other qualities she deserved, and for her to tell him gently that she wished to finish their relationship. If he left it much longer, he thought grimly, she might do that anyway!

He was nobody special, he knew that. But to her, he *was* special. He knew that as well, because she'd told him. He smiled to himself as he thought of her last letter.

Whatever anybody else thought about him, and his suitability (or lack of it) as husband material - and although privately he might agree with those members of her family who felt she could do a lot better - the only opinion that really mattered to him was hers, and to her it didn't seem important that he wasn't, say, a doctor, or a teacher, or a lawyer, or a highly paid merchant with power and influence in Liverpool. Danny was accepted and loved for himself. And what could be more precious to any human being than that?

When he finally began to write, the words almost fought each other in their haste to cover the sheets of cheap writing paper. And he didn't stop writing until it was time to start his next shift.

THREE: MID ATLANTIC

1

The ship's newspaper, discarded on one of the tables in the Smoking Room, reported under the heading 'Movements of Liners' that RMS *Berengaria* was now 1,500 miles west of Bishop's Rock. With New York another 1,500 miles to the east, she was mid-way across the Atlantic.

And while tensions continued to build in the kitchens, in the Smoking Room there were tensions of a different kind as the occupants waited for the announcement of the daily ship's pool result.

This, Sam discovered as he sat quietly watching and listening, was a competition for passengers to guess the number of sea miles covered by the ship between noon one day and noon the next, over distances varying between five and six hundred miles, at speeds varying between twenty four and twenty seven knots, and in weather conditions varying from clear sunlight to freezing gales. Or thick fog. Or driving snow.

For the passengers it provided an extra daily bonus of excitement and anticipation. And for Cunard, anything that added to the allure of an Atlantic crossing and provided favourable publicity was greatly encouraged. The prize, if travelling from New York, was $1,000, or with an exchange rate of $4.87, nearly £250 if sailing from Southampton.

It was always an occasion of raucous celebration when the winner was announced, and when Lexie Stonefeather learned he was today's winner he punched the air with a triumphant yell, eyes gleaming with pleasurable anticipation.

(And Jack Dalton's eyes, as he sat piously reading his Bible well within earshot, gleamed with even greater pleasurable anticipation.)

Lexie revelled in being the man-of-the-moment, with much hearty backslapping and 'My round, fellas, what'll you have?'

Being toasted by some of the most powerful and influential men on either side of the Atlantic was every bit as intoxicating as the whisky he enthusiastically replenished. In fact he was in such an expansive mood that he didn't even mind when the conversation moved on to other topics, and someone began reminiscing about one particular voyage on which he'd spent a good deal of time with the sweetheart of the day, Mary Pickford, and her husband, the equivalent male heart-throb Douglas Fairbanks.

'Wouldn't mind meeting her myself,' grinned Lexie. 'I could match old Dougie Fairbanks' performance any day, given half a chance!'

The newspaper proprietor in the group winked. 'Couldn't we all!'

There were loud guffaws amid general agreement. Sure thing. They could *all* match old Dougie Fairbanks' performance any day, given half a chance.

Lexie found all this men-of-the-world camaraderie invaluable. He could make good use of Lemuel in New York, and the newspaper man's son was apparently a friend of the Prince of Wales, so was also worth cultivating because you never knew where contacts could lead. But Lemuel was the one he really needed to butter up, cement the Us-Big-Cheeses-Of-The-World-Gotta-Stick-Together for useful introductions to people of importance - the sort of people far removed from irritating small-time contractors in London, whingeing about piddling little bills for work carried out not being paid on time. Or not being paid at all, if he could help it. Honourable dealings, like any form of kindness, were weaknesses to be exploited. What did it matter whether or not they went out of business, as long as he didn't? Let them damn well wait until he was ready to part with his money; they were lucky to get it at all. Effing nuisances, the lot of them.

He drifted back to the conversation going on around him, which had now moved on to binoculars because the ship's newspaper had announced that the *Aquitania* would soon pass them on her journey eastward. His new friends were discussing the merits of various types and makes - which was another useful opportunity to show off, because it appeared he was the only one among them who'd brought binoculars with him. He broke in to air his knowledge of Zeiss field glasses, and then had an even better idea: why not ratchet up the starring role a few more notches by producing them?

He drained his glass, set it down on the table, and, adopting the air of a genie about to grant three wishes, announced grandly, 'Tell you what, gentlemen, I'll nip down to my suite and get them and you can try them out for yourselves. How about that? Back in a jiff!'

2

There was a sudden surge of excitement along the deck.

The *Berengaria* was no longer a solitary vessel steaming across the vast Atlantic; a distant plume of smoke above a tiny dot had been spotted on the western horizon, and the word quickly spread. RMS *Berengaria* and RMS *Aquitania* would shortly pass each other.

Caroline decided to pop down to the suite for the new Leica camera she'd bought in London during her visit. It should make some interesting and quite iconic shots, the *Aquitania* approaching, passing them mid-Atlantic, and then receding eastwards towards Southampton. She'd become very interested in photography in recent years, to the point where it was progressing from fascinating hobby to serious art form.

She'd need the camera for Sports Day anyway, so she might as well make good use of it beforehand. Also, she'd adorn the pale mauve dress she was wearing with one of the deep purple flowers nestling in the two latest additions from the ship's florist. (Sophie had been right about a stupendous bouquet from Cyril arriving on the Early Morning Tea tray. What she hadn't expected was for it to be joined by an equally stupendous twin. But then she hadn't stayed at last night's Carnival Dance long enough to see Caroline punish Cyril for his lack of attention in the pool by spending time with another arrival on the scene: Luigi, the Rudolph Valentino look-alike with brooding Italian eyes, whose family were something to do with motor cars in Italy.)

'I'll come with you,' decided Sophie. 'I could do with combing my hair and powdering my nose.'

'Yeah, I thought you might,' nodded Caroline archly. 'Because I see from the programme that a certain ship's officer is jointly organising the Sports Day games - the one you actually danced with *twice* at the Sailing Night Ball, you Jezebel you!'

'Don't be ridiculous,' said Sophie impatiently. 'It's got nothing to do with the fact he may be there. I just don't want to look a mess on any photographs you take, that's all.'

It was true. Just the same, she was glad she hadn't mentioned anything about seeing him by the shops yesterday, because although she had no regrets about confiding in her sister about the extent of her unhappiness and disastrous state of her marriage, it didn't mean Caroline was now free to take on the role of matrimonial/romantic interest advisor. All these silly comments about attractive men were beginning to grate. She'd made it quite clear she was not interested in lighthearted flirtations, and Caroline should respect that.

Caroline grudgingly acknowledged she'd crossed the line between sisterly concern and interfering.

'Look. I know you've made the decision to stick with all this Countess of Knotworth nonsense. And you know I think it's the wrong decision -'

'Yes. So there's no point in talking about it.'

'Think about it, Sophie, and be honest with yourself even if you won't be honest with me. When you danced with him, wouldn't part of you have liked to have taken it further?'

Sophie had been dreading this conversation. The Sailing Night Ball had been... well, who wouldn't find it a magical experience to dance with one of the most attractive officers on board, and end the evening on a flower-garlanded deck gazing at the moonlit ocean? But it had merely been a superficial break from reality, and after the initial novelty, when Clive's very maleness had acted as a sort of antidote to seven years of Aubrey, it became increasingly clear to her that there were deeper reasons to reject divorce in addition to practical ones such as wasting Pop's money and returning to New York to admit failure.

Such as, self-respect. Integrity. And conscience.

'No. I enjoyed dancing the polka, and that's all there was - and is - to it.'

'Hm.' Caroline fixed her with a steady gaze. 'And tell me, do you think slobbery, snobbery Aubrey is pining for you right now? All lonely and sad?'

'Probably not. But just because he chooses to behave like an alley cat doesn't mean I'm going to do the same.'

Caroline shrugged. 'What a shame. Ending up a dried-up old prune, lying in state on your stately Weedmoor Hall deathbed, thinking, 'If only I'd gotten laid all those years ago aboard the *Berengaria* by a real man', for some creep who doesn't even love you!'

Sophie turned away in disgust. 'Quite apart from the fact that two dances hardly demonstrate a desire on either his part or mine for a racketing love affair, I hate that particular expression. It's vile!'

'Not as vile as living a lie with that selfish -'

Sophie determinedly cut Caroline off. 'Look. I've made my decision, and that's it. I made a promise in my wedding vows: for better or worse.'

Caroline merely laughed. 'Oh, don't be such a sanctimonious pain-in-the-neck, Reverend Sister Sophie! You're only the Countess of Knotworth, honeybunch, not the Virgin Queen! Although it wouldn't surprise me if some of those society folk you count as friends call you the Virgin Countess behind your back.'

'This conversation is getting more absurd by the minute, and I've had enough of it. I've told you, I'm not interested in romance with anyone. And I've had enough of you pushing boundaries.'

'Oh? And what about the boundaries some of your aristocratic friends pushed when they tried it on with me? Probably because they thought I was easy meat, being American?'

Sophie looked at her sharply.

'I know you didn't believe me.' Caroline imitated Sophie's indignant tones: *'You're making it up! Lavinia's husband*

107

wouldn't do anything of the sort!' - but I was telling the truth. He did. But to come back to what we were saying - I think it would do you good to have a wild fling, honeybunch.'

'Oh you do, do you?'

'Yes.'

Sophie sighed. Obviously she'd been wasting her breath. 'And what if there was "issue"? Have you thought of that?'

'Well it rather puts the ball back in his court, doesn't it. Does he accuse you of adultery, and say it couldn't possibly be his because, well, you know, and have all his private business public knowledge for yet more society gossip? Or does he say nothing, accept the child as his, and just feel relieved he hasn't had to be part of its creation? Don't tell me similar things haven't happened in the past!'

'Whether it has or it hasn't, as far as I'm concerned -'

Caroline gave her another penetrating look. 'Incidentally, what *does* snobbery slobbery Aubrey have to say on the subject of producing heirs?'

'He never -'

'No. He never mentions it, because he's too busy thinking about his boyfriends to give any thoughts to you, or your happiness.'

Sophie turned away.

'Do you really want to go through life childless just for the sake of a title, Sophie?'

'D'you think I need you to spell that out for me?' Sophie's voice was thick with tears. 'It's hurt me for the last seven years! *Of course* I don't want to go through life childless!'

This conversation was becoming too painful by far, and there was no point in continuing it. The decision was made. She'd stay with Aubrey and keep to her marriage vows, even if it meant never having a child of her own. And she'd behave with the propriety expected of a Countess, and ignore Caroline's unwanted and unwise advice regarding shipboard romances. She'd also forbid any photographs being taken of her and Clive if they happened to meet up this afternoon at Sports Day -

especially with Theodore and Daphne on the alert to pick up the merest hint of gossip, should she be seen in the company of dashing ship's officers. (Although ironically, she admitted sadly to herself, Aubrey would probably find this particular one even more attractive than she did.)

As she set off, leaving Caroline to follow, yet again she had the strangest sense that this voyage, as well as being the crossing of an ocean to a different continent, would be a significant journey to her own destiny. She shook her head impatiently. She'd had enough of all these ridiculous premonitions or whatever they were. *She'd* decide how her future would turn out, and these unexpected fanciful notions, so totally out of character, could go right back to wherever they'd come from.

And stay there.

3

As Lexie was approaching his suite Elsie Parkinson came out of the one opposite, where she'd obviously just finished changing the sheets and cleaning the room.

He looked her up and down and whistled. 'My my, aren't *you* a pretty girl!'

Elsie tried awkwardly to edge past him. 'Excuse me, sir...'

'Hey, what's your hurry?' He grinned, looking pointedly at the bundled sheets and bed linen, then back up at her.

She avoided eye contact, looked at the floor. 'Excuse me sir, I have to -'

'What's the matter? Am I embarrassing you?'

How on earth was she supposed to deal with this? Back at home she'd put him in his place, and if he didn't learn where that was she'd soon show him with a carefully aimed jerk of the knee. But she wasn't at home, and the dice was loaded in his favour; he was a first class passenger, she a stewardess who'd never again be employed on any Cunard (or any other) ship following a complaint to the Chief Stewardess. And she knew instinctively that he'd be vindictive enough to do just that, should his pride be injured.

'Listen kid, I'm in the film industry,' Lexie announced importantly. 'And funnily enough, I'm looking for someone like you to be in my next movie.'

She said nothing. If he thought she was stupid enough to be taken in by that one, he'd picked the wrong stewardess.

'Tell me...' He looked at her through lowered eyelids. They had three purposes, the female sex: decoration, recreation, and procreation. This one, pleasing to the eye as she was, fell into the first two categories. And if she fell into the third one as a result, that was her problem. 'How would you like to be a film star?'

'Excuse me sir, I must -'

'I bet you'd jump at the chance, eh?'

Again she tried to edge past him. 'I'm sorry sir, I -'

'Because believe me, I could make things happen for you!'

Too true, thought Elsie. Everything from pregnancy to the sack.

'Now, you come along to my suite when you go off duty, and we'll discuss business, all right? We'll have an audition, just acting out a little scene I have in mind, and then, once I've checked you have the talent -'

'I'm sorry, sir, I -'

Lexie smiled reassuringly. 'Now don't be nervous, there won't be anyone else watching. Just you and me, that's all.'

'I really have to -'

'Let's have a little kiss here and now, just to show we've got a deal!'

She made another determined effort to pass him.

'Ooh, you are a little tease, aren't you!' He joined in the game, chortling as he dodged in front of her while she, clutching the bundle of dirty linen protectively in front of her and feeling utterly ridiculous and increasingly desperate, sought to evade him.

He pinned her playfully against the wall, his hands either side of her shoulders. The overpowering smell of stale cigar smoke filled her nostrils.

'Gotcha! Now then - let's have this kiss...'

4

The *Aquitania* was drawing nearer.

The Atlantic was still choppy, and although the wind had abated slightly and they'd left behind a few squally showers, the sky was overcast, threatening rain. But even a torrential downpour wouldn't have deterred the excited passengers now lining the rails of both ships in readiness for the *Berengaria* and *Aquitania* to greet each other with a series of exuberant hoots as they passed. The promenade deck was festooned with flags, balloons, and bunting to add to the gaiety of the occasion.

For Theodore, there was an added dimension: the spectacle meant his long overdue invitation to dine at the captain's table. It was entirely fitting, he mused as he and Daphne stepped out of the Winter Garden on to the promenade deck, that the *Aquitania* - the very ship on which his elder brother had received *his* invitations - should make amends for the lamentable oversight of himself and Daphne not yet receiving theirs.

But Theodore had an ace up his sleeve. He'd recently taken a course in Navigation, so was now ably equipped to discuss the subject with someone who'd be suitably impressed by the depth of his knowledge.

Such as, the captain. Over dinner.

And the two factors needed in order to bring this about were now almost in place. The first of course was the *Aquitania,* or, more specifically, the opportunity she provided to air his navigation expertise. And the second was the right person to air it to, which was where the ship's officer striding purposefully along the deck came in. Nice chap; he'd spoken to him in the purser's office. And everyone knew the purser's responsibilities included passing on information to the captain (with a quiet influential word where appropriate) regarding suitable dinner invitation candidates.

He casually positioned himself and Daphne in the path of the approaching officer, a satisfying scenario drifting into mind as he watched the man stop briefly to answer someone's enquiry by nodding, smiling, and pointing up at the bridge: years hence, when the captain published his memoirs, how gratifying to read that, of all the Great and Good on whom this honour had been bestowed, it was he, Theodore, who stood out as one of the most entertaining dinner guests of all time. He read the accolade in his mind's eye: 'Yes, I've dined with Royalty, high society, university professors, bankers, politicians, eminent scientists, sporting celebrities... But the most rewarding conversation was with a chap who could discuss navigation with so fine a grasp of his subject that one felt almost a sort of kinship...'

Perfectly straightforward, you see. All it took was a shared interest in Navigation. And ensuring it was duly noted and passed on.

The man drew almost level. Theodore steered Daphne forward and greeted him with a friendly smile.

'Grand sight, isn't she!'

The officer slowed down politely. 'She certainly is, sir.'

'Now, correct me if I'm wrong,' went on Theodore, secure in the knowledge that he wasn't. 'But wasn't the *Aquitania* the first British liner to be fitted with electrical compasses?'

'You're absolutely right, sir,' complimented the officer, his eyes flicking surreptitiously towards the crowds at the rails. Bob Smythe was perfectly capable of performing the Sports Day opening ceremony and beginning the programme on his own, but he was co-organiser and it wasn't fair to leave it all to one person for too long.

Theodore smiled, preparing to launch contentedly into the principle of Newton's Laws of Motion applied to the combined forces of gravitation and the earth's rotation. And then another - extremely unwelcome - voice cheerily joined in.

'Never mind electrical compasses, if youse knew some of the things that went on in the shipyard as she was being built...'

Theodore closed his eyes. Oh *no*! Not that infernal nuisance turning up *now,* of all times!

Daphne glared indignantly. Did this ghastly man assume he could just barge in on a private conversation?

The officer looked at him with interest. 'Oh, where you involved in building her, sir?'

'Aye, all nine decks of her, from start to finish.'

'Really?'

'Aye. Ah'm lucky Ah'm still here! I mind when a hot rivet fell fifty feet from an upper deck and just missed my head!'

What a pity, thought Theodore, glaring at the grizzled, bullet-like head and thick muscular neck. It wasn't as if you didn't present a sufficiently obvious target.

'How regrettable,' he murmured, an obligatory tut of sympathy covering the dual meaning of 'regrettable'.

The officer looked at him sharply.

Sam, unaware of the uncharitable alternative interpretation, carried blithely on. 'Aye. Even more so for some of the others. One lad was working above the engine room wi' a sheer drop below him when someone higher up slipped and dropped a heavy bag of tools that hit him.' He indicated the waterline area. 'Fell the full twenty foot onto the engine room floor.'

The officer shook his head in sympathy, and Daphne stared balefully at the *Aquitania*. Trust this uncouth lout to dampen the celebratory occasion by introducing the totally unnecessary topic of injuries to some labourer who happened to have worked on her. Of course one didn't wish to appear unsympathetic, but...

Sam shrugged. 'It was work. I remember the keel blocks being fitted, before any work on the ship started at all. We all knew it meant jobs for hundreds of men.'

'Well, there we are then,' said Theodore vaguely, and drew breath for another attempt. 'Anyway. As I was saying. The advantages of electrical compasses -'

Sam, staring transfixed at the grace and beauty of the finished product on which he'd spent so many hours labouring as she steamed towards them, again innocently carried on. 'Aye, there's many a memory in that ship. I mind the day her keel was laid -'

'Yes. I'm sure you do.' Theodore rolled his eyes. 'But to come back to the advantages of the gyro-compass over magnetic compasses -'

He was interrupted by the *Aquitania's* foghorn releasing a jubilant whoop-whoop-whoop, accompanied by a belch of steam from one of her four funnels. The two ships were now drawing level, and it was the signal for the crowd on both ships to go wild, laughing, waving, and calling to each other, although nearly half a mile separated them.

Sam grinned delightedly, and shook his head in admiration. 'Look at her! And if you'd seen the size of her keel, you wouldnae believe she'd ever float! A huge, massive girder lying there, almost the entire length of the slipway...'

If this nincompoop, thought Theodore, resisting the urge to throttle him, mentions that dratted keel once more...

He'd jolly well nip this in the bud right now, before an intelligent discussion on navigation degenerated into a maudlin reminiscence of the *Aquitania's* keel. He had a far more important topic to discuss, on which hinged an invitation to dine at the captain's table - and he wasn't going have it sabotaged by all these interminable tales of keels in Glaswegian shipyards.

He laid deliberate emphasis on his words. *'As I was saying.* I feel the importance of the gyro-compass can't be -'

Again he was interrupted, this time by the *Berengaria's* answering burrrp-burrrp-burrrp. The frenzied waving and calling of the crowds at the rails of both ships grew to a crescendo which, to Theodore's frustration, threatened to join the foghorn in drowning out his voice altogether.

And Sam was just getting into his stride.

'Ye wouldnae believe what we got up to. I mind one day not long after she was launched, a few of the lads dived in to the

115

river from the main deck for a bet! Freezing water, and nae towels to dry themselves with. So they just put their clothes back on and got on with the job. They were riveters, like me'.'

Daphne's response to this unwanted information was to give a dignified wave to the people on the distant corresponding promenade deck, which, together with the boat deck, were the only ones that mattered. Whatever alien territory existed beneath these decks was inhabited by an unknown species. Best it remained so. She had no wish to become acquainted with whoever might reside in the depths of the ship.

Theodore rallied his forces yet again, and pointedly addressed the officer.

'To come back to what I was saying about navigation -'

Sam, who wouldn't normally interrupt when someone was speaking, was distracted by the noise of the crowd and carried on, oblivious.

'And we had other ways of making a few quid, an' all. Pitch-and-toss, illegal gambling dens during the lunch break behind the sulphuric acid tank... I won ten bob one day, and two-pounds-seventeen-and-six the same week! Aye, I mind that cheered me up in a freezing blizzard. There was no shelter, y'see. No light, no heat... Aye, we were oot in the open, riveting in all weathers, hail, rain, and snow.'

To Theodore's intense irritation, the officer seemed genuinely interested in all this drivel. He grinned and held out his hand to Sam.

'Clive Willis. What a remarkable coincidence it must be for you to see her crossing the Atlantic! I should be rushing off - my colleague will be starting Sports Day soon - but I'd love to hear more about the actual building process. I'm absolutely riveted. Excuse the pun!'

Sam shook the outstretched hand, surprised that a couple of spontaneous remarks prompted by the close proximity of ship he'd laboured on should amount to anything other than passing interest, but happy to relate more if requested. One glance at Daphne's face, however, and he felt it might be wise to skip the more unsuitable shipyard humour that came to mind, and keep strictly to educational facts.

'Er... Aye, well, y'see the carpenters and platers, they begin at the bottom of the ship, working the side-framing up into position. First amidships, and then out towards the bow and the stern.' He indicated the *Aquitania* as she sliced gracefully through the Atlantic waves. 'Then more platers follow the carpenters, then the riveters follow the platers, then the caulkers follow the riveters -'

'Dear me,' broke in Theodore with a mirthless smile, 'All this information! So invaluable in our everyday lives! We'll all be qualified to build our own ships after this, won't we. But it's the navigation aspect that interests me. Now Clive, I'd like to come back to the advantages of the gyro-compass -'

He broke off, frowning; he suspected the officer's mind was beginning to wander elsewhere.

He was right. Irritating as it was to have been commandeered by an unwanted conversation that was repeatedly and determinedly dragged back to Navigation - not his favourite topic - it provided Clive with the opportunity for an unexpected idea to form in his mind.

Unlike the obvious choice of highly qualified ship's architects and marine engineers who were automatically invited to dine at the captain's table, here was someone whose practical hands-on experience gave an unusual perspective to the creation of the *Aquitania.* After all, not many shipyard workers were to be found sailing first class on the *Berengaria.* Could Sam, as a totally novel and quirky - but highly entertaining - possible candidate be considered for an invitation? That a guest should be interesting and amusing company was taken as read, but as a change from the customary list, every now and then the captain liked to invite someone slightly out of the ordinary; a whimsical eccentric or a colourful character with a story to tell, such as the American scientist on a recent voyage who had some strange theory about splitting atoms, which would cause an explosion of such energy that just half a pound of hydrogen and an atom-

117

smashing machine could provide the power for the *Berengaria* to cross the Atlantic.

Added to that, on this particular trip there was, unusually, a scarcity of glitzy film stars and other show-biz personalities, so the invitations for the Last Night at Sea Dinner had yet to be decided. And added to *that,* Sam would certainly make a refreshing change from the usual queue of twopenny-halfpenny yachtsmen who'd taken courses on navigation and dropped what they considered to be subtle hints for invitations because they'd managed to get from Southampton to the Isle of Wight.

He rubbed his chin thoughtfully as he concentrated once more on the current conversation.

'...Because I really do find Navigation a most engrossing topic,' droned Theodore, 'And I'd welcome the opportunity to...'

Clive chose his words carefully, to avoid causing any offence.

'Ah, yes. Navigation. Another equally interesting aspect - once we've got a ship to navigate, eh, sir? Fascinating to hear about the actual building of the very ship we see being so ably navigated eastwards to Southampton, isn't it?'

Theodore gaped at him open-mouthed. Good heavens, here was a golden opportunity to hold an intelligent conversation about the intricacies of navigation with one of the few passengers who knew anything about it, and the chap seemed more interested in listening to this old fool wittering about a gang of labourers in a shipyard!

Sam saw the look on Theodore's face, and felt ashamed. He hadn't realised... The chap obviously wanted to talk about navigation, and here he was, hogging the conversation. He self-consciously shuffled back a step and signalled for Theodore to speak, then saw Mary waving from the crowd, and beckoned her across.

There was an audible groan from Theodore. Weren't things bad enough already? Were they now to be subjected to a two-pronged attack?

As the introductions ('We've already met!' snapped Daphne) that followed included the inevitable information that this was Sam and Mary's Fiftieth Wedding Anniversary treat, Clive made the decision; he'd put their names forward as a suggestion for a dinner invitation at the captain's table before they arrived in New York. It was unlikely, he admitted privately, to be taken up. But at least he'd try. It would all depend on the available mix of weighty VIPs and amusing lightweights.

'Theodore,' Sam explained to Mary, 'Was just talking about navigation. Sorry tae interrupt, Theodore.'

'Yes. To return to the subject of gyro-compasses...' Theodore gave an expansive smile. At long last, the platform was his to air his knowledge on a subject close to his heart instead of suffering yet more mind-numbing Tales From The Shipyard.

He gave an exasperated sigh as yet another frenzied cheer from the rails drowned his voice; the *Berengaria* drawing away from the stern of the *Aquitania* was the signal for the festivities heralding Sports Day to begin in earnest.

He determinedly began again. 'Gyro-compasses...'

Clive knew that although Bob Smythe wouldn't be happy about being left to organise the games on his own, he'd understand his predicament. They all got waylaid from time to time. It went with the job. Resisting the temptation of bored captive audiences from time immemorial to fidget, he risked another glance along the deck, caught sight of Tom Burnett loitering nearby, and gave him a rueful wink. Being stood up was a novel experience for handsome young ship's officers. Tom, however, obviously didn't intend waiting any longer. He raised a philosophical eyebrow in return, put the waste of a good part of his salary on flowers for Caroline down to experience, and strode off.

It was sheer bad luck that as soon as he disappeared, Sophie and Caroline emerged from the Winter Garden and hurried through the crowd, distress showing clearly on both faces.

So Caroline hadn't stood him up after all, thought Clive. Something was wrong. And whatever it was, it was welcome, because it gave him a legitimate excuse to escape a never-ending monologue on the advantages of gyro-compasses without any accusations of being ill-mannered. He made a brief polite bow to Daphne, Mary, Theodore, and Sam.

'Do please excuse me, I must...'

The others followed his glance. It was obvious that Sophie and Caroline required assistance of some sort, and even Theodore had to grudgingly admit that the first duty of any available officer (and any other crew member) must of course be to attend to whatever was causing the slightest worry or inconvenience to a first class passenger.

'Aye,' said Mary, her voice full of motherly concern. 'On ye go, son!'

'So nice to meet you... I do hope we can continue this interesting talk on another occasion.'

He was gone.

Theodore stared after him, seething. It really was *too bad!* First this dim-witted clown rambling about keels and rivets and idiots diving into the Clyde (pity they didn't stay there; they'd be in good company with a few dead cats and rats) and now Clive rushing off because the dratted Countess of Knotworth and her insolent American sister had probably locked themselves out of their suite, or caused some other equally ludicrous emergency.

Most annoying of all, however, the officer on whom he was depending to remedy the state of affairs regarding their long-overdue dinner invitation to the captain's table had left him marooned in the company of the two people with whom he and Daphne least wished to spend time: Sam and Bloody Mary.

5

The rumours filtered down, as rumours invariably do despite whatever preventative measures are put in place to quash them by higher authorities - in this case the purser, who would have been aghast had he known that the information he was at such pains to ensure went no further was already common knowledge among the catering crew.

According to the initial unofficial telecommunications network, two female passengers had arrived in one of the first class corridors in time to witness a male passenger and a stewardess in a compromising situation.

It was old Reg who filled in the spicy details. He'd been working nearby at the time but, being hard of hearing, was initially unaware of anything untoward, or he would have stepped in and sorted things out himself with no loss of face to either party. As it was, he informed them, the Countess of Knotworth and her sister discovered Lexie grinning and pawing at Elsie as she was pinned helplessly against the bulkhead. Alerted by the commotion (and knowing Elsie was now in no physical danger), he decided, with the wisdom that comes from years of experience of life and human nature, to remain uninvolved but quietly stop work and listen, because despite being slightly deaf he had no difficulty in picking up raised voices.

Especially in an incident such as this.

There had been a blazing row, with the Americans tearing into Lexie and demanding he apologise to the stewardess, and Lexie responding that the girl had encouraged him and flirted with him, and the two women retorting that this was clearly rubbish and accusing him of molesting her, and he ridiculing them, asking if they seriously thought he intended raping the stupid bitch there and then in a public corridor when all he was doing was giving her a friendly kiss, and the Countess of Knotworth scathingly responding with a colourfully expressed description of how his very presence made her skin crawl.

The only voice he hadn't heard in all this was Elsie's.

It had ended with the Countess of Knotworth announcing that the matter would be reported, and three sets of footsteps departing the scene; the first stumping off followed by an angrily slammed door, another lighter set hurrying in the other direction, and two more marching resolutely back in the direction from which they'd come.

You didn't have to be a clairvoyant to hazard a pretty accurate guess that the incident would produce some irritated sighs and grimaces in the purser's office…

Old Reg wasn't the only one with years of experience of life and human nature, and it was a tribute to the diplomatic skills of the purser that both Lexie and the Countess of Knotworth left his office wholly satisfied that he'd been genuinely sympathetic to two opposing points of view.

The Countess of Knotworth and her sister were invited into his private office immediately after the incident, and came away reassured that the matter would be fully investigated.

'A most unpleasant individual, a really nasty piece of work,' Sophie reiterated as they departed.

Lexie, issued with a similar invitation a little later, also came away greatly reassured. The purser had focused on his version of events to the exclusion of everything else, because of course Lexie's reputation was of far more importance than some apparent problem with landing cards (without which it was impossible to disembark) for the second class passengers.

'Couple of over-excitable women reading too much into the situation. You know what they're like. Must be their time of the month, or their hormones or something,' he smirked as he stood up to leave, confident this trivial misunderstanding could now be safely laid to rest.

The purser, of course, had little choice but to placate both parties. Although RMS *Berengaria's* renown thrived on juicy scandal, it was *acceptable* juicy scandal, which enhanced her aura of glamour. This unfortunate incident could cast a sleazy slur, which Cunard could on no account allow.

However, now that both versions of the event had been given his full attention, a discreet veil could be drawn over the affair as far as the passengers involved were concerned. But he still made his way up on deck to have a quiet word with Clive, who had returned to take up his Sports Day duties.

Calling him aside, he murmured that - as Clive was on Sports Day duty anyway - it might be an idea if he paid special attention to the Countess for the rest of the day, devoting time and energy to ensuring that no sour aftertaste from this regrettable affair affected her overall view of the *Berengaria*.

It was essential that first class passengers left the ship eager to book the next passage, quite apart from making sure every possible opportunity for glowing publicity was taken advantage of. So any negative memories - in fact anything remotely unfavourable - must be replaced with the wholly favourable... and the end justified the means. (Although quite obviously this conversation would be denied as ever having taken place. And should things go from bad to worse, well, let's just say it wouldn't do anything for his career prospects...)

And if that meant the administrative chores Clive was due to resume following his Sports Day duties being delegated to Stuart Murray while Clive concentrated his efforts on the Countess of Knotworth, well...

Clive smiled to himself as he pictured Stuart Murray scowling in the corner.

'And for heaven's sake, Mr Willis,' was the parting shot. 'Make absolutely sure that Stonefeather character doesn't come anywhere near either of them!'

And Clive, tongue firmly in cheek, agreed to abandon the administrative work he'd been so looking forward to resuming, and apply himself most diligently not only to ensuring that the

Countess thoroughly enjoyed Sports Day afternoon, but the Carnival Dinner and Fancy Dress Ball to follow.

Tedious job at times, but somebody's got to do it.

6

Cunard's level of concern for the Countess of Knotworth's distress didn't extend to Elsie, who was dispatched to the Chief Stewardess' office. She found the experience every bit as unpleasant as the predicament she'd just escaped.

'Do you mean to stand there and tell me you're making all this fuss over somebody trying to kiss you?' demanded the Chief Stewardess, outraged.

'I wasn't going to make a fuss -'

'Well I hope you're satisfied! All the trouble you've caused!'

'I wasn't going to make a fuss -'

'Who d'you think you are? Getting the purser involved in it all!'

'I wasn't going to make a fuss -'

'Don't you think he's got enough to do without some silly little attention-seeker making a fuss about nothing?'

'I wasn't seeking attention! I wasn't going to make a fuss -'

'You think you deserve preferential treatment, do you?' The Chief Stewardess looked at her in disgust.

'I wasn't going to make a fuss -'

'Oh grow up! All that...' The Chief Stewardess waved her hands vaguely, 'Is just part of life, and you're going to have to get used to it. Coming in here like Lady Mulligatawny, making all this fuss over nothing!'

'I keep telling you, I wasn't going to make a fuss -'

'Don't you answer me back!'

Elsie stayed silent. It was obviously one of those least said, soonest mended occasions.

'And don't stare at your feet like that. Listen to me when I'm speaking!' The Chief Stewardess gave her a prod in the arm.

'You're nobody special. Get on with it, like the rest of us have had to do. Making all this fuss!'

'I wasn't going to make a fuss!'

'I've had to put up with that sort of thing for years!' the Chief Stewardess declared. 'I wouldn't have *dared* to make a fuss!'

'I wouldn't have said anything,' protested Elsie, 'If the Countess of Knotworth and her sister hadn't arrived.'

There was a pause.

'Well in that case,' said the Chief Stewardess triumphantly, 'You couldn't have been in all that much danger, could you?'

Elsie said nothing.

'And anyway, he said you were willing!'

'Well I wasn't! He was lying!' So much for the Countess of Knotworth's unbiased evidence that Elsie had been an unwilling participant, assaulted against her will.

'Why didn't you call for help if you were in some sort of danger? You weren't making a fuss *then*, were you?'

You can't win, thought Elsie. In one breath, don't make a fuss. In the next, why didn't you call for help? Damned if you do, and damned if you don't. Or the other way round. She understood Billy's impotent fury; the slightest complaint made by a passenger against you, and there'd be a D/R in your Discharge Book without your side of things even being heard, and never employed by a shipping company again. But make a complaint against a passenger - 'I do not wish to be groped at, or have somebody's foul-smelling tongue stuck down my throat as I carry out my duties,' - and you were told not to make a fuss, grow up, get on with it like the rest of us have had to do.

And as if things weren't bad enough, after feeling queasy all morning, she was finally about to throw up. She grabbed an empty vase from the Chief Stewardess's desk, her legs almost giving way under her.

'I... oh!'

That old cliche about seasickness was true, she thought miserably; at first you were frightened that you were going to die... then you were frightened that you weren't.

126

The Chief Stewardess was unsympathetic. 'Half the crew have to contend with seasickness, not just you. Take ten minutes to sort yourself out, then get back on duty. There's work to be done!'

Elsie fled thankfully to the washroom, taking the vase with her to wash out. She was definitely having second thoughts about a seagoing career. She'd looked forward to a life of adventure and excitement, meeting the rich and famous, and found the reality was emptying chamber pots and spittoons full of other people's vomit as she struggled (unsuccessfully) not to throw up herself.

Retching, morning, noon, and night... Staggering along trying to keep upright as the ship rolled... Sleeping in a tiny, hot, stuffy cabin off a main corridor almost next to the engine room with the incessant noise of the turbines preventing sleep, and sharing with other stewardesses she didn't particularly like...

She'd never get used to this. It had been the biggest mistake of her life, and if somebody offered her a magic carpet to escape, she'd fly away this instant.

But what else could she do? What was there back home?

Nothing.

7

Danny braced himself against the ship's rolling and, balancing a tray of tea and dainty cakes, headed towards the couple shrouded in blankets on the deck loungers they'd insisted must be placed as far away as possible from the noise and excitement of the Sports Day activities.

The man poked his nose out of the blankets.

'Ah. Thank you.' He looked around as the tray was placed in front of them. 'One more thing. Should anyone be looking for us - a Scottish couple, for example - please *do not* tell them we're here.'

'They're *haunting* us!' groaned his wife, also peering from a cocoon of blankets and inspecting the plate of cakes before reaching out a plump hand to select the largest. 'It's too, *too* aggravating, it really is!'

Danny produced the required sympathetic tut, but was privately more concerned about what might be happening in the kitchens. Sports Day for the catering crew was a day of non-stop, exhausting drudgery, and there hadn't been a spare minute to speak to Joey, but he'd seen Alec Baxter deliberately making a point of inspecting whatever Joey produced, the implication being that it was likely to be sub-standard and unacceptable, and his friend once again looked near to breaking point from strain and fatigue.

'The result of the latest encounter,' complained the woman as she waved permission for the tea to be poured, glaring at Danny as if he personally were to blame, 'Is the most debilitating stress-induced headache I've ever endured!'

Theodore nodded. The whole thing would be absurd if it were not so damned infuriating. If he and Daphne had had no contact with the pair from the start they could simply avoid them and there'd be no problem, but because the Countess of Knotworth's infernal sister - dratted woman! - had insisted on introducing them, they'd somehow got it into their heads that some sort of friendship had resulted and were now impervious to every effort to shake them off. Hints, coolness of manner, curt dismissals, even direct insults... *nothing* he or Daphne said or did seemed to have the slightest effect.

He reached out to take the cup and saucer. 'Yes. So please take note: we are not to be disturbed at all. By *anyone.* Do you understand?'

'Yes sir, I quite understand. Sports Day isn't for everyone,' agreed Danny automatically.

'It's not Sports Day we want to avoid,' snapped Theodore. 'It's being bothered by unwelcome intruders!'

'*No one* is to come anywhere near us!' emphasised Daphne again. One had to labour the point, because those idiotic Glaswegians would probably assure a waiter they were close friends and so an exception could be made.

'Very good, madam.' Danny turned to go. 'I'll do my best.' Or not, as the case may be, he added under his breath. How exactly was he supposed to prevent anyone from going anywhere near them? Set up an invisible ring of steel around them?

'Please do. Thank you.'

Danny nodded obediently. 'I'll make quite sure all the other waiters know you're to be left strictly alone, madam.'

Daphne watched him zig-zag off as the ship rolled, and looked around for the book she'd borrowed from the ship's library.

'Oh *drat!* Darling, I've left my book on the bed!' She peeled away the mound of blankets and levered herself off the recliner. 'I'll whizz down and get it. Back in a jiff...'

Theodore nodded, sank back, snuggled into his blankets, and gradually relaxed. The day Daphne 'whizzed' anywhere was the day he'd eat his proverbial hat. She'd be twenty minutes at the very least. He let out a contented sigh, and his eyes closed.

Peace at last.

There was a slight noise. He became aware of a shadow, a presence hovering at his side. He opened one eye.

A tall figure in an old-fashioned floor-length black coat was bending towards him. Her face, half obscured by a flowery folk-art headscarf, loomed over him.

''Ello.'

Theodore opened the other eye and gaped in consternation as she lowered herself, uninvited, onto Daphne's deck recliner.

'American? English? I am Russian...'

Theodore's eyes widened in horror as bony fingers began to edge towards him over the blanket.

'Russian men...' She shook her head dismissively. 'Always drunk!'

He looked around in desperation, but his and Daphne's instructions had been carried out to the letter. There wasn't a soul in sight.

'*Ty mne mravisha*... I like English men... '

He could hear screams of laughter, shouts of encouragement, and whoops of victory from the crowds on the far deck where Sports Day now in full swing, but here there was nobody; no help at hand, no waiter conveniently hovering, no lackey at whom he could click his fingers for this bizarre plight to be instantly remedied. It seemed his quest for undisturbed isolation had been a bit *too* successful.

He shrank from the woman's questing fingers. He didn't understand Russian, but whatever it was she'd said sounded a bit too close to 'ravishing' for comfort. Theodore was urbane and possessed his full measure of self-assurance, but this was one of the few occasions in life when even he was nonplussed. What on earth was the correct etiquette for dealing with a clearly unhinged amorous Russian?

Did you show sympathetic understanding? Best not; that might convey willingness, and mean that every time Daphne disappeared for five seconds she'd lie in wait and pounce again. Indignation? Best not; it might tip her over the edge and cause

130

her to become violent, and everyone knew that lunatics had the strength of ten men. Russian women probably had the strength of another ten (all that shovelling snow, and humping machinery around factories during the Revolution) and this particular one looked sufficiently muscular under the enormous coat to lift him bodily and heave him over the side. What if Daphne returned to find his recliner empty? It would never occur to her, or anyone else, that he might be thrashing helplessly in the cold Atlantic, screaming, 'Help! Man overboard!'

Fingers twitched at the blankets once more '*Ty mne mravisha*... I like you...'

Urgghh!

He attempted to lean away from her, stealthily moving his hand out of range.

Damn Caroline for introducing them to those dratted nuisances and landing him in this ridiculous predicament. Because if they weren't so obviously incapable of realising that an afternoon of relentless good humour and memories of shipyards was neither to his nor Daphne's taste, there'd be no need to lurk out of sight on this lonely bit of deck like lepers. Even more infuriatingly, he wouldn't have banished the waiter with strict instructions not to return under any circumstances.

The whole thing was beyond belief. He'd finally managed to shake off the Glaswegian slum-dwellers, only to find them replaced by an insane Russian nymphomaniac.

8

One of the deckhands was sent to tell Tom Burnett that Caroline had been unavoidably delayed, but was now on deck and hoping to see him if he wasn't too cross about being kept waiting.

It seemed he wasn't too cross. He appeared almost immediately.

Clive could now concentrate on ensuring that the earlier unsavoury episode was banished from the Countess of Knotworth's mind. Cunard owed him some free time anyway; he'd put in a lot of extra hours during recent turnarounds in Southampton. Particularly on the last occasion, when the ship just missed a night tide and had to dock the following morning, which meant nearly a thousand entries being altered on the wages sheets in time for the pay-off of the crew who were then due an extra day's pay, as well as overseeing the cargo report before the Port Sanitary Authority, Customs, and Harbour Board officials were due on board. So why feel guilty about taking advantage of a legitimate excuse to enjoy himself?

But whereas a few years ago he'd have found it highly amusing to be given official permission to dally with an attractive female, he now admitted privately that there was something distasteful about turning on the charm for Sophie as a sort of damage limitation exercise, as opposed to the uncontrived meeting she assumed had come about naturally.

He glanced at the sisters as they were reduced to fits of giggles by a riotous Bolster Bar Fight between two overweight men. From what he knew of Sophie she'd prefer honesty, and for him to say, 'Look, sorry, I've been detailed to watch over you and make sure you enjoy yourself following that Stonefeather unpleasantness,' instead of this deceit.

What surprised him was that he was sufficiently bothered to care. After all, his views were widely known; women were all very well, but his career came first every time. He gave himself a brisk mental shake. This occasion was no different. He'd been assigned a job, and he'd do it, without any further pointless soul-searching about its morality.

There was a round of applause, and more laughter. One of the contestants was finally knocked off the bar, and the victor was dancing a jig of triumph which the ship's barber was capturing on film, having set up a dark room as a lucrative side-line to develop and print his own and passengers' snapshots when the Barber's Shop was closed. Clive noticed Caroline also busily snapping events, and suspected she'd included a couple of him helping Sophie to her feet when, encased in a canvas sack stamped C.S.S. Co. Ltd. LINEN BAG, she'd lost her footing and rolled on the deck, helpless with laughter during the Sack Race.

'Come on, Lady Goody-Two-Shoes! Have a souvenir caricature done, like the rest of us,' Caroline was persuading her sister as an off-duty A.B., an expert cartoonist who had likewise turned his hobby into a profitable sideline and whose work was greatly prized as a unique souvenir of a *Berengaria* voyage, indicated that he had a free slot.

Sophie shot him a brief self-conscious glance, and sat down in the chair while the man's pencil skimmed over the paper and he signed the work with a flourish.

Clive smiled at the result. It was enchanting; the A.B. had skilfully captured her air of timid vulnerability... he hastily gave himself another mental shake before announcing the next Event, the Three-Legged Race, over the loudspeaker.

No point in feeling uncomfortable about this sort of thing at this stage in his career; he had a job to do, a Countess to keep happy, and a Carnival Dinner and Fancy Dress Ball to charm his way through before the evening was over.

9

The inoffensive little clergyman, popular with children, ready to take a joke against himself as he came last in the Egg and Spoon Race, the Obstacle Race, the Sack Race, and the Potato Race, nearly choked to death in the Biscuit and Whistle Contest, and was effortlessly knocked off the boom he was sitting astride in the Pillow Fight, endeared himself to old and young alike. Quite obviously far from athletic, he presented no threat at the start of each race as the contestants eyed each other to assess the chances of finishing first. Or avoiding the shame of trailing home last.

Who could fail to show cordial encouragement when it was obvious that if he managed to finish at all, he'd trail harmlessly in behind everybody else? How sporting of him to enter a race which clearly he had no chance of winning. There was something very appealing about this inoffensive parson; dear little fellow, doing his best to join in the spirit of the games! Who could fail to be beguiled by his unworldly demeanour, bless him - such a trustworthy, *ethical* manner about him, so rare in today's avaricious world - when he possessed not an ounce of competitive spirit?

But beneath the genial all-round-good-egg camaraderie was a carefully thought out reserve strategy just in case anything went wrong with the main target: Lexie Stonefeather. Always wise to have a few more to fall back on, in case unforeseen circumstances such as illness or a sudden conversion to clean living and rejecting the evils of gambling scuppered his plans at the last minute. Because work had to begin in earnest during the next couple of nights, with Lexie ripe and ready to be shown the full extent of Jack Dalton's card skills.

Or to put it another way, fleeced.

So the vicar continued to twinkle his way through the Three-Legged Race, the Veterans' Race, and the last event on the programme, the Treasure Hunt. And it was, in fact, the Treasure Hunt that unexpectedly came to Theodore's aid.

The first group of shouting, whooping children flooded his patch of deck like cavalry to the rescue, followed by a crowd of excited adults - including, inevitably, Sam and Mary.

'Oh, here you are!' exclaimed Mary, as the apparition he had been at such a loss to know how to deal with glided furtively away. 'We've been looking for you everywhere!'

'Turn our backs for two seconds, and ye vanish!' teased Sam.

'Never mind, we've found you now.' Mary gave a reassuring nod. 'And we know where your wee bolt-hole is for next time, don't we!'

Sam grinned. 'That's blown the cover for your wee bit peace and quiet, eh?'

Theodore didn't know whether to laugh or cry.

'Where's Daphne?' Mary looked around. 'I don't want to hurt her feelings, thinking we didnae look for her!'

Theodore managed a strangled grunt, shook his head to assure her there was no danger of Daphne's feelings being hurt by Mary and Sam not looking for her, and gestured towards the Winter Garden Pavilion with a long-suffering shrug to indicate she'd vanished on some mysterious errand he hadn't quite fathomed.

And whereas normally he would have been incandescent with rage that his express demand for privacy and seclusion had resulted in his refuge being invaded by unbridled pandemonium and a gaggle of rampaging children, on this occasion he actually managed to summon a tolerant smile and gingerly pat the head of the child who discovered the next clue, which was hidden underneath an adjacent recliner.

'Are ye *sure* Daphne won't be disappointed or hurt?' persisted Mary as the crowd eagerly set off again in search of the next clue, with Sam panting gamely after the vanishing horde.

'Please don't give it another thought. I do assure you she won't be,' said Theodore firmly.

'Mind, I'm not sure we'll follow them much further oorsels,'' Mary confided. 'None of us are getting any younger, eh? And it seems to go on and on…'

It had taken one of the junior pursers hours to lay the trails for the Treasure Hunt, which took the participants a total of four miles up and down the ship before finally arriving in the Smoking Room, where the treasure was hidden in the coal scuttle.

Theodore, glancing apprehensively around lest the black-coated Russian reappeared, bared his teeth in another smile as he nodded in agreement and waved her impatiently away.

And the smile became genuine; a smile of heartfelt relief as Daphne clumped back out through the Winter Garden Pavilion doorway with her book; solid, unwraithlike, dependably irascible, and clearly capable of making short work of an entire harem full of Russian nymphomaniacs.

10

The entire ship was ablaze with lights from bow to stern.

The Carnival Dinner had given way to RMS *Berengaria's* legendary Fancy Dress Ball, and the ballroom was festooned with a riot of multi-coloured fairy lights, bunting, and balloons. Exotic and highly scented flowers graced every table; the ship's gardener had excelled himself, and no alcove or public area was without a bower of the most delicate blooms, each arrangement more eye-catching than the last.

The orchestra was in full swing, and the ballroom was now full of Wild West cowboys, highwaymen, Regency dandies, baggy-trousered gypsies, villainous-looking pirates, Apache chiefs in feathered head-dresses, bejewelled Indian rajahs, Arab sheiks, bell-boys, and caricature Scotsmen in kilts. Others in full evening dress danced with fabulously gowned women; *haute couture* Paris creations blended with Arabian princesses, squaws in fringed tunics, South Sea island beauties in grass skirts, masked Venetian adventuresses, giddy flappers, Southern belles in crinolines, Roman goddesses, sultry gypsies... it was the ultimate backdrop for a thousand frivolous, enchanting, carefree shipboard romances.

And it had started with another spat between Sophie and Caroline, who'd tartly suggested that her sister turn up in sackcloth and ashes as the tamed, dutiful wife, because that was how she deserved to end up if she was stupid enough to waste the rest of her life on the chinless wonder she'd married, condemning herself to years of unhappiness instead of just accepting the whole thing had been a disastrous mistake and making a new start. Oh, and another thing: although naturally Caroline would keep to the unwritten code of conduct regarding men, i.e. you didn't poach from your own sister (no danger of that where Aubrey was concerned - who'd want him?), as Sophie had made it quite clear she had no interest in the PDH who'd been so attentive all afternoon, he was now fair game to be added to her own collection of male admirers. Was that understood?

Sophie had shrugged and nodded, surprised it had taken her sister as long as this to set her sights on Clive.

But it was impossible for ill-humour to stay around for long at a *Berengaria* Ball. It was as though a sort of unspoken decree: "Only fun, festivities, and frolics allowed in here!" monitored the entrance, and the comic policeman escorting the gangster's moll back to their table after a particularly energetic Charleston was finding it necessary to remind himself that he was actually on duty.

How easy it had all been! Superficial small talk at the start of the afternoon had moved on to laughter and easy banter at the Sports Day antics, then progressed to more intimate and meaningful conversation at the Carnival Dinner, before continuing here at the Fancy Dress Ball. In fact it was all so easy that he was becoming increasingly uncomfortable about the deception. It was obvious she'd relaxed with him purely because he was a ship's officer and therefore to be trusted as being no more than a friendly companion; someone who wouldn't make a pass at her. Or deceive her in any way.

Well, he'd just have to add this to all the other sins he'd be called upon to pay for one day, far off in the future when he was old and decrepit - something he probably had in common with her sister, he thought as Caroline, attired seductively as a Greek goddess, fluttered her eyelashes at him before smiling at the Arab sheik with whom she'd danced earlier, and then turned back to Luigi, who could be heard making some comment about the perfectly sprung dance floor as they finished a waltz.

Clive watched the Arab sheik, a Californian involved in the film industry called Frank (they'd been introduced earlier) glare balefully at Luigi. Caroline was gazing into the Italian's eyes as he moved on from the perfections of the dance floor to an

138

inventory of far more interesting perfections: her own. She listened, clearly enthralled, to his audible compliments about her eyes (pools of deep flashing sapphire), her mouth (the most kissable he'd ever seen), and her hair (spun silk; how did she expect him to resist running his fingers through it?)

Clive smiled faintly. He'd spouted similar drivel himself in his time, but even he could take lessons from this Italian.

He concentrated once more on Sophie, holding her chair as she sat, thanking her for the dance as the orchestra announced a short break, and enquiring whether she'd like a drink.

She shook her head. 'No thank you. D'you know what I'd rather do?'

He groaned inwardly. If she was typical of the usual American heiresses, he was only too able to guess what she'd rather do; what was coming could vary from a request to conduct the ship's orchestra to wheedling entreaties to go onto the bridge and take the wheel - followed by a fit of girlish giggles as he gently advised against it because (depending on the time of year) there may be the odd iceberg around they'd be wise to avoid. His job tonight was to come up with a plausible excuse, couched in the most diplomatic of terms, as to why whatever bizarre whim he was presented with wouldn't be possible. And then to keep her, the rest of the passengers, the crew, and the ship itself, safe in one piece.

Sophie laughed. 'Don't look so worried. Just because I've come as a gangster's moll doesn't mean I want to raid the ship's bank. But I'm hot, and it's too windy to go out on deck. I'd rather have a swim than a drink.'

He couldn't hide his look of surprise. First time he'd heard *that* one!

She laughed, and checked her watch. 'It was just a joke, Clive. I'm not seriously suggesting a swim when it's almost midnight, and the pool's closed!'

The smooth, confident ship's officer automatically swung into action. (At least she didn't expect him to arrange the lowering of a lifeboat so she could swim in the Atlantic!) If the Countess of Knotworth wanted a swim at midnight, then a swim at midnight was what the Countess of Knotworth would have, and the purser could sort out any problems about it next day.

'Well, what are we waiting for?'

It was Sophie's turn to look surprised. She'd merely meant it as a flippant throwaway quip.

'You mean, *now?*'

Clive smiled as he held the door open for her. 'I think it could be arranged.'

Sophie couldn't be bothered digging out the dark red bathing costume from the wardrobe drawers. The new golden brown one was still in its Ladies Fashions bag, where she'd thrown it on the chaise-longue when they'd come in from the shopping expedition yesterday. That would do.

She shook it from its wrappings and hurried to meet Clive, who popped to his cabin for his well-worn Johnny Weissmuller-style one piece. And as she descended the grand staircase, feeling like a truanting schoolgirl, she once again experienced that strange sixth sense of something she couldn't quite put into words. It was as if she had one last chance to turn back while she still could… or go on to whatever lay ahead.

She shook her head; this was getting out of hand. She determinedly dismissed this latest ridiculous flight of fancy from mind; for heaven's sake, it was only a swim, not some dramatic event with repercussions that would affect the rest of her life!

11

Lexie had drunk a few whiskies and brandies too many, even for him.

Worth it, though, because he'd managed to persuade Lemuel Hoffmann to arrange a meeting with his co-directors immediately they stepped ashore in New York, which meant, as he'd already set up one important meeting before leaving England, he now had two on arrival day. Everything was going nicely to plan!

It had taken some doing. Lemuel hadn't been keen at first, grumbling that it had better be worth his while and pointing out that he couldn't spare long because he was heading straight off to sort out some problem at his California branch early the next day, but - Lexie winked at his reflection in the dressing table mirror - he always got his own way in the end.

'Lemme assure you, Lemmie old son - ha ha! - you definitely won't regret it!'

Of course, he'd put Lemuel on the spot so he'd appear churlish if he refused this favour to the jovial fellow who'd been so generous with his rounds; the back-slapping good guy with whom they'd all spent so much time building an affable bond of friendship.

And then that stupid old priest or vicar or whatever he was had to put the dampener on things by announcing that he was tired, and was off to bed.

'I'll bid you all good night, gentlemen,' he'd yawned, and withdrew.

It was contagious. It set everybody else off. One by one they drifted away until Lexie was left by himself, and reluctantly he too returned to his suite.

But he wasn't tired. His mind was active, contemplating what he'd wear for the New York meetings. So, although it was now well after midnight (so what? If he decided to issue orders at three, four, or five o'clock in the morning regarding his embarkation requirements and what he wanted valeted, it was the steward's job to take them) he rang the night bell to summon the flunky. He'd have some sandwiches sent along as well.

'Come!' he called, downing another mouthful of whisky as Billy knocked and entered. He glanced round. 'I'll have some chicken sandwiches - *chicken,* not roast beef, not pork, or anything else you decide to bring. But first, let's get clear what's to be ready for going ashore in New York…You listening, boy?'

'Yes sir.'

'My navy striped suit. Everything immaculate from top to toe, waistcoat, shirt, socks pressed, shoes polished to mirrors, trilby brushed, and so on. And before you start telling me that *Berengaria's* valeting standards are the highest in the world so I needn't worry, *I'm* telling *you* they'd better be. Understand?'

'Yes sir.'

'I hope you effing well do, because I don't want to have to repeat all this again. Everything else is to be packed away in the trunk, and delivered direct to my hotel.'

'Yes sir.'

'Well, don't just stand there! I'm waiting for my sandwiches!'

Billy turned for the door, then, remembering the porridge incident - Lexie was still holding a half-full whisky tumbler - hesitated. Porridge splattered on a uniform was one thing, losing an eye if someone threw a glass at you quite another.

'Go on, get out!'

Billy was only too glad to obey.

Lexie turned complacently to the mirror and slicked his hair, seeing himself in his mind's eye as he stepped nattily ashore amid the fireworks, the photographers' flashing bulbs, the waiting press jostling to interview VIPs and celebrities, the

142

crowds in their thousands eager to spot the rich and famous, the honking cars and taxis, the gawping unskilled workers waiting to meet emigrant steerage relatives... He'd give them all a cheery wave as, attracting admiring and envious glances from all sides, he strode off to bring about his lucrative business deals.

Thinking about disembarking made him feel restless. Changing his mind about the sandwiches - couldn't be bothered waiting for that half-wit steward, who'd probably bring the wrong ones anyway - he decided to go up on deck for a smoke.

He made his way past the top of the grand staircase to the promenade deck, then stopped. Voices were approaching from further down the stairs, and he recognised one of them; that sanctimonious Countess who, with her big-mouthed sister, had reported him to the purser. He listened more intently, and heard her laugh. The other voice, interestingly, was a man's.

Hmm. A man's voice, eh? Well, as they were still some way below him, they were either coming from one of the staterooms on E or F deck, or the swimming pool. He concentrated even more carefully, and picked up the word 'water' and 'pool'. Aha! So the two of them had been down in the swimming pool together, had they? At this time of night? While it was closed? With all those rest rooms full of comfortable couches at the side? He smiled grimly. Complain about *him* doing a spot of fornicating, would she? Looked as though the whiter-than-the-driven-snow Countess had been busy herself in that department. The hypocrisy of it! He stood ready to let them see him as they came up. He'd enjoy watching her squirm.

And then he had an even better idea.

Here was the very opportunity to pay back the interfering busybody for running to the purser with tales about him amusing himself with that stewardess, like a prefect reporting a naughty schoolboy to the headmaster. Let *her* feel what it was like to be tutted at in disgust for a change! It was time someone reminded her of that old saying - that dim-witted clergyman who was always hanging around the Smoking Room probably

143

knew the exact words - about being concerned with the mote in someone else's eye while ignoring the plank in your own. Well, Lexie Stonefeather would happily oblige, and in the most satisfying way imaginable: he'd start the gossip circulating in unstoppable momentum.

And he knew the very people who'd be most interested in hearing it - that prissy couple she and her sister had been talking to at the Sailing Night Ball, who were evidently friendly with her husband, so were well placed to ensure he was made fully aware of his wife's midnight shenanigans...

He smiled as he stepped out onto the promenade deck. A win on the ship's pool, a business meeting with Lemuel Hoffmann's associates, and now the most devastating retaliation he could inflict on Lady Virtue-Personified for crossing him, because the subsequent gossip ashore would of course destroy her reputation for good.

Yes, fate was definitely smiling upon Lexie Stonefeather.

12

Elsie needed to get away from the claustrophobic quarters in the depths of the ship, and the clinging whiff of stale seasickness she could never quite shake off.

Most of all, however, she needed to consider the future, and that wasn't going to be easy, given the lack of opportunities for women and her own lack of skills.

She had ambition. She just didn't know how best to channel it. Or even what she wanted to do. All she knew was what she *didn't* want to do: be a stewardess, which she'd found consisted of little else than never-ending drudgery to be carried out regardless of her own debilitating sea sickness. No time off for trivial irritations like that - get on with it like the rest of us have had to do, and stop moaning.

But neither had she any desire to go back to living in Southampton, enviously watching the great ocean liners depart from the quayside. In her mind's eye she saw again the waving crowds, the military band, the gangway being pulled clear, the last mooring ropes being cast off, and the stern tugs pulling the ship away from the quay to back out into the fairway before the bow tug swung her round so her nose pointed towards the sea, carrying the rich and famous - and the poor and ordinary, like her - on a voyage filled with thrills and adventures before arriving in the Promised Land with its countless opportunities.

America... Stateside... New York... The very names conjured up excitement and a sense of destiny. And yet sadly, despite all the anticipation and sewing of uniforms for a career that allowed her to travel and see the world, it seemed she wasn't cut out to be part of the world of transatlantic romance after all. Not much glamour in mopping up someone else's vomit while spewing up your own.

But if Southampton held no attraction either, what did that leave? And where?

She felt a strong urge to breathe in the clean tang of the ocean, and search out a quiet spot to sit and think. And yet, what good would that do? All the thinking in the world couldn't bring a solution where there wasn't one. She couldn't go forward, she couldn't go back, and she couldn't stay where she was - especially now, with the Evil Eye of the Chief Stewardess firmly fixed on her following the Stonefeather incident.

Well, as all other options had failed... might it be worth considering the seemingly fatuous suggestion her mother had made some time earlier regarding her future? She'd ridiculed the idea of having a chat to God about what to do with her life in prayer, but let's face it, she hadn't made much of a success of it herself so far, and things could hardly be much worse than they already were. But then why should He care where she was or what she did? It wasn't as though she'd been His most devoted supporter. She'd only set foot in church to see friends after the service, using it as a sort of social club to gossip about whose boyfriend had proposed and whose, like hers, hadn't.

But the desire for solitude and fresh air was so overwhelming that she decided to go up on deck anyway.

13

It was one of those coincidences in life which, while improbable, everyone experiences from time to time. Danny, Elsie, and Billy Saunders all happened to make their way to the deserted aft mooring deck within minutes of each other.

Billy arrived first, punching open the door because that's what he felt like doing to the pasty face of the passenger he'd grown to detest more than anyone else he'd ever met on a ship. Mister Stonefeather, after summoning him in the middle of the night to tell him what he wanted valeted (even though the navy blue suit and its ensemble hadn't been worn since the previous valeting) and order sandwiches, was nowhere to be seen after he'd trekked half way round the ship to produce them.

Danny, in much need of his last-thing-at-night fresh air, appeared almost immediately.

'Aye-aye,' he greeted Billy, who looked like a fire-eater who'd breathed in too many flames. 'Now what's happened?'

Billy let rip with what he'd like to do to Lexie Stonefeather and his navy blue suit, instinctively breaking off as he heard a slight noise behind him.

It was Elsie.

She blushed, self-conscious and shy to find Billy and Danny in the refuge she'd sought for herself. Suppose Billy thought she'd followed him out here?

Danny smiled a welcome as she hesitated by the door.

'It's OK, it's work-related, don't worry. Billy's just making a list of some extra services he'd like to provide for your favourite passenger.'

(Not only was fraternisation between male and female members of the crew forbidden, friendship between counterpart catering staff was tolerated only for work-related purposes.)

'My favourite…? Oh, *him*. Huh. I'd poison him if I thought I'd get away with it!'

'Quite a night for inventive ways of getting even, isn't it,' remarked Danny. 'All we need now is Joey Smith turning up and telling us he's carved Alec Baxter into a vegetable sculpture with a kitchen knife.'

Despite the flippancy, Danny was aware that an explosion was simmering on some menacing back boiler in the kitchens, with Alec watching Joey like a cat relishing pouncing on a mouse whose luck was finally about to run out. Or the mouse getting in first and GBH-ing the cat, which would have an even worse result. Joey hadn't said any more since their talk on the first night, and it was obvious he wasn't going to, but the nagging suspicion that there was a lot more to it all than met the eye, and - even more worrying - that it was only a matter of time before the whole thing erupted with terrifying consequences, was impossible to shake off…

Billy, meanwhile, was turning over an idea in his head. He already loathed Mister Stonefeather on his own behalf, but even more so for exploiting his first class status to abuse a stewardess who couldn't fight back. He recalled hearing some of the long-serving crew members describing, with much ribald laughter, something called the *Berengaria* blessing.

He turned tentatively to Elsie. 'How are you at sewing?'

'I'm very good at sewing. Why?'

'Because,' said Billy slowly. 'I reckon kindly, caring Mister Stonefeather deserves an extra-special valeting touch known as the *Berengaria* blessing, as a mark of our great affection and esteem for him. Would you be interested in contributing to it?'

Elsie looked blankly at Danny, who obviously understood the meaning of Billy's enigmatic invitation. But even as he quietly warned her that if she had any sense she'd turn and run before Billy even explained what he was talking about, let alone got involved in such dangerous stupidity, he could see he was wasting his breath.

She couldn't wait to be a part of it.

FOUR: THE TEA DANCE

1

Lexie surfaced slowly. Something wasn't right. Why did he still hear the sound of snoring when he was no longer asleep? Moving quietly from his side to lie on his back, he squinted sideways, and gazed in horrified revulsion at the strange face on the pillow next to him. Pale, thin, unattractive...

She gave a slight cough; her breath stank of stale vodka. Whoever said vodka had no smell had never met Madam Don't-Mind-If-I-Do here. He lay still, struggling to recall what had happened last night. Who on earth was she? Where had he picked her up?

It slowly started to come back. He'd been drunk, but he definitely remembered heading towards the boat deck for a last cigarette. And on the way, he'd discovered that self-righteous Countess and her boyfriend coming up from the swimming pool, where they'd apparently been indulging in the sort of activities she'd been so quick to criticise *him* for.

But then what?

He remembered someone accosting him on deck. That was it, a Russian woman, going on about how she liked Englishmen. He'd chatted to her. Did she happen to know Prince Whoever-He-Was, whose smoked sturgeon was prepared specially by Mister Smith? He vaguely remembered a drunken, incoherent explanation about which Romanoffs (not that any of them meant anything to him) had escaped the Revolution and were now living in Paris, but that didn't explain how she'd ended up in his bed. From what he could see, she was naked...

He gingerly shook her shoulder. She mumbled something in Russian, swatted at him with her hand, turned over, and went back to sleep.

Oh no you don't, madam. Bad enough 'Who's been sleeping in my bed?' without finding not mummy, daddy, or baby, but a *Russian* bear. He thought of the wartime poster, all fangs dripping blood and vicious claws, and eyed her apprehensively. One way and another, he wanted her out of here quickly; the fewer people who knew about this, the better. He gave her a slightly more robust prod between the shoulder blades, and the mumbling grew louder, punctuated (he guessed) with a good sprinkling of swearwords.

'Good morning,' he began awkwardly. What else did you say to a strange Russian woman you woke up to find next to you in bed? A polite observation about the weather?

At the sound of an unexpected English voice she was suddenly wide awake. She sat up, blinked, and stared at him. Another torrent of Russian, then she leapt out of bed, stark naked.

'My clothes! Where are my clothes?'

He gestured at the arm chair, where both sets of clothes had been flung in an untidy heap.

More agitated Russian, panic creeping into the tone as she rummaged through the pile. He looked at her questioningly.

'My husband! I must return quickly! Before he wakes up!'

'Well he's not likely to do that, is he. You said he was dead.'

'Dead?'

'Yes. Last night you said he was dead.'

'No! I said he was *in bed! Drunk!*'

Lexie stared at her, aghast.

'He is very jealous man! He kill us both!'

'Effing hell!'

He leapt out of his side of the bed and grabbed his underpants. Everyone knew what the Bolsheviks had done to the Cossacks during the Revolution. Or was it the other way round? Not that it mattered. The entire country had been full of homicidal maniacs hacking each other to death with hammers and sickles - and here he was lying in bed next to the wife of one of them!

'You have not introduced yourself,' she rebuked him as she pulled on her underwear. 'What is your name?'

Then, before he could think of an excuse not to tell her so the sickle-wielding husband wouldn't know whose bodily parts to slice off, she announced solemnly, 'I am the Grand Duchess Anastasia, only surviving daughter of the Czar Nicholas.'

Yeah. And I'm the Queen of Sheba, thought Lexie, looking at her in mounting horror. He'd bitten off more than he could chew here all right; she was bonkers. As soon as she was dressed - he glanced across to see a large shapeless flowery dress go over her head - he'd bundle her out of here and then bolt straight down to the dining saloon for breakfast, a sort of belated alibi. And if he ever clapped eyes on her again (or more importantly, the husband, who was probably as nutty as she was, and getting fired up on vodka right now), and anything came of this, he'd deny all knowledge and swear he'd never set eyes on her before. Fortunately there were no witnesses. Nobody need ever know...

There was a knock at the door.

He jumped. He'd forgotten he'd told that idiot steward to bring Early Morning Tea. He glared at the 'Do Not Disturb' sign hanging on the doorknob on his side of the door, which with hindsight he should have hung outside immediately he woke up and discovered Her Eminence lying next to him.

'Go away!' he shouted urgently, hopping on one leg as he pushed the other into his underpants.

Too late; the door was already opening. Billy Saunders stood there with his tray. But instead of apologising and backing respectfully out as one would expect, the steward calmly leaned against the doorframe, taking in the scene before him with interest.

'I said, *go away!*' snapped Lexie.

The woman grabbed her coat, held it protectively in front of her, and released another torrent of hysterical Russian, then, realising neither of them understood a word, switched back to English.

'Young man! Do not tell anyone! My husband, he is very jealous man!'

Lexie, still hopping on one leg and glancing down in frustration at his underpants which had somehow got twisted, tried simultaneously to shield his modesty from Billy's view while presenting the dignified and authoritative presence of a first class passenger addressing a subservient underling.

'I don't want any tea! *Go away!*'

The problem was that in the last thirty seconds Billy had ceased to be a subservient underling. He continued to lean against the doorframe observing events, an unwanted bystander, calm and infuriating.

Aware that his uncovered rear end was in full view of the open door, Lexie tried to pull the counterpane off the bed to cover himself, only to find it was tucked in too tightly and refused to budge. Concealing as much as he could with the other hand - what was *wrong* with these effing underpants! - he turned his upper torso towards Billy threateningly.

'Will you effing well *get out!*'

He didn't like the look in Billy's eyes at all. Here he was, issuing orders to some no-count who should jump to it the moment a command was uttered... and the man stared coolly back at him and didn't move an inch! Meanwhile, the whole farcical nightmare was visible to whoever might pass by in the corridor. The thought of a collection of interested observers gathering in the doorway (with the Countess of Knotworth heading the queue) made his blood run cold. Gossip of this kind spread like wildfire; he imagined those denizens of the Smoking Room with whom he hoped to carry out important business transactions roaring with laughter as this juicy tale was related, with more spicy details added on each subsequent telling.

'D'you hear me, you cretin? *Get out!*'

No response.

Lexie was almost apoplectic with rage. If he wasn't hampered by these blasted underpants... *'Go away! Shut the effing door!'*

As he bent down to sort out the underpants problem, the ship rolled, taking him with her; he lost his balance and ended up in an undignified heap on the floor. He looked up to see the steward standing composedly by the wide-open door, taking it all in with a malicious glint in his eye and making not the slightest effort to come to his aid. Momentarily there was eyeball to eyeball contact between them, and he remembered Billy slipping over in a mess of vomit...

The woman, meanwhile, shoved her large feet into a pair of man-sized shoes by the bed, snatched up her bag, grabbed her headscarf, flung on her voluminous black coat, drew from its pockets a wad of dollar bills, stuffed them into Billy's mess-jacket pocket, put her forefinger to her lips, and fled.

Lexie hadn't expected much help from her, but the sight of that lackey staring insolently at him as he struggled stark naked on the floor instead of either discreetly closing the door and coming to help him or, even more preferable, closing it and going away, sent his blood pressure soaring. But mortifying as the loss of dignity was, what concerned him most was the fact that this steward had seen the apparition with whom he'd spent the night.

For more reasons than one this saga had to stay muffled, and if that meant (temporarily) adopting a let's-you-and-me-be-best-mates attitude, Lexie had no scruples about it.

His tone changed.

'Listen, What's-Your-Name... Billy, is it? Well listen, Billy boy. Not a word about what you've seen in here to anyone, and I'll make sure you're in line for a good tip when we get to New York, all right?

Billy smiled sardonically and said nothing. Firstly, Lexie Stonefeather disgusted him. Secondly, he didn't trust him an inch, and didn't believe a word of it. And thirdly, even if he *was* telling the truth, if he thought payment would wipe out everything Billy wanted revenge for, he could forget it.

Stuff his money. Billy wasn't for sale.

As for any complaints about standing at the door without giving assistance, he'd tactfully bring up the issue of Mister Stonefeather's treatment of a defenceless stewardess, in view of which he felt his first priority, his moral duty, was to ensure the safety of the woman in the suite. Because Mister Stonefeather was, unfortunately, already in a state of agitation when he arrived. Would the Chief Steward - in the presence of Mister Stonefeather, of course - like him to identify the woman, to corroborate his version of events? After all, she was witness to the fact that he'd said he didn't want any tea, wasn't she? So there was no point in actually going into the room, was there? As for not helping Mister Stonefeather to his feet, she would also confirm Mister Stonefeather's repeated instructions that he should go away, which he took to mean that his assistance was not required. When the woman left the room, so did he, once satisfied that Mister Stonefeather was not actually injured or in need of medical help.

And then he'd ask innocently if he had not followed the correct procedure after all in ensuring the woman's safety was uppermost in his responsibilities?

Get out of that one, Chief Steward. Billy's back was safely covered.

He hadn't uttered a word throughout. He hadn't needed to. The look in his eyes said it all; open dislike, undisguised scorn, and utter contempt. With one last malicious stare at Lexie he finally withdrew, tray still in one hand as he closed the door with the other.

Lexie collapsed on the bed, tangled underpants still around his left ankle. And just as he thought things couldn't get any worse, the door opened again, with no preceding knock this time.

The woman poked her head around, blew him a kiss, and hissed, '*Ya lublu teby, mily!*' (I love you, darling!) I come back tonight! Yes! And tomorrow night also!

155

2

Danny, having given the order for Lexie's breakfast (Wiltshire ham and two eggs, sunny side up - carefully repeated and confirmed in the hearing of others; no possibility of wrong orders) caught Joey's eye and motioned him across with a slight jerk of his head.

Joey reluctantly came to the counter. 'What is it? I can't talk now, he's -'

'I need something, Joey.'

'What?'

'Camembert cheese. Not much, but nice and ripe.'

Alec Baxter glanced across. Joey flicked at an imaginary speck of dust on the counter.

'Come back after we've finished cleaning the kitchens.'

Danny nodded. 'But that isn't all.'

'What else? Hurry up, he's -'

'You wouldn't be avoiding me by any chance? How come we've had hardly any chance to speak on this trip?'

Joey turned away. 'I've told you, Danny, leave it. We'll meet up in New York if I can get away. OK?'

It would have to be. That, as far as Joey was concerned, was the end of the conversation. Also, Lexie's breakfast arrived, and Alec Baxter was beginning to take an interest in what was so special about ham and eggs that required the attention of Joey Smith, who had quite enough to do on the fish section.

Lexie glanced furtively around as Danny positioned his breakfast on the sparkling damask tablecloth.

But so far, all was clear. No sign of any wild-eyed Cossacks or Bolsheviks making straight for him, sickle at the ready. Gradually he began to relax, tucking into his Wiltshire ham with gusto. All was well. He'd regained control over the situation, and now he could put his mind to making plans for the day, which would re-establish his authority over events…

He'd dawdle over breakfast, enjoy a few freshly-baked croissants over a leisurely cup of coffee, and then make his way down to the safety of the Smoking Room.

And that effing steward could whistle for a tip, because he wouldn't be getting one. Tradition that anyone winning the ship's pool gave the bedroom steward ten per cent, huh? Well, this was one tradition Lexie wouldn't be keeping alive.

As for the Russian problem, Grand Duchess Raving-Mad, hopefully she was joking about turning up again tonight (by which time the husband would probably have been promoted to Czar Nicholas, who hadn't really been shot at Ekaterinburg and dumped down a mineshaft after all) but just in case she wasn't, he'd make damn sure he was nowhere around for her to find him. Wouldn't be difficult. Bound to be a poker school or baccarat game in the Smoking Room. And tomorrow would be even safer because, being the last night of the voyage, it was sure to involve serious players, and take place in the privacy of someone's stateroom.

Don't you worry about that, muttered Jack Dalton under his breath when, later that morning, Lexie raised the possibility in the Smoking Room.

It will do. You can bet your bottom dollar on it.

Not that you'll have one left to bet with by the end of the night.

3

'I'm gasping for a cup of tea,' grumbled Sam as Mary preened her hair in the bathroom. 'How long are you going to be?'

No reply.

'Why can we no' just send for the stewardess to bring us tea in bed, like everyone else?'

He got a reply to that all right. Mary darted to the door. 'Because the poor wee lass has enough to do without waiting on us!'

'But it's her job,' Sam pointed out.

'That's what I mean.' Mary vanished back into the bathroom. 'She hasn't time to bring us tea, she's too busy.'

As Sam scratched his head, pondering a response to this unanswerable logic, he heard a slight noise at the door. He looked across hopefully. Had the stewardess brought a tray of tea after all as a surprise, without being asked?

No such luck. An envelope was pushed under the door, and the noise ceased.

'Here! Somebody's sent us a letter!'

'A *letter?* Don't talk daft! You don't get letters at sea!'

'Well Ah'm telling ye, one's just come under the door!'

Mary bustled from the bathroom, patting her hair in place. What was the daft galoot on about? He'd probably dropped a piece of paper and it had slid in the direction of the door.

Then she, too, spied the envelope.

'Oh aye... so we have. I wonder who it's from?'

Sam hopped out of bed and picked it up. 'It's got *Berengaria* stamped in the corner...'

They looked at each other. Had they, as they clumped through the minefield lying in wait for anyone unsure of first class procedures, committed some breach of etiquette so serious in nature that somebody found it necessary to pen a letter of rebuke? Even worse, had their son suddenly gone bankrupt? Was this telling them to vacate the stateroom, they'd been relegated to steerage forthwith?

'Well, open it,' urged Mary.

Sam looked round for his reading glasses. 'Where's my glasses?'

'Wherever you left them! Och here, give it to me!'

She carefully opened the envelope, took out the high quality writing paper, scanned the contents, and gasped. Her hand flew to her mouth.

'What is it?' asked Sam curiously.

'Is this some kinda joke?'

'What is it?'

She passed him the letter. 'Here. Read it yourself.'

Sam squinted at the letter, holding it at arm's length. 'Captain... requests... pleasure... Eh?' He looked up in disbelief, then continued reading. 'His table... Last Night At Sea Dinner...'

They gaped at each other.

'Och, it's a mistake,' shrugged Sam. 'It's obviously meant for someone with a similar name, and whoever delivered it must have pushed it under the wrong door.'

Mary checked, re-checked, and checked again. There was no mistake. It was *their* name, *their* passenger reference number, and *their* stateroom. Bewilderment changed to panic. Her eyes widened in horror.

'I've got nothing to wear! We cannae go, Sam! *I've nothing to wear*!'

She saw the look of disappointment in her husband's eyes, but it couldn't be helped.

And Sam didn't even attempt to argue. Even if the Fiftieth Wedding Anniversary celebrations ended up in divorce, she wouldn't budge on this one. No way would she appear at the captain's table in the home-made grey dress, or any of the frocks she'd bought on the market. He could argue until Kingdom Come that they looked perfectly all right to him, it wouldn't make the slightest difference.

They wouldn't be going, and that was that.

Theodore tried to hide the fact, or at least make it less obvious, that he couldn't help continually glancing towards the door... until he saw Daphne surreptitiously glancing towards it as well.

It really was most annoying. The anticipated envelope containing their invitation to dine at the captain's table for the Last Night At Sea Dinner hadn't arrived yet.

Of course, one appreciated that the purser's office would be working flat out, tomorrow being the last day of the voyage. But still, thought Theodore, surely invitations issued to the captain's guests took priority over other, more mundane matters? After all, it didn't take long to write out a few favoured names, the pleasure of whose company the captain desired at his table for dinner, did it? And it was pretty much a foregone conclusion that he and Daphne *would* be invited. Quite apart from his interest in Navigation - always a scintillating topic at any dinner party at which there were fellow nautical enthusiasts - it so happened that this particular voyage was comparatively low on well-known celebrities. On their last voyage the Prince of Wales had been on board, and on previous trips Noel Coward and his theatrical set, an Indian Rajah, a couple of ambassadors, and a sprinkling of some obscure Eastern European aristocracy... Well, of course, one quite appreciated that procedures had to be observed. But on this occasion...

His reverie was interrupted by his wife's clipped upper-class English tones as she replaced her freshly-squeezed orange juice glass on the tray for Elsie to collect.

'Don't worry, darling. It's bound to be delivered later. They're probably tied up with one thing and another at present...'

160

4

'You're very quiet this morning,' remarked Caroline.

No response.

'Well?'

'Well what?'

'I said, you're very quiet.'

'I didn't know there was a law saying we've all got to be as noisy as you.'

Caroline was becoming impatient. 'Now just a cotton-pickin' minute, honeybunch. There certainly is in this suite, because I want to know *why* you're so quiet! And where did you get to last night?'

A knock on the door saved Sophie from further interrogation. Elsie came in with a tray of tea, biscuits, and the two lavish bouquets which were now the norm, deposited the tray on the dressing table, and opened the curtains.

'Morning, Miss P,' greeted Caroline. 'Say, you're looking a bit green around the gills! You all right?'

'Oh, just a touch of seasickness, Miss Caroline. I'll be fine. Shall I pour the tea?'

'Yes please, if you'd be so kind,' said Sophie. The interruption couldn't have been better timed. The inquest into where she'd got to last night, and with whom, couldn't be avoided indefinitely, but first she needed to reflect on it herself. Something very strange had happened and she needed to allow her brain to process events.

'I hope you'll feel better soon,' Caroline was saying as she reached a languid hand for the cards. 'Neither the Countess nor I suffer from *mal de mer*, but it must be pretty dire if you have to work through it. Can't you lie down for a while?'

'I'll be fine, thank you, madam,' murmured Elsie, hoping as she poured the tea that they wouldn't guess how close she was to lying down there and then on the floor and refusing all commands and threats by the Chief Stewardess to get up again until they reached dry land.

Caroline's attention moved on from the stewardess's seasickness as she read the first card.

'Oh. Frank. The Californian.' She turned to Sophie. 'You know, the Arab sheik. He wants to meet up at the tea dance this afternoon.'

'That's nice,' said Sophie automatically.

She lay back on the silk pillows and closed her eyes, vaguely aware of Caroline chatting to Elsie about the flowers. Good. It distracted attention away from her, and gave her time to think. And she needed to do a lot of that.

Take it from the basics. It was perfectly natural to go over the memorable events of the previous day. Who didn't enjoy looking back on a happy occasion, and think fondly of the person with whom they'd shared it? Nothing wrong with that at all. Perfectly normal behaviour.

What wasn't normal was this deep ache, the feeling that a part of her was missing, instead of merely appreciating Clive's company as just one of the ingredients that had gone to make up a delightful day. Memories to treasure and all that. Certainly nothing that should cause this sense of acute loneliness. *Why?* Had she fallen victim to some ridiculous teenage infatuation? No. She definitely wasn't infatuated. She knew the symptoms well enough - everybody did, there was no need to remind herself of the racing heartbeat, the dry mouth etc - and she'd gone through all that with Aubrey. This was... she felt as though she was slowly finding her way through fog swirling around her brain. And somehow she knew that when the fog eventually cleared, she'd wish it hadn't.

'Thanks, Miss P,' Caroline was saying, as Elsie handed her a dainty bone china cup of Assam tea with a slice of lemon in the saucer and a biscuit on a matching side plate. 'Now you be sure to get some rest today, you hear? Or we'll have to go back to the purser's office and insist that nobody makes you work while you're ill!'

Two pairs of eyes looked at her in horror - Elsie because she could imagine the Chief Stewardess' face if another complaint was made on her behalf ('Not *you* again! D'you mean to stand there and tell me you've been whingeing to passengers about being seasick? The rest of us just have to put up with it! I wouldn't have *dreamed*...' etc), and Sophie because, to her shame, her first thought had not been for the discomfort of another human being, but sheer joy at the thought of seeing Clive again.

It was then - as Elsie poured milk into her tea, causing Caroline to wrinkle her nose in disgust - that the fog suddenly cleared. The strange premonitions she'd had regarding the gold-brown bathing costume and the swimming pool came sharply into mind, and at last she understood the significance. It was far, far worse than some ridiculous teenage infatuation.

The high-principled, I've-made-my-vows-and-I'll-keep-to-them-no-matter-what-the-cost Countess of Knotworth, the morally upright paragon who had resolved to make the best of a disastrous marriage resulting, as she was the first to admit, from her own ambition, had somehow managed to fall hopelessly in love with the most inappropriate, incongruous, and inadvisable man on the entire planet.

As if things hadn't been wretched enough before!

But at least until last night they'd been relatively manageable and uncomplicated. Now what?

Well, she may as well face it. Now nothing.

All that had changed was that as well as being in a sham marriage with a man she didn't love, and who didn't love her, she'd complicated the situation even further by falling in love with someone else. And as if that wasn't bad enough, a man who, albeit for different reasons, was even less likely to love her than Aubrey.

163

How trite it sounded, 'falling in love with someone else.' Some people - her sister, for example - fell in and out of love with mystifying regularity. But she wasn't made to love indiscriminately. She'd thought she was 'in love' with Aubrey when he'd first courted her (or rather, her money) so ardently, but she'd been young and naive then. This was altogether different, and a lot more serious. Because in spite of knowing Clive for only a matter of days... she loved him. *Really* loved him. And more deeply than she'd have thought possible.

How doubly ironic then, that the man to whom her heart had decided to give itself, against the advice of her brain which was only too ready to point out the futility, probably gave his to a different woman on each trip.

Southampton - New York: Oops, fallen in love, Clive. Cute brunette.

New York - Southampton: Oops, here we go again, Clive. Stunning blonde this time.

And something else niggled: had Clive sought out her company for its own sake, or been detailed to placate her after she'd complained about that horrid Stonefeather man molesting Elsie? Because the more she thought about it, the more strange it seemed that someone from the purser's office - the very someone she'd complained to, no less - should have so much time off during the voyage. Very strange indeed.

Well, there was only one way to handle this appalling mess, and that was to say nothing to anyone - *certainly* not Caroline - and for self-preservation's sake, go into denial about the whole thing and forget last night ever happened.

Clive was well used to being teased in the Purser's Office after spending time with a desirable female passenger, but on this occasion he didn't rise to it, and after getting no response to make it worthwhile the subject was quietly allowed to drop. They all had plenty of work to do anyway; nobody wanted to be the cause of embarrassing delays because of incomplete paperwork when the ship was due to dock.

He stared at the invoices and receipts spread across his desk, and saw instead *Berengaria's* swimming pool as it had been last night. He'd seen it hundreds of times before, but there'd been a clearness, a freshness about it last night, as though he'd seen it for the first time.

Of course, the decorative cascades that kept the sea water constantly changed and fresh had been switched off, so the water was bound to be as quiet and still as the feeling deep within him in that moment just before she dived in, when everything, including his brain, had decelerated to a state of slow-motion... but it didn't matter how much he tried to rationalise it, there was no escaping the fact that it wasn't the actual appearance of the pool that was different; it was him. The famous verse from the Rubaiyat of Omar Khayyam floated into mind: *"The moving finger writes, and having writ, moves on, nor all thy piety nor wit shall lure it back to cancel half a line, nor all thy tears wash out a word of it."*

Well, the moving finger had written something in the Pompeian pool last night that he wouldn't have believed possible. How could he - *he*, of all people, whose career was the only important thing in his life - have been so stupid as to let this happen? Indeed, how could anyone, let alone Clive Willis whose flair for extricating himself from any romance that looked like becoming a bit too intense was legendary, fall so unbelievably rapidly - and so deeply - in love? This hadn't been part of the plan at all. It was unbelievable - and it had the potential to blow everything he'd worked for sky high.

He had no intention of becoming emotionally involved with anyone, let alone the wife of a powerful aristocrat. Enmeshed in an adulterous love affair, with an enraged husband in England citing him in divorce proceedings? Oh no... Juicy scandal was highly entertaining, as long as it didn't centre around oneself.

He absently shuffled a couple of invoices, glad there was so much to get done. It meant there was no chance of accidentally meeting Sophie today. He could take the coward's way out and avoid her, while convincing himself it was purely because he was kept so busy in here. Even more important, there'd be no time to think.

Which was just as well, because the subject repeatedly coming into mind, crowding out the things he should be concentrating on such as cargo manifests, returns, and balances of cash, was one he didn't want to think about at all.

The full irony of it hit him: the time had come far sooner than he'd expected to start paying for all the sins he'd chalked up, starting with the latest one of misleading Sophie, and then working steadily backwards over the years. Each and every one of his careless affairs, cavalier wooing, and shrugging aside of infatuated females now queued up to present him with the bill. It was time to pay them all in full, with interest; the smooth-talking, always-in-control, career-focused ship's officer, whose courteous charm and film star looks had set a-flutter so many feminine hearts - and who made sure any flutterings stayed strictly within female hearts and that his own was never similarly affected - had somehow managed to fall deeply in love with the most unlikely, unsuitable, and unavailable woman on the planet.

Well, the only way to deal with this was to scrub the whole thing completely from mind and forget it ever happened.

And that's exactly what he'd do.

5

Sam and Mary gaped at each other in disbelief when the results for the mid-day ship's pool were announced in the Winter Gardens. What? *What?* What was that he said? Sam had won the ship's ... *Sam* had won the *ship's pool?*

There must be some mistake. They'd never won anything in their lives, apart from Sam's small amounts at the shipyard. He hadn't even told Mary he'd entered for it, because he knew she'd hit the roof about throwing money away.

But they'd won! They'd actually won! And the prize would be... well, something like two hundred pounds!

While Mary was still speechless with shock, Sam struggled down on one knee by her chair.

'Mary, will ye marry me?'

'Och get up, you fool!'

'But ye haven't said whether ye'll -'

'Well I'm hardly likely to say no, am I, after fifty years. Get up before your knees lock and you're stuck doon there, making a holy show of the pair of us!'

Knees creaking, hanging on to the arm of her chair, Sam hauled himself back up. 'Right. First on the list, a trip to the jeweller's!'

And once the result had been officially confirmed and the money deposited at the ship's bank, first on the list it was.

Mary eyed the display tray of engagement rings in the window in rapt attention, her gaze lingering on the biggest and brightest on offer while Sam stood hoping whatever she selected wouldn't wipe out the entire winnings. They had a week in New York in front of them yet, and it was a safe bet she'd be in and out of shops buying presents for friends and relatives, as well as the entire clientele of the fish and chip shop, which meant nearly half of Glasgow.

'What d'you think o' that yin?' wondered Mary, pointing to a sparkling temptation on the bottom row.

'Aye, well, whatever one you want,' agreed Sam, rubbing his chin. They all looked much the same to him. Apart from the price, that was.

They entered the shop, and were immediately greeted like visiting royalty. Mary was seated on a brocade-covered chair while the senior salesman snapped his fingers for the display case to be produced for her perusal by a minion.

And that was when she came back down to earth with a bump. It was immediately obvious that these rings were designed for the sort of dainty fingers that would never know drudgery or toil; their size took no account of the rheumatism which had caused her knuckles to swell during her years working in a cold, damp factory. What was the point of trying any of them on? She may as well try and get one of them over the bandage on her thumb.

The senior salesman rescued the situation with an irritated clap of the hands to summon the minion, who had disappeared into the recess of the shop.

'Mister Brown! This tray is for display only - please bring the appropriate selection, with sizes to fit a wide range of hands!'

And the minion, a fast learner, soon worked out the coded message for 'Get the larger sizes quick, you numbskull!' and hastily produced a replacement tray.

Finally, after much deliberating - these things can't be rushed, she'd waited fifty years for this - she made her choice. To Sam's relief, it turned out to be a twenty guinea diamond solitaire rather than the more ostentatious number in the window.

'Aye. That one looks all right,' he nodded, relieved.

The ring was duly tried on. It fitted.

Mary admired it from all angles on her finger, watching the light catch the expertly cut stone and the colours reflected in it.

168

Then, embarrassed, she let her hands drop onto her knees. The contrast between their aged appearance and the newness of the ring was all too obvious, and the bandage on her left thumb stayed visible no matter how much she tried to hide it under the palm of her right hand.

But Sam, in a rare moment of perception which was all the more precious to her because it was so unexpected, reached over and covered both hands with his.

'All those things those hands of yours have done for other people over the years,' he said quietly, 'Now it's their turn tae get something back in return.'

And then, to her amazement, he lifted her left hand and kissed it.

The salesman tactfully withdrew, motioning the minion to leave the couple in privacy for a few moments before bustling forward again to complete the transaction and put the ring back in its box... when Mary finally got around to taking it off her finger.

'Now, would Sir like an inscription inside the ring?'

'An inscription?'

'Yes. A few special words engraved inside it?'

No. It turned out Sir wouldn't. Any special words Sir wished to say to his wife, he was more than capable of saying himself. For free.

'Here! What d'you think ye're doing?' demanded Mary, as the salesman's hand automatically reached out to take the ring.

He blinked in surprise. 'I thought -'

'I've waited fifty years for this. It's staying right where it is!'

'As Madam wishes. I just thought Madam would want me to put it in its presentation box, so that -' He got no further.

'Listen, son. The only thing going in a box around here,' warned Madam, closing her right hand firmly around her left, 'Will be anyone daft enough to try and take this off my finger!'

They'd been to the Gentlemen's Outfitters for the white shirt, where it was Sam's turn for the ushering-to-the-brocade-chair treatment, and now it was time for Ladies' Fashions, where Mary eyed the coffee and cream tea gown in the window and, leaving Sam sprawled on one of the luxurious settees, opened the shop door with a flourish and entered the fairyland within.

The senior saleslady, flanked by two juniors, smiled a welcome, and she was once again ushered to an ornate chair. How may they be of assistance to her?

Surrounded by sumptuous accessories, gloves, scarves, exquisite fripperies of every kind, and a posse of eager salesladies, Mary blinked and gaped at them, and her courage failed. Marooned in the shop without a clue what she wanted (other than the dress in the window, which her own common sense told her was too small anyway) or what to say when she got inside, she became increasingly hot, flustered, and aware of her mouth hanging open like one of the fish on the slab waiting to be gutted.

The need to escape was overwhelming. She stood up abruptly, and headed towards the door.

But the senior saleslady was kind, patient, and sensitive. With some gentle probing, she drew the problem to light. Mary and her husband, it seemed, had been invited to dine at the captain's table tomorrow night, and... and she had nothing suitable to wear, so they couldn't go, and her husband was disappointed and couldn't understand why the dresses she'd brought with her weren't good enough, and... her eyes strayed to the coffee and cream dress in the window.

Ah.

Well, that particular *sample* gown, explained the senior saleslady with an instructing glance at the junior salesladies, although suitable for this afternoon's tea dance, would not really be appropriate anyway for what Mary had in mind. She laid emphasis on the *suitability* angle, to divert attention from the fact that the sample model in the window wouldn't fit Mary's generous frame anyway. But all was not lost; what might Mary choose to wear from her own wardrobe?

Mary looked at her, shamefaced, and explained about the home-made grey dress.

The senior saleslady nodded with understanding and tact.

'I wonder if you'd like to bring it along?' she suggested, 'One of our assistants, Miss Harris here,' She signalled one of the junior salesladies forward. 'Has quite a gift with attractive accessories, and with the addition of one or two, I think we may be able to surprise you...'

6

Elsie was seasick again.

I can't stand much more of this, she thought as she retched once more in the stewardess' washroom.

Her previous voyage, in the Nursery, had taken place in relatively calm weather. She hadn't realised the Atlantic could be battered by winds varying from Force Five to Force Nine day after day, with no let-up. She hadn't realised the Chief Stewardess would expect her to report for duty, fit or not. She hadn't realised the conduct of some first class passengers could fall far below acceptable norms of behaviour to people like Billy and herself, who earned their living in a service capacity. And she hadn't realised what it felt like to be unremittingly seasick, day after day. She was beginning to detest the *Berengaria.*

She raised her head and looked at herself in the mirror over the washbasin - pale, gaunt, hollow-eyed. No wonder Billy hadn't looked at her twice. And how ironic, because her ashen appearance certainly hadn't put off Lexie Stonefeather, whose attentions she *hadn't* wanted.

Thoughts of Billy took her back to last night. She hadn't expected to meet anyone, let alone Danny and Billy when, forlorn and wretched, she'd sought solitude on the aft deck. It had meant, of course, that the planned chat with her Creator hadn't taken place. In fact she'd completely forgotten about Him in the excitement of being part of Billy's plan.

(Had she really agreed, like a child excited at the prospect of belonging to a juvenile Secret Society, to be a part of his preposterous plot? Yes, she had. And she needn't come on all Goody-Two-Shoes about it either, she told herself wryly, because she hadn't taken much talking into it. She disliked Lexie Stonefeather as much as Billy did.)

Perhaps it was just as well that 'chatting to God' had been swept from mind by Billy's irresistible temptation. You couldn't very well pray to a caring Creator, who taught forgiveness and turning the other cheek, when you were busily planning a most un-Christian retaliation like this. It was a text book horns-versus-halo battle - and the horns won, hands down.

But somehow, at some deeper level than this rubbing of hands in glee at getting her own back against Lexie, the desire to pray was even stronger, and when she returned to the sleeping quarters she'd finally given in to an outpouring of contradictory emotions - the desire to be above childish pranks like this, despite the stubborn determination to do it anyway - as she lay in her bunk, the air fetid, the sounds the other stewardesses made in their sleep intrusive, and the incessant throb of the ship's engines almost intolerable. And yet it was there, in that most uncongenial of surroundings, following a disjointed, irrational prayer, where she'd experienced an overwhelming sense of peace. Not so much about the present (how could there be, when she was guilty of relishing the exact opposite of every Christian value there was!) but an undefinable sense that, long term, all would be well, and she'd end up where she was meant to be in life. Strange. Very strange. But nice strange; comforting strange…

The ship lurched, she was overtaken by yet another bout of seasickness, and last night's events were temporarily forgotten in the awfulness of the present.

She splashed her face with cold water, rinsed her mouth, and cleaned her teeth. She felt weak, washed out; all she wanted to do was lie down and rest. Anything else was beyond her, and would remain so until she finally staggered on to dry land.

No. Not quite anything else.

She wiped her mouth slowly with the towel, and again stared at her reflection. Things had changed since last night. She was no longer a lonely alien who didn't fit in on the ship. She had

173

fellow-conspirators, and she trusted them. She now had *friends.* And one of them was Billy.

Also, it was her turn to have three precious hours off this afternoon, instead of having to be on call. And having washed her uniform and tidied her bunk, it was now time to go up to the aft mooring deck with her needle and cotton, and a blouse that needed a button sewing on. She'd need that to act as a sort of decoy; a cover, in both the literal sense of the word and as smoke screen, for the real purpose.

She almost, but not quite, managed a smile, still not quite able to believe she'd actually agreed to being a part, with Danny and Billy, of this ludicrous plot. Well, she didn't care how ludicrous it was, or - despite last night's genuinely heartfelt prayers - how contrary to the ideals of Christianity she hoped (one day) to aspire to. If she was entirely honest with herself, she couldn't wait to do it.

The aft mooring deck wasn't the most secluded place to carry out the sort of activities you didn't want the rest of the ship to know about, but short of a stewardess turning up at the strictly out of bounds stewards' glory hole with a cheery, 'How do, fellas. Don't mind me, just dropping in to commit a quick felony. Won't be long!' this particular skulduggery had to take place in the only area available to all the crew.

And so Elsie appeared on the aft deck and shyly met up with Billy. Danny, who wasn't blind to the way the wind was blowing between these two - he'd seen the interested glances Billy sent in her direction when he could keep his mind off what he'd like to do to Lexie Stonefeather long enough to notice her - kept a discreet distance and leaned over the rail, watching the ship's wake and hoping Joey might appear and join them so there'd be an opportunity for a quiet conversation. But Joey, usually good company and always ready for a laugh, seemed to have deliberately turned into a recluse on this trip.

Danny squinted at the far horizon. He was becoming seriously worried; when he'd collected the Camembert, Joey had looked

174

under more strain than he'd ever seen him, even after that terrible voyage to Australia. But short of confronting Alec direct - and that, obviously, would be counter-productive; Alec was hardly likely to pour out his soul to Joey's mate, and Joey would never forgive him for interfering - there was nothing he could do, other than look on the bright side; at least the explosion he'd expected to happen before now hadn't taken place. The worry was whether Joey's determination to resist provocation would, in the long term, cause even more problems.

But for now, as there was no positive action he could take anyway, he may as well concentrate on what was going on here...

Although there were other crew members about, it was quite possible, under the pretext of a harmless 'Good afternoon,' and other pleasantries, for what needed to be discreetly transferred from one to another taking place without anyone realising that villainy was afoot, and Billy was now casually depositing at Elsie's feet a linen bag containing Lexie's navy blue suit, which he'd kept separate when collecting the items for valeting while Lexie was at breakfast.

Skulduggery, Phase One, completed satisfactorily.

Danny likewise silently passed on to Elsie his lump of Camembert cheese.

Skulduggery, Phase Two, completed satisfactorily.

And Elsie herself had brought, together with a blouse that needed a button sewing on, the third item required; needle and cotton.

Skulduggery, Phase Three, about to take place.

She attracted no attention as she sat quietly sewing, and although Billy's linen bag had drawn a few curious looks there had been no outright comment; everyone had a uniform to repair from time to time, and some preferred to do it in the fresh air. If they brought it in a bag, so what?

Only Danny and Billy heard Elsie's anxious whisper, 'Are you sure the laundry crew won't be blamed for this?'

175

'Don't worry. If anyone's going to be blamed, it'll be me,' Billy promised as she transferred Lexie's suit from the linen bag onto her knee, covering it with the folds of her skirt and the decoy blouse. 'But it won't happen, because he'll know what to expect if it does: the Ship's Newspaper will have nothing on me. I'll make sure *nobody* misses hearing every last detail of his starring role in the cabaret act with the Russian tart...'

He related Lexie's Early Morning Tea saga, with the offer of a bribe to keep his mouth shut about his overnight companion. (Danny gave a wry smile. So the Russian had got lucky after all, had she? Or unlucky, depending on how you looked at it.)

'I'm glad you didn't take his money,' shuddered Elsie.

Billy grinned. He hadn't needed to. Lexie's seductress had stuffed a wad of dollar notes in his pocket, and he'd been too intent on Lexie's discomfort to bother shoving them back at her and telling her he didn't want it, which would probably only have resulted in some endless ridiculous pass-the-parcel pantomime anyway.

He'd planned to include Danny in the three-way share out, but Danny waved the offer aside; he'd been a bedroom steward himself in the past, and remembered his own experiences with the odd obnoxious passenger giving him a hard time. So that just left Elsie and Billy to enjoy the windfall - and Billy calculated there'd be enough for a slap-up meal and a Broadway show in New York, where it was nobody's business whether a steward fraternised with a stewardess or not. He intended asking Elsie out as a Thank You for this, and then (assuming she said yes) he'd make sure it was the best date she'd ever had, and that she forgot the misery of seasickness, Lexie's assault, and everything else that had made her trip on the *Berengaria* so obviously unhappy. She needed feeding up after eating almost nothing for most of the voyage, and a few laughs wouldn't go amiss either. Well, he'd never been able to afford to go to a Broadway show himself until now, so why not treat them both?

But he was getting ahead of himself. First, the Skulduggery.

He looked at her levelly. 'If anything goes wrong I promise I'll take full responsibility. You and Danny won't be mentioned, or involved in any way.'

They smiled slowly at each other, a smile of trust, of fellow conspirators with a common aim. But there was something else: silent acknowledgement of mutual attraction.

All doubts and misgivings faded for Elsie, even though she knew perfectly well it was an unworthy, childish, and utterly pathetic thing to do. It was also the one thing that had brought a smile to her face during this interminable voyage.

Billy Saunders' thoughts ran along similar lines. This whole escapade was immature, despicable, low, he didn't deny it - but neither could he stop the grin spreading from ear to ear. After all, Lexie Stonefeather had described him as a moron. Wouldn't this be just the sort of moronic revenge someone who fitted that description would carry out? Billy's would probably be the first name that sprang to Lexie's mind as the culprit - and that was just how he wanted it. His job was quite safe, because without definite proof who was responsible the Chief Steward couldn't authorise a D/R in his Discharge Book. As for morality, let those saintly souls who had higher ethical standards than he possessed be above revenge. He had no such delusions about himself. Guilty as charged, Your Honour. He didn't care how childish it was, he liked the unspoken message it contained. And it saved him the bother of shadowing Lexie for a spot of old fashioned assault and battery in a dark New York alleyway.

He winked at her, then moved away so as not to draw attention to them chatting. Elsie watched him go, taking in the way he held his head erect, the set of his shoulders, and the way he walked, with the distinctive rolling gait of a sailor...

And then bent to the task in hand. She unpicked the lapels of Lexie's jacket and waistband of his trousers, smeared a small dollop of Camembert inside each, neatly sewed them up again, and, carefully folding the suit to avoid creasing it, replaced it in the linen bag.

Skulduggery, Phase Four, completed satisfactorily.

177

7

'Oh, just ignore her. She's been like this all day,' grumbled Caroline as she whirled off with Frank-from-California-who's-in-the-film-industry for the first waltz of the tea dance.

It was true. Sophie *had* been preoccupied and distant all day. Probably because they were fast approaching New York, where reality would set in, guessed Caroline. A picture came to mind; Sophie, youthful, with a healthy enthusiasm for life, before she became Countess of Knotworth. An apt name indeed, because in her view marriage to Aubrey was definitely not worth the effort.

She'd been right to drag it all out of her sister early in the voyage. Each sea mile they travelled had brought a lessening of the damage done by Aubrey's wounding indifference, and the ship's frivolous distractions would, by temporarily banishing long-term problems from mind, actually help make clear the wisest course for the future: whether to divorce, or try to make a go of the marriage. As Pop said, no point worrying about the past. It's gone. No point worrying about the future. It's unknown. Just concentrate on the present, because that's all you can do anything about.

Caroline's own wish, should a genie with a magic lamp conveniently happen by, would be for some event to force Sophie's hand and make the decision for her. Not that it was likely to happen, given her sister's determination to avoid the merest hint of scandal. (Wasn't all bad. It gave *her* license to behave with enough lack of decorum for them both...)

Caroline, however, was wrong. Sophie's preoccupation with reality setting in might have been true yesterday; now it was the additional complication that was too private to share with anyone.

The whole thing was unbelievable. Only two days ago she'd insisted she'd keep to the vows made on her wedding day, vows Aubrey obviously regarded as meaningless, but she did not. Now everything had changed. Could she, in all honesty, stay with Aubrey now? Wouldn't the whole thing be a lie? But then, weren't they already living a lie? What did one more matter?

What a mess.

Well, she'd just have to obliterate last night from mind altogether, and make sure she never saw Clive again. As for living a lie, Aubrey had done it for the last seven years. Now it was her turn.

Something drew her eye to the doorway. She turned away as Lexie Stonefeather made his entrance and looked around.

He, seeing the Countess of Knotworth sitting alone at her table, smiled slowly, made his way to another table nearby, sat down, nodded politely to her, ordered a drink, and raised his eyebrows as she ignored him.

Well, let's just see how holier-than-thou she was in about, oh, let's say fifteen minutes time.

He settled down in comfort to watch the dancers, and relish choosing the moment to detonate his bombshell in her face. It was admittedly a very attractive face, but one with eyes that saw a lot more than they needed to, a nose that was too ready to poke into other people's business, and a mouth that did too much unnecessary talking.

This should sort out the problems with all three.

8

As Theodore and Daphne took to the floor for the waltz, they were spotted by Mary and Sam.

'Yoo hoo!' Mary waved enthusiastically as they swept past.

'Ignore them,' hissed Theodore.

'I fully intend to,' Daphne hissed back. 'Honestly, I've never been so mortified in my life!'

Both looked determinedly in the opposite direction. They'd already been dealt one infuriating blow today, without this pair adding to their chagrin.

The non-appearance of an invitation to dine at the captain's table was of course all due to the dratted Countess of Knotworth appearing just as the *Aquitania* was sailing past, and distracting the junior purser with some imagined drama which he then had to investigate. Something to do with a stewardess, and that ghastly Stonefeather creature. Not that it mattered; the end result was that Theodore's qualities as an eminently desirable captain's table dinner guest had been completely driven from the chap's mind by the interruption.

It really was too, *too* bad.

Also, Julian and Arabella were temporarily confined to their suite with a touch of *mal-de-mer* (keeping that young stewardess on her toes, by all accounts!). However, one thing that could always be relied upon to lift one's spirits was *Berengaria's* celebrated *the dansant,* which never failed to leave one with an all's-well-with-the-world afterglow following an enjoyable few hours.

'If Cunard pursers don't take the trouble to sift through passengers sufficiently thoroughly to provide the sort of intelligent and stimulating conversation in which one assumes the captain chooses to engage with his dinner guests,' Daphne had sniffed as they made their way to the flower-bedecked Grand Hall, 'I think we should jolly well book with White Star in future.'

'I agree with you,' Theodore nodded. 'We'll travel on the *Olympic* next time.' There was a slight pause. 'Because quite honestly, much as it pains one to admit it, the tone does appear to be lowering on the *Berengaria*...'

There was no need to elaborate on the type of passenger who had contributed to the lowering of *Berengaria's* tone. Daphne, nodding in agreement, understood his meaning perfectly. One just had to cling to the forlorn hope that those responsible weren't intent on lowering it still further at this afternoon's tea dance. Which was why one's heart sank into one's boots at the sound of that raucous 'Yoo-hoo!' across the dancefloor...

But it was impossible to disregard Mary's cheery waving, and, aware they were attracting more attention by ignoring the couple than by smiling a polite greeting and carrying gamely on, Theodore bared his teeth and prepared to whirl past.

Unfortunately, the dance finished just as they were level with the table.

'Sit yoursel' doon here, hen,' invited Mary, indicating two empty chairs obviously intended for their new pals.

Lexie Stonefeather watched all this with amusement. He'd already observed Mary and Sam's overtures of friendliness being received with frigid disdain, and guessed that under normal circumstances any approaches he made would be similarly received. But these weren't normal circumstances. Mr and Mrs No-Riff-Raff-Please were clearly seeking a timely escape from the Glaswegians, which meant that right now was the ideal moment to make his own move. So, as the orchestra struck up 'The Blue Danube', he approached Daphne with a courtly bow.

'May I have the pleasure?'

Daphne tutted under her breath. Really, it was *too* tiresome. If it wasn't those infernal nuisances it was this equally undesirable character. However, he was the lesser of the two evils; at least dancing with him could lead to the possibility of a more distant table. With an agonised glance at Theodore, she accepted.

Theodore, in turn, made his apologies to Mary and Sam.

'It would be diabolically rude of me not to dance with the Countess of Knotworth, who is on her own. Do excuse me.'

'Och aye, on ye go,' said Mary goodnaturedly. 'We'll see youse later.'

Lexie held Daphne close - far too close for comfort, but there wasn't much she could do about it without causing an attention-drawing scene - as they joined the rest of the dancers and glided in stately procession around the dance floor.

'How gallant of your husband to dance with the Countess of Knotworth,' he began smoothly.

Daphne gave a non-committal grunt to deter him from further conversation. Bad enough being imprisoned in his vice-like grip without having to talk to him as well.

'But,' went on Lexie, completely undeterred. 'I expect he's trying to cheer her up. Poor lady, sitting all alone, pining for her lover.'

'Her husband wasn't able to accompany her,' Daphne informed him with a sniff, to indicate that the amount of polite small talk she was prepared to tolerate was now at an end.

'Oh, I didn't mean her husband. No, I meant...' He looked at her in apparent surprise. 'Or hadn't you heard?'

'Heard what?'

'Oh dear! I thought it was common knowledge.'

'I'm afraid I don't know what you're talking about.'

'Well, you're the only one who doesn't. The whole ship knows about it.'

'Knows about what?'

'Oh,' Lexie shook his head. 'I shouldn't have said anything. I'm sorry, I assumed you knew. Forget I mentioned it.'

'Mentioned *what?*'

'Nothing. Nothing at all.'

Daphne looked at him sharply. 'It can hardly be nothing at all if the whole ship knows about it!'

'No. I'm sorry,' Lexie shook his head firmly. 'I've said too much already. I might have my faults, but gossiping isn't one of them. Anyway, it might not even be true. Forget I said anything.'

'Now look here -' Daphne slowed down, then moved on again abruptly as the couple behind bumped into them. 'So sorry,' she apologised, and turned back to Lexie. 'I happen to be a personal friend of the Earl of Knotworth -'

The couple behind them tutted audibly, and they broke into an undignified trot in an attempt to fill the empty gap ahead and catch up with the other dancers.

'- And in that capacity...' Daphne, a little breathless from the sudden exertion, tried not to pant, but was determined to root out whatever this despicable Stonefeather person knew, and she didn't. 'If there is something he should be aware of, I think the only honourable thing you can do is to tell me.'

Lexie gave a regretful sigh, and leaned a little closer.

'Oh dear. You've put me in rather an impossible position, haven't you? Under those circumstances I suppose I can't refuse to tell you what's already common knowledge. You're bound to hear sooner or later, anyway.'

'Bound to hear *what*?'

Another sad sigh; the well-meaning friend having the truth unwillingly dragged out of him. 'Well... while the rest of the ship was enjoying the Fancy Dress Ball, your friend's wife was down in the - ahem - deserted swimming pool area...'

'Swimming pool area?'

'Yes. Long after midnight, according to reliable sources.'

'What on earth was she doing down there?'

Lexie gave a delicate shrug. 'Well of course one can't speculate on that. But rumour has it she was seen coming up the grand staircase... with a man.'

Daphne stared at him.

He would have like to have spun things out a little longer, but the orchestra was reaching the final rousing crescendo of 'The Blue Danube' and the dance was nearing its end.

'And they were both quite blatantly laughing. Didn't seem to care who heard them.'

Daphne blinked. Aubrey's wife having some sort of tawdry assignation with a man - well, scandalous as it was, one could at a pinch overlook it; that sort of thing happened regularly at most country house weekends and went unremarked as long as it was kept discreet - but this! The grand staircase on the *Berengaria*! And blatantly *laughing*, if you please! In full view! Good heavens, it was tantamount to actually advertising the fact.

And *that* was unforgiveable.

Lexie nodded in mournful sympathy at her shock, and released his hold.

'I'm so sorry to be the one to tell you about all this unsavoury gossip. But as I say, it may not be true... I shall leave you to draw your own conclusion.'

And Daphne, of course, drew exactly the conclusion he'd intended her to draw.

As soon as her partner bowed and sauntered off across the dance floor she marched over to where Theodore was courteously escorting Sophie to the empty table next to Sam and Mary, and confronted her.

'You *slut!*'

Sophie gaped at her in amazement. Slut? A waltz at a tea dance with boring old Theodore? Good heavens, she hadn't even wanted to dance with him; she'd accepted his invitation purely out of good manners.

'How *dare* you!' Daphne was shaking with rage. 'I hope you're not going to ask me not to tell Aubrey about this!'

Even Theodore was taken aback by the onslaught.

'I say, steady on, old girl! It's all perfectly respectable. Merely a waltz at a tea dance. Aubrey won't mind in the least!'

'Oh, don't be so ridiculous!' snapped Daphne. 'I'm not talking about you two dancing together!'

'Well what -?'

Daphne stared into Sophie's face. 'I'm referring to the salacious gossip that is currently circulating the entire *ship!*'

'What gossip?' asked Sophie, mystified.

'Don't you dare play the innocent with me!' Daphne was working herself into a self-righteous frenzy. 'The whole *ship* knows about your sordid little secret!'

Sam and Mary looked at each other, unsure how to react.

'Poor, poor Aubrey!' Daphne shook her head dramatically. 'That it should come to this!'

'Come to *what*, darling?' Theodore was as mystified as everyone else.

'Yes, what on earth are you talking about?' frowned Sophie.

'*You* know what I'm talking about!' Daphne pointed an accusing finger at her. 'And before you plead with me not to not to let poor Aubrey know about it, I must tell you that as long-standing and utterly loyal friends - of *his* - Theodore and I are duty bound to warn him before he hears about it in far more hurtful ways, from other far less caring sources! Heaven forbid! The least we can do is save him from that!'

Caroline, who could hardly miss Daphne's indignation, arrived at the table with Frank-the-Californian-who's-in-the-film-industry in tow. 'This all sounds very interesting. Duty bound to warn poor Aubrey about what?'

Daphne, shaking with emotion, turned on her. 'I think the situation is already dire enough without you flippantly making light of poor Aubrey's shock when he hears -'

'Darling,' broke in Theodore gently, 'What on earth has happened?'

'It appears,' Daphne drew herself up to her full height, 'That the whole ship knows what the Countess of Knotworth got up to last night!'

'I wish I did,' said Caroline.

'Oh, she's been trying to keep it from you as well, has she? Well let me inform you. Your precious sister,' announced Daphne, quivering with indignation, 'Has betrayed her husband.

Publicly!' She turned to face Sophie. 'How could you be so cruel - so utterly heartless?'

'Betrayed Aubrey? Publicly?' Theodore blinked at his wife. The mind boggled. Good heavens! *Publicly?* Where on earth...?

'Yes. She was seen coming up the grand staircase, from the deserted swimming pool, in the middle of the night - with a man! As near as dammit *in flagrante delicto!'*

Sophie closed her eyes. Oh no.

Of all people, it would have to be Daphne. And how ironic - she'd spent seven years watching Aubrey setting off on adventure after adventure with his current male favourite, yet she was the one who was cruel and heartless, for daring to take a midnight swim. She could protest her innocence of anything more than that from now until she drew her last breath, and it wouldn't make the slightest difference. She knew perfectly well it wasn't the possibility of adultery itself that so scandalised Daphne, as much as the unforgiveable realisation that everyone knew about it. Which was why she and Theodore would be barely able to wait until they could contact Aubrey and, as long-standing and utterly loyal friends, acquaint him with the fact that his wife had been fornicating with all and sundry in the ship's swimming pool. And *everyone knew.*

Caroline was looking at her in amazement. 'Is it true?'

'Well it's -'

'Oh, it's true all right,' nodded Daphne. 'They were *laughing!'*

'What on earth were you doing in the swimming pool at that time of night?'

'I went swimming.'

'Swimming?' snorted Daphne.

'Yes.'

'Do you seriously expect us to believe,' went on Daphne incredulously, 'That you went down in the dead of night to the swimming pool - to *swim?'*

'Yes. What else would I go to a swimming pool for?'

Daphne snorted again, louder.

186

'If my sister says she went swimming,' said Caroline, her voice rising in defiance of the accusation, judgement, and anticipated punishment Daphne managed to convey with every word, 'Then she went swimming. Nothing else.'

Daphne gave a disgusted tut. 'Oh please! Don't insult my intelligence!'

Caroline's voice rose to match Daphne's in volume. 'Unconventional as it may be to go swimming at night, it's not a crime as far as I'm aware. Nor is it proof of adultery, as you seem to think.'

'My hearing is not impaired, thank you,' retorted Daphne. 'There's no need to shriek like a common fish wife!'

'Eh? Excuse me!' Mary, who had listened in bemused silence until now, had no intention of letting that pass. 'I'm no' standing by while you look doon yer ugly big conk at fish wives!'

Daphne turned to her, outraged. Who did this vulgar woman think she was, daring to speak to her like that?

Mary nodded vigorously. 'You criticise fish wives tae me, missus, and ye're asking for trouble!'

Danny, arriving with a tray of dainty Afternoon Tea cakes and biscuits, struggled to keep a straight face, and dawdled as long as possible arranging plates on the table to hear whatever might come next.

He wasn't disappointed. Having once started, Mary got into her role of defender of the reputation of the world's fish wives with gusto, and was now drawing breath for the next broadside. She'd spent enough time trying to befriend someone who obviously didn't hold fish wives in high esteem; if Daphne could air her views on fish wives, then Mary could air her views on Daphne.

'Some people who've never done a day's work in their lives want to try earning their living gutting fish themselves instead o' sitting there criticising the folk that do - they'd have a bit more respect for fish wives then, allow me tae tell you!'

Daphne looked as though she was about to faint.

187

'Aye, ye might well look shocked!' Mary gave another belligerent nod. 'You think you're better than fishwives, do you? Away and pee yer breeks!'

'I -' gasped Daphne.

'You might think ye're above the rest of us, missus, but fish wives, they'd throw rubbish like you away wi' all the fish heads!'

Theodore had had more than enough. High time to reassert the authority of a mature, responsible male, and bring this mortifying spectacle to an end. He closed his eyes and held up one hand, like a policeman directing traffic.

'Could we please dispense with these inane observations about fish wives, which even the most obtuse among us will appreciate have no bearing on my wife's disclosures regarding the conduct of the Countess -'

'Is that so, pal?' said Sam, rising from his chair. He might not understand Theodore's fancy words, but there was no mistaking the condescending hostility in his tone, and Sam didn't like it. Nor did he like anyone belittling Mary, who'd never done anything to hurt either of them.

Danny couldn't drag out arranging plates and cakes and biscuits indefinitely. He collected a tray of empties from the neighbouring table, and set off to the kitchen to provide some light entertainment for the other waiters.

Meanwhile, the open warfare at this particular table was beginning to attract curious glances from the dance floor, and the Head Waiter, keeping a wary eye on developments from the sidelines (An altercation? At one of *Berengaria's* renowned afternoon tea dances? It was unheard of!), signalled the orchestra to start the next dance quickly to drown out raised voices. This unseemly row couldn't be allowed to besmirch the ship's reputation. Interesting spats between celebrities was one thing; free-for-all brawls - especially with a Glaswegian rough-neck who looked likely to pick up a chair and swing it down over his opponent's head like they did in Wild West bars in cowboy movies - quite another.

The orchestra obediently plunged into a particularly enthusiastic Charleston. Attention shifted back to the dancers once more, and the Head Waiter breathed more easily; the combatants wouldn't be able to make themselves heard above the music, and the band leader was sufficiently experienced to follow the Charleston with another waltz to calm everyone down again.

Theodore and Daphne, outraged - the unbelievable *awfulness* of it! - stalked away from the Grand Hall, tight-lipped.

Mary and Sam, still seething - they'd actually tried to *befriend* these pains-in-the backside! - glared after them.

Caroline, concerned for Sophie - so the genie with the magic lamp *had* happened by and granted her wish after all! - gave her sister a gentle hug.

Sophie stared bleakly - wait until Aubrey hears about *this!* - at the table.

And Lexie Stonefeather, highly amused by the whole thing - went even better than he'd hoped! - stood, and, with another polite nod at the Countess, sauntered out of the Grand Hall.

Spread a little sunshine all around, that was Lexie's motto.

FIVE: LAST NIGHT AT SEA

1

'You know, gentleman, I did so enjoy our little game the other day,' the clergyman told his new friends diffidently in the Smoking Room. 'I wonder... would any of you care to come to my stateroom tonight for a few more games, before we all part company in New York?'

Lexie glanced at Lemuel Hoffmann as he lit another cheroot.

One born every minute, eh. The vicar was going to be in for a Very Interesting Time when he arrived in New York, came to his senses, realised too late that he'd lost his Convention dough, and had to explain to the church authorities where it had gone.

'Glad to, Reverend,' Lexie assured him, snapping his fingers for another whisky.

The clergyman nodded, and gave them all a benign smile.

'Medicinal purposes,' Lexie explained briefly as he downed his whisky. Although actually it was the truth on this occasion. His throat had begun to feel increasingly tight as the morning progressed. Sure sign of the beginnings of a cold.

It wasn't surprising. What with that Russian she-wolf on deck in a freezing Atlantic gale, then that effing steward with the door open and a drought blowing in on him stark naked, it was no wonder he'd started with the sniffles. Damn the pair of them! Hopefully a few more whiskies would shift it, because he needed to be on top form for his meetings tomorrow.

But he wasn't going to miss tonight's fun, sniffles or no sniffles. He gave an anticipatory chuckle, finding the prospect increasingly amusing. So amusing in fact that he failed to see the gleam in the clergyman's eyes as, under his breath, Jack Dalton recited one of his favourite phrases: Won't you come into my parlour, said the spider to the fly...

They'd learn the rest of his favourite phrases tonight.

Mary couldn't believe it. The grey home-made dress had been transformed.

A dusky rose sash had replaced the pale grey one she'd wrapped around the hips, and was fastened with a large artificial flower at the front. Garlands of matching smaller flowers hung from the right shoulder, and the skirt had been caught up over the right knee in graceful drapes and now displayed two or three inches of a skilfully inserted matching dusky rose scarf, which served as an under-panel.

As Mary inspected her now unrecognisable dress - in just twenty four hours Ladies Fashions had performed a miracle - the junior salesladies were despatched to bring from the mahogany drawers at the back of the shop a selection of beaded head-dresses, hair adornments, and evening bags to complement the outfit, all in the most enchanting shade of dusky rose.

She rejected the head-dresses ('Och, I'm no' trying to look sixteen, hen,') but found a small hair slide irresistible. And a dusky rose evening bag equally so. And the nicest thing of all was, she could peel off a few notes to pay for all this finery without guiltily calculating the number of hours she or Sam would have to work to accumulate it.

She returned to the stateroom and displayed the dress proudly for Sam to admire. He muttered something about women's fripperies; it had looked perfectly all right to him as it was, but if the alterations made her happy that was all that mattered.

'Aye, well they do,' said Mary, hanging it carefully in the wardrobe to keep it fresh and clean for tonight. 'It'll give me a bit of confidence. I need all the help I can get to get me through a' this Captain's Table malarkey. I'm that nervous I'll no' be able to eat a thing!'

3

Mary wasn't the only one attending to clothes in wardrobes.

Billy Saunders packed away in Lexie Stonefeather's enormous trunk every item of clothing except those he'd been instructed to leave ready for tomorrow's embarkation, and he and old Reg between them lugged it to the holding bay. Once there, stacked among all the other trunks, it was inaccessible; there could be no changing of minds about which suit to wear.

And then, smiling to himself, Billy took the suit from its laundry bag and hung it in the wardrobe. As yet there was only the faintest whiff of Camembert; certainly not enough to arouse either old Reg's or anyone else's suspicions. But the room was pleasantly warm, because Lexie had left a note instructing the heating was to be left on as he was starting with a cold.

Bless his poor little cotton socks, thought Billy with malicious pleasure. Let's hope his nose is nicely blocked up as well.

Skulduggery, Phase Five, completed satisfactorily.

The Last Night At Sea Dinner was always a special occasion, and tonight was no exception.

Unfortunately, Daphne and Theodore were slightly late. It was all the fault of that *monstrous* debacle at the tea dance yesterday; they'd both needed to retire and rest again this afternoon, and had only just surfaced.

'My nerves will take weeks to recover from it,' Daphne had complained as she sent for the stewardess (Miss Parkinson, or whatever her name was) to bring another lavender-scented handkerchief to dab on her temples. 'Those awful, *awful* people!'

'The only positive outcome,' agreed Theodore, swallowing another aspirin, 'Is that at least we'll free of the sight of them for the remainder of the voyage.'

But the shock awaiting them when they'd recovered sufficiently to head for the dining saloon was enough to make them wish they hadn't bothered to get out of bed, because this was enough to send them straight back.

'I can't believe it! I simply can't believe it!' gasped Theodore, as Danny held the chair for Daphne to sit down. '*Look!*'

Daphne looked, blinked, looked away, and then looked again. It was true! Those odious brutes were sitting among the other guests at the captain's table!

Theodore waved Danny away impatiently. Who could possibly concentrate on making the choice between *Consommé Grimaldi* or *Ris de Veau Osielle* after this latest shock to the system?

Daphne stared in repelled fascination at the grey dress, which, for all the dusky pink alterations and adornments, was clearly the home-made effort the woman had already worn more than once. And Theodore, outraged, took in the new white shirt and slightly ill-fitting double breasted dinner jacket Sam was wearing, which had obviously been hired from the Men's Outfitters.

And these scarecrows had actually been invited to dine at the captain's table, if you please! Why? In heaven's name, *why,* when the ship abounded with far more worthy guests? Not that he was implying that he was one of them... but...

'Well, it's to be hoped he's interested in hearing all about keels, and rivets, and all the rest of the shipyard tediousness,' he commented sourly, glaring at the captain.

'And the life and times of our glorious fishwives.' Daphne's tone was equally bitter.

But evidently he was - because the most shocking thing of all was that the captain, leaning towards Sam as he chattered quite unselfconsciously, was laughing heartily at whatever it was Sam had just said. Theodore watched, dumbfounded, as the conversation halted momentarily as a whole roasted oxen and grilled antelope was wheeled in for the next course, accompanied by the orchestra playing Elgar's Pomp and Ceremony March No 4.

Daphne shook her head, closed her eyes, and raised a protesting hand when Danny arrived once more to take their orders for Joints and Roast.

'No. No, I'm afraid I simply couldn't face anything at present.'

'Neither could I. We'll just have some light refreshments sent along to our stateroom instead,' decided Theodore, signalling permission for Danny to assist his wife to her feet.

The whole thing really was enough to put one off one's grilled antelope.

'My wife is feeling most unwell.' The tone implied that Danny was in some way to blame.

'I'm sorry to hear that, sir,' said Danny politely. 'I hope you'll be feeling better soon, madam.'

Theodore grunted in rebuke; recovery from trauma of this magnitude was hardly likely to be speedy.

'As for attending the Ship's Concert or Farewell Party, I'm afraid it's out of the question.' Daphne shook her head. 'You're absolutely right darling, I'm *decidedly* unwell!'

'I think an evening of seclusion would benefit us both,' agreed Theodore.

'I shall write my postcards,' decided Daphne. There was a slight pause, then she added peevishly, 'If I didn't have such a charitable nature, I'd send one to Lady Cunard, advising her that if things go on as they are, it will be only a matter of time until people start referring to the *Berengaria* as the *Bargain Area!*'

'And if I didn't have any scruples about sinking to the level of the lowest common denominator responsible for that state of affairs,' replied Theodore grimly as he took Daphne's arm to escort her from the dining saloon, 'I'd sign it!'

5

Sophie sat deep in thought as the Rodney Hudson Dancers high-kicked their way through *'Sweet Georgia Brown'*.

The Ship's Concert was in full swing, to be followed by the Farewell Party. But unable to face the possibility of bumping into Daphne and Theodore or, even worse, Clive, Sophie had refused point blank to attend either. Caroline, of course, immediately pointed out that her absence would be taken as proof of guilt by Daphne and Theodore, Sophie retorted that as far as they were concerned conclusive proof of guilt already existed, and the atmosphere between them had once again become strained.

But she finally agreed to attend the Concert, which she'd always supported in the past because of the collection taken at the end for various seamen's charities, with Caroline and Frank-from-California-who's-in-the-film-industry, who had obviously emerged as clear favourite as the voyage neared its completion. (Tom, Cyril, and Luigi had obviously been consigned to the forgettable ranks of suppliers of daily fresh flowers, and the Polish count and German princeling had faded from the scene altogether.)

The Ship's Concert was the highlight of every voyage, always popular because famous musicians, film and theatre stars, opera singers and so on, willingly gave performances free of charge. In addition, various members of the ship's crew took part from time to time, so each concert was a delightful surprise and passengers never knew who they'd see perform. But tonight Sophie was unable to concentrate on the performance...

As far as Aubrey was concerned, she knew exactly what his reaction would be when informed that his wife's adultery was the subject of widespread gossip on the ship. He'd be completely indifferent as to whether or not adultery had actually taken place. That was irrelevant, of no importance whatsoever. All that would matter to him was the fact that 'everyone knew' - because Daphne and Theodore, of course, would make it their business to make sure everyone who mattered did know. And *that* was what he wouldn't forgive.

The orchestra swung smoothly from *'Sweet Georgia Brown'* into *'If You Knew Susie'*, and she tried to concentrate once more on the Concert because irritatingly, after deliberately making an appearance to trumpet her clear conscience, there was so sign of Theodore and Daphne to trumpet it to.

The other irritating thing was, she felt increasingly like a gooseberry - the proverbial spinster aunt, tolerated but ignored as Bright Young Things chattered and giggled together at a those-in-the-know party. She could neither concentrate fully on the concert because of their intrusive tete-a-tete, nor concentrate on what they were saying because of the concert. All in all, she wished she'd just made an anonymous donation to the seamen's charity and stayed in the suite.

She made another attempt to join in with Caroline and Frank. From the snatches of conversation she managed to hear, they were discussing the making of *'Phantom of the Opera'* in 1924.

'Why don't you come out to California for the preview in October, Caroline?' suggested Frank. 'Don't wait until general release in November!'

He broke off as the chorus line high-kicked their way off stage to enthusiastic applause, and one of the A.B.s was introduced on stage. A Greek, called Aris Rouvas. He stood in front of the orchestra and began a popular Al Jolson song, *'All Alone'*.

Caroline listened for a few moments, then re-directed the conversation back to previews and the film industry.

'October…?'

She rather fancied the idea of finding a niche in the glamorous movie business - not that she needed financially to work, but her abundant creative energy needed to be channelled, and photography was a keen interest - and Frank had already suggested coming out to Los Angeles because he had numerous contacts she would find useful to meet.

'Yeah. You just gotta see it! Lon Chaney did all his own make up,' enthused Frank. 'Painted his eye sockets black, enlarged his nostrils with black paint, then put a set of jagged false teeth in his mouth, and his face looked like a horrible skull with a few wisps of black hair on his head!'

Don't know why he bothered, thought Sophie. They could have just got Aubrey. He'd have done nicely, and he wouldn't have needed any make-up. Then, ashamed and horrified at herself, she drew away from Frank and Caroline and a conversation she didn't feel part of, and concentrated on the singer. The Greek A.B. was gifted with a good singing voice, and injected great feeling and honesty into each word.

'Just like a melody that lingers on, you seem to haunt me night and day...'

The tears welled up, and she stared resolutely up at the ornate ceiling in a futile attempt to stop them rolling down her cheeks. Her sham marriage of formal indifference had been tolerable - or at least bearable - until now, but Theodore and Daphne's threat altered everything. She knew what lay ahead; she'd experienced the silent treatment before, when she'd committed some breach of etiquette she wasn't even aware of until it was too late. This far more serious sin, the sin of *'everyone knowing'*, would result in tepid formality becoming permanent frigid dislike.

What a mess. What an absolute mess it all was.

If only she hadn't come on this voyage... If only she hadn't met Clive... If only she and Aubrey were happy together... If only Daphne and Theodore weren't both childhood friends of Aubrey's... If only they weren't here on the *Berengaria*... If only she hadn't told Clive she'd like to swim after the fancy Dress Ball... if only the unknown witness who'd seen them coming up the grand staircase hadn't leapt to the wrong conclusion... If only...

What a mess.

Well, sitting here trying not to cry wouldn't solve anything. May as well at least let Caroline and Frank enjoy the evening without spoiling it by her miserable presence.

She stayed until the Concert finished, made a generous contribution, then, instead of attending the Farewell Party, retired back to the suite. And she'd almost reached it when Lexie breezed out of his door.

Oh no. Not him. Not now, of all times.

There was no way to avoid him other than a childish and undignified turning on her heels and retracing her steps. She prepared to pass him without a word.

Lexie, who'd popped back to his suite for another clean handkerchief to sneeze into, was setting off back to the Smoking Room to continue the congenial warming-up poker session before the serious business began. He saw her hesitate, and smiled. This was turning into a very gratifying evening. For one thing, there'd been no sign of the away-with-the-fairies Princess Whoever-she-Was(n't). An altogether more desirable siren, Lady Luck, was smiling on him tonight, and he was going to double what he'd already won the ship's pool courtesy of the vicar. He couldn't wait for that to happen.

On second thoughts, yes he could, because here came another unexpected bonus: the opportunity to gloat at the sanctimonious Countess of Knotworth. He was sure Lady Luck wouldn't mind waiting a minute or two while he relished this.

'Good evening!'

No response. Sophie attempted to pass him.

'Oh, don't be like that, your Ladyship. I only wanted to give you a little piece of friendly advice.' He leaned closer, and stared at her. The smile was replaced by a look of undisguised vindictive malice; the voice became hostile and threatening. 'Next time you're coming up from the swimming pool with your boyfriend, keep the noise down. Attracts all sorts of people you don't want it to, noise, when you're having a bit of innocent fun.' There was a pause while he let that sink in.

'That's been my experience, anyway. Just thought I'd pass on some good advice to you. Goodnight. Sweet dreams.'

He strode off, whistling.

So that was who'd seen her. Out of nearly four and a half thousand people aboard the *Berengaria,* he had to be in the vicinity of the grand staircase as she and Clive came up from the pool.

She knew straight away that the story about it being the talk of the ship was rubbish. He'd targeted the people who could cause the most damage to her, and if the rest of the ship started gossiping about it as well it was an added bonus. He'd set out to pay her back for that unsavoury stewardess business and, in the most effective and damaging way possible, he'd done it.

Clive was working far into the night with other members of the Purser's Office, attending to records and documents required by the health authorities, immigration officials, and myriad other port, harbour, and dock departments concerned with the liner's arrival.

It was important there were no delays.

From the shipping company's point of view, the speedier the voyage and turnaround time in port the better. Fares paid by passengers not only had to cover all the expenses of running the ship while at sea, but meet the costs of time spent ashore, and an extra day in port meant more dock and harbour charges to pay as well as an extra day's pay for the crew.

From the first class passengers' point of view, depending on whether a business meeting was scheduled or the trip was purely for pleasure, while there were few complaints if the hedonistic luxury aboard was prolonged for an extra day, it was still preferable that the trip didn't drag on to the point where it became a little *too* long.

From the second and third class passengers' point of view, it was a case of being philosophical about any delay because there wasn't much they could do about it.

From the immigrants' point of view the sooner they were out of steerage the better. Whatever awaited in New York had to be an improvement on being imprisoned in cramped, comfortless conditions, with total lack of privacy and the ever-present stench of seasickness.

And from Clive's point of view, it didn't matter how much work there was. He'd willingly be chained to his desk throughout the entire night if it meant there'd be no time to think about anything else.

6

Danny's feet were throbbing. Last Night At Sea was always a long, exhausting night. After the Ship's Concert was the Farewell Party, and passengers were always reluctant to go to bed after that; there were goodbyes to be said, addresses to be exchanged, business and social engagements to be arranged, and so on.

But there was a brief lull, which meant a short break for the waiters. Most of the others collapsed gratefully onto the boxes that served as seats in the store room, and grabbed a sandwich and a cup of tea, but Danny just wanted some fresh air. There wouldn't be enough time to trek to the aft mooring deck, however. Was it worth the risk of going out on the promenade deck?

Common sense gave the obvious answer straight away: no, it wasn't. It'd be just his luck for an irate passenger to find a waiter taking a breather. But he didn't have the energy to traipse to the aft deck...

He quietly opened the door. It was deserted. He breathed in a few lungfuls of clean sea air, padded across to the rail... then became aware of the door opening behind him.

He stiffened, looking round in dread, then relaxed slightly as he recognised Sam stepping over the coaming. If he was any judge of character, the Glaswegian was unlikely to report him, but it as was obvious he'd be spotted he'd just have to brazen it out and hope for the best.

Fingers crossed. 'Good evening, sir. I was just, er...'

'Oh! Och aye, me an' all, son, me an' all.' Sam was equally relieved that his fellow fugitive on deck was not someone had had no wish to see (in his case, Theodore or Daphne) and nodded good-naturedly. 'I needed to escape thae Flamenco

Dancers at the Concert, a' that shouting and bawling and stamping and banging. Gie' me a good pipe band any day... Is that you finished your work, aye?'

'No,' admitted Danny guiltily. 'Better get back inside.'

'Oh. Late night, eh?'

'Always is, Last Night at Sea. Goodnight, sir.'

'Aye well. 'Night, son.'

It was only later - much later - that he wished he'd gone below and talked to Joey instead.

7

The whisky bottle was already on the table, and the cards set out for his own particular favourite: Faro.

Jack Dalton gently ushered his new friends into his stateroom.

'Please don't think me presumptuous, gentlemen,' he said as they hesitated in surprise at the doorway, 'But how would you feel about a little change from poker? It's just that I've been reading about Faro, and it struck me as rather an interesting game.'

'Faro?' scoffed Lexie. 'We're on the *Berengaria* in the twenties, not some Mississippi riverboat in the last century!'

Lemuel Hoffmann also found the idea amusing. 'Why Reverend, have you only just heard of Faro? Where've you been for the last twenty five years? Nobody plays Faro these days!'

'Went out with the Ark,' nodded Johnny Greaves, another London business man who'd spent most of the voyage in the Smoking Room, and tagged along to make up a foursome.

'Don't know about the Ark, Reverend,' chuckled Lemuel. 'But I reckon it certainly went out with Wyatt Earp and Doc Holliday!'

Jack Dalton laughed along with them, but made sure he got in quickly before anyone could add Soapy Smith to the Rogue's Gallery of yesteryear. There was no need for them to know that his childhood heroes just happened to be the gamblers of the Mississippi riverboats and saloons of the wild west, Wyatt Earp and Doc Holliday among them. But his biggest hero of all was Soapy Smith who ran the Tivoli Club in Denver, where every game played was fixed in Soapy's favour. Lexie Stonefeather may never have heard of him, but Lemuel, being American, certainly would have done.

'I guess it is a bit unfashionable,' he agreed pleasantly. 'Sounds an interesting game though, doesn't it. I believe it has other names, like, er, bucking the tiger?'

'Oh, that was just because the cards had pictures of a tiger on the back,' explained Lemuel.

'Ah. I see. I find it all fascinating. Anyway... what d'you think?'

He flapped his hand vaguely at the table, so their attention focused on the whisky bottle rather than the green baize on which it stood, hoping none of them had picked up the copy of Hoyle's Rules of Games in the Smoking Room and seen the disclaimer at the beginning of the Faro section, warning readers that no honest Faro bank actually existed in the United States. Because the other thing there was no need for them to know was that if he was banker - which of course he would be - by the end of the night it'd be clear that none existed on the *Berengaria* either.

Johnny shrugged. 'Oh why not, Reverend, if it makes you happy.' He chose the chair nearest the whisky, settled down, and made himself at home. He didn't really care what they played as long as the whisky bottle was near to hand.

Lexie, thrown by this unexpected development, wasn't happy. He didn't want to swap games at this stage in the proceedings. Switching to Faro was an unsettling interruption in the pattern, and who wanted to change tack in the middle of a winning streak? And yet, frustrating as it was when he was winning and the clergyman losing (as Jack Dalton made it his business to do at the warm-up games), he'd find it an anticlimax if they all trooped back to the Smoking Room because he objected to Trev the Rev playing Faro. Especially when the whole point of leaving it was for the sole purpose of getting into Trev's stateroom to relieve him of his convention money...

He sneezed. That was another annoying thing; he hadn't managed to fight off this cold despite all the whisky. If tonight hadn't been the last night on the ship he'd take himself off to bed, but he couldn't let a cold get in the way of his plans now.

Also, he couldn't risk another encounter with that crackpot Russian female, and he'd be safe here; she'd never find him in a vicar's stateroom. So he'd humour the clergyman, let him get this Faro nonsense out of his system, and then, when the novelty had worn off, they could get back to poker. As long as by the end of the night the sucker's money was safely in Lexie's pocket, what did it matter what they played? If he was as clueless at Faro as he was at poker, there shouldn't be any problem.

Lemuel Hoffmann was also initially slightly taken aback to see the table laid out for Faro, but (as Jack Dalton was well aware, having banked on his knowledge of human nature) as he was now in the awkward situation of having accepted an invitation to his host's stateroom, he couldn't very well turn round and walk out without appearing churlish. And he was curious about Lexie Stonefeather, who had more or less press-ganged him into a business meeting in New York on their arrival. He wanted to find out a bit more about the character of the man before doing business with him. Convivial get-togethers in the Smoking Room were all very well, but they provided too many opportunities for people to show themselves in a good light, and it was always sensible to have as much insight as possible before finalising any agreements. This was a useful way of doing it.

Jack Dalton, still keeping up the appearance of an inept amateur who was punching above his weight where the other three were concerned, filled all four glasses with whisky, loosened his dog collar, and smiled at them. If they wanted to continue playing poker but were too polite to object to the change, that was their problem. He was here to make money, not fiddle round entertaining them with games of their choice. *He'd* be the one to decide when they changed back from Faro to poker. Or blackjack. Or seven card monte, another lucrative favourite. He had the necessary deck containing a double-faced card all ready for that.

'Talking of old-timers, gentlemen,' he smiled, sipping his whisky to reassure the others there was no dastardly plot to get them drunk while he remained stone cold sober, 'You've probably heard one of Mark Twain's sayings that I particularly like. But just in case you haven't, allow me to quote it for you.'

He held his glass up in a toast. '"A dollar picked up on the road is far more satisfactory than the ninety-nine you had to work for, and money won at Faro, or in stock, snuggles into your heart in the same way."' How true. I'm sure we'd all go along with that, gentlemen?'

Surprise, surprise, he was right. From the general murmur of agreement it seemed that yes, they all went along with that.

'I thought so.' He gave one last mild-mannered naive clergyman's smile before the mask finally came off for the serious business ahead. It was going to be a long night.

'So... are we all ready to play?'

8

The knocking at the door was quiet but insistent, and Sophie wasn't sure how long it had been going on because it intruded into a dream at first. Gradually she realised she was no longer asleep. Someone really was knocking at the door.

A voice, hoarse, guttural, deeply accented, called furtively through the keyhole.

'*Milliya moya* (my sweet)… It's me! I come for our night of passion! Open the door, my English lover…'

Good heavens, who on earth was this?

She looked across to Caroline's bed, which was empty. Was that her sister outside, fooling around because she'd had too much to drink?

Another salvo of knocking. Another croaked endearment from the other side of the door.

'Open the door! *Ya teby lublu, mily!* (I love you, darling!)'

Sophie's eyes widened, and she instinctively pulled the silk counterpane up to her chin. Whoever was outside the door definitely wasn't Caroline.

'It's me, darling! I come to you, *lubov moya* (my love)… Open the door!'

The unknown presence at the door rattled the handle. There was another drum percussion on the mahogany panels, another hoarse exhortation to let the night of passion begin. Sophie cowered in bed, frozen with horror. Was the door safely locked?

The handle rattled again. 'It's me! I am here! *Ya lublu, mily!*'

Another rattle, more robust this time. Sophie looked around helplessly. What should she do? Scream? Pretend to be asleep? Stay calm and unruffled, and ignore it until they got tired and went away?

Again the voice croaked through the keyhole. *'Celuyu!* (Kiss me!) *Obozhayu!* (Embrace me!) Oh, let me in!'

'Go away!' screamed Sophie, and immediately regretted it; she'd now put the last two options firmly out of the question. She began to panic. *'Go away at once, do you hear?'*

There was a moment's silence, then an outburst of loud, hysterical Russian.

Whoever was out there obviously wasn't going to quietly go away. There was yet another onslaught on the door, louder and even more insistent, and another stream of Russian.

Better ring for the stewardess.

She got out of bed, pulled her silk dressing gown around her, and rang the bell, wondering if an attack of hysterics might deter the unwelcome visitor. Unlikely; whoever was on the other side of the door sounded more than able to outdo her in that department, if the hysteria already in the voice was anything to go by…

What to do until the stewardess arrived? If she didn't open the door, whoever was outside sounded as though they were likely to break it down anyway. The stewardess was on her way and would be here at any moment, so she was in no real danger. She inched open the door warily, and peeped round.

A woman, tall, lanky, dressed in an old-fashioned long black coat with a bright, flowery folk-art headscarf partly obscuring her face scowled back at her.

'Suka! (Bitch!) Slut!' spat the apparition.

Sophie blinked. This was the second time she'd been called a slut on this voyage. But why on earth should this unknown woman launch an unprovoked attack in the middle of the night?

The stranger hadn't finished.

'Who are you? What are you doing here?' she demanded imperiously. The tone became even more threatening. 'Where is he? *Where is he?'*

He? Sophie instinctively went into Countess of Knotworth mode. 'Who are *you*? What are *you* doing here? I don't know

210

who you're looking for, but there is no man in here. This is my suite!'

Her tone was obviously genuinely indignant, the words indisputably the truth. The woman stared at her, frowned at the number on the door, then blinked, her mouth hanging open.

'Oh!' More incomprehensible Russian, then the long pale face unexpectedly broke into a smile. *'Izvinite, izvinite* (I am sorry).'

Sophie, who spoke no Russian, glanced down the corridor - if she'd known the stewardess was going to take this long to arrive she'd never have opened the door - and edged backwards.

Another bout of muttering, then the figure lunged forward and enveloped her in a rib-crushing hug. Overwhelmed by the mixture of vodka fumes and halitosis, Sophie again desperately tried to disentangle herself from the woman's voluminous coat.

'I come to the wrong door! I remember... His room, it is *that* side!' The Russian released her with another bright smile. *'Izvinite!'*

Speechless, Sophie reeled against the door frame. The woman patted her hand reassuringly, then turned and began knocking on Lexie's door instead.

'Milliy moya, my sweet. It's me! Open the door. Let me in!' she hissed through the keyhole.

'Are you lost?' enquired Sophie tactfully. It was obvious the woman needed to be handled with sensitivity, but surely *no* female, however emotionally or mentally disturbed, would knock on Lexie Stonefeather's door from choice? Presumably the poor soul was confused, had lost her way to her own accommodation, and assumed she was speaking to her husband. 'The stewardess will be here in a moment. She will take you back to your suite, to your husband.'

There was a vehement shaking of the head, and more frantic hammering on Lexie's door. A hand flapped in Sophie's direction to quieten her. Sophie looked at her helplessly, and peered along the corridor... Where on earth was the stewardess? Would she never get here?

The woman turned to her.

'I have come to my English lover again. He is asleep...' Another enthusiastic pounding on Lexie's door. 'I wake him... *Milliya moya,* wake up!'

Finally, to Sophie's relief, one of the stewards arrived, hurrying breathlessly down the corridor towards them.

'I'm sorry for the delay, madam,' apologised Billy Saunders. 'The night-duty stewardesses are all busy at present, attending to a pregnant lady who needs help. The doctor is with her. Can I be of assistance to you in the meantime?'

He looked curiously at both women, immediately recognised the tall Russian at Lexie's door, and took a shrewd guess at the cause of the disturbance. Lexie's visitor also recognised Billy. For the second time she put her finger to her mouth, winked, took another sheaf of dollar notes from her pocket, and stuffed them into his mess jacket pocket.

'Sshhh!' she hissed. 'Do not tell my husband again!'

'This lady knocked on my door by mistake,' explained Sophie. This whole thing was rapidly descending from bizarre to surreal. Why was this strange woman stuffing notes in the steward's pocket and asking him not to tell... *again…?*

And that was when things *really* descended from bizarre to surreal. Later, both Sophie and Billy were to describe events from then on as nothing short of farcical.

Lexie Stonefeather, glowering, frowning, sneezing, muttering a stream of profanities, and obviously drunk, stumbled into view around the corner. The Russian saw him and immediately swooped towards him, arms outstretched and coat flapping, bat-like.

'*Lubov!* Darling! I come to you! All day I think of you! We have another night together, *milliy moya!*'

Lexie still couldn't believe what had happened in that effing vicar's stateroom, where instead of relieving the clergyman of his convention money, the clergyman had, with clinically ruthless efficiency, relieved him of his ship's pool money. So

212

this definitely wasn't the moment for a woman he had no desire to see anyway to fling herself all over him.

He shrugged her off and cursed her, the words slurred but venomous.

And as he did so, a towering giant of a man, broad, muscular, mane of black of hair flowing behind a ferocious face, strode down the corridor from the other direction, ignored both Sophie and Billy, and, before either of them realised his intention and could do anything to stop him (not that Billy - or Sophie either, if she was honest - had any desire to do so) swung his fist full into Lexie's jaw.

'You stinking English dog! You think you can impregnate our Russian women, huh? And you think you get no opposition from us Russian men, huh? *You think Russian men stand by and do nothing while you lust after the flower of virtuous Russian womanhood, huh?*'

The words, while laughably melodramatic and theatrical in themselves, nevertheless rang true because of the raw emotion in the man's voice. The accent was rather an attractive blend of French and Russian, thought Sophie, slightly surprised that she should even notice.

Lexie, taken unawares and knocked off balance, gasped as he stumbled against the bulkhead, but before he could right himself the giant was already aiming the next blow; the huge fist made contact with his face a second time, crunching into his right eye.

'I will show you how Russian men protect our women!'

Billy knew he should intervene, and fast. But there are some temptations even the most saintly among us find impossible to resist, and Billy was the first to admit he wasn't up there with the saints. Such blissful moments of revenge happen but rarely in life, and he was going to savour every second of this one; the Russian had done what he'd been itching to do and couldn't, and whereas a ten-a-penny steward would instantly be imprisoned if he dared to touch Lexie Stonefeather, the Purser's Office would have to tread a very diplomatic path in an incident

213

involving a first class passenger mounting an understandable assault against a man who'd slept with his wife - especially as there'd already been a separate complaint made against Mister Stonefeather by another first class passenger regarding his less than gentlemanly behaviour with one of the stewardesses. Fate had provided Billy with a ringside seat for this entertaining spectacle, and he was savouring every moment.

He tried to suppress a grin, exchanged a brief glance with Sophie, and immediately knew there'd be no complaints from her about him not wading in without delay to stop the Russian attacking Lexie Stonefeather.

Lexie's erstwhile admirer was also momentarily stupefied, but quickly recovered and gazed at the giant openmouthed, hands clasped to her bosom in rapturous delight. Lexie obviously having been dismissed completely from mind, she unleashed another torrent of Russian, this time addressing the raven-haired avenger of wronged Russian womanhood. And by this time, Sophie had picked up enough of the language to be able to work out from all the *'milliy moya', 'lobov moya',* and other unmistakeable endearments that it wouldn't be long before marital harmony between the two was fully restored.

She and Billy watched the pair stagger off arm in arm down the corridor, leaving Lexie Stonefeather, equally stunned, slumped against the bulkhead, gingerly patting his right eye and jaw in turn.

'Don't just effing stand there!' he snarled at Billy. This was the second time that steward had stood staring at him with undisguised amused malevolence when he needed help. He began to haul himself upright. 'Help me! And then get the effing doctor!'

'Of course, sir. Straight away.' Billy made a half-hearted attempt to hold out his arm for Lexie to grasp, and then, as the man reached out to clutch it, withdrew it as if it had just occurred to him that fetching the doctor was his most immediate priority. 'Oh. Just at the moment he's attending to a lady who's pregnant, but I'll report what's happened and he'll

214

be with you as soon as possible. Especially as those injuries to your face may be serious, sir.' With luck, he added under his breath.

Lexie's eye was swelling and closing. He sneezed, half expecting to spit out a couple of teeth, and tentatively felt his jaw... at least his teeth all seemed to be in position. But he was beginning to have second thoughts about involving the doctor, which would mean the incident being recorded in some kind of official log book, which in turn meant his amorous adventure with the flower of virtuous Russian womanhood becoming common knowledge. He wished he'd never set eyes on the old crow.

The fewer people who knew about this whole business, the better. They'd be arriving in New York soon anyway, so it might be wiser to lie low, sort out his wounds himself, and make sure he was seen as little as possible, explaining to those he couldn't avoid meeting that he'd stumbled in the bathroom after rather overdoing the whisky in the Smoking Room, so his injuries would be overlooked with a tolerant man-of-the-world smile.

Bad enough the night had been an absolute catastrophe as far as that clergyman was concerned without this assault by a crazed Russian being the talk of the ship. Because as well as losing every last cent of his ship's pool money to that blasted vicar - who'd turned out not to be a vicar at all but an effing card sharp - he'd now have to conduct his important business meetings with a black eye and heavily bruised jaw, like some thug who'd been in a cheap bar brawl.

However...

A cunning look came into his eye. Maybe he could turn the whole thing to his advantage? The Russian was obviously wealthy. If he sued for damages ashore he should more than recoup his losses...

'You needn't bother the doctor,' he decided, in a tone of generous concern for the pregnant woman. 'But I'll be suing that maniac for damages, and you're both witnesses to the fact that he tried to kill me. It was a completely unprovoked attack!'

'Oh believe me, I'll be only too ready to do my duty as a witness,' replied Sophie. Her tone changed. 'But you won't like what I'll say, because I don't agree it was an unprovoked attack. You took advantage of a vulnerable woman.'

'Are you as mad as she is? Vulnerable?! You saw what she was like! *She* was making all the running - *she* was after *me*!'

'Which proves that you took advantage of her vulnerability,' Sophie pointed out coolly. 'The poor lady is obviously emotionally disturbed.'

'She's more than emotionally disturbed, she's raving mad! She thinks she's the Grand Duchess Anastasia!'

'All the more reason not to have taken advantage of her then. Which you must have done, because I distinctly heard her say she was returning for *another* night with you, indicating she'd spent at least one.'

'The effing bat's insane, anyone can see that. She's imagined the whole thing!'

'She didn't look as though she was imagining it. Are you denying that you spent a night with that man's wife?'

'Of course I'm denying it! I've never seen her before in my life! I can't help it if she imagines things!'

Billy cleared his throat.

'Perhaps the knock he gave you caused a bit of concussion and affected your memory, sir? Yesterday morning, when I brought the Early Morning Tea, that lady was in your bedroom. Do you remember now?'

Lexie glared at him. If that blasted Countess of Knotworth wasn't here taking everything in and poking her nose where it wasn't wanted yet again...

'Listen, you effing little... when you join the line-up for tips...' He left the sentence unfinished. Everyone knew stewards relied on tips to make their meagre salary up to a living wage.

Billy said nothing. Mister Stonefeather could see quite plainly from the expression on his face what he could do with his tip.

216

A sudden onset of tiredness hit Lexie like a sledgehammer. The whisky consumed during the session he'd just left, added to what he'd drunk in the preceding hours to throw off his cold, meant his brain was befuddled, unable to function properly; the adrenalin rush had passed, the cold was draining his energy, his eye hurt, his jaw hurt, and all he wanted to do was sleep. He had important meetings tomorrow. He couldn't stand here wasting time with these idiots. He gave Sophie one last insulting leer, and turned away.

'Eff the lot of you, I'm going to bed,' he announced sourly, then had a last minute thought. Johnny Greaves had accidentally knocked a glass of whisky over, and some of it had spilt down his suit, and splashed his shirt.

He glared at Billy again.

'I want these things,' he indicated his suit and shirt, 'Valeted, and sent on to my hotel. And bring some steak for my eye. Hurry up about it, I'm tired!'

He sneezed again, set off unsteadily, then had an afterthought, turned, and narrowed his eyes at Billy. 'My navy blue suit and everything all ready for going ashore?'

For the first time since he'd come aboard, he saw the steward become almost animated. Definitely a spark of willingness in his eye. The threat of not getting a tip had obviously done the trick. (Not that he'd be getting one!)

'Oh yes, sir,' Billy assured him, nodding respectfully. 'Your navy blue suit is all ready and waiting for you in the wardrobe.'

The well-groomed look for today's dapper man-about-town. So absolutely *you,* Mister Stonefeather!

217

9

Joey Smith took off his chef's whites and hung them by his bunk as usual.

Normally he'd have washed them first, because he was running out. He'd only been able to afford three. They weren't provided, even with an advance; you had to supply your own before you signed on for the voyage.

But who cared about unwashed whites tonight.

He stuffed the letter he'd written earlier into the bottom of Danny's bunk, where it would be found when the bedding was stripped after the ship docked. Only one letter, and that was short and to the point. As far as everyone else was concerned, actions spoke louder than words, and let them make whatever they wanted of it. There'd be no heart-wrenching final letter for Clara. They'd said all they needed to say to each other in Southampton, before the ship sailed.

Nobody else would miss him. His parents had died in the Spanish flu epidemic, and his only other relative was an older brother, also seagoing. They'd never been close.

But he and Danny went back a long way, and he owed his friend this at least.

Also, he wanted the pay he was due up to tonight to go to Clara. It wasn't much; it was the gesture, rather than the amount itself, that was important to him. So he'd asked Danny in his letter that, should Alec Baxter claim what was due on Clara's behalf as her future husband, whilst acknowledging that Danny wouldn't have any influence regarding private and personal matters between the purser's office and the dead man's former fiancée, he would nevertheless make this known among his shipmates. Alec Baxter wouldn't have it all his own way.

And he'd asked him to visit Clara in Southampton and make sure she knew, as well. It mattered to him; it was important. The actual amount may be laughable when compared to Alec Baxter's superior wages, but he still wanted her to know he'd done his best to ensure it went to her, not her future husband.

As for his whites, whoever wanted them could have them. There was nothing else to leave, and no one else he wanted to write to.

Then, as everything had to appear normal, and it was important that as far as all the rest of the occupants of the glory hole were concerned he was fast asleep in his bunk, he climbed in, pulled his blanket over his ears as usual to muffle the incessant noise of the propeller and the sounds made by the others as they got ready for bed, and waited.

There was no danger of him drifting off to sleep in the intervening hours, although his mind was calm, composed, and, at last, free from all worry and stress. He'd come to the decision a while ago, but wanted to confirm it in his heart as well as his head; to be completely sure. And now he was.

He quietly got out of bed, padded out of the glory hole, and made his way up on deck. The place was deserted, as he'd known it would be at two o'clock in the morning. The look-out was on duty of course, but look-outs can't train their eyes in every direction at once, and anyway there were blind spots if you knew where they were. As for anyone else turning up, there was no need for any explanation beyond a mumbled comment about not being able to sleep and wanting a smoke.

He looked at the reflection of the ship's dimmed lights as she ploughed on through the inky sea. Everything was quiet now; the sounds of music and laughter from the first class passengers' Farewell Party had long since died away, and everyone had retired to their suites and staterooms. Or other people's suites and staterooms, as the case may be. Well, good for them. No doubt in steerage the immigrants had also held their own farewell party, but for different reasons.

Well, as this was a night for farewell parties, why not hold one of his own? And why not invite himself as guest of honour?

'Lovely to see you, Joey. So glad you could come. What'll you have? Champagne? Sure! Help yourself! So anyway, how's things? I understand you're leaving for what might be called pastures new?'

'Yes, that's right. Time to be off.'

'Oh, that's too bad, Joey. What does Clara think about it?'

'Well, you'd have to ask her that. When she actually gets to know about it. But then, you'd be lucky if she finds time to answer, what with the wedding coming up and all.'

'I didn't know you'd set the date, Joey. Congratulations!'

'Oh, not to me. No, she's going to be Mrs Alec Baxter.'

'But... But I thought...'

'So did I. So did she. But that was before Alec decided he wanted her, and as you know Joey, what Alec wants, Alec gets. So he raped her. Couple of months ago now. She's pregnant, of course.'

'Oh no!

'Oh yes.'

'How that must have hurt you, Joey.'

'Well yes. Not quite how I'd expected things to work out.'

'It must have preyed on your mind very heavily, Joey... You kept it quiet, didn't you?'

'Too true. There's enough gossip about it at home, without half the ship tittle-tattling about it as well.'

'Well, I can understand that. Some things are too private, too deep, to be fodder for other people's gossip... Oh, your glass is empty, Joey. More champagne? Canapés? Or how about some of Mister Smith's celebrated smoked sturgeon?' (Danny had related the tale as they'd shaved a couple of days ago; they'd both laughed at the notion of only Mister Smith's creations being acceptable to Lexie, whose proud boast it was that the man who could pull a fast one on him had yet to be born.)

'Thanks. He's certainly a whizz with the smoked sturgeon, Mister Smith, isn't he?'

'Oh, all those things and more. Such a nice bloke as well. Handsome, too. But to come back to what you were saying... couldn't you marry her and bring up the child as your own?'

'Sounds such a simple solution, doesn't it. Of course I would if he'd left her. But good ole' Alec's got that covered; he's threatened to kill her and the child rather than let anyone else - in other words, me - have either of them. And she knows he means it.'

'He's evil. I'm surprised you haven't laid him out before now. Why haven't you, Joey?'

'Another simple solution, eh? I held myself back, for two very good reasons. The first is, that's exactly what he's been waiting for. I wouldn't give him the satisfaction of seeing me dragged down to the hold and chained up, then losing my job, and prison, which is just what he wants. The second one is, I'd half kill him gladly if it was just me that got half killed in return. But it's not as simple as that, as you know. I don't want him using his fists on her on my account.'

'I can well believe he'd knock her around, Joey.'

'Oh, that's only the half of it. Alec Senior just happens to be the landlord of most of the houses in the street. Clara's dad's unemployed - he got shell-shock in the trenches, and it damaged his head - her mum's frantic with worry, there's two younger ones, and they've got nowhere to go if they get kicked out. If she does things Alec's way, they all get to stay in the house. She and Alec move in next door. All one big happy family, eh?'

'If you ask me, Joey, he sounds the sort of bully who'd kick them out anyway if he had a mind to, whether she married him or not. I wouldn't trust him as far as I could throw him.'

'I don't.'

'The other thing is, Joey, people will call you a coward if you go ahead with this.'

'I don't doubt it. Let them. Some of them will feel sorry for me as well; shake their heads and say, 'Poor Joey. Loser in life, wasn't he?' Well, they can keep their opinions to themselves. It's nobody's business but mine what I do with my own life.'

221

'But they'll say you couldn't have been much of a man if you didn't stay and fight for her.'

'I know that as well. They'll say all sorts of things. I did fight. I lost. Simple as that. I tried everything I could. And I'd carry on fighting if it'd do any good. But she won't let her family be hurt. There's no way round it without him causing more pain than he already has.'

'But all this noble stepping aside... that's not the way to handle it, surely.'

'No, it probably isn't. If I was cleverer, or richer, or had more clout, maybe I'd have handled it better. Then again, maybe not, I don't know. One thing I do know, she's made up her mind to marry him. And she won't change it.'

'How can you be so sure?'

'Because he's got that all sewn up as well. The shame angle - fingers pointing at her, the fallen woman. She's the local Jezebel now. He's made sure everyone knows she's in the family way and he's the father, who wants to do the right thing by her, stand by her in her shame. The kind-hearted rough diamond who's doing the honourable thing.'

'That must really stick in your craw, Joey!'

'It does. Because the minute she opens her mouth about him raping her - not that she'd be believed - the rest of them start piling what few belongings they've got on to a wheelbarrow and head for the workhouse.'

'Oh, it's not called the workhouse now, Joey.'

'All right, the "poor law institution". To all intents and purposes it's the workhouse, and they know it.'

'But Joey, tragic as it is, is it worth...?'

'Here's the fact of the matter. If she turns Alec down, the whole lot of them will be vagrants. I've gone over and over all the options until I can't think straight, because there aren't any. As for tragic, Joey, well, it's just the way things are. I've been thinking a lot lately, and you know what conclusion I've come to?'

'No, what?'

'Life's more trouble than it's worth.'

'Don't ever say that, Joey!'

'Why not? It's the truth.'

'But you never know what's round the corner.'

'Look Joey, I know you mean well and all that, but there aren't any corners in the ocean. It's straight down.'

'But wouldn't you like to have one last word with Clara before deciding...?'

'No.'

'But have you really thought this through, Joey?'

'Yes.'

'But...'

'But nothing. Well, nice chatting to you, Joey, but I must be getting along.'

'Is this really what you want to do?

'It is. Thanks for the farewell party, Joey.'

'Pleasure's all mine, Joey. Well... All the best then, if your mind's made up.'

'It is.'

'You're sure?'

'Quite sure.'

'Nothing I can say to make you change it?'

'I think you've already said everything there is to say, haven't you, Joey.'

'But I hate to finish on such a sad note...'

'Me too. Don't let's, then. No point in toasting the future, but I tell you what Joey, I really enjoyed that smoked sturgeon. Best I've ever tasted! My compliments to the multi-talented... the irreplaceable... the one and only... Mister Smith!'

The lights twinkling from the stern of the ship grew fainter, and the noise of the engines and propeller screws gradually gave way to the gentle swish of the sea's surface waves. Joey allowed the movement of the sea to flip him over, swimming a few strokes before turning onto his back again to watch the ship, visible now only when the swell lifted him.

223

Surprisingly, the water wasn't as cold as he'd expected it to be. He vaguely remembered being told about someone who'd fallen in next to an ice floe, yet found the water quite warm; apparently it depended on the drift of the Arctic current or the Gulf Stream. Gradually, however, the cold began to seep into him, but with it came a sort of detached indifference to the fact that there was no shout of alarm from the ship, no searchlight scanning the water, no lifeboat launched to rescue him. He was alone. Just him, the sea, and the night sky with its broken cloud obscuring the moon from time to time (the ship no longer counted), and yet instead of the terror he'd expected to feel, it seemed his very helplessness, and the fact that there was no longer any point in fretting about the best course of action to take, because he was no longer in any position to take any action at all, brought its own respite from worry.

A small wave sloshed across his face. He instinctively spat out a mouthful of salt water, and took another gulp of cool night air, imagining the uproar if he'd been seen; the liner, having almost crossed the Atlantic, would now have to stop to search for some stupid kitchen worker who'd gone and fallen overboard, inconveniencing everyone with a delay while the engines went from Full Ahead to Stop, and they lowered a boat, carried out the search, and picked him up.

'Don't bother. It'd inconvenience me a lot more to be dragged back on board than it would you,' he told the silvery wake which was still visible when the moon put in an appearance.

Another wave lifted him, and he saw the ship, further away now, her lights fading in the undulating horizon. The cold seeped relentlessly into his body, slowing the instinctive swimming motions his arms and legs made as he lay on his back.

He had no regrets, no second thoughts. It was as he said - just the way things were. Some lives were long, some were short; his was finishing right here. And he couldn't care less.

And yet it seemed appropriate to mark it in some way, so that his time on earth had been of some relevance, if only to him. If

224

he'd died from natural causes ashore, a Requiem Mass would be said for him. *Requiescat in pace* - 'May he rest in peace.' Well, that was all he wanted now, to rest in peace. Strange how the Latin always came back...

Vague memories from his Catholic childhood floated into consciousness just as he felt that consciousness gradually beginning to fade - Sunday Mass, Catechism, prayers learned by rote, the Irish priest in his horrible long black dress who knew everything about everyone and glared at you if you were late for Mass... and the knowledge, drummed into you with the rest of the never-ending list of do's-and-don'ts, that suicide was a sin. A cardinal sin. A sin that was beyond all forgiveness, because you were throwing God's gift of life back in His face.

Well, he'd committed it now. It was too late to change his mind, too late to say he was sorry. Anyway, that wouldn't be true; he wasn't sorry. If there turned out to be a God and he was about to be judged... well, he'd long since turned his back on church and religion, and he was honest enough to admit that it was a bit late to come crawling back to God now his life was about to end and judgement awaited. So he'd just have to say, 'I'm sorry God, I'm afraid I just didn't believe in you. And life, a gift? Well, I didn't want your gift. I found the whole thing more trouble than it was worth. Could I maybe swap with someone else, give them my life - well not *my* life obviously, but could someone who actually wants to live, but who faces death at the very same moment as me, have life instead of me?'

So - no Requiem Mass, no priest mumbling Latin over his coffin. Not that he'd have a coffin anyway. Just the sea. So he'd do it himself: he'd commit his soul to God, if God existed, in the four or five minutes or so of life he had left.

He said it aloud, without feeling foolish or self-conscious, because there was nobody around to hear him. No fancy words, no long rambling prayers, just the truth from his heart: 'Here's my soul, God, if you're there; I entrust it to you. I'm sorry I've made such a mess of my life. And I'm sorry for any hurt I've caused people during it. And no hard feelings on my side for

225

Alec Baxter; just the way things worked out, I guess. And, er, if you do happen to exist, God… er, Jesus…? I could do with you being here right now, because I don't think I'm going to like the next few minutes very much.'

And as he said the words, he knew beyond all doubt that the rules and rigmarole that had been made so much of - which he suddenly saw quite clearly had had the effect of preventing him from getting to know God instead of learning to trust Him as a loving father and caring friend - were not what God was about at all. For other people, those things may well be the way. But not for him. For him, regulations and rituals weren't where God was. God was right here, right now, on the ocean with him. He knew it without the slightest doubt; he'd never been more certain of anything in his life.

How strange to feel such utter certainty *now*, of all times, when he only had a few minutes of that life left! And how unbearably sad that he'd never experienced it before, when life was ahead of him and it wasn't too late to actually benefit from it - and to realise that by turning away for so many years from all the off-putting surface flaws and defects, he'd deprived himself of the riches hidden far beneath…

And it was in that moment the thought came to him, like a spotlight suddenly throwing light on something he'd known deep down but hadn't realised until now - what he wanted was not the end of life itself, but the end of the life he was living at present. He didn't want to be a chef on the *Berengaria*, he didn't want to go back to England, and to his surprise he realised he didn't even want Clara any more. He'd felt sorry for her, and he was fond of her, and they'd sort of drifted together because she was an obvious choice for a wife, but he didn't really love her. He never had.

And then he knew something else: it wasn't his time to die. And that he'd been forgiven for throwing God's gift of life back in His face and saying He could keep it, it was more trouble than it was worth. Because he was overwhelmed by the most surprising sense of utter peace, and deep tranquillity.

Something brushed against his hand - a gentle touch, not frightening, not threatening, but solid and tangible. The moon was hidden behind another cloud so it was difficult to see properly, but as he reached curiously towards it he realised it was the branch of a small tree that had presumably been uprooted and washed out to sea from some river, perhaps in a storm. He groped his way to the trunk. It hadn't been in the water long; it was strong, and it floated.

The moon came out from behind the cloud, and it was then that he saw it - a small bobbing light away to his right, which meant to the north. A fishing craft, probably. And although he was cold and stiff, he knew there'd be enough strength left in his limbs to swim towards it, because it felt as though he was being carried along by some invisible current in the direction of the boat.

As he got within calling range, and his strength finally gave out, and the tree started to lose its buoyancy, he saw the name emblazoned in large letters on the stern.

She was called *'The Kindly Light'*.

SIX: ARRIVAL

1

At long last, thought Elsie as she splashed her face and cleaned her teeth. Almost the end of this nightmare.

Was it worth trying to find out about jobs in America while she was here?

But how and where did you find out about things like that, apart from hopefully seeing adverts ashore? She couldn't risk asking the other stewardesses, who all seemed to get on better with the Chief Stewardess than she did. They might report it. The Chief Stewardess regarded it a privilege to work for Cunard, and would view any desire to leave as the ultimate disloyalty, which could be dangerous because until she got another job she couldn't afford to leave this one, no matter how much she detested it.

And would she be granted entry to America? She knew that before 1914 there'd been a million steerage passengers a year, but numbers were restricted now. There was no longer an unlimited choice of jobs for those seeking a blank canvas and a new beginning.

Anyway, she had to return to England. She'd signed on at Southampton, and that was where she'd be discharged. The term 'voyage' meant, for the crew, a double-passage, out and home; other than in exceptional circumstances you couldn't just decide to jump ship in New York. But did she continue as a stewardess and hope she'd learn to cope with seasickness, as many other seafarers had to do, or... or what? Or nothing, because she already knew what the alternatives were: low-grade skivvying or factory work.

She dried her face, and headed to the kitchens. Better hurry, or she'd be late for the Early Morning Tea Run. Again. No point in antagonising the Chief Stewardess more than she had already, or there mightn't even be the option of re-signing on the *Berengaria*, whether she wanted to or not.

But in the kitchens, shocking and terrible news awaited.

One of the commis chefs had jumped over the side during the night.

Elsie knew the missing man by sight, and she knew his name, Joey Smith. He was nondescript, insignificant, didn't stand out in a crowd; you'd hardly notice him. But he was kindly. And he was a friend of Danny's.

And Danny was making sure that everyone knew what Alec Baxter had done to Joey's fiancee. He'd discovered a letter from Joey at the foot of his bunk, and it was taking all Billy Saunders' strength to restrain him from flaying Alec Baxter senseless with his fists.

'Leave it, Danny, it's not worth it,' Billy was saying, to try and calm him, while Danny - Danny, who wouldn't kill a fly - struggled to free himself and leave Alec as dead as his friend might have been. 'Especially as Joey's been saved.'

He was right. Tragedy had been averted.

A wireless message had been received, informing the *Berengaria* that a member of the crew had been picked up by a fishing vessel, and was alive.

2

A sullen, uncomfortable quiet pervaded the kitchens. There was none of the usual irreverent banter between waiters and chefs, and Danny's fury was still raging as preparations took place for Luncheon.

Things had to come to a head. And they did.

Danny had started a whip-round to help pay Joey's costs while ashore. He guessed that one of the men from the fishing vessel would be caring for him in his home until he'd recovered, and knew, if that was the case, that Joey would want to reimburse the man and his family, as well as show appreciation to the rest of the crew.

Alec Baxter, face uncharacteristically blotchy, approached Danny to offer his contribution.

'Go to hell,' spat Danny. 'I don't want it.'

'Look, I didn't know he was going to something like that.'

'What did you think he was going to do? Appear at the wedding and give her away, with his blessing?'

Alec looked at the floor. 'Like I've said, Danny, I want to contribute -'

'And like I've said, go to hell. You've put Joey there often enough, try experiencing it yourself!'

Alec's voice was quiet. 'I have done.' He looked at the hostile faces next to Danny. 'No matter what he said in the letter, I didn't rape her, and that's the truth.'

'Why would he say you did, then?'

'I don't know. I didn't know she'd told him that. I thought she'd just told him she wanted to finish. Maybe she felt guilty about the fact she got pregnant, and it was easier to tell him I raped her? Maybe she felt guilty about breaking off the engagement? I don't know why she told him that, but it isn't

231

true. She was more than willing, whatever he says, and my conscience is clear..'

'*Your conscience is clear?* I don't believe I'm hearing this!' Danny's voice was scornful. 'He said you'd threatened to kill her and the baby rather than let him have either of them!'

'That's rubbish, and before you ask me I don't know why she said that either. All right, I'm a bit possessive, but -'

'That why you knock her about then, is it?'

'I've never hit her, and that's the truth as well.' Alec sighed heavily. 'Look. Leave Clara out of it. That's not why I'm feeling bad about all this. It's the way I treated Joey that's bothering me -'

'Yeah. I think it bothered Joey a bit as well. Why d'you think he jumped over the side?'

'Look, Danny. I can't put right what's happened, but at least I can say I'm sorry and try to make amends to him. If Clara really wants to marry him, I wouldn't stand in her way, and I'd take care of the child financially -'

'Oh, that's very decent of you. So Joey can look after the bastard you've given her, can he? With all the neighbours laughing at him for being so stupid?'

'*Will you pipe down and let me finish!* You've made your feelings clear enough, now it's my turn. I've told you, it wasn't rape, no matter what he says, or what she says!'

One of the bystanders snorted in derision. Alec faced them.

'It's the truth. I'm no rapist, whatever she told him. And he's wrong about me holding homelessness over her as a threat, as well. I've been thinking about that a lot, and I've come up with a way that will prove it's a lie - to her, to Joey, to everyone else, and most importantly, to me.' He nodded. 'I'll prove it, once and for all. I'll get my dad to make the deeds of the two houses over to her. He won't like it, but he'll do it. *She'll* own the house, and the one next door for her mum and dad and brothers and sisters.'

He turned back to Danny, who obviously didn't believe a word.

'And you can take that look off your face, Danny. I admit I wouldn't go giving houses away willy-nilly ordinarily, but the thought that Joey tried to end his life because of the way I treated him - well, that's something I don't want on my conscience. All the other stuff, the Clara side of things, that isn't on it because none of it's true except for the fact she's pregnant, and it's mine, and I proposed, and she accepted, and she told me she'd break it off with Joey. That's it. She's made up the rest, or exaggerated it out of all proportion. I don't know why. But I haven't threatened them with homelessness - and there's the proof.'

'Aye aye!' Danny's tone was scathing. 'The big, powerful, rich landlord, buying your way out of trouble because you've got more money than him?'

'Well what else would you have me do?' Alec shook his head. 'I'm trying my best to put things right, so think about it before you tell me to stuff my contribution, Danny. Three people have been given second chances here; Joey; Clara, because she could sell the house and move away for a fresh start with Joey and the baby, if that's she really wants; and me. And I'm taking mine. I want to see Joey while we're ashore, to -'

'Here we go again. *You* want? What about what *he* wants? You think he wants to see you? The whole point of him going over the side was to get away from you before he battered you senseless and you made sure the rest of his life was ruined because of it. Now *you want* to see him, he's still supposed to jump to your command, is he? Well, he's ashore, he's his own man, he's not under your authority now, and he doesn't have to listen to -'

Alec interrupted. 'Yes, all right, I admit I was wrong to goad him. But all the Clara rubbish about rape and homelessness and knocking her about was just that. Rubbish. And that's the truth. It's how I was with Joey I want to put right. That's why I want the chance -'

Danny was losing patience. 'Yeah, to wheedle him into forgiving you, let's be best mates Joey, let bygones be bygones, it was just one of those things, me just happening to get your fiancee pregnant while you -'

One of the senior chefs finally stepped in.

'That's enough! Joey's been saved, and that's the end of it. Sort this out between you in your own time. Preferably ashore.' He turned to Danny. 'You. Get back to work.'

Regardless of whether half the crew jumped overboard and the entire catering department needed to unburden crises of conscience, the ship's standards had to be maintained, and first class passengers tempted to toy with today's range of choice on the *Carte du Jour* Luncheon menu.

Chefs had to get on with preparing it, waiters had to get on with fetching it, and nothing was allowed to get in the way of it.

Like the man said, that was enough.

3

'It's the busiest time of the trip for the Ladies' Hairdressers,' announced Mary, 'But I've managed to get an appointment.'

She frowned at her hair in the mirror. She'd always considered a Marcel Wave an extravagant and unnecessary waste of money and done her best with a sort of poor-relation attempt at finger waves, but now they'd won the ship's pool... well, why not luxuriate in the most magnificent hairdressers she'd ever seen?

She turned and scrutinised Sam.

'You want to get yersel' along to the barber's an' all, get spruced up for when we go ashore. You cannae meet somebody with a name like Sylvia looking like a scruff!'

It was a long time since they'd seen their son, and she wanted them both to look smart for the occasion. He'd met a nice girl in America, and things were getting serious. Sylvia had written to them herself, popping her letter in with one of Michael's, saying how much she was looking forward to meeting them and showing them around her home town. Mary couldn't wait to meet her prospective daughter-in-law and her family, wanted to make a good impression, and wanted Michael to be proud of his parents.

'Anyone would think I was one o' thae prehistoric ape things, tae hear you talk!' grumbled Sam.

'Aw, ye're no' exactly that bad,' conceded Mary.

'Gee, thanks!'

'But we're no' turning up looking like a pair o' hooligans after a rough night in Sauchiehall Street, so get yersel' doon there!'

Sam muttered under his breath that it was worse than being in the Army, but Mary was adamant, and off they set, she to the hairdresser, he to the barber.

But the barber's was full, and couldn't fit him in, so Sam wandered off to fill in time until Mary could trim his hair herself with the scissors she'd brought with her 'just in case'. Just in case of what, he never worked out, but since she'd packed half of everything they owned he might as well make use of them, because she'd cut his hair with those scissors all these years and it had been good enough for him - and Michael - up until now. In any case, she'd be paying top whack in that fancy hairdresser's. Better to keep what was left in reserve to make sure they had enough for when they actually got to America. He didn't want Michael stumping up for everything; he wanted to be able to hold his head high, stand his round, pay his way, and not sponge off anyone while they were there.

And as he'd never been in a gymnasium before - he'd always got enough exercise at the shipyard, as well as the walk to and from work - the thought occurred that he may as well have a go while he was still on board, where everything was provided, from horizontal and parallel bars to fencing sticks, boxing gloves, punch balls, horse-riding machines, and even camel-riding machines.

The gymnastic instructor welcomed him. This was the quietest morning for the gymnasium; most people were packing, doing last-minute shopping, visiting the ship's bank, enquiring at the purser's office about future travel arrangements or hotel bookings, or up on deck awaiting their first sight of the awe-inspiring New York skyline.

'What would you like to try, sir?' he offered.

Sam was at a loss. The only thing he recognised were boxing gloves and the punch ball, which he indicated with a shrug.

The gymnastic instructor was a garrulous individual, and as he fixed the gloves on Sam's hands and stepped back for him to take the first swing at the punch ball, he chatted about the other apparatus available. How about sampling fencing, for instance?

236

'Aye, all right, why no'?' agreed Sam, taking his eye off the punch ball for the one vital fraction of a second that it mattered. It caught him in the eye.

So not only had he failed to get his hair cut, he'd end up with a black eye, which should impress the prospective in-laws no end when introductions were made: 'And this is my Dad...' Unspoken information: the hooligan who's spent a few too many rough nights in Sauchiehall Street.

Which meant that not only would he be told in no uncertain terms that the engagement was now off (not that she'd part with the ring, of course), he'd probably end up celebrating his Golden Wedding with a divorce as well.

4

Lexie slept through the morning and awoke to find his cold worse than ever, which meant that he had no sense of smell. He decided to go to the dining saloon for lunch - he'd long since missed breakfast, and although if he wished he could have whatever he wanted brought to his suite, he wasn't in the mood to see that steward again.

So he ran his own bath and, after a brisk scrub, donned his clean underwear, crisp white shirt, waistcoat, navy blue suit, and shining shoes, and sauntered up to the dining saloon.

However, aware that his black eye and bruised jaw may be cause for comment and possibly even the odd ribald snigger should any of his Smoking Room pals spot him, he decided to keep a low profile. And he'd make sure he kept well clear of Madam Rasputin (if she'd told him she was Rasputin's sister instead of Grand Duchess Anastasia he'd have believed her, because she was a walking female version of the mad monk, minus the beard) and her maniac husband, even though he hadn't seen either of them in the dining saloon throughout the voyage so far. They were like vampires, seemed to only come out at night.

So he chose a more secluded table from his usual one, which meant a different waiter.

Tony was a Liverpudlian, and hadn't been on the ship long. He politely held the chair as Lexie sat down, trying not to grimace; the guy stank to high heaven. If waiters were expected to keep themselves clean and smart with their limited washing facilities (and a bucket to wash the uniforms which were always expected to be spotless), you'd think someone in the lap of first class luxury, with stewards running baths and full valeting services whenever required, could manage to wash themselves now and again.

Lexie sniffed, snuffled, sneezed, perused the *carte du jour* Luncheon Menu, and decided on smoked sturgeon to start.

'Smoked sturgeon,' he ordered. 'And I have it done especially for me by Mister Smith.'

Tony looked at him, puzzled. 'Mister Smith?'

'Yes, *Mister Smith*. The chap who does it for a Romanoff prince. I don't want anyone else doing it.'

Tony might be inexperienced, but he knew better than to open his mouth when he wasn't sure how much it was wise to say. Or not say, as the case may be. He knew nothing about Mister Smith doing special smoked sturgeon for Romanoff princes. Did this smelly individual mean Joey, who churned them out for whoever wanted them? And if so, did he explain that, er, unfortunately Mister Smith wasn't here today, without getting obvious reply: 'What d'you mean, not here? He can't have gone far, can he? The ship's still at sea!'

Or did he nod obediently, bring a common-or-garden smoked sturgeon done by Joey's replacement, Howard Langton, and hope for the best? But if he did, would the man know someone else had done it, because Joey's smoked sturgeon had some special characteristic that he'd recognise? And would he then complain that the waiter had got above himself and not heeded his specific instructions?

'I'll put a special request in with the *poissonnier* about it, sir.'

Better get clarification about this from higher up. Especially after this morning's news about Joey Smith.

'Bloke out there wants his smoked sturgeon done by, er, Mister Smith, who does them in some special way for Romanoff princes,' he informed Alec Baxter in the kitchens.

Danny, who had just arrived through the 'In' swing door, pricked up his ears, groaned inwardly, and willed the *entremetier* to get a move on with the *Potage Dauphine*.

'Mister Smith?' repeated Alec suspiciously.

'Yes.'

239

'...And he does smoked sturgeon in some special way for Romanoff princes?'

'Yes. That's what he said.'

Danny shuffled uncomfortably, and fixed his gaze on one of the chefs in the furthest part of the kitchen.

'What's he talking about? It's done exactly the same way for everyone!'

'Well, he says he doesn't want it done by anyone else.'

Alec narrowed his eyes at Tony. First he'd heard about Mister Smith doing special smoked sturgeon for Romanoff princes. What had been going on here?

Danny became aware of Alec's head turning towards him, and felt a sudden penetrating stare. He determinedly avoided eye contact.

Tony felt it might be wise to give a bit more information.

'I don't think he's all there, to be honest. He keeps staring round the room, all shifty. Well, he does with the eye he can actually see out of - someone's given him a good poke in the other one, from the look of it. And a good sock in the jaw. And I don't think he's had a wash since he's come on board - he stinks like cheese that went off a week ago.'

'Don't you be cheeky about the passengers,' Alec rebuked him automatically, his mind more on whatever jiggery-pokery had been going on under his nose and had inadvertently just come to light. Smoked sturgeon... Romanoff princes?

Danny's *Potage Dauphine* arrived. He took it without a word, and hurried through the 'Out' swing door before it could occur to Alec to ask where the passenger usually sat, and which waiter had attended him until now.

Alec watched him thoughtfully.

'Who's his usual waiter?'

'Danny,' said Tony.

Danny. He knew it.

If this had happened yesterday, both Joey Smith and Danny would have had a D/R in their Discharge Books. But things had changed...

He called an instruction to Howard Langton.

'*Oui,* chef,' acknowledged Howard, and busily set to work.

'Tell the passenger,' said Alec slowly, with what Tony later described as a very old-fashioned look on his face, 'That Mister Smith's smoked sturgeon is indeed fit for Romanoff princes... but unfortunately he's indisposed at present (there was no need to elaborate either on the nature of Mister Smith's indisposition, or his whereabouts while he was indisposed), so the *poissonnier* will personally ensure the finished result is of a standard that is equally acceptable.' There was a slight pause. 'That's all.'

5

It was always difficult to keep to the routine on the last morning of the trip. And especially difficult on this occasion, because a Do Not Disturb notice hung outside Lexie's door all morning, so it was only when he went for lunch that Billy and old Reg could gain access.

When they did, Reg's language, normally free of blasphemy of any kind, came near to matching Lexie's, quickly followed by a gasp of horror when he remembered that Elsie was working within earshot in the suite opposite. He sniffed the fetid air and surveyed the germ-ridden handkerchiefs strewn all over the opulent red carpet.

'The stink in here! I've never smelt anything like it! It's as if he's released a canister of nerve gas!' He sniffed again. 'Has he been hoarding cheese in here, or what?'

Billy smiled to himself and said nothing.

'And as for throwing these filthy things all over the place…'

Billy shrugged. 'True to form to the last.'

'I hadn't realised how bad it would be in here!' Reg shook his head. 'That carpet will have to be replaced before anyone else can use the room. And all the paintwork re-done, since he's somehow even managed to chip that. It'll need new curtains, too, because they'll never get these properly clean. And how we're going to get rid of that terrible cheesy smell, I don't know. The place will have to be fumigated.'

'And disinfected,' added Billy. 'It's full of germs. He's got a cold.' He opened the door to create a draught and allow the contaminated air to escape.

'A cold?!' exclaimed Reg, knees creaking as he bent to collect the array of dirty handkerchiefs left for the steward to pick up and the laundry crew to wash. 'I hope he's got bubonic plague!' He hastily modified his wish. 'I mean, as long as *I* don't get it from these things!'

Billy, motioning the old man upright and gathering the handkerchiefs in his place, made no comment. The more old Reg, who'd been with Cunard for more years than anyone could remember, expressed his revulsion at the state of Lexie Stonefeather's suite, the less importance would be attached to any last-ditch complaint Lexie might still decide to make about Billy Saunders.

'Cunard won't have made much money out of this one,' went on Reg. 'In fact it'll probably cost them more than he's paid in his fare to put it right.' He watched Billy throw the handkerchiefs in a large canvas laundry bag. 'I know his sort. If I was a betting man, Billy, I'd say don't hold your breath for a tip, because there won't be one.' He shook his head again. '*Nobody'll* get a tip out of this one!'

But for once, old Reg was wrong.

6

Lexie finished his lunch, dabbed his mouth with his Irish linen napkin, sneezed, dabbed his mouth and nose again, pressed a small tip into Tony's hand, and detoured across the dining saloon to speak to Danny.

Danny, heading to the kitchen with an armful of empty plates and the order for a couple of dowagers' dessert courses, looked at him, surprised.

'This,' announced Lexie grandly, stuffing a ten pound note into his breast pocket, 'Is for you! A little token of appreciation for getting my smoked sturgeon done by that guy who does them for the Romanoff prince!'

Danny tried not to gag at the smell emanating from Lexie's suit and willed him to keep his voice down, glancing apprehensively at the Head Waiter who, fortunately, was engrossed in conversation with a middle aged couple near the entrance.

'Oh... There's no need, sir. It was a pleasure.'

'No, it made all the difference.' Lexie shook his head dismissively. 'That one I had today was nowhere near as good. Not the same standard at all.'

Again Danny glanced at the Head Waiter, whose attention was still fully taken up with the couple. He began edging politely away, body language clearly indicating that much as he'd love to stand talking to Lexie, he was obliged to make his first priority getting to the kitchens and collecting the next order.

'Well, I'm surprised to hear that, sir.'

'Oh, I'm not one to make a fuss,' shrugged Lexie, oblivious to the hint. 'Not my style to complain about anything. Easy-going sort of guy, that's me.'

'Just as long as everything is to your satisfaction, sir,' murmured Danny, continuing to edge towards the kitchens. Thank heavens Lexie was pouring out all this bilge to him, and nobody else! But he couldn't relax, because if the couple who'd collared the Head Waiter moved off just as Lexie drew alongside, and he decided to continue praising Joey Smith's skills to a higher authority...

'Yes. I hear he's indisposed, by the way?'

'Er, yes, sir.'

'Well, I always make a point of rewarding good service. Pass this on to him with my compliments and best wishes for a speedy recovery, will you.'

Well aware that a generous tip would be discussed between staff - and cause maximum humiliation to Billy Saunders, who wouldn't be getting one - Lexie pushed another ten pound note into Danny's pocket.

'I will indeed sir. Most kind. Thank you!' nodded Danny as Lexie sneezed again, turned, and marched from the dining saloon, trailing a smell of rancid cheese behind him.

Daphne and Theodore, explaining at great length to the Head Waiter why they felt it preferable to make their gratuity direct to him in order to provide educational benefits for the waiters, broke off, took in Lexie's black eye and bruised jaw, and wrinkled their noses in disgust as he passed.

'That *dreadful* man!' grimaced Daphne with an eloquent sniff, 'Look! He's been *fighting* with someone!'

'So he has,' observed Theodore. 'Well, let's hope he got the worst of the encounter.'

The Head Waiter stood politely, knowing any conjecture about Lexie's injuries would merely be a temporary interruption to the matter in hand.

'Anyway,' Daphne returned to her theme, which, on balance, was of greater immediate interest than Lexie's black eye (they could find out the details about that later). 'As we were saying - it might be a rather novel idea to provide some communal mind-improving facility such as the Encyclopaedia Britannica

245

for *all* the waiters to browse through during their leisure hours, rather than bestowing money on individuals to squander on whatever dubious pastimes may appeal when they go ashore.'

The Head Waiter diplomatically suggested that individual waiters might prefer the freedom to use any gratuities passengers wished to give as they chose; for example they may prefer to supplement their income for their families, to whom a set of the Encyclopaedia Britannica on board the *Berengaria* at sea would be of little benefit.

'I take your point,' acknowledged Theodore. 'Nevertheless, one wouldn't want it on one's conscience if - shall we say, the more unworldly among them - were lured by the more morally corrupt into spending money on questionable pleasures ashore.'

He caught sight of Danny, grinning from ear to ear at apparently nothing as he resumed his journey to the kitchens.

'Now there's a case in point.' Theodore nodded towards him. 'That fellow, smiling vacantly at the world as he goes about his tasks; he's the sort of guileless innocent I mean. I do feel we have a moral responsibility to protect the more naïve among them from being led astray by the more unscrupulous among their number.'

'I agree, darling,' nodded Daphne earnestly. She studied Danny as he tried, unsuccessfully, to keep his face straight, and a thought struck her. She frowned. 'Although on reflection, a set of Encyclopaedia Britannica would probably be a complete waste. I mean - let me put this delicately - one can hardly expect waiters to match the intellectual level of, you know, the diners upon whom they wait, can one?'

7

RMS *Berengaria*, accompanied by her welcoming flotilla of smaller craft and greeted with blasts from the horns of tug boats, ferries, lighters, and all the regular port traffic, was beginning to make her stately way upriver to Cunard Pier 92.

They'd passed the Ambrose Light, they'd passed Sandy Hook, they'd stopped briefly at the Quarantine Point near Staten Island to take on board the State doctors who checked for anyone with contagious diseases, they'd come through the Narrows and stopped in the Inner Harbour for the Ellis Island Inspectors to climb aboard and meet the captain, purser, and ship's surgeon, they'd left behind the Statue of Liberty and Governor's Island, skirted the tip of Manhattan, and turned into the Hudson River.

Crowds were gathering to give her a tumultuous New York welcome. Reporters and photographers, cameras ready to snap a possible procession of European royalty and aristocracy, Far Eastern potentates, the famous, the rich, the newsworthy - anyone, in fact, who'd fill newspaper columns and sell papers - mingled with friends, relatives, well-wishers, enthusiasts entranced by the magic of the great liners, and the curious who always attach themselves to any gathering or event. Honking taxis and cars added to the carnival sense of occasion, streamers and banners were displayed along the pier to welcome the ship, and the band was playing.

Mary, who had forgiven and forgotten Sam's black eye the moment the distant skyline of New York appeared out of the mist, spotted Michael in the crowd as the great ship edged towards the quayside, and was going mad with excitement.

'There he is! *There he is!*'

She'd brought a green jumper with a white collar up on deck with her. She'd have more chance of him seeing her if she waved the colours of the football club he supported.

'Michael! Michael!'

Sam joined in, also waving enthusiastically. '*Michael!*'

Daphne, stepping out on to the boat deck with Theodore, gestured towards Sam's black eye.

'Look!' she hissed, aghast. 'Good heavens, *that's* who that dreadful man in the dining saloon was fighting with!'

'Well,' replied Theodore. 'As they're both equally obnoxious, let's hope the pair of them knocked seven bells out of each other. Because quite frankly -'

Mary's antennae picked up on the fact that Sam's black eye was the subject of Daphne and Theodore's conversation. She glared across.

'Aye, have a good look doon yer big snotty conk! Ye want one yersel'? Jist say the word!'

Daphne and Theodore hastily moved out of range, and Mary resumed calling her son.

'Michael! *Michael!*'

'The *impudence* of it!' gasped Daphne, outraged. 'That abominable woman, screeching like the proverbial fish wife - which, of course, she is - and actually *threatening* us!'

'Oh, I expect that's just everyday parlance for these people. They probably threaten each other as a form of greeting,' surmised Theodore.

'Yoo-hoo! *Michael!*' yelled Mary again.

'However,' added Theodore, flinching at the sound, 'Out of consideration for the rest of humanity, one would assume that anyone afflicted with such a voice would elect to have their vocal chords cut to spare an assault on the eardrums of -'

Mary became hysterical as a young man in the crowd picked out the green jumper, still being dementedly waved like a flag, and waved back, laughing, pointing, and nudging the girl beside him.

'MICHAEL!'

248

Even Sam, who had himself been shouting to catch the attention of his son, felt enough was enough.

'Michty me, wumman,' he grumbled, holding his ear. 'Ye near shattered my eardrum! Keep some of yer blether back for while we're in America!'

Mary didn't even hear him. '*Michael!* MICHAEL!'

'*Haud yer wheest*!' Sam flapped a hand at her. 'You'll lose yer voice altogether, the way ye're going on!'

'Well all I can say is,' remarked Daphne to Theodore with a sniff. 'Thank heavens for that. The sooner, the better!'

'Quite so,' murmured Theodore, and added drily, 'What a pity she didn't actually spot him while we were still in the English Channel...'

8

The derricks had been raised, the bo'sun had called the sailors to Stations, the for'ard gang were preparing to throw the main mooring ropes, and the first of a host of officials and other permitted visitors were ready to swarm aboard; Customs, more port doctors and immigration officials, Cunard office staff, railway and travel agency staff, photographers, reporters, hotel representatives...

Elsewhere on the ship, first class passengers were preparing to disembark and, as the gangway was lowered, it was time for the traditional line-up of stewards and stewardesses to say farewell.

This was something of a euphemism, because both passengers and stewards knew perfectly well that although the friendly goodbyes were genuine in themselves - many stewards built up affectionate relationships with passengers, and kept up correspondence with Christmas cards and news of families etc - there was an underlying secondary purpose.

Tips.

A passenger showing monetary appreciation for excellent service was important; it made the difference between subsistence level and a living wage. And although some left a discreet envelope in first class staterooms or suites, many preferred to slip a little something into a steward's hand at the line-up. So it was necessary for the more sensitive among them - usually new stewards, embarrassed by the blatancy - to develop a thick hide about accepting what a passenger, who could well afford it, wanted to give. It went with the job, and you had to get used to it.

Either that or hide away and do without, as Elsie had chosen to do.

She'd been fortunate. Sophie and Caroline had each given her a very generous tip when she'd packed for them earlier ('And you must take all these flowers for your cabin as well,' Caroline insisted), and she preferred to forego the line-up, too shy to smile expectantly at the other passengers she'd looked after.

Mary and Sam, who'd already presented Danny with a lavish tip in the dining saloon, looked for Elsie in the line. But there was no sign of her, and fond as they were of their favourite stewardess, every minute spent with their son after such a long absence was precious beyond measure; the week would fly by too quickly as it was without a last minute search for Elsie eating into what little time they'd have with him.

So they approached the Chief Stewardess with a fat envelope bearing Elsie's name, and asked her to pass it on with their best wishes and thanks for everything she had done for them.

And then, with unselfconscious yells of sheer exuberance, excitement, joy, and overwhelming love, Mary and Sam became the first passengers to rush down the gangway onto American soil and the emotional reunion awaiting them on the quayside.

9

Jack Dalton was also among the first to go ashore.

No longer dressed as a clergyman, he was now wearing a well cut suit and smoking a fat cigar. He rewarded his steward, old Reg, with a bulging envelope, which Reg accepted with a grin and the usual feigned surprise.

'Oh! ...Oh, thank you, sir!'

'Pleasure, Reg!' The meek, mild, murmuring clergyman was replaced with confident geniality, and an answering grin.

'Have a good time ashore, sir!'

'Oh, I will. Enjoy your run ashore too.' There was a wink. 'Don't forget, tell Stavros Jack Dalton sent you, in a certain speakeasy.... Thanks again for all your help, Reg; for everything you've done for me.'

'Pleasure's all mine, sir.'

'See you next time then.'

'Look forward to it, Mister Dalton,' Reg leaned forward, his voice lowering. 'Or whatever name it happens to be on the next trip.'

Jack Dalton laughed, winked again, looked along the row, picked out Billy Saunders, and headed towards him. Billy looked at him, surprised; this man hadn't been one of his passengers. He was well aware there'd be no tip from Mister Stonefeather, and wouldn't want it even if there was, so apart from a small gratuity from some of the others he wasn't expecting anything. In his case it was a genuine appearance to wish his passengers well, and say goodbye.

'Am I right in thinking you were Mister Stonefeather's steward?'

Billy shuffled uneasily. What was this? Some kind of last vindictive gesture by proxy?

'Yes sir.'

They assessed each other silently for a couple of seconds.

'Well, I know he thought particularly highly of you. He mentioned you once or twice in the Smoking Room.'

Uh-oh. Here it comes. Billy stayed silent. Self preservation; say nothing until it's clear what the threat actually turns out to be.

'And you and I both know what a delightful, thoughtful character he is, don't we. A true paragon of generosity and kind-heartedness. An example to us all in the ways of moral rectitude we aspire to tread. Wouldn't you agree?'

Billy gaped at him, unsure what to say. 'Er...'

'So I know he'd be most upset if I didn't make sure you got the ten per cent traditionally passed on to the steward when a passenger wins the ship's pool.'

Billy, known throughout the catering department for his quick-witted perception, was still not sure what was happening.

'Because you see, unfortunately he hasn't got any of it left now. Between you and me he lost it all in a card game. But being the high-principled soul that he is, he'd still very much want you to have this. In fact, bless his tender-hearted benevolence, he'd *insist* on you taking it! So here you are - ten per cent of Mister Stonefeather's ship's pool win, with my compliments.'

He shoved an equally bulging envelope into Billy's hands, winked, strode briskly down the gangplank, and vanished into the crowd.

It was only as Billy caught a brief glimpse of him hailing a taxi, which stopped briefly at the U.S. Customs Inspectors check point before roaring off towards downtown Manhattan, that he recovered sufficiently to realise he hadn't even said thank you.

10

Lemuel Hoffmann, pressing an envelope into the hand of his bedroom steward, groaned inwardly; Lexie, smart in his navy blue suit and shiny shoes, and sneezing into his handkerchief, was joining the throng.

He was regretting being railroaded into agreeing to Lexie accompanying him to the office for a business meeting.

It wasn't the sinister black eye or bruised jaw. Not that he believed the cock-and-bull story about falling against a doorway any more than anyone else (a likely tale!) when Lexie popped into the Smoking Room for one last whisky 'for the road'. He'd already noticed the gruff Glaswegian with a matching black eye coming up from the gymnasium, and joined in the laughter when one wag made a jocular comment about the pair evidently not being able to see eye to eye about something, each with one eye almost closed.

No, it was the smell.

He couldn't allow the office to be filled with that appalling stench. He pictured his co-directors and office workers sniffing in disgust, too polite to say anything - or at least, to say anything openly - and he wasn't prepared to allow his own standing to be diminished by bringing this foul-smelling individual into their midst, because despite looking the part on the outside due to his steward's valeting, Lexie obviously couldn't be bothered to carry out basic bodily cleansing underneath. In fact it was incomprehensible that he wasn't asphyxiated by his own stink.

And that was another thing. Who wanted someone sniffling and sneezing all over them, and passing it on?

Nobody.

So he may as well get the business of disappointing Lexie over right now, because whatever project Lexie had in mind to discuss, he had no intention of listening to it.

'Lexie -'

'Lemmie! Hey, old buddy!' Lexie rubbed his hands, and reached out to clap a hand on his shoulder. 'Are we ready to do business together, or are we ready to do business together!'

Lemuel edged safely out of reach and shook his head regretfully. 'Sorry. Something's come up, Lexie. I'm afraid I'm not going to be able to make it after all.'

Lexie looked at him, shocked and disbelieving. Sorry? Something had come up? *How,* pray, when they were both still on the effing ship?

He frowned as Lemuel backed away from him. He'd noticed others as well, sniffing, staring at him, and creating a sort of space around him. Anyone would think he had raging halitosis, and hadn't bathed for a week! What was the matter with them all? It wasn't as if he had some terrible contagious disease - it was only a cold, not the plague or Black Death. And his black eye and discoloured jaw might be a bit off-putting, but not to *that* extent. (In fact it added to his air of mystery; gave him that frisson of danger so irresistible to women, the sort of thing you could brag about at the right time and in the right company, with an Aren't-I-the-lad wink and a sly grin, to an appreciative male audience: 'Did I ever tell you about the time when I was attacked by a jealous husband on the *Berengaria*? Ha ha!')

But right now, with Lemuel effing him about and calmly cancelling their business meeting, certainly wasn't the right time or place.

'Oh? But I thought we had an agreement, Lemmie?'

Lemuel looked at him. He didn't like being called Lemmie, and he was beginning to dislike his erstwhile Smoking Room companion more by the minute.

'One of those things, I'm afraid. Maybe some other time? Now, I know you have another important business meeting later

255

on, Lexie, so I won't hold you up. Nice meeting you anyway. All the best!'

He was gone. It was as abrupt as that. Not even a handshake! Lexie couldn't believe it. After all the money he'd spent, buttering the louse up and buying him drinks!

Seething, he glared round, and his fury increased as he saw not only the line of stewards taking everything in with keen interest, but passengers saying their goodbyes and giving their tips, including the snobbish pillar of society he'd danced with to pass on the news about the Countess of Knotworth's nocturnal swimming pool adventures.

And there in the line-up, taking it in with even keener interest than the rest, was that insolent pipsqueak who'd witnessed both the Early Morning Tea farce and the subsequent assault when the incandescent husband had appeared from nowhere, swooped down the corridor like some sort of deranged avenging angel, and probably would have killed him if there hadn't been witnesses present.

Well, since they were all so interested in his private business, he'd give them something to gawp at. He may not be able to force Lemuel Hoffmann to keep to his gentleman's agreement, but he could, and would, deliver a lethal blow to that brazen steward; he'd annihilate him in full hearing of everyone present, including the Chief Steward, with a scathing summing up of his incompetence and - even more unforgiveable in Cunard's view - insolence to a passenger. Let's see how entertaining he found *that*.

He turned, and started grimly towards Billy Saunders.

And Billy, guessing rightly that after this humiliation Lexie would be out for blood - and as the easiest target would be a bedroom steward who couldn't answer back, it wasn't difficult to guess whose blood would do nicely - prepared for war in earnest.

Lexie had power and money, even despite last night's gambling losses which wiped out his ship's pool bonus. But Billy was more than equal in mental agility. There'd been no silver spoon for him, no limitless trust fund to cushion life's blows; conditioned from childhood to develop a survivor's instinct for thinking on his feet and anticipating an enemy's next move, he was also a shrewd judge of character. And he'd had enough opportunities to see how Lexie's mind worked, and to prepare for whatever was likely to come next.

And then make sure he got in first.

He greeted Lexie with a beaming smile.

'Enjoy your stay in New York, Mister Stonefeather.' (Stuff the 'Sir'. The trip was over; Billy Saunders called nobody 'Sir' unless he had to. If the Chief Steward, who was standing a few feet away, rebuked him, he'd say he was so overwhelmed with gratitude that he momentarily forgot himself.) 'And thank you so much for such a generous tip!'

He displayed the envelope, waving it in Lexie's face with another broad grin. 'Glad you had no complaints, and enjoyed your time aboard the *Berengaria*!'

Lexie Stonefeather stared at him. Enjoyed his time aboard the *Berengaria*? He'd ended it with a black eye, a painful jaw, a cold, a cancelled business meeting, a complaint made against him to the purser by two interfering women, complete strangers treating him as though he had leprosy, and minus every penny of the ship's pool money he'd won as well. So no, he hadn't enjoyed his time aboard the *Berengaria*. And what was all that rubbish about a tip? What was he talking about? He hadn't given him a tip, nor was he going to, and the lackey knew it.

'What tip? I haven't given you a tip, because -'

Again Billy cut in before Lexie could continue.

'Oh, not personally, no! No, I meant you kindly requesting your fellow card player to pass ten per cent of the ship's pool money he won from you on to me. Most thoughtful of you. Thank you very much!' Again he waved the envelope in front of Lexie's face. 'And I just wanted to let you know that he did as you asked. He passed it on to me, with your compliments.' He turned to the line-up for confirmation. 'Didn't he, boys?'

257

The chorus of affirmation and nods of agreement were obviously genuine, and included the Chief Steward and old Reg, both of whom were renowned for their honesty, integrity, and total trustworthiness.

Lexie hesitated.

'The sign of a true gentleman,' went on Billy in a tone of fawning admiration, eyes glinting with a dislike equal to Lexie's and holding the envelope tantalisingly in front of his adversary. 'A gallant loser, gracious in defeat.'

The rest of the line took this broadside swipe at face value - a gentlemanly acceptance of losing at cards, while still nobly ensuring his steward didn't miss out because of it. Only Billy and Lexie knew there was another layer to this conversation, a more subtle and significant meaning to the word 'defeat'.

Old Reg glanced at Billy. He may be hard of hearing, but he wasn't stupid. There was more to this than met the eye; a battle of some sort was taking place between Mister Stonefeather and the steward, and whatever it was about went deeper than the surface reason of a steward's natural revulsion at having to face, day after day, the results of Mister Stonefeather's choice of lifestyle. He sensed the assault on the stewardess might have something to do with the contempt in Billy's voice as well. But, as on numerous occasions in the past, he stayed quiet and kept his thoughts to himself.

Lexie also stared at Billy. Could he get away with a dramatic accusation that this insolent swine had given him the bruised jaw and black eye? No. The steward would immediately insist that the Chief Steward check with the Purser, who would check with the Countess of Knotworth, who would no doubt take great delight in making known the full details of why, where, when, and how, the wronged husband had exacted his justifiable revenge.

Even as his mind processed events on one level, on another he was aware that almost the entire line of stewards, unimportant flunkies as they may be, were sniffing at him, a look of disgust on some of their faces. He sneezed again. What the eff was wrong with them? Hadn't they ever seen anyone with a cold before? What *was* this mystifying habit everyone seemed to have developed of sniffing and recoiling from him as if he was some sort of walking bad smell?

More pressing, however, was the need to settle the score with Billy. He'd announce that, out of sheer compassion, he'd generously organised the tip because only someone with a very limited mental capacity could be as abysmally inefficient as Billy Saunders.

He began confidently; an assassin with an invincible weapon, aiming at a stationary target, with ample time to ensure the shot found its most accurately lethal mark.

'Ah yes. The tip. Or to be more precise -'

Billy tensed. There was obviously a below-the-belt deathblow on its way. Well, if that was how Mister Stonefeather wanted to play it, Billy was ready; two could play at that game.

And then Lexie broke off mid-sentence.

Like a deflating balloon shrivelling haphazardly in one direction before changing course and boomeranging back, the battle was suddenly and unexpectedly over - and it was all due to the arrival of Madam Rasputin, still shrouded in the long coat and folk-art headscarf, but now clinging adoringly to the arm of the black-haired giant. Her cheeks were flushed, her eyes bright, her smile radiant, and there was a definite spring in the step of both of them.

Lexie expelled a lungful of air in frustration, abruptly turned on his heel, and strode towards the gangway. Would you effing believe it! Trust that psychopathic thug and his delusional trollop to turn up *now*, of all times! He couldn't risk another encounter with them in full view of half the ship, no matter how his fingers itched to wring their necks.

What with that pair of lunatics, and the effing steward, and everything else that had happened... he cursed the *Berengaria* and everyone aboard her under his breath.

Cunard were in for a shock if they thought Lexie Stonefeather would put up with the experiences he'd been forced to endure on this trip without making sure they were fully aware of his displeasure. And as a letter of complaint would merely be brushed off with courteous but meaningless flannel, he'd ensure his dissatisfaction was made clear in a way *nobody* could ignore…

Billy couldn't stop the grin spreading across his face as, with a disdainful glance at Lexie's hunched back scurrying down the gangway, the woman broke contact with her husband, headed towards him, and shoved another wad of dollars into his mess jacket pocket.

'Dosvi-daniye, fseevoh-khahroh shevo, spa seeba!' (Goodbye, all the best, thank you!) she bid him with a mischievous wink, before nestling back into the giant's arms.

'Thank you very much, madam. Enjoy your stay in New York!'

The Russians nodded and smiled, the man's arm sliding protectively around his wife.

Out of the corner of his eye Billy saw Lexie succumb to another spasm of coughing half way down the gangway.

'And may I wish you the best of luck with your other business meeting later today, Mister Stonefeather?' he called with innocent sincerity as, with another violent sneeze, Lexie finally staggered off the gangway onto the quayside.

No answer.

11

The stock of engagement rings at the jewellers had diminished during the crossing, and the proprietor added another to the total during the morning. Experience had taught him to stay open as long as possible on the last day of the trip; it was often particularly lucrative.

'Well, honey,' said Caroline to Frank-from-California-who's-in-the-film-industry, wafting her left hand to admire the new adornment on the third finger, 'I guess we'd better break the news to my sister - who'll say (she imitated Sophie's scolding voice), 'But Caroline, you've only known each other for a couple of days! How can you be sure?'

She was wrong. When they joined Sophie to disembark, her sister said nothing apart from a wistful, 'Congratulations. I hope you'll both be very happy.'

Caroline looked at her in astonishment. Was that all she had to say? Not even a rebuke for being absent all night, and all morning until now? What about, 'But you've only known each other a couple of days!'?

There was no way she could know that Sophie's lack of conversation, whether to scold or be enthusiastic, was because her mind was too preoccupied with wishing Clive had done likewise and proposed to her, and that she was free to say Yes. Because even though *she'd* only known *him* for a few days, she'd never be more certain of anything in her life.

Turning away, Sophie looked at the familiar landmarks with mixed feelings. It felt good to be home again. She'd looked forward for a long time to this period of escape from Aubrey. And yet now, instead of the carefree joy she'd anticipated, she was unable to shake off a sense of deep disquiet, loneliness, and longing to be near Clive, and she'd gladly swap the Manhattan skyline for the sight of him hurrying towards her, smiling.

But that wasn't going to happen. She may as well try and slide down a rainbow.

There were two separate issues here - three, if you counted the ridiculous notion of falling in love with someone you'd only just met - and there'd be no fairytale happy ending to any of them. The first was, she wasn't free to love anyone else. And the second was, regardless of whether or not she was free, the fact that she'd fallen in love with Clive didn't automatically mean he'd fallen in love with her in return. So this sojourn in New York was going to be a brief respite from Aubrey, and the icy, aloof hostility she'd face from now on, and that was all. The changes that had come upon her on the ship had to be left on the ship.

The tears welled up, and she turned her back on the stupendous Manhattan skyline to watch the activity on the ship. No doubt things were equally busy in the Purser's Office, but part of her - the part that dreamed of sliding down a rainbow and finding Clive at the end - had secretly hoped...

It was no good. She'd just have to be stern with herself. Self-discipline and backbone; that's what she needed. Clive must be left behind on the *Berengaria* and forgotten, for all time.

There was no other way.

The Purser's Office door was open.

The place was overrun, which meant Clive got his wish; there wasn't a spare moment to concentrate on anything other than the turmoil as a dozen people clamoured for his attention at once.

Both Tom Burnett, dealing with a reporter from the New York Daily News: 'Who would you like to interview? We're a bit short of movie queens on this trip, but we've got the usual captains of industry and the idle rich...' and Clive, answering a passenger's enquiries about train times from New York to Boston, happened to glance momentarily out to the

262

boarding/disembarking area just as the Countess of Knotworth and her sister, preparing to leave the ship, were framed in the doorway. Caroline was chatting animatedly to Frank. Sophie was quiet, slightly apart.

Tom frowned, thinking of the money he'd wasted on flowers. He tried to be philosophical: Oh well, worth a try, even though he'd known she was out of his league; win some, lose some, there was always next time, and all that.

Huh!

It didn't work. He could have treated himself to a slap-up meal and the theatre with what he'd spent on that flighty American piece. Well, he'd learn from the experience, and be more cautious about who he frittered away his hard-earned salary on next time.

Along the counter, Clive froze. He'd checked earlier to see if or when she was returning to England on the *Berengaria,* but there was no booking, which meant she was probably travelling back on a different ship.

So it was now or never.

Did he leap up like some crazy jack-in-the-box who'd either taken leave of his senses or was drunk on duty, abandoning the passenger mid-sentence to rush out and gabble frantically that he couldn't let her go without telling her he'd fallen in love with her?

He pictured her gaping at him in amazement before hurrying down the gangway with other bemused passengers, leaving him to stare after her amid the incredulous looks of his fellow crew members. From the purser down to the brass-buttoned cabin boys on hand to help with hand luggage, and taking in the sailors working nearby and line-up of stewards on the way, there'd be a chorus of deriding sniggers and catcalls - and he was honest enough to admit that if he saw anyone else doing what he had to physically hold himself back from doing, he'd be the first to laugh as well.

He was aware of the train enquiry passenger looking at him in consternation as he stood at the counter, motionless and mute...

The moment passed. He'd kept his dignity, his self-respect. He'd stayed in control, he hadn't rushed out to her like some pathetic love-sick adolescent. He was safe.

Bereft, but safe. Except that a more apt description might be safe, but totally bereft.

12

The dining saloon was empty, and the thorough clean that always took place in Southampton or New York about to begin.

Tony was comparing his tips with the others, and grumbling that the passengers on this trip hadn't been as generous as he'd expected, which meant he wouldn't be able to paint the town as red as he'd hoped. There were the inevitable comparisons with previous voyages, and the all-time record was brought up again. One of the bellhops had been given a hundred dollars by the head of multi-national corporation a few voyages back. It had been the talk of the ship.

'A hundred bucks!' marvelled Tony, looking at the modest collection in his hand. 'And look what I've got! A few measly quid!'

'Think yourself lucky you haven't ended up with a set of Encyclopaedia Britannica to browse through in your leisure hours,' said the Head Waiter caustically.

'Encyclopaedia Britannica? What's that?'

'Leisure hours? What are they?' echoed Harry Watts, in a slightly more sarcastic tone.

The Head Waiter ignored him.

'Books,' he explained to Tony. 'They give you information. Tell you things.'

'Information?' queried Tony, with a puzzled frown. Then understanding dawned. His brow cleared. 'Oh, you mean like where to get a drink during Prohibition? I already know that, thanks. Danny told me.'

It's just as well, thought the Head Waiter, Danny isn't standing in front of me right now.

Danny, in the kitchen-cleaning squad, was thinking much the same thing about Alec Baxter.

He didn't know what to make of things at all. He believed what Joey had said, and Joey obviously believed what Clara had said - and yet he had to admit Alec's version of events came across as plausible as well. It sounded as though Clara had been manipulating the pair of them, and playing them off against each other. In fact, he thought as he changed the water in his bucket and added more soda, it sounded as though she and Alec were made for each other. And deserved each other. And were welcome to each other.

There was a particularly loud cheer from the quayside, where the band was playing and crowds shouting excitedly. Not that it distracted him; Danny had seen it all before, and the arrival and departure of the *Berengaria,* spectacular as it was, held no great relevance for him. The only person he wanted to be waiting for him at the end of a voyage was in Liverpool, and the only person he wanted to see in New York was Joey Smith, who wouldn't be in the crowd.

But as soon as the work was done and he was free, he'd try to find out where Joey was, what had happened to him, and, if possible, visit him. The only news passed down from the higher echelons was that a brief radio message from a fishing vessel had informed the ship that a member of the crew had been picked up, and was alive.

Danny knew that very few fishing boats were equipped with radio, so this was obviously one of the larger vessels, which meant she might be at sea for a lengthy period. And if so, Joey would have to stay on board until she returned to port, because she wouldn't turn back just on his account. But it was all conjecture at this stage.

However, he had friends in New York, and once ashore there were ways and means of finding out a lot more information. And if all else failed, there was the Seamen's Church Institute which the previous year had opened an emergency homeless shelter for seafarers. Someone there would have heard something, especially since the fishing boat had radio.

In the meantime, the already clean kitchen equipment had to be scoured yet again, following the time-honoured tradition that you never took a dirty ship into port. Every inch of paintwork had to be scrubbed, the stove tops burnished until they gleamed, copper pans and other pieces of equipment likewise polished, every utensil inspected and if necessary sent for repair, every fridge, cold store, and store room thoroughly scrubbed, and every empty bottle and package collected for return to the suppliers.

So - the sooner they got on with it, the sooner they'd be finished.

SEVEN: NEW YORK

1

'Guess what I found out?' Stuart Murray grinned around the purser's office.

'What?' asked Tom Burnett, scowling.

'Well, according to a naturalist making a trip to the U.S. to identify wild flowers, apparently there are seven different types of bramble.'

Bob Smyth looked up briefly from last-minute administration work. 'Is that a fact. Well, when he comes back, tell him I've probably got all seven growing in my garden. Would have saved him a trip to America.'

'Yes. And there's probably another seven in my garden that haven't even been discovered yet,' added Charlie Johnson.

Tom, who still hadn't got over parting with the astronomical sum he'd spent on flowers for someone who probably tossed them in the bin the following morning - if not the same day, after receiving a more impressive offering - tutted.

'Huh. I wish I'd given that American floozy a bunch of brambles instead of wasting good money on her. Never again! I'll have to recoup it by selling my whisky allowance.'

The others murmured their sympathy. They'd all fallen prey to similar futile extravagances in the past, and taken full advantage of the system operated by the shipping line whereby officers could purchase up to three bottles of whisky for their own use, which made a tidy sum when sold on to the Press photographers - no questions asked about where it may end up in Prohibition New York. (Clive privately decided to drink his entire allowance himself. And that was just for starters.)

But gradually, one after another set off on various errands, and he was left on his own with the remaining batch of cargo consignment notes.

The last of the passengers had left the ship, and the emigrants in steerage were now being transferred on to small steamboats and ferried to Ellis Island for the Immigrant Examination. Some went eagerly, excited at the prospects of a new life and 'the lady with the spikes in her head' welcoming them to the promised land; others were filled with dread and apprehension, and left the *Berengaria* reluctantly - the last tenuous links with home. The middle-aged man Danny had seen boarding the ship in Southampton in obvious misery was one of the last to leave, heartbreak and exhaustion clearly etched into every line of his face.

Clive, who happened to go to the door for a breath of fresh air as the man was climbing aboard the steamboat, felt for him. They were both in a similar situation, in that they'd made a decision, for good or bad, and now was the time to live with it and try and make the best of it if it turned out to be the wrong one. As, he now admitted, had been the case for him when he'd deliberately avoided Sophie following their swim, then compounded that mistake by staying silent as she disembarked because he was more concerned about losing face in front of the crew.

And if he hadn't been man enough to do it on the ship, it'd be even more out of the question to make enquiries about where she was staying in New York, and turn up unannounced on the doorstep. What on earth would he say?

'Oh, good morning. Remember me? We went swimming together on the *Berengaria*. I happened to be passing this way so I thought I'd just pop in to tell you that, erm, I've fallen in love with you.'

No. Even in free and easy, uninhibited New York, that would be one step too far. As for trying it in England, the butler would have him arrested before he'd even got over the doorstep; he'd be certified insane. It was the moving finger thing again - he'd had his chance, and made his choice. Now, like the unknown emigrant, he'd have to make the best of things, cut all ties, and make a fresh start.

He returned to his desk, and looked at the bills of lading and consignment notes for the cargo. He'd wanted his career, and now he had it, so he'd better start concentrating on it. He picked up the pen, stared at the paperwork, then laid it down again.

Had he imagined the whole thing? Was this love he felt, or some weird sentimental wishful thinking now she was safely out of reach? All he knew was, he'd never experienced this sense of desolation and loneliness after any of his previous shipboard romances. Not that this counted as a 'romance' anyway. Maybe that was the problem? If things *had* progressed to 'romance', would he now feel as he had at the end of the road (voyage) with all the others - pleasant memories to look back on in his old age, but nothing more meaningful than that? Was this just unfulfilled lust? The attraction of the unattainable?

He sat back in his chair, put his hands behind his head, and listened to the activity on the ship. The U.S. Customs rummage crews were on board in the eternal contest to see who could outwit whom, seamen having far more time and ingenuity to take advantage of the ship's complicated design to find the cleverest possible hiding places for contraband than the rummage crews had to discover it. Gangs of workmen were erecting the deck gear, removing coamings from the tops of the hatches, and fixing the net stretching from the topmost deck to the quayside as protection against the hull of the ship as huge canvas laundry bags, loaded with over 100,000 items, were landed en-route to the laundry. He listened to the throb of the dynamos supplying power to the winches, and heard the creaks and groans of the cargo gear as the stevedores began to unload what was to be stored in the dockside sheds and warehouses.

Again he picked up his pen and absently cast his eye over the consignment notes for the cargo, which on this occasion included valuable antique furniture and pictures carried in the strong room, but for the most part consisted of household goods: carpets, pottery, silver, bronze, glassware, fabrics, woollen and cotton goods from the mills of Yorkshire and

271

Lancashire, steel and electro plate goods from Sheffield, hats, shoes, toys, coats, ties, leather goods… the list went on.

Oh, what was the use. He couldn't concentrate.

He left his paperwork, trotted down the majestic grand staircase passing gangs of cleaners ministering to the carpet and ornate Louis XIV style balustrades, and walked to the deserted pool. He sat on one of the marble seats, no longer warmed by interior copper piping, and stared at the water, now dimly lit, quiet, and still, and his mind went back to the swim after the Gala Night Dinner.

For her, it was probably just one of those pleasant but forgettable interludes in life; the sort of thing recalled at dinner parties when the conversation turned to vaguely remembered people during transatlantic travel.

'Oh yes,' she'd say. 'Believe it or not I once sneaked off for a midnight swim with a ship's officer in the swimming pool on the *Berengaria!*'

There'd be appreciative laughter from the others, her husband joining in with a mock-shocked tone: 'I don't seem to recall you mentioning anything about *that*, darling?'

And she'd laugh. 'Let me think, what was his name again? Began with a C. Clive, that was it. We cooled off after a Fancy Dress Ball.'

More laughter, before another guest took over.

'Yes, we have fond memories of the dear old *Berengaria* too. Such a jolly ship. But did I ever tell you about the time we were on the *Olympic…*'

'What is it,' he asked aloud, 'About one particular human being that has this effect on another? Especially when you don't want it to!'

But either the swimming pool decided to keep the answer to itself, or it could no more provide an explanation than the philosophers who have puzzled over the same phenomenon since man first walked the earth.

He sighed and stood up. Better get back to the consignment notes. Perhaps they'd know the answer.

2

'The Glaswegian couple in D18 asked me to give you this.' The Chief Stewardess held out the envelope as Elsie presented the card all stewards and stewardesses must sign to confirm nothing had been left behind in any of the suites or staterooms. 'They'd hoped to say goodbye to you in the line-up, like everybody else.'

'I, er, wasn't feeling well,' mumbled Elsie uncomfortably.

It was true. She'd expected to feel better once the ship docked, and to a certain extent she did. But not being able to rest when she'd needed to during the bouts of seasickness, and forcing herself to keep going for the duration of the trip, meant exhaustion was now catching up with her. And although all she wanted to do was lie down and sleep, just because the ship had docked didn't mean she could finally relax. The major spring-clean of the suites and staterooms had to be completed first.

'Mm. Well, I won't keep you from your work.' The Chief Stewardess filed the card away.

'Thank you,' Elsie mumbled again, pocketing her envelope and turning to go.

She was called back. 'Just a minute. There's something else arrived for you, in the post. It was addressed care of the Cunard office.'

She held out a second envelope. Elsie looked at it in surprise. She didn't know anyone in America. Who on earth had written to her c/o the Cunard offices in New York? She looked more closely. Had someone from home...? No, it definitely wasn't from anyone at home, because as well as the writing being unfamiliar it bore an American stamp and a New York postmark.

The Chief Stewardess was also extremely curious to know who had written to one of her stewardesses, and looked expectantly at Elsie. But Elsie had no intention of opening it until she could do so in private, on her own. She pocketed it with Mary and Sam's envelope, and turned to go.

Once safe on the other side of the door she took it out and examined it, but resisted the temptation to open it; the Chief Stewardess could appear any moment, and whatever this turned out to be, it was going to remain confidential until she knew more about it herself. She made her way to the first of the empty suites to be cleaned - the chambre de luxe the Countess of Knotworth and Caroline had occupied, still filled with Caroline's admirers' flowers - and hurried though the salon and bedroom to the small enclosed verandah, making a few banging noises on the way so that old Reg, working with Billy in the suite opposite, would assume she was safely engaged in her tasks. Then she sat on the cushioned rattan sofa and looked at the two envelopes.

First she opened the one from Sam and Mary, and was astounded to find they'd left ten per cent of their ship's pool winnings for her. This was the equivalent of over three months' wages! She was rich! She gasped, fingering four five pound notes and four one pound notes in turn. This meant she could start saving for... well, something. Something bound up in her future, even if only freedom from financial worries for a short period between one job and the next.

She folded the money and said a silent heartfelt Thank You, because there was no address on the envelope for her to write and thank the Glaswegians and tell them how much their gift meant to her. Maybe she could follow the example of the mystery writer, and contact them c/o the Cunard offices?

She looked at the second envelope, and frowned. Was this going to be something else to worry about? Some ominous unknown enemy lying in wait in New York? But who? She didn't even know anyone. Well, there was only one way to find out...

She carefully opened it, and unfolded the good quality writing paper inside.

It was hand written; large, confident handwriting, signed with a flourish. The surname was vaguely familiar, but not immediately recognisable. Her eyes skimmed quickly down the page, and odd words leapt out: New York... children's books... job... interview...

Her hand shot to her mouth. She blinked, and with a sharp intake of breath read it again, properly.

It was from the parents of the nine year old child in the Nursery on her first voyage, telling her how impressed they'd been when she'd sketched simple objects for the children to colour in, and how their daughter had enjoyed it. The husband ran a publishing house in New York, specialising in children's books, and had the idea of printing small 'colouring-in' booklets with simple pictures for a wider range of young children - and because they'd been impressed with her work, they were considering offering her a job, drawing the sort of thing she'd produced for the birthday party on the ship. As her skills progressed, there may be an opening for an illustrator for some of the other children's story books they published.

Would she be interested? If so, they may be able to help with her immigration application. Maybe she'd contact them when next in New York, so a suitable time could be arranged for an interview, where, if all went well, they would formally offer her the job?

Elsie slumped on the sofa, mouth open, mind racing, all thoughts of work completely forgotten. She lifted her eyes from the letter and stared through the verandah window at the Cunard piers, totally oblivious to the bustle and activity on the quayside, then read it again. And again. It was unbelievable.

This meant that not only would it be possible to leave this detested job for another one - and one she'd truly enjoy doing - but she'd actually be living in New York as well!

And not only that. Sam and Mary's tip meant that instead of having to work a few more trips to save the money for her steerage passage, plus enough to rent a small room on arrival, she'd now have sufficient when she added it to the wages she'd be paid in Southampton.

So there was only the home leg of this trip to get through now - and with the promise of this undreamed-of offer dangling in front of her she'd cope with another week at sea, whatever the weather. The home trip would give her time to take it all in properly, and allow her mind to digest and process every aspect of this amazing good fortune. And then, in Southampton, she'd tell relatives and friends about this terrific job opportunity, her decision to take it, and how important it was to her to know she went with their blessing. Because of course it wouldn't be goodbye for ever. She'd write often, and save up, and who knew, hopefully in a few years she'd have enough for a visit. First class on the *Berengaria* of course - nothing less!

The other thing she'd enjoy doing would be to tell the Chief Stewardess that she wouldn't be signing on for another voyage, thanks all the same.

She heard old Reg calling along the corridor, and stood up, folding the letter and money carefully into her pocket. The sooner her work was done, the sooner she'd be free to leave the ship, because even the Chief Stewardess couldn't keep her cooped up in here forever, and New York with all its attractions and opportunities was waiting out there! As well as a date with Billy - exciting enough in itself - she'd be able to arrange and attend the interview. And from the sound of things, that appeared to be more or less a foregone conclusion. They'd already seen the sort of thing she'd drawn; they wouldn't have written the letter if they weren't serious.

She wondered what Billy would say about it all when she told him.

Thinking about Billy brought her back to the night when she'd felt a great need to go on deck and talk to God about what to do with her life, and how best to use the few talents she had. She hadn't done it, of course; everything had been flushed out

276

of mind by the presence of Billy Saunders, and the irresistible temptation of taking part in his plot.

So where did that leave her resolution to become a better Christian and turn the other cheek? She shuffled uncomfortably. Best gloss over that one, and leave it for some time in the future when she was a better person; the person she'd like to be, rather than the person she was now. In the meantime, gratitude and wonder sat uneasily alongside guilty conscience. The whole thing was so entirely unexpected! Never in her wildest dreams had it occurred to her that this amazing solution to her problems might be waiting for her in New York.

Well, she'd been quick enough to pray when she was in need; the least she could do now was to say thank you, even if she couldn't quite manage 'sorry'. Because there was no point in lying about it, she wasn't a bit sorry about the part she'd played in getting even with Lexie Stonefeather. Maybe she'd feel contrite about it one day. A long, long way off from now.

But for now, well, she *had* spoken to God later that night in her airless, noisy cabin, and couldn't deny the sense of utter peace that followed her prayer of desperation. Whatever else she was guilty of, she wasn't too proud to get on her knees and say Thank You.

And there, in the enclosed verandah of a first class suite on RMS *Berengaria,* as old Reg bustled along the corridor and the noise and activity of New York continued heedlessly outside the confines of the ship, she did just that.

3

The fishing boat that picked Joey up had in fact been returning to port.

Joey, via a somewhat circuitous route, had ended up in the Seamen's Church Institute, still weak and prone to spasms of shaking, but nowhere near as badly damaged or injured or affected by his immersion in the sea as he might have been.

The SCI, or 25 South Street as it was also known (the Post Office at the SCI was one of the most recognisable addresses in the world), provided cheap but safe accommodation for sailors. It housed nearly six hundred men, contained a dining room, a place to store baggage, a reading room stocked with books, magazines, and newspapers in numerous languages, and even a Centre for Seafarers' Rights with legal advice available. And, of course, a chapel.

Danny and Joey greeted each other in the reception area, but after superficial small talk over a cup of tea Joey suggested moving on to somewhere slightly more secluded, and they made their way to a speakeasy managed by a former seaman friend. They sat at one of the tables in the basement of a harmless-looking drug store, reached by a series of doors and stairs and passageways at the back of the main shop area and fitted out like a pub, with a fully stocked bar and waiter service.

A friendship that went back years meant safe topics of conversation and an unthreatening skirting round the subject of Joey's attempted suicide should he not wish to discuss it. But it was inevitable that sooner or later one of them would mention it, and in fact it was Joey who brought up the subject, couched in the self-mocking black humour that would shock and offend anyone less than an old and true friend.

'Go on then, say it - couldn't you even manage to get *that* right?'

Danny grinned. 'What went wrong? So much alcohol on your breath you even put the sharks off?'

Joey laughed, but Danny was one of the few people he felt able to confide in; to speak with total honesty about the strange and profound insights he'd experienced while in the sea. He hesitated, swilling his drink around his glass. If he was going to tell anyone what happened just before he reached the point of drowning, it would be Danny.

'Keep this to yourself, Danny. Nobody else would believe it anyway. And why should they? I wouldn't believe it myself if it hadn't happened to me. I don't want people to think I've turned into some sort of religious maniac.' He looked at Danny. 'But God was there with me in the ocean. I *knew*. There was absolutely no doubt about it.'

Danny was silent. The last thing anyone could accuse Joey Smith of being was a religious maniac. For as long as he'd known him, Joey hadn't set foot in a church. And everyone knew he'd been round the block a few times in his youth, and then some.

'Well.' Joey shrugged. 'I don't blame you for not believing me. You probably think I've gone crackers; all that salt water affected my brain. But I can't deny it happened, and I won't.'

Danny studied him. There was something different about him; all the worry and tension had left his face, and the eyes were steady and clear.

'I'd heard of "The peace that passeth all understanding," but never thought I'd actually experience it - especially after telling God what He could do with all His religious rubbish.'

'Well,' admitted Danny, 'You certainly look in a lot better mental state than you did on the ship. Not that it'd be difficult!'

'I've had to do a lot of thinking, Danny. I'm not going back on the *Berry,* I'm going to make my life here in the States. One of the lads who picked me up has a brother who needs a farmhand, bit of a way from New York. He's promised to help me with all the immigration rigmarole.'

'Well, if that's what you want, Joey -

'It is.' The tone was definite, positive.

There was a pause.

Danny filled it. 'I found the letter you left. I'd already made sure everyone knew about Alec and, you know, Clara, before we heard you'd been picked up.'

'Oh. Clara.' Joey sighed. 'That was something else I discovered while I was in the sea. I didn't want to marry her anyway. I never really loved her, I just sort of went along with things because... Oh, it was just how things were.'

Danny stared at him in amazement. If it was anyone else but Joey dropping this bombshell he'd think they were insane. One minute jumping overboard because of a broken romance, next minute he didn't want to marry her anyway? Well, this certainly put a different light on the whole thing, especially as Joey had asked him in the letter to visit Clara...

That would be some visit!

It was one thing to comfort the grieving fiancee and hand over the whip-round all the lads had contributed to; quite another to break the news that actually, having survived the suicide attempt he'd made because of her, Joey wasn't all that bothered about marrying her anyway. In fact, to be honest, he didn't want to. He'd never really loved her. Oh, and he was going to start a new life in America as well, so he wouldn't be coming back to England. If Clara *had* been playing the two of them off against each other, this would stop her in her tracks!

So... did he tell his friend about Alec's protests that he had no intention of making her homeless, that accusations of rape were rubbish, and that she'd happily accepted *Alec's* proposal of marriage while she was engaged to Joey? How did you tell someone whose suicide bid could so easily have been successful that it sounded as though she'd been spinning him a line all along? It was all getting a bit too complicated. A hornet's nest indeed.

280

Well, he'd take things one step at a time, starting with the astounding news about Alec promising, in front of a host of witnesses, to make the deeds of two houses over to Clara, and agreeing to pay for the upkeep of the child should she and Joey still want to get married. Because that fact might change things, and Joey needed to know about it.

He glanced up and stiffened as two traffic cops came into the speakeasy, then relaxed as they sat at a nearby table and ordered drinks. Nice to see they took Prohibition so seriously.

'I can tell you, Joey, Alec Baxter was really shaken up by it all,' he began tentatively. 'He was as white as a sheet.'

'Well, well. That's interesting.'

'If you think that's interesting, try this for size. He said he's going to make over the deeds of both houses to Clara, and pay for the upkeep of the child if you and she got married.'

'Did he indeed,' said Joey grimly. 'Did he also tell you they've probably already paid more in rent than those scummy slums would be worth if they were put up for sale? And that it'd take more than the value of the house to sort out the damp, and everything else that's wrong with them? Don't be taken in; he wouldn't give away something that had any value. Mouldy bricks and leaking roofs on a couple of falling-to-bits two up-two downs with no electricity, a tin bath in the kitchen, gas lights, and a backyard privy? Very generous.'

'If they're paying rent to live there, they may as well live there without paying rent,' Danny pointed out. 'However bad a state the houses are in, at least they can't be thrown out if they own them.'

'He'll find some way of making sure he doesn't lose out on the deal, don't you worry.'

'I could be wrong,' ventured Danny, after a long pause. 'But I think he's been struck with remorse. Especially about the way he treated you, picking on you all the time.'

Joey snorted. 'Am I supposed to feel sorry for the poor misunderstood innocent?'

Danny hesitated again. 'He wants to see you, Joey. I told him where he could stick that idea, but I couldn't put him off.'

Joey stared into his drink.

'Well,' he said slowly. 'All right. I'll see him. There's things I need to say to him anyway.' He looked up at Danny. 'I was going to ask a favour, Danny. I've written a letter to Clara while I've been in New York, explaining things. Will you see that she gets it?'

'Sure thing.'

'Right. Well, I've got one or two alterations to add after what you've just said.'

Joey went to the bar, had a word with the barman, and came back with a pen and a page torn from a notebook. He scribbled a few sentences, folded it in with the letter already inside the envelope, sealed it, and handed it to Danny.

'I'll tell him you'll see him then,' said Danny, pocketing it. 'Where d'you want to meet? Here? 25 South Street? Or somewhere else?'

'The SCI. I don't want him knowing about this place. It's not as if I want to be best buddies, drinking together, all palsy-walsy. What I've got to say won't take long.'

'Right you are then.'

Joey frowned. 'Also, I want what you've said about him promising to make the deeds over to Clara put down in writing and signed. If he's at the SCI, I can get someone from the legal department to witness it; make sure it's done properly, all above board and straightforward for the paperwork to be sorted out in England. There'll be no wriggling out of it at the last minute with some stupid excuse. I don't trust him an inch; I'll make damn sure he doesn't go back on his word on this. At least then if things go wrong between them in the future she'll have some security.' There was a pause, and he nodded at the letter. 'And it makes me feel better about not wanting to marry her.'

'Right you are then,' said Danny again, checking his watch and finishing his drink. He decided against passing on Alec's version of events and protestations of innocence; he had more

282

respect for Joey than to let him know Clara had evidently been two-timing him all along. And whatever would be said between him and Alec at their meeting was none of his business. They'd said enough on the subject. It was time to drop it, move on to happier topics, and re-affirm friendship.

'I never told you, Joey, what with you hogging the headlines with all your drama, but I'm leaving the *Berry* myself when she docks in Southampton. I'm going to propose to Norah, and try and get a Liverpool based ship.'

Joey grinned. 'About time!'

'I know.'

'Best of luck - but tell her I said she wants her head examined if she takes you on!'

Danny replaced his glass on the table. 'Tell her yourself when you've made your first million, with ranches from here to California, and you book a first class passage on the *Berry*. Mind you, the service won't be as good. Can't get the waiters these days, can you? Anyway, I'd better be getting back, Joey. I want to do some shopping first. Buy a nice present for her.'

Joey became serious. 'Stay in touch.'

'You bet.'

'Thanks for the drink, Danny.'

They nodded to the other occupants of the room, including the barman (and traffic cops), and made their way through the labyrinth of passages and doors to the drug store front. As they came out on to the street, and Joey was about to return to the Seamen's Church Institute, Danny fished in his pocket and drew out an envelope.

'Oh, I nearly forgot. Mister Stonefeather - you remember, the nobody-pulls-a-fast-one-on-me smoked sturgeon connoisseur?'

'Oh aye? The one you wanted the Camembert cheese for?'

'That's the one. Billy Saunders got one of the stewardesses - nice young lass, Elsie, you might remember her -'

'Yeah, I remember. Something brewing there with Billy?'

'That's her - to sew it into his suit as a sort of leaving present. A lovely scent of *eau de* rancid Camembert. Serve him right.

He tried it on with her, and made Billy's life a misery as well. Anyway, to show his appreciation for his preferential treatment, he wanted me to give you this, with his compliments and best wishes for a speedy recovery.'

Joey opened the envelope, drew out a ten pound note, and gasped. The standard rate for tips was between one and five pounds.

'Tell you what Danny, this'll come in very handy. I'm a bit short, as you can imagine, until I can start working and get a job. But next time you're in New York, I'll treat you to a drink to celebrate your engagement. How's that?'

'Next time I'm in New York *I'll* treat *you* to celebrate my engagement.' Danny pulled out another ten pound note from his waistcoat pocket, and waved it in front of Joey. 'As a thank you for getting the one and only Mister Smith to do his smoked sturgeon a la Romanoff princes, he gave me one as well! I'm taking Norah out somewhere special to propose.'

They both laughed as they turned in different directions, neither of them making any dramatic gestures of friendship or emotional goodbyes.

Danny waited until Joey had walked a few paces, then called him. 'Hey, Joey!'

As Joey turned, Danny tossed him another envelope.

And as Joey instinctively reached out to catch it, Danny called, 'The lads had a whip-round.'

Then, before Joey could say anything, or refuse to take it, he turned, lifted one hand in salute, and walked off. It wasn't nearly enough for Joey's needs, but unless a kindly fairy godmother appeared with a magic wand and tossed some more into the coffers, it was the best he could do.

4

In order for the carefree pleasure, romance, cocktails, superb food, and profusion of fresh flowers available at all times during the next crossing of the Atlantic (for first class passengers anyway), the liner spent three clear days in New York in addition to the portion of twenty four hours on Arrival and Sailing Days - and every minute was fully occupied with preparations for the next voyage, to refuel, re-victual, and repair.

The ship's surgeons used time in port to ensure the dispensary was fully re-stocked. The ship's gardener sent faded blooms ashore and took in fresh stocks to make up the six thousand plants he tended. The librarians acquired the latest novels, papers, and magazines, and supplies of stationary, postcards, and postage stamps for the thousands of postcards dispatched. The ship's bank transferred cash and carried out other necessary transactions with the parent office ashore. The printers ensured the equipment was in good working order to print the ship's newspaper and daily menus. The barbers and ladies' hairdressers ordered fresh supplies of shampoo and other products. And the shopkeepers re-stocked as much as they could for the next round of shopping sprees.

Internal and external painting was carried out, together with any repairs necessary to the navigational gear, decks, and boats. Upholstery and fixtures in suites and staterooms were deep-cleansed, re-painted, or replaced, and linoleum, carpets, and curtains repaired or replaced in the first class sleeping and public areas, and second class public rooms and cabins.

Electricians and plumbers checked the gymnasium equipment and swimming pool. Clean linen arrived back on board, with every item of returned laundry checked. In the crockery department a stock-take took place for about 100,000 items of china, glass, and earthenware, and 26,000 pieces of silver.

To cater for around four thousand passengers and one thousand crew, fresh perishable goods were received, examined, and counted; oxen, calves, lambs, pigs, hares, thousands of chickens, ducklings, turkeys, partridges, grouse, pheasants, pigeons, quails, plovers, and snipe; salmon, sturgeon, plaice, trout, halibut, brill, soles, herrings, sardines, lobster, oysters, clams, even a couple of turtles; potatoes by the ton and sacks of other fresh seasonal vegetables, crates of apples, oranges, melons, peaches and every exotic fruit a passenger might request; tons of butter, gallons of fresh milk, cream, cheeses of every variety, thousands of eggs; every existing variety of flour, dried fruit, spices; the list was endless.

Most importantly, as a 52,000 ton liner travelling 3,000 miles across an ocean couldn't afford for anything to go wrong once at sea, a thorough overhaul took place, with engines and boilers being opened up for inspection and cleaning. Miles of electric cables were checked, and eight thousand tons of oil pumped from an oil tanker alongside the ship into the tanks. Machinery was kept going while the ship was moored to the quay to provide power for electric lighting, refrigeration, and the winches taking on cargo for the United Kingdom, and bringing on board the huge quantities of fresh water required.

And the company's shore officials paid visits of inspection to ensure everything went well. Cunard couldn't afford to keep the ship idle any longer than necessary.

But despite all the activity there was still some free time for the crew, and Billy and Elsie finally put the arduous voyage behind them with a celebratory date; they'd enjoyed a fabulous meal at Vincenzo and Eugenia Sardi's Little Restaurant, been to see 'Charlie's Aunt' at Daly's Theatre, and were now strolling along Broadway in companionable silence, taking in the sights and sounds around them.

'All these people out enjoying themselves,' marvelled Elsie, looking round. 'Half of New York must be here.' A thought struck her. 'I hope Mister Stonefeather isn't among them!'

'What if he is? We're as entitled to walk along Broadway as he is.'

'I know, but I still hope we don't meet him. I never want to see him again.'

They moved over to the side to allow a crowd of boisterous young men to pass, college students from the look of them.

'Billy,' she continued hesitantly.

'Yeah?'

'Talking of Mister Stonefeather... D'you ever feel guilty about what we did? Do you have any regrets about it?'

'Putting cheese in the bas - I mean, in his suit? No, I don't,' answered Billy firmly. 'I'm not a doormat for people to walk over. I'm more a sort of human mirror - however people treat me, good or bad, they get the same behaviour back. Simple as that.'

Elsie nodded. She felt much the same herself.

'Why?' He looked at her. 'D'you think *he's* feeling guilty about the way he treated you?'

'Highly unlikely,' admitted Elsie.

'As for regrets,' Billy went on. 'The only one I've got is that we didn't put pickle in as well!'

Elsie grinned. The more she got to know Billy, the more she liked him. He made no pretence to be a saint, which was comforting - saints can be daunting, and anyway she could hardly claim sainthood herself after taking part in his childish plot - and you knew exactly where you were with him. A dangerous enemy but a good friend, loyal and dependable. Billy was a gentleman at heart, but definitely someone you'd better have respect for, and be straight with.

So it was time to let him know about the interview she'd arranged for tomorrow, which would hopefully lead to an exciting new job in New York. Not wanting to spoil the evening with reminders of work, she hadn't broached the subject before now, but if left much longer it could become loaded with 'Why didn't you tell me about it before?' recriminations.

She drew in a long breath.

'I've got a bit of news to tell you,' she announced.

'Oh aye? Don't tell me you sewed some pickle in with the cheese after all? You're even worse than I am, young lady!'

She laughed. 'No, don't be daft, it's nothing to do with him. I didn't say anything before now because I was too busy enjoying every minute, but -'

The bravado defence mechanism leapt into action. Billy was ready to get in first if she was about to announce that he shouldn't read anything into the date because when they got back to Southampton she was going to accept the marriage proposal of some overpaid pen-pusher with a cushy job.

'But you're not enjoying it now?'

'Of course I am! But... as well as enjoying the best evening I've ever had, there's something I'd like to share with you, Billy; to get your take on it.'

Billy looked at her, but said nothing.

'There was a letter waiting for me when we arrived in New York, sent to the Cunard offices. It was from the parents of one of the children on the last trip. I drew some pictures for them to colour in. It turns out that the parents publish children's books in New York - and they've offered to give me an interview for a job.'

Billy stopped in his tracks and grinned. 'Well gee whizz!' He affected a New York accent. 'Ain't dat sumtin? That's swell!'

Elsie laughed. '*Swell*?'

'When in Rome, or in this case, New York.' Billy winked at her. 'You'd better get used to people talking like that if you're going to be living in this town! They won't say (he put on a mock upper class English accent), 'But that's simply marvellous, darling!'

Elsie laughed. She'd been unsure how he'd take the news, and it would have soured the whole evening if he'd been in any way

288

resentful or jealous. He wasn't. He was genuinely delighted for her.

'But I'm not joking now. It's wonderful news, Elsie,' he said quietly, and gave her arm a gentle squeeze. 'Because I got the impression you weren't keen on being a stewardess, even without Mister Stonefeather's input.'

'You're right,' she agreed. 'I *was* keen, until I actually started doing it. Then, well, I didn't know what I wanted to do. All I knew was, I didn't want to do that!'

She felt shy about mentioning her prayers in the stewardess's cabin. Billy probably didn't believe in 'all that rubbish' and wouldn't hesitate to say so, and because tonight had been so special she couldn't bear even any minor differences of opinion to cast any shadows or, even worse, for him to ridicule, or dismiss as sheer coincidence, something so totally unexpected and amazing that she was still shaking her head in wonder.

'I'm glad things have worked out for you. And I'll look forward to meeting up when the ship's in port, to hear how your exciting new life is going!' He looked at her as she tried not to yawn. 'But for now, I reckon it's time you got some sleep, isn't it. Fancy a nightcap before we get a taxi to the hotel?'

'No thanks.' She shook her head. It had been a wonderful evening, but she'd been working until late afternoon, she *was* tired, and it was important to be at her best for the interview tomorrow. 'I'm still full. I'm just looking forward to lying in a proper bed with a floor that isn't moving, and no bunks above and below me with people snoring and coughing and muttering in their sleep. And no ship's engines making that horrible noise all the time. And cool fresh air.'

'Me too. Come on then, let's go,' said Billy, waving down a taxi. He held the door open for her, helped her inside, and jumped in himself.

The thought of a quiet room that didn't have to be shared with a dozen other stewards and communal laundry hanging all over the place appealed to him as well. They both relished the thought of a good night's sleep, of being able to rest after a hard day's work without the additional strain of night duty, on constant alert to attend to the next bell-call. So it was extremely satisfying - and appropriate - thought Billy with a smug smile, that this should be provided courtesy of Lexie Stonefeather's ship's pool winnings.

Because he'd booked them a room each at the newly opened Gramercy Hotel to enjoy the luxury of a proper bed in quiet surroundings and utter comfort, following a slap-up meal and a Broadway show.

And all at Lexie's expense.

5

Old Reg had gone up on the aft mooring deck for a smoke. It was quiet; he was alone. He stared at the lights reflected in the river, and lit up a cigarette.

And then someone else appeared. It seemed the Chief Stewardess also had an urge to take the night air before retiring. Reg leaned on the rail, exhaled, and smiled a welcome.

'Pleasant night, Miss Atkinson.'

'Indeed it is.' She spoke clearly, aware of his slight deafness.

'Strange you should come up. I was just thinking about you.'

'Oh?'

'Yes.' He hesitated. 'May I speak frankly?'

She'd never known him do anything else. Reg was a seafarer of the old school who dealt in straight talking, no skirting round the subject.

'Of course, Reg. We've known each other too long for either of us to take offence at whatever this may be about. What's troubling you?'

She looked at him, expecting some business they needed to discuss; which flowers for a particular passenger, the likes and dislikes of a regular passenger regarding tempting delicacies provided in the first class suites, and so on.

'Well... I won't beat about the bush, Miss Atkinson -'

'Please don't, Reg. We've both been doing this job for more years than I can remember, and neither of us has bothered beating around any bushes up to now.'

'True, true. We're both old hands at this game, Miss Atkinson. We've given our lives to Cunard, you and I...' He looked down at the glow of his cigarette. 'But I for one won't be able to do it for much longer.'

She frowned slightly. As he said, they'd worked well together for years, and always spoken freely in the past. What on earth was bothering him? As she was on the point of telling him to get on with it and spit it out for goodness sake, he took a deep breath and plunged on.

''Well, here's what I wanted to say. I've been thinking about what I'll do with this old life of mine when I leave the sea. It's hard, because this is all I've ever known. I've got no family - I never married - but I can't go on doing this forever.'

She nodded sympathetically. She dreaded thinking about the future herself; where she'd go and what she'd do when the time came for her to retire. She had no family either.

Fortunately, she hadn't done badly for tips on this trip. It all added up, and it was just as well that it did, because all that was waiting when she could no longer work was a lonely old age. She'd lost the energy and vitality she'd had when she'd started out, seeing the job as a kind of passport to adventure and opportunity, like Miss Parkinson probably did now; it had been a long, hard slog to get promoted, because most other Chief Stewardesses either knew somebody high up in the Cunard offices or were qualified nurses, but she'd done it - she'd pulled herself up by her own boot straps, with no help from anyone else.

'Well, as you may know, Miss Atkinson, the Old Age Pension is five shillings a week if you're over seventy - and I'm not far off that now. If you pass the annual means test, of course -'

She shifted uncomfortably. Her own future situation looked increasingly unappealing the more she thought about it, and she didn't want to have to examine it too closely until it became absolutely necessary.

'And neither of us are what you might call spring chickens -'

'Er, no,' she agreed, wondering where all this was leading, because it didn't seem to have much connection with flower arrangements or which champagne and chocolates to provide in which first class suites for which passengers.

'Well - I've got a proposition to make to you, Miss Atkinson. We're very alike, us two, and we know how each other works. We're not like these young ones today, expecting everything on a plate. We've had to work hard all these years, you and me.'

She nodded again, thinking of Elsie grumbling about being seasick and wanting to lie down. He was right, they *had* had to work hard, under the most unbelievably brutal conditions, without whingeing about it to anyone. And if Miss Moaning Minnie Parkinson lasted in the job for as long as she had, then she could guarantee that Miss Parkinson would end up every bit as hard-bitten as she'd had to become. And every bit as unsympathetic about having to work while coping with the misery of seasickness, and men trying it on. It was called self-preservation.

'Well, I reckon I've managed to save up enough over the years to buy a small house - a modest little place, but something that could be turned into a guest house, a boarding house.' Reg hesitated, then carried on in a rush. 'And I was wondering... what would you say to maybe coming in on it with me, running it together? I know this must be a terrible shock and sound a real cheek, and you've probably already got plans for your retirement - not that you're anywhere near retirement age yet of course...'

He began to flounder. He was aware of her looking at him in amazement.

Oh dear. He'd done this all wrong. Fancy jumping straight in like that, no finesse, no leading up to it or anything; what on earth must she think of him? He threw the cigarette overboard in self-disgust. He hadn't got around to smoking it anyway.

'Forget I said anything, Miss Atkinson. I'm sorry if I offended you. I've probably spent too much time with sailors, and not enough with women.'

Still she said nothing.

He glanced at her anxiously; was she about to slap him in the face for his impudence, or even more humiliatingly, ask if he'd taken leave of his senses?

Finally she spoke.

'Reg, I... Well. Like you say, we're alike, us two. We work well together, we make a good team. And it's quite remarkable that you should mention the possibility of a guest house, because strangely enough, that thought has occurred to me from time to time as well. But in my case it's simply wishful thinking, because I'd never be able to afford to buy a house.'

He was about to interrupt, but she shook her head.

'Let me finish, Reg, this is important. I will not sponge off anyone. Self respect comes into it. I'd want to pay my way; earn my keep.'

Again he opened his mouth to interrupt; again she shook her head.

'I have some savings of course - we have to provide for our old age, don't we - but certainly not nearly enough for a house. I will not take out of any business arrangement we might decide to make more than I put in, Reg. However, on the strict understanding that your input didn't exceed my savings - in other words, we both contributed an equal amount, I'd be prepared to consider your suggestion.'

Reg, who was beginning to hyper-ventilate, felt his breathing settle down to a regular rhythm as relief flooded through him. At least she hadn't laughed in his face. Or slapped it.

'Well, I'm glad you're not dismissing the idea out of hand, Miss Atkinson. Maybe we could discuss it more fully when we're off duty? Chew over a few details, see if it's something we could think seriously about, whether we could make it work together? No need to feel committed in any way, of course. What would you say?'

There was another silence, but definitely not a disapproving or discouraging one; more the silence of someone weighing up a totally unexpected proposition, and finding it increasingly attractive.

Reg might be a seafarer who dealt in straight talking, and lacked a silver tongue that could trip off a spiel of courtly flannel, but he was honourable, and kind, and she was confident they could get on well together and make a go of this possible joint venture. It was a most surprising solution to the dismal prospect of a lonely old age for both of them - and all the more agreeable for that.

The light wasn't great, but there was enough for Reg to see the Chief Stewardess was smiling.

'I'd say Reg, if we're thinking of going into business together, it might be an idea if you were to start calling me Deborah instead of Miss Atkinson. Strictly off duty, of course.'

'Of course.'

Some silences can be awkward, others can be easy and companionable. This one was definitely easy and companionable.

6

The telegram was couched in deceptively affectionate terms, and arrived just after the guests had left the luncheon party.

The Countess of Knotworth, her father, and her sister (who was already wondering whether Frank-from-California-who's-in-the-film-industry might be better as a short-term fling than a long-term commitment), had enjoyed a convivial lunch with Sam, Mary, Michael, and Sylvia, but the house was quiet now. Caroline and Frank had gone to visit friends.

Pop watched Sophie intently as she opened the envelope, unfolded the telegram within, and started to read.

'DARLING REQUEST YOU CURTAIL STAY IN AMERICA STOP DISTURBING NEWS FROM DAPHNE STOP BOOK RETURN PASSAGE WITH ALL HASTE STOP MISSING YOU' (The word 'stop' was used in telegrams to indicate the end of a sentence.)

She read it through again. The carefully phrased message, ostensibly from a lovelorn husband missing his wife, was, she knew, no heartfelt 'request', but a command to return home to face his fury as her fall from grace became common knowledge. (Daphne certainly hadn't wasted any time in ensuring that poor Aubrey knew all about his wife's scandalous behaviour on the ship; it had obviously been right at the top of her 'To Do' list.)

'Darling... Missing you...' Oh, Aubrey. If only! If only it had been true, even for a minute. Well, it hadn't been true during their seven years together, and it certainly wasn't true now. In fact it was downright insulting. Did he really think she hadn't sufficient intelligence to see through this insincere tripe?

When he finally spoke, there was great tenderness in Pop's voice.

'This marriage has been a mistake, hasn't it, Sophie? You're not happy, are you?'

Before meeting Clive, she'd have denied it. Now, there was no point.

She shook her head. 'He despises me, Pop.'

There. She'd said it. She'd put into words what she hadn't wanted to admit to anyone, least of all Pop. She looked at him, shamefaced.

He didn't try to persuade her that she was mistaken. He just nodded sadly.

'The sort of people who use people often *do* despise them.' He reached for her hand. 'Caroline told me about the state of affairs in your marriage, Sophie. She told me everything, but I was waiting for you to say something yourself.'

She couldn't look at him. She'd let him down, disappointed him, brought humiliation; the grand marriage he'd been so proud of had been a sham all along, and now the most private aspects of it were about to be publicly laid bare. His daughter would become society - and newspaper - gossip fodder, with a subject matter no loving father would want to read.

His hand was warm, large; her own hand felt as though it was being enveloped in a comforting blanket, and she suddenly realised just how deeply Pop loved her.

'Obviously the pool nonsense is just the catalyst. The main issue, as far as I'm concerned, is that this is not, and on his part never was, a marriage of love. As for his crony's hysterical accusations at the tea dance, I'm no expert on law, but they'd be laughed out of court. Especially when the ship's officer in question…'

Sophie didn't hear the rest. *Court? The ship's officer in question…?* Her head spun; she thought she was going to faint.

Her voice held a note of panic. *'Court?* No! Absolutely not, Pop. I couldn't bear it!'

He stayed silent. He wouldn't agitate her further. His role was to protect her, and ensure the best legal minds in New York sought the least painful way of ending this marriage. He took the telegram from her other hand, studied it for a few moments in silence, then spoke again.

'Stay here, Sophie. You don't have to go back to England.' His voice was firm. If that bullying jerk expected her to jump to his every command, let's see his reaction to Annulment on the grounds of Non-Consummation! 'You don't have to do anything you don't want.'

Stay here. You don't have to go back to England... Oh, how tempting it was. But hiding here (not quite) out of Aubrey's reach was just putting off the inevitable.

'There'll be gossip and tittle-tattle,' he went on. 'But at least it'll be temporary, then you'll be free. Which is worse, short-term gossip, or long-term unhappiness? Do you really want that for the rest of your life? Because believe me, there'll still be gossip if you go on living a lie. People will see right through it.'

She nodded miserably.

'And there's a valuable lesson waiting to be learned from this, Sophie. There always is in times of trouble. You'll see who your real friends are.'

Friends? Well, she didn't have many in England, that was for sure. In fact the most loyal friend anyone could have was standing right next to her: Pop, whose money she'd siphoned off by the cartload to pay for her husband's extravagant restoration work. She thought of the army of interior design consultants with their swatches and samples, the nursery she'd lovingly prepared in readiness, all paid for by Pop's generosity...

Guiltily she turned to him. 'Pop -'

He cut her off. 'I know what you're going to say. Forget the money, Sophie, it doesn't matter. And I'd still say the same thing if I were penniless, in debt for the rest of my days to pay it off. It's your happiness I care about, not money... Cut loose, Sophie. Don't waste your entire life because of a mistake.'

A mistake. That's what this marriage had been, for her and for Aubrey. And now it was time for each of them to admit it, and deal with the aftermath as best they could. So she *would* return to England as 'requested', but not for the reason he was expecting.

The longer she put off the inevitable confrontation, the more difficult it would be. She'd have to face him some time. Best get it over with as soon as possible, taking full advantage of the new-found courage that had resulted from honest soul-bearing with Pop, rather than let it hang over her.

However, "booking return passage with all haste" presented an unforeseen complication: Clive.

The only available ship on which she could book an immediate passage home was the *Berengaria*. She could wait for the *Aquitania* of course, but it meant fielding awkward questions as to why it should be so important to avoid the ship's officer involved. Also, it was possible that Daphne and Theodore might be on board the *Aquitania*; she knew for a fact they wouldn't be on *Berengaria's* return crossing.

So - the *Berengaria* it would be. She'd face whatever awaited in England, and then put it behind her for once and for all, and try to build a new life for herself.

As for Clive, she'd make absolutely sure she didn't see him during the trip by staying in her suite and avoiding all social occasions.

7

Lexie Stonefeather had been doing a lot of thinking since coming ashore, and the more he thought, the clearer it became that the blame for each and every infuriating disaster that had happened on the *Berengaria* lay entirely with Cunard.

Take the first night for example, when that purser's assistant came into the Smoking Room to warn them about card sharps. Of course Cunard would naturally deny responsibility for Lexie's losses, pointing out that, having given warnings, they couldn't be held accountable if passengers then chose to play card games for money in private staterooms. Nor had they any control over whether or not the winner decided to give ten per cent to a steward that he, Lexie, happened to dislike.

But Lexie's point was that it was morally indefensible of Cunard to allow the sort of scheming villain who deliberately set out to fleece unsuspecting victims on board in the first place. Yet paradoxically, they seemed to think they could high-handedly appoint themselves custodians of passengers' morals when it came to the poking of female passengers' noses into other peoples' private affairs. As for being attacked by that Russian psychopath, it would serve Cunard right to be dragged through the courts, because if there was one thing he couldn't stand, it was bullies intimidating defenceless underdogs.

But mere litigation was too lenient, and in any case they'd employ some silver-tongued lawyer to wriggle out of it. How much more satisfying - and amusing - to take inspiration from the irreverent nickname he'd heard recently for the '*Berengaria*': the '*Dead'n'bury'er*'. Now *there* was a name to give you ideas! If whoever thought that one up only knew how apt an epitaph the jokey witticism would become for this effing ship. They couldn't have come up with a more appropriately descriptive title!

He made discreet enquiries among his more questionable contacts, and learned of a German who'd been involved in the production of explosives between 1915 and 1918 and now made his living as a demolition expert. A deal was struck after assurances that he'd pay handsomely for a particularly spectacular celebratory firework - if the man got his meaning - timed in advance to provide a surprise grand climax when everyone would be having a lovely time at a tea dance next Friday afternoon. (Unfortunately, what Lexie didn't know was that the man, who had no intention of supplying for a complete stranger the sort of thing he constructed only for known and trusted clients, had soldered together a few unwanted bits and pieces which, to an ignorant eye, looked like a miniature version of an electrically initiated vibration/pressure sensitive land mine.)

And as there was no time like the present, Lexie headed towards Pier 92, attired in his natty brown suit because the navy blue one hadn't brought him the success he'd expected at his meeting (he couldn't understand it at all; they'd sniffed at him as though they couldn't wait to get rid of him. Although actually, he'd begun to notice a slight whiff himself as his cold passed its peak and his sense of smell gradually started to return. Must have spilt something without noticing. Oh well, easy enough to buy a new one and give the navy number to some homeless bum; nobody could say Lexie Stonefeather didn't have a generous nature!), and reached the dockside just as Danny was approaching from the other direction.

Lexie smiled to himself. Perfect! This gullible waiter was the ideal choice for his plan, because he could pile on the flattery and gratitude for excellent service. And if that didn't work, the tip would. It would be well worth twenty five dollars (that seemed about right; no point in arousing suspicions with an over-generous amount) for the satisfaction of ensuring that what he had in mind for RMS *Berengaria* came about.

He greeted Danny effusively. 'Well hello there, Danny! It *is* Danny, isn't it?'

Danny looked at him in surprise. Why would a first class passenger loiter on the dockside while the ship was in port? Not that there was restricted access to the public, although Pier 92 was technically private property; it just wasn't the sort of place you'd expect to see anyone other than those attending to the ship's business.

'Yes, sir.'

Lexie lowered his voice and produced from behind his back a bulky Schwarz Toy Shop bag that was obviously heavy. 'Well, I've got a little business proposition to put to you, Danny. I thought of you especially, because you did me a good turn, and I always like to repay good service.'

Danny smiled politely. So that was why he was skulking on the dockside. Wasn't hard to guess what was coming next. He eyed the bag curiously.

'And because this is a very important task, I need someone I can trust... someone like you... to carry it out. There's a hundred dollars in it for you - twenty five now, the other seventy five when you've delivered a parcel I want to send to a business partner in England. Interested?'

Danny looked at him levelly. It wasn't unheard of for people to approach crew members to transport goods from one port to another - one shipmate had brought four baby alligators in a box into the U.K. for someone on their last trip - and there wasn't usually any problem getting items on board, especially after liberty time ashore when the crew often went shopping anyway. The real problem came in getting it off again at the home port, where U.K. Customs rummage crews were known even to empty a coal bunker if they suspected there was something hidden beneath the coal. But quite apart from the fact that he'd be doing no favours for Mister Stonefeather whatever the payment, if this smarmy creep thought Danny was easy meat with his 'Twenty five dollars now and seventy five *after delivery*' baloney, he could think again.

'As a result of an important business meeting,' Lexie went on (well, it *was* important. It was important to him, and what could be more important than that?), 'It's vital my business partner gets this as soon as possible. It's a prototype of a new gadget we're planning to market. I haven't time to go through the usual freight channels, bills of lading and all that rigmarole. And I can't return yet because I've got other meetings to attend.'

Danny peered inside the Schwarz Toy Shop bag and saw a bulging unwieldy lump wrapped in brown paper. Prototype of a new gadget about to hit the market? Hm. Maybe, maybe not. At a guess, from his knowledge of the man, it was more likely to be something illegal, that shouldn't be on board at all. Not that it mattered, because whatever it was, he had no intention of delivering it. However, if he could up the price... Fairy godmothers with magic wands and wads of dollars come in all sorts of unexpected shapes and sizes.

He looked at the address - some obscure place in London - and continued to say nothing.

'By Jove, you're a tough negotiator, Danny,' flattered Lexie, getting the message. 'All right. Because it's you, and I like you, let's make it fifty now, and fifty on delivery.'

That was more like it. Although sixty would be even better...

Danny knew Joey would never accept charity. But the money could be a loan, perhaps to be repaid in the future as a donation to the SCI, or as funds for some other destitute seaman. There was still time to nip back and leave an envelope without actually seeing him, so he wouldn't know about it until it was too late to refuse it.

Lexie, slowly counting out five ten-dollar bills from a large wad, looked at him slyly.

'Have I picked the wrong guy? I thought you looked like a resourceful lad who could think of somewhere safe for it to go?'

Out of the corner of his eye, Danny saw Alec Baxter approaching. It was decision time. Either he refused to have anything to do with this and told Mister Stonefeather to stuff his prototype gadget, or he took the bag and the fifty dollars right now, because there wouldn't be another chance, and it was obvious Lexie wasn't going to go any higher. Fifty dollars was better than nothing at all.

He nodded. 'Oh yes, sir. I could.'

Such as, over the side the moment we leave New York, he added silently. If he ever saw Lexie again he'd explain that, unfortunately, the parcel had been discovered and confiscated; he'd already seen that this self-important smarty-pants could be hoodwinked by a mere waiter, and there was nothing in this verbal agreement that said he'd have to return the fifty dollars in the event of non-delivery. Anyway, he never *would* see Lexie again, because he wouldn't be on the *Berengaria* should Lexie come hunting for him when she next arrived in New York.

He quickly pocketed the dollar bills, indicating Alec with a jerk of his head and reaching for the bag. He was startled at the weight; whatever was in it seemed to be made of solid lead.

'I'll see to it for you, sir. Leave it to me.'

Lexie grinned to himself, picturing the Cunard offices frantically wiring the captain of the *Berengaria* when they got his letter informing them about a bomb when the ship was at the furthest point from land. Of course, there was no guarantee the waiter would actually store it below the water-line. That was a chance Lexie would have to take, because obviously he had no plans to be on board when the thing went off. But even if it was hidden where it couldn't actually rip a hole in the hull, it should hopefully cause the next best thing: a fire at sea. And if that effing steward happened to be near the explosion and ended up with a limb or two blown off, so much the better.

And if all else failed, the damaging publicity alone should hit Cunard where it hurt most.

Danny turned away, leaving Lexie to scurry away himself because naturally the fewer witnesses to this particular transaction the better, quite apart from the fact that it was obvious he wanted to avoid Alec.

But Alec was equally intent on catching up with Danny, and called him as he hurried up the gangway. 'Oi! Danny!'

Danny didn't answer.

Alec called again, louder. *'Danny!'*

'What?'

Alec glanced without interest at the Schwarz Toy Shop bag.

'I decided to take a walk along to the SCI in the hope I might see Joey. I was lucky, he arrived back while I was there. I gather you two had just met up somewhere?'

Danny said nothing.

'So I thought you might be interested to know what he said?'

'I hope he said what I feel like saying,' answered Danny shortly, starting up the gangway again. Now that Joey was no longer under Alec's authority and fearing for his job, he was more than capable of speaking for himself, and Danny had no desire to prolong this conversation.

'Look. What's done is done, and I can't undo it.' Alec was equally determined to prolong it. 'But I told him I'm going to look after Clara and do my best to make her happy.'

Danny halted momentarily.

'What am I supposed to say? Well, lucky old Clara, spending a lifetime with you! Will that do?'

'Forget Clara. What's important is, I've made my peace with Joey. And that's the end of it.'

They walked in silence to the top of the gangway, then Alec looked at Danny. 'But I was telling the truth, no matter what she told Joey. Whatever else I'm guilty of, I'm no rapist; Clara told me she had feelings for me. And that's the truth.'

He strode off.

Danny lowered the Schwarz Toy Shop bag to the deck and stared after him. If Clara had 'feelings' for Alec Baxter, well, all he could say was, she had a very strange taste in men.

But then it was a very strange business altogether and he still didn't know what to make of it, other than drawing the obvious conclusion that this pair sounded as though they were made for each other.

And he still didn't like Alec Baxter. He never had, and he never would.

8

Twelve hours before the ship was due to sail the general inspection took place to ensure all the first class areas of the ship were fit to grace a king's palace; every crystal chandelier sparkling, every marble pillar polished, every inch of chrome gleaming, every carpet without blemish, every silver receptacle untarnished, every plush settee welcoming.

New carpets had been laid where necessary in the public rooms and first class staterooms (the suite Lexie had occupied had been fumigated, refurbished, and repainted throughout), the elevators had been serviced and were fresh-smelling and immaculate, whistles were tested to ensure they were clear, the ship's machinery was warming up, the engines given a turn to ensure everything was in excellent working order, the cargo (including a motor car belonging to a stock market millionaire) winched on board and stowed away, last minute stores taken in, and the muster of the crew had taken place for boat, fire, and bulkhead door drill.

The sense of anticipation increased as the activity continued; in the kitchens the butchers were already cutting up meat and preparing poultry for the first of the meals, and the first batches of bread were ready to be baked, and in the first class staterooms the stewardesses were arranging baskets of exotic fruits, decanters of sherry, and beautifully wrapped chocolates...

It wouldn't be long before the passengers started to arrive.

EIGHT: HOMEWARD BOUND

1

"A Berengaria *sailing is tempestuous, with the exploding of flashlights, the pursuit of reporters - everything about the* Berengaria *is on the grand, opulent scale. She is sensational; sensational people board her."*

'Humph,' thought the second steward, casting a cynical eye over the passenger list as he sat at a table with the seating plan of the first class dining saloon spread out in front of him. He had long since formed his own opinion - which he kept strictly to himself - of some of the sensational people who paid a fortune to spend best part of a week overeating, oversleeping, overindulging in amorous adventures, and playing the sort of deck games his nine year old daughter would consider boring.

There were one or two muttered comments along similar lines among the A.B.s as the winches brought on board the last of the cargo and heavy luggage, but these were swamped by a tidal wave of excitement among the crowds on the quayside as reporters duly pursued and flashlights duly exploded.

Stewards, lined up ready to welcome the passengers on board, helped with hand luggage as fashionable flappers and wealthy playboys, having temporarily interrupted farewell parties for the journey to Cunard's Pier 92, danced up the gangway to resume even more boisterous parties on board the ship. Not for nothing was RMS *Berengaria* nicknamed 'Hollywood Afloat' by Cunard, and described as a gleaming and bejewelled ferryboat for the famous and titled.

Up the gangway they tumbled; the billionaires who laughingly gave their address as No Fixed Abode as their lives were spent travelling around the world in ultimate luxury, and the usual sprinkling of European aristocracy, bankers, industrialists, film stars, and celebrities (among whom on this occasion was Josephine Baker and the cast of *'La Revue Negre'* who would be leaving the ship at Cherbourg for the Theatre des Champs Elysees in Paris). The more mature *haut monde* and dowagers filed up in dignified fashion behind them.

Then, as midnight approached, stewards moved through the crowds, striking gongs and shouting, 'All ashore that's going ashore! All visitors ashore!'

And for any that hadn't quite got - or were reluctant to accept - the message, the ship's ear-splitting whistle let out a blast, and the marine superintendent announced that the order for the gangway to be lowered was imminent. Friends and relatives shook hands and parted, sweethearts broke off bitter-sweet embraces, and all non-passengers finally made their way off the ship. The captain and pilot were on the bridge, the last formalities were carried out in the purser's office, passengers leaned on the rails to wave farewell, the marine superintendant ashore oversaw the casting off of mooring ropes and hawsers, and, to whoops of the ship's siren, deafening cheering, and waving of countless handkerchiefs, the mighty ship edged away from the quayside and backed out into the Hudson River.

And standing slightly apart from the crowd was Joey Smith, quietly watching proceedings. He waved to no one; the only people he'd choose to wave to would be too busy working to see him, and anyway Danny would know he'd got the extra fifty dollars in addition to the whip-round and Mister Stonefeather's tip. He was no longer a part of all this.

It was a strange feeling.

When he'd joined the ship in Southampton he'd had no idea that he'd take the decision to jump overboard, no longer wanting to live... only to find a completely new life awaiting him in a new country, with new opportunities, and new friends. He'd changed... life had changed... everything had changed.

But the biggest change of all was that no matter how convincing the arguments to the contrary from those intellectual superiors who'd win a logical debate every time, no matter how patronising the politely-expressed, 'Well of course, you're entitled to your beliefs...' with the rest of the sentence 'However far-fetched or absurd...' left unspoken, no matter how sceptical the observations about religion causing more wars than anything else (with which he agreed, while no longer necessarily linking the one with the other), no matter how loud the ridicule - in short, no matter what anyone else's opinion was on the subject - after his experience in the sea he could not, and would not, ever again doubt the existence of God, who for some unaccountable reason had chosen to make His presence known in the most unexpected way, at the most improbable time, and in the most unlikely location on the planet.

2

Clive, hurrying past a group of young American men-about-town on the elliptical staircase that wound down through a total of five decks, headed towards the purser's office with details of tomorrow morning's lifeboat drill, then stopped dead. Further down the staircase a woman with tawny hair was ascending towards him. He sternly told himself to get a grip; he couldn't carry on like this every time he saw someone with tawny hair.

He started down again, still watching the woman intently.

There was something very familiar in the way she moved, in the way she held herself...

Common sense again took hold, and he gave himself another talking to. Of course it wasn't her! How could it be? Obviously she wouldn't be travelling back the U.K. again the moment she landed in America. He'd already seen the passenger list; he knew perfectly well she wasn't on it.

She glanced up and saw him.

He froze. He wasn't mistaken.

It was her.

He vaguely remembered hearing something about someone making a last-minute booking to return home because of some family crisis, but he'd been concentrating on another matter at the time and missed the name...

He began to move down the staircase in what seemed like slow motion, his eyes never leaving her face as she stood stock still, looking up at him. He was oblivious to group of young men and the other passengers on the staircase (and the lifeboat drill instructions, impatiently awaited in the purser's office), and had to hold himself back from putting both arms around her and telling her how thankful he was that he'd been given a second chance.

But sometime during this trip, he knew that he *would* tell her…

Sophie stiffened, tensed, and then relaxed.

Hide out of sight throughout the entire voyage to make sure they didn't meet?

As if.

Although she'd honestly tried, before boarding, to remain firm in her determination to avoid any possibility of meeting Clive, convincing herself that what she felt for him was just some weird unwanted infatuation, intuitively she knew she was meant to make this voyage. And to spend time with him.

Things were going to come to a head anyway regarding Aubrey, and there was nothing she could do about that. This was a separate issue altogether.

She looked at Clive, and felt all the tension gradually drain away as he approached, his face breaking into a smile of such tenderness that the forthcoming unpleasantness with Aubrey no longer held the dread and terror that had consumed her ever since the telegram arrived.

3

Elsie and Billy both had more sense than to openly flaunt Cunard's "No Fraternisation" rule. They didn't need to. Both of them were content to let things progress at a natural pace, in which any potential future relationship would either run its course and die a natural death or, depending on future time spent together in New York when the *Berry* docked and Elsie had time off from her new job...

A couple of trips back, a passenger who'd taken to him had offered Billy a job as a steward at a new golf club currently being constructed on the outskirts of the city. So, if things went well, and if at some point in the future he decided to leave the sea and begin a new life in the States... who knew.

And for the moment, who cared.

They'd had a great time together in New York, and they'd meet up properly in Southampton, and until then there'd be enough opportunities to give her a big wink and a wide grin whenever their paths crossed. As he'd make sure they did.

And neither the Chief Steward nor sour-faced Miss Atkinson could complain about that.

And if they did, thought Elsie, who had heard that the weather forecast was sufficiently 'moderate' to escape the miseries of sea-sickness for at least part of the trip, she'd draw caricatures of them as the wicked witch and evil goblin in the children's story book she was already planning to write and illustrate.

4

Danny stood in the line of waiters for the short but inevitable pep talk that took place at the beginning of every voyage, regardless of how often they'd heard it before. The Head Waiter held at arm's length a book entitled 'The Art of the Table' by C. Herman Senn MBE and, after clearing his throat importantly, quoted the passage they all knew by heart.

"'It would be easier to fit a square peg into a round hole than mould into an ideal waiter a person of slow intellect, disobliging and tactless disposition, and bad manners...'"

Danny's mind began to wander as he watched Alec Baxter fussing around a decorated whole salmon while the veg chefs arranged ornate fruit and vegetable sculptures to amuse the passengers: a pair of leaping dolphins carved from a water melon, exotic flowers, fish, birds, rabbits, and dogs, sculpted from aubergines, carrots, oranges, peppers, and onions; even a flock of sheep fashioned from cauliflower heads.

It had been a strange trip, and a deeply poignant turnaround in New York. Life can certainly throw up some surprises… It was difficult to know who had been more deeply affected by Joey's attempted suicide, and its unforeseen outcome.

Elsie's life had also changed dramatically; they'd all heard how she and Billy painted the town red to celebrate the terrific job she'd landed.

And the trip certainly hadn't ended as Alec Baxter had expected - two houses down, and a wife who wasn't worth having!

His own life would change too, at the end of this voyage. If he signed on another New York-bound ship, rather than Montreal or Quebec, he'd keep in touch with Elsie, see how things worked out for her as time went on. And for Billy.

He wondered idly whether any of the passengers' lives had changed as well, during the trip. Or the ship's officers…

The Head Waiter was glancing sternly over his spectacles, and he resisted the temptation to join in with the lecture.

'"...There should be at all times a pleasant manner, everlasting patience, and self-control to restrain any outward expression of annoyance under the most trying circumstances"' The Head Waiter took off his spectacles. 'And there'd better be, if you don't want to join the dole queue. That's all. To your posts. The passengers will be on their way for refreshments any moment.'

And indeed they were.

One of the first faces to appear was vaguely familiar, although the manner of dress was at first confusing; an unremarkable sober suit, the sort favoured by university professors and learned dons, worn by a slight, balding, nondescript figure who would blend easily and unobtrusively with the inhabitants of the Smoking Room.

Danny smiled to himself. He wondered what name Jack Dalton had booked his passage under this time.

The academic gentleman gave a brief smile of recognition, then turned to study a spectacular model of the Eiffel Tower created from spun sugar, and a swan carved from a block of ice. He'd given Danny a generous tip before going ashore, but he was in work mode now, and absent-minded professors don't greet waiters like long-lost cousins.

And Danny was also in work mode - although as he headed to his section, he found himself thinking that if there was the slightest chance he'd get away with it, he'd slip in among all the exhibits a caricature of Alec Baxter's pasty moon face sculpted out of Camembert.

Perhaps he should write his own instruction manual for waiters: 'One Hundred And One Uses For Camembert Cheese'?

Despite the lateness of the hour and the fact he'd be on duty again at 6AM, Danny needed some fresh air when he finished work. There was no chance of escaping onto the promenade deck tonight because merrymakers, over-stimulated by the

Berengaria's departure (champagne corks were still popping as the ship, accompanied by the usual flotilla of smaller craft to wish her Bon Voyage, made her way past the brightly lit skyline of Manhattan), were in no hurry to retire to bed.

But he hadn't yet had a chance to dispose of the mysterious, and probably illegal, contraband Mister Stonefeather had gone to such lengths to have smuggled on board.

And he wanted rid of it.

He collected the Schwarz Toy Shop bag with its lead-heavy contents from the glory hole and made his way to the aft mooring deck. He had a brief moment of guilt - he'd taken the man's money, after all - and wondered about the so-called 'prototype gadget'. He fingered the unwieldy object shrouded in sheaves of brown paper curiously, and frowned; it was a similar size and shape to a wartime mine. What on earth was it? Every housewife's dream, a mine-shaped casserole dish? The thing had a sinister, malevolent feel to it…

He didn't trust Mister Stonefeather, or his prototype gadget. And he wouldn't have taken the money if he hadn't had a very strong sense - no proof maybe, but certainly intuition - that he was being used for a purpose that was in some way harmful, malicious, or just plain bad. So whatever this thing was, it wouldn't be staying on the ship.

He glanced round. He was alone.

He heaved it on to the rail and let it balance for a moment, remembering Billy's fervent wish that he could sling every item of uniform contaminated by Lexie Stonefeather's vomit over the side. Well, he couldn't make that wish come true, but this was the next best thing, because whatever lay hidden beneath all the brown paper was contaminated by association. His first impression Sailing Night crystal-ball-gazing had been accurate; Mister Stonefeather had caused enough trouble on the outward trip without his continued presence by proxy, in the form of his Schwarz Toy Shop stand-in, causing yet more mayhem on the way home.

Over it went.

He leaned on the rail and watched as it was tossed about in the ship's wake before eventually sinking out of sight.

There.

Job done. Your prototype gadget has just had its very own Grand Launching Ceremony, Mister Stonefeather.

Put your fins together for a big round of applause, fish!

After dismissing the last vestiges of Lexie Stonefeather from mind with a silent 'Good Riddance to Bad Rubbish', Danny became quiet, still, and reflective, watching the movement in the water as it swirled past beneath him.

On to more important things. Deeply important things.

He sat down to write to his Love. He stared at the sea for a few moments more, then, on impulse, instead of the usual news and gossip about the ship, decided to try and express his feelings for her in a way he'd never attempted before.

He took his pencil and paper, and slowly started to write.

You Are the Love of My Life

Life would be nothing for me without you,
Kindness and loving in all that you do,
This is a love only given to few -
You are the love of my life.

Together we'll face every low, every high,
If life knocks us down, we'll get up and get by,
You are the one I will love til I die -
You are the love of my life.

I know you so well, you're as fine as could be,
You are so special, so precious to me,
I adore you, my dearest, it's easy to see -
You are the love of my life.

He signed it as he signed all his letters: 'Rain or shine, Dan.'

He read it over. People who wrote 'proper' poetry would scoff and scorn at his efforts. Well, let them. It wasn't written for them. It wasn't written to impress anyone. It was written for her, and for her alone. She wouldn't scoff, and that was all that mattered. She'd know it came from his heart, and that he'd tried to put into words how he felt for her as honestly, but as poetically, as he could.

He'd done well for tips on this trip, and he'd been saving for a while now in order to provide and care for her in the new chapter that would begin in their lives if she said Yes.

Whatever the future may hold, whatever adventures may lie ahead as they created their own family, and watched that family grow - as long as she was by his side as life unfolded, to share laughter, loyalty, and the spontaneous joys and inevitable sorrows that went to make up treasured memories over the years, what did anything else matter?

He stood up and leaned over the rail, staring at the ship's wake.

Homeward bound…

He felt the restlessness of the ship, of the sea itself, and shared it; three thousand miles of the Atlantic ocean, in all its moods, to cross, before collecting his Discharge Book in Southampton and making his way to Liverpool to be with her again and see her face, her lovely face; to see her smile when he quietly handed her the poem he'd written for her … and got down on one knee to propose.

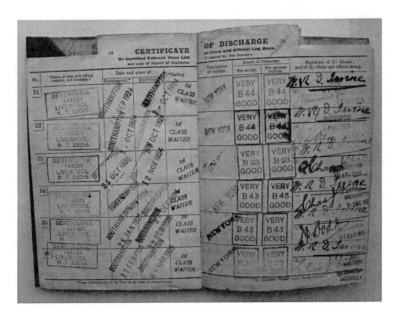

Danny's Discharge Book